"[A] rich, ambitious debut novel . . . Each character gives Card a fresh opportunity to play with form: Chapters shapeshift here into historical fiction, there into folklore. . . . Card's ghosts bracingly remind us that no family history is comprehensive, that some riddles of ancestry and heritage persist beyond this lifetime."

—*The New York Times Book Review*

"Card, who works as a public librarian, delivers a novel overflowing with unadulterated humanity. . . . Card is a natural storyteller. Whole family histories are compressed into two pages, stories building upon stories like strata of earth. . . . The result is a rich stew, teeming with grudges, humor, doubt, loss, and love."

—*The Washington Post*

"An epic novel haunted by the ghosts of colonialism . . . Card's book joins a literary tradition that challenges imperial records of history by imbuing the present with voices from the past. . . . [A] vivid debut."

—*The Atlantic*

"[A] lyrical, ambitious debut . . . Card is a restless writer. Her first chapter delivers a stunning series of second-person character portraits; they build into a centuries-spanning epic about race, trauma, and the weight of a lie."

—*Entertainment Weekly*

"Across generations, a family reckons with the ghosts of enslavement's legacy in this stunning, kaleidoscopic debut. . . . Card invites readers to imagine themselves as a series of characters, one by one, in the moments before [a] revelation upends their identities, and such inventive narrative techniques continue throughout the novel. . . . A fantastic debut."

—*Booklist*

"A rich and layered story . . . A wonderfully ambitious novel: It sprawls in time from the uncertain present to the horror of slavery on a Jamaican plantation, examining racism, colorism, and infidelity and how they obscure and fracture a lineage. . . . An intriguing debut with an inventive spin on the generational family saga."

—*Kirkus Reviews*

"[A] profound, assured debut . . . Through a fluid blend of patois and erudite descriptions of Jamaica, Card offers a kaleidoscopic portrait of a troubled but resilient family whose struggles are inscribed by the island they once called home. This masterful chronicle haunts like the work of Marlon James and hits just as hard."

—*Publishers Weekly*

"[A] radiant debut . . . Card is a beguiling storyteller, and *These Ghosts Are Family* is layered with fraught family relationships arising from the complicated legacies of the racial divide in Jamaica and in the United States. Card's characters—even the ghosts—are vividly drawn and compelling. [Card] is a public librarian and now one of our brightest new writers. There is magic in these pages."

—*BookPage*

"Card weaves a multigenerational narrative that tackles racism, colonialism, slavery, immigration, infidelity, and family ties—and just about every other issue of the modern age."

—*Library Journal*

"A dying man has kept a secret for three decades that will change the course of his family's life and alter everything they thought they knew. The story sweeps across time and location, from Jamaica to Harlem, to reveal the background of his choice and the effects it has had on everyone he's encountered."

—*Electric Lit*

"Spanning the generations of the Paisley family from colonial Jamaica to present-day New York City, *These Ghosts Are Family* traces the impact of Abel's deception on his entire family and demonstrates how the choices a person makes can resonate for many years to come."—*She Reads*

"A gripping tale of generational trauma and what happens when it goes unaddressed . . . This may be your next page-turner."—*Refinery29*

"I've admired Card's writing a long while, and in *These Ghosts Are Family*, a Jamaican family contends with a faked death, a stolen identity, and the revelation of decades-old secrets."

—R.O. Kwon

"Maisy Card's remarkable debut is for anyone out there with family drama or trauma and for those who have tried to make their own way despite—or in spite of—it."

—*MS.* magazine

"*These Ghosts Are Family* operates on two levels: it pursues the personal (e.g., infidelity, lies, betrayal) while also exploring the universal; through the lens of one family, it confronts the enduring traumas of colonial history, slavery, and forced migration."

—*Lit Hub*

"[Maisy Card] wrote this book like it was an abstract work of art. . . . This book is a must-read."

—*Livre Cafe*

"A breathtaking story that sweeps across continents and time."

—*Debutiful*

"Absolutely haunting . . . Card's writing is inventive and captivating, dipping into different narrative styles and playing with magical realism and folklore."

—*BuzzFeed*

"This electric and luminous family saga announces the arrival of a new American talent."

—*BookRiot*

"A solid debut novel from author Maisy Card that engages the reader from the very beginning right up to the end. If Maisy keeps writing novels like this, she will be a force in the book industry for years."

—*Red Carpet Crash*

"[A] compelling debut . . . [The novel is] presented asynchronously, actively engaging readers in piecing together the puzzle of a family that doesn't know how or if they all fit together. . . . [Card's] personal understanding affects and authenticates the characters and events in *These Ghosts Are Family*. Card is a powerful new voice, and readers will eagerly await her next effort."

—*Shelf Awareness*

"Trust the buzz for this haunting novel about a Jamaican family."

—*Apple Books*

"One of the buzziest books of the year . . . Spanning decades, this moving tale . . . chronicle[s] one family's story from colonial Jamaica to modern-day Harlem."

—*PopSugar*

"One of the year's buzziest books."

—*Bustle*

"Maisy Card has written a spectacular intergenerational novel . . . She's such a lyrical writer that I found myself rereading paragraphs for the sheer pleasure of letting her words wash over me. . . . A magnificent story, a family saga in which racism is threaded into its tapestry, ghosts live among us, and somehow, each person in this family tree is relatable. . . . This tale mixing history and folklore earns a place in the canon of magnificent intergenerational novels."
—NJ.com

"A masterful novel that spans from Jamaica to England to America and weaves together a tale about a family that was faced with slavery, emigration, bitterness, guilt, and ultimately atonement. . . . An explosive novel about how one man's lie can change everything for the people who once loved and cared for him."
—Book Reviews By A Book Lover

"These Ghosts Are Family presents Jamaica as a people, a history, a physical place, an unplottable scape, imagination, and memory."
—The Book Slut

"[A] sweeping family saga."
—IHeartRadio.com

"Card captures lightning in a bottle with this book."
—The Rumpus

"Maisy Card's debut novel is cat nip for those who love to feast on the dysfunction of family . . . This is worth a read."
—Paper magazine

"[A] generational saga of this sort is a beloved genre, and These Ghosts Are Family by Maisy Card blows open the previous limitations of this kind of writing . . . Card deftly weaves in a ghostly element that continues the flow of the story rather than disrupts it. It infuses the dramatic moments with more weight, keeping the readers at a safe distance but piquing a different kind of curiosity."
—I've Read This

"Colorful and complex. Readers will be intrigued by a story that is as intricate as the realities its characters face. . . . Not only bold and ambitious, but also honest and real, as it accurately reflects the challenges descendants of slaves face when attempting to trace their genetic lineage and history. The novel, appropriately, feels like a puzzle, much like the jumbled origin stories of the African diaspora."
—The New Orleans Review

"An expansive portrait of history, family, and the inextricable ways the two shape perceptions of who we really are . . . *These Ghosts Are Family* stares down the history of colonialism in Jamaica and its continued legacy of colorism in stark, heartfelt prose."

—*Guernica*

"An absorbing story, and the ability of the author to tie her characters together is masterful."

—emissourian.com

"Card's writing is wonderful . . . She weaves in history and cultural elements with a touch of majesty."

—*Bowling Green Daily News*

"At turns painful, mesmerizing, amusing, and haunting."
—*Wesleyan University News*

"Card's hauntingly beautiful debut novel pivots around this subterfuge to spin the story of Abel/Stanford's ancestors and descendants, as well as figures from their shared history. She maps colonialism, racism, and infidelity in complex, rewarding storytelling that reflects the many truths of being human."

—*Austin 360*

"Maisy Card is a great writer. [Her] compelling debut . . . evokes the richness of culture and the inevitable impact of generational secrets, full of magnificent characters that continue to haunt me."
—Nicole Dennis-Benn, author of
Patsy and *Here Comes the Sun*

"Every family's got secrets but Abel Paisley's secret is monstrous and mesmerizing. *These Ghosts Are Family* begins with energy and intrigue and, really, never lets up. This book is painful and shocking but it can be funny as hell, too. What a talented writer. Maisy Card has written one of the best debut novels I've read in many years."
—Victor LaValle, author of
The Changeling

"Through Maisy Card's immersive storytelling, *These Ghosts Are Family* explores the intersections of generational trauma, love, and long-held family secrets, showing what it means to build a life in the face of history. I was hooked from page one."

—Lisa Ko, author of *The Leavers*

"I suspect many readers will talk about the consequences of unspoken generational trauma in *These Ghosts Are Family*, but I'm most amazed by the deft use of characterization, place, and embodiment here. This book is a master class in writing home as a collection of odd spirits and a mobile metaphor."

—Kiese Laymon, author of *Long Division*

"In this fascinating debut, Maisy Card reveals her spectacular range and scope. Part immigrant narrative, part ghost story, part historical fiction, part family drama, *These Ghosts Are Family* explores and illuminates the complexities of race and lineage in Jamaica and the United States. This is a bold, gripping, compassionate book."

—Helen Phillips, author of *The Need*

"Maisy Card's relentlessly inventive debut is a thrilling exploration of family, memory, and which pasts we choose to haunt us."

—Kaitlyn Greenidge, author of
We Love You, Charlie Freeman

"This spirited narrative is grounded in a devastating history; and yet, somehow, *These Ghosts Are Family* generates a sense of possibility about the future—for these characters, and for the reader as well."

—Tope Folarin, author of
A Particular Kind of Black Man

"How do actions reverberate across multiple generations? In Maisy Card's stunning novel, people live and die and lose and love and make their way through this chaotic but profound experience we call life. Her luminous prose lights a way even in the darkest moments. *These Ghosts Are Family* will haunt you long after you finish it."

—Michele Filgate, editor of
What My Mother and I Don't Talk About

"Written with the brand of Jamaican humor I know and love, *These Ghosts Are Family* is a book I didn't know I needed to read, which might be the best kind of book. Maisy Card is a wonderful arrival for Caribbean literature."

—Alexia Arthurs, author of
How to Love a Jamaican

"*These Ghosts are Family* by Maisy Card will enchant readers completely with a fascinating cast of characters, each more bewitching than the last. This book is destined to become 2020's most beloved debut novel."

—Julia Fierro, author of
The Gypsy Moth Summer

THESE
GHOSTS
ARE
FAMILY

A NOVEL

MAISY CARD

Simon & Schuster Paperbacks

New York   London   Toronto   Sydney   New Delhi

Simon & Schuster Paperbacks
An Imprint of Simon & Schuster, Inc.
1230 Avenue of the Americas
New York, NY 10020

First Simon & Schuster paperback edition January 2021

SIMON & SCHUSTER and colophon are registered trademarks of Simon & Schuster, Inc.

For information about special discounts for bulk purchases, please contact Simon & Schuster Special Sales at 1-866-506-1949 or business@simonandschuster.com.

The Simon & Schuster Speakers Bureau can bring authors to your live event. For more information or to book an event, contact the Simon & Schuster Speakers Bureau at 1-866-248-3049 or visit our website at www.simonspeakers.com.

Interior design by Carly Loman

Manufactured in the United States of America

1   3   5   7   9   10   8   6   4   2

The Library of Congress has cataloged the hardcover edition as follows:
Names: Card, Maisy, author.
Title: These ghosts are family : a novel / Maisy Card.
Description: First Simon & Schuster hardcover edition.
New York : Simon & Schuster, 2020.
Identifiers: LCCN 2019038809 | ISBN 9781982117436 (hardback) |
ISBN 9781982117443 (paperback) | ISBN 9781982117450 (ebook)
Classification: LCC PS3603.A7325 T47 2020 | DDC 813/.6—dc23
LC record available at https://lccn.loc.gov/2019038809

ISBN 978-1-9821-1743-6
ISBN 978-1-9821-1744-3 (pbk)
ISBN 978-1-9821-1745-0 (ebook)

For my mother

somebody was afraid we would learn to cast spells
and our wonders were cut off
but they didn't understand
the powerful memory of ghosts.

—Lucille Clifton

FAMILY TREE

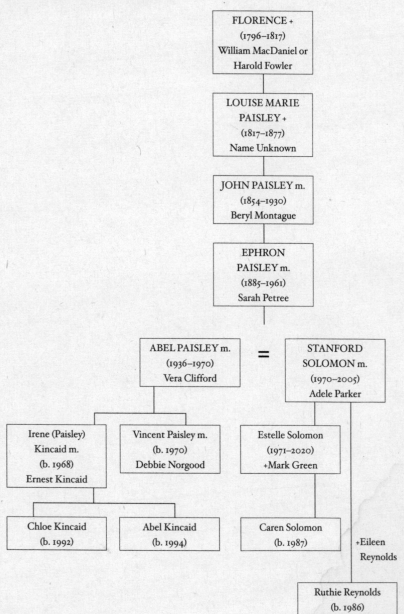

FLORENCE +
(1796–1817)
William MacDaniel or
Harold Fowler

LOUISE MARIE
PAISLEY +
(1817–1877)
Name Unknown

JOHN PAISLEY m.
(1854–1930)
Beryl Montague

EPHRON
PAISLEY m.
(1885–1961)
Sarah Petree

ABEL PAISLEY m.
(1936–1970)
Vera Clifford
= STANFORD
SOLOMON m.
(1970–2005)
Adele Parker

Irene (Paisley)
Kincaid m.
(b. 1968)
Ernest Kincaid

Vincent Paisley m.
(b. 1970)
Debbie Norgood

Estelle Solomon
(1971–2020)
+Mark Green

Chloe Kincaid
(b. 1992)

Abel Kincaid
(b. 1994)

Caren Solomon
(b. 1987)

+Eileen
Reynolds

Ruthie Reynolds
(b. 1986)

CONTENTS

THE TRUE DEATH OF ABEL PAISLEY

Harlem, 2005

Let's say that you are a sixty-nine-year-old Jamaican man called Stanford, or Stan for short, who once faked your own death. Though you have never used those words to describe what you did. At the time you'd thought of it as seizing an opportunity placed before you by God, but since your wife, Adele, died a month ago, you've convinced yourself her heart attack was retribution for your sin. So today you have gathered three of your female descendants in one house, even the daughter who has thought you dead all these years, and decided that you will finally tell them the truth: you are not who you say you are.

You have spent the last twenty years of your second life living in a brownstone in Harlem, running a West Indian grocery store. Recently, you shuttered the store. You have given up on fighting your arthritis pain and are finally sitting in the wheelchair Adele picked out. You are looking out of your parlor window, waiting for your daughter, the one who thinks you are dead, to arrive. It's been thirty-five years since you've seen her, so you study each woman who passes your house for reflections of yourself. You haven't bothered to shave, press your clothes, or comb your hair.

You are ready to be still and rot. You imagine the death of Stanford Solomon, unlike the abrupt end of Abel Paisley, will be achingly slow; already it feels like you are losing small pieces of yourself daily. To you, old age is the torture you deserve, a slow, insignificant death, your matter dispersing into the air like dandelion seeds until the day there's nothing left.

When you died the first time, you were still a young man in your thirties and had been working in England for less than a year. It wasn't easy for an immigrant, especially a black man, to find a decent job back then, but through a boy you'd known back in primary school, Stanford, you'd gotten a room and a job on a ship. You had no idea it was just the beginning of your streak of good luck.

You and Stanford were the chosen wogs they allowed to work alongside the white men. Stanford complained often about London. He hated the cold. He missed his grandmother and the tiny village, Harold Town, where you'd both grown up back in Jamaica. You'd already escaped the countryside for Kingston, and from there, London. You felt free. That sense of freedom and joy only dampened when you thought of the family you left behind. Your first wife, Vera, wrote you long letters weekly about how you'd abandoned her and left her to become a dried-up old spinster. But you both knew perfectly well that it was her idea for you to go to England, where she thought you'd somehow become a better provider. Your son, Vincent, was still in Vera's womb when you sailed off. Your daughter, Irene, a stumbling toddler. You had barely settled in when Vera's first letter arrived, with the list of things she wanted you to buy and send to them. With every letter the list grew longer, and you worried that you would never be enough.

The day you died, you were running along the dock because you were late for work while a container was being lowered onto the ship. You stopped short when the container fell, dropped from the crane, and thundered against the deck. You were close enough to hear the screaming.

"Who was it?" you heard someone shout.

"One of the wogs!" another answered. "It's Abel!"

For a moment you were confused, hearing yourself pronounced dead. It was like one of those movies where the dead person's spirit stands by watching as a crowd gathers around his body. But no, you were certain, it wasn't your body, so you boarded the ship. The captain approached you immediately and said, "I'm sorry, mate. No way Abel could have survived that."

You almost laugh now when you think of it—the one time racism worked in your favor. The captain had gotten his wogs confused, looked you right in the eye, and mistaken you for the other black guy. Abel was dead, crushed under the container. Unrecognizable. But you, Stanford now, could turn and go home.

Perhaps it's telling about your nature that you did not hesitate. You nodded and turned and walked away, quickly, from Abel and all his responsibilities, before any of the others had a chance to recognize you. Back in your room at the boardinghouse, you riffled through your roommate's things and learned what it really meant to be Stanford. You and Stanford actually did look alike, which made it a little easier to forgive the fact that all the white people had trouble telling you apart. You were the same height, the same light-brown complexion, the same lanky build. You, Abel, did not arrive dressed for an English winter, so you had even taken to wearing Stanford's clothes.

Of course, you thought of your family. Your wife, Vera. You thought about the two life insurance policies you'd purchased. The one she'd made you take out before you left, and the one the company made mandatory. You decided that you were worth more to her dead. Vera was beautiful. She would find a new husband, a richer one; the children were young enough to embrace a new father, and they would finally live the life Vera thought that she deserved, the one she had no qualms about constantly demanding of you.

Stanford had little family. No wife. No children. That was what clinched things for you. Stanford was raised by his grandmother, who was in her seventies and losing her eyesight. You could continue writing her letters, sending her a little money, and there was no bother there. What surprised you was how right it felt. At least then.

When you met Adele shortly after you became Stanford, you connected with her immediately. Like you, she was Jamaican and had left her family to work in England, though at nineteen, she was almost fifteen years younger than you. You were as drawn to her as you had been to your first wife, and she to you. The difference was that Adele did not try to remake and mold you. When you told her the truth, the very first night you spent together, that you had taken your friend's name, she did not try to dissuade you. Instead, she avoided the subject until you proposed, and she said yes on the condition that you live in America. As if leaving that country would leave the lie behind.

Later, the guilt would hit her first, a few years after coming to the U.S. She had started to go to church multiple times a week and suggested that you atone. You remember having laughed at the thought that getting down on your knees could redeem you. But since the day that she collapsed in the store, you've been thinking about your past. You've been thinking about that word, *fake*, and you decided you were right to never use it to describe what you've done. You are a thief, pure and simple. It wasn't Stanford's life you had stolen, for he would have lost that regardless. It was his death. Where is his soul now? Circling the world, looking for a grave that does not yet exist? Isn't it about time you give him his due?

Your granddaughter has taught you to use the computer to kill some of your idle time. It was easier than you thought to find your first daughter, to track her journey from Jamaica to New York.

You are thinking of the grave that bears your real name and all of the people who needlessly mourned you when Irene finally arrives, the daughter who thinks you are dead. She is under the impression that she has been called to your house to care for an old man in a wheelchair. That old man is you. You didn't realize just how little you've thought about her all these years until you watch her climb the stoop, and all the feeling you should have had for your firstborn suddenly rushes through you.

When she enters, you see her mother Vera's wide, obstinate mouth, her large, slightly bulbous hazel eyes, her flaring nostrils. You can sense immediately, before she even speaks, that she also has her mother's brutal tongue. You are intimidated. She has a look that says she is a frayed rope one tug away from snapping, and it occurs to you to wonder if, when you tell her the truth, she will kill you. In that moment, your death—your real death—flashes in your mind.

You have never had a premonition before, but now the certainty of it causes you to slump forward in your wheelchair. You have a vision of a woman supporting your weight as you make your way up the flight of stairs, bringing you all the way to the top, and then just letting you go, as if she'd just remembered she was supposed to be somewhere else.

Your daughter, who moments before had introduced herself as Irene, the name you gave her, bends down and asks, "You alright, Mr. Solomon?" You sit up straight, or as straight as an old man with scoliosis and arthritis can, and say, "You can call me Stanford."

❧

Now let's say you are a thirty-seven-year-old home health aide named Irene whose father faked his own death, but you don't know it yet. Today is the day he will tell you. All you know is that he died when you were very young. You have no memory of him whatsoever. You recognize his face only as a young man in photographs. Though your mother always told you your father was timid and spineless, in one photo you remember a square-jawed man with reddish hair, face lightly freckled, dressed in a police uniform, one hand on his gun, his eyes so astute and focused it felt like they were alive and could see into you. You don't recognize that face when you meet the old man who is your new client, for his red hair is white, and as far as you know, aging after death is impossible.

You do think it's strange that this man called the agency and asked for you by name. He claimed another client recommended you, which you find unlikely. You do your job, but you don't make much effort to be nice. You've lived in America for seven years and the only reason you came here at all, the only reason you agreed to do this miserable job in the U.S., was to get away from your family. Your brother and your mother. It seems ironic that you spend your time caring for other people's parents, when you couldn't stand the thought of doing so for your own.

Your husband left you and went back to Jamaica after the first month in Miami, but you stayed because you have two children who you'd sworn to keep away from the cancer that raised you. Instead you moved to Brooklyn where you had a childhood friend to help you. But Vera, your mother, died just a year later. Sometimes you regret not waiting. You would at least have inherited her house if you'd stayed in Jamaica. Now you are living in a basement apartment with your two kids, working nine hours a day, six days a week, changing colostomy bags and spoon-feeding strangers to stay afloat.

You misunderstand the look the old man gives you when you introduce yourself. You worry that he's another pervert, that he'll sneak pinches when your back is turned or when you're on your knees, bent over cleaning. It happens so often you're not even surprised anymore. You are grateful that he's in a wheelchair—at least he can't sneak up on you—although it means you'll probably have to help him to the toilet. You might have to pull down his pants for him, which can lead to all kinds of undesirable propositions.

You are scrutinizing his features, speculating what kind of man you have in front of you, when the image of your father, dressed in a tweed suit, too hot for the Caribbean, that he had specially made for his journey away from you, flashes in your mind, but you don't know why. It is the only photo you have of the two of you. He is standing under a mango tree with you in his arms. That tree became your favorite growing up. That tree became your father. Whenever you sat under that tree, you asked for things, and even though you rarely got them, you still imagined he could hear you.

It's always been clear to you that your father's death was the dividing line between hell and heaven. Even if you do not remember much about those days or years before he left, you know you had seen your mother smile, you carry the physical memory of being picked up and held, you swear there was laughter. Before he died, you didn't know what it meant to be mishandled, to be jerked, to be shoved, to be slapped, to be pinched or even choked by her. You know because you remember the first time Vera did each of these things to you. Each time, afterward, you sat under the mango tree and asked the man in the picture who you thought was dead and therefore held some supernatural power to please protect you. He never did. Today you will finally know why.

You have always wondered who you'd be, where you would be, if he'd never left, if he had lived. You don't think you would have run away from home and down the aisle with the first man who stood in front of you. Later, after he reveals his true identity to you, if you were to "accidentally" let him fall down the stairs, knowing the life you've lived, a life he caused, would anyone blame you?

৶

Never mind. Instead, you are a thirty-four-year-old heroin addict named Estelle Solomon whose father once faked his own death. He did it before he had you, but you don't know it yet. Today is the day that he'll tell you. Sometime in the late afternoon. For now, you are lying, unaware, on a daybed in the basement of your family's Harlem brownstone, where you've lived for the last eight years, since a judge made your parents the legal guardians of your daughter. You had begged your father to let you and Caren move into the garden apartment, right above you, because it has windows. But he screamed, "Is what you need windows fah? Why, when you spend fi yuh whole life asleep?" Instead, they kept your daughter upstairs with them and left you to stay in the basement. Your father seems determined to keep you alive but just as eager to bury you.

You weren't always such an embarrassment. You worked very hard to become one.

You have been an addict for many years now. But before your mother died, you were also an artist. You could still hustle. You were taking and selling pictures. Occasionally, someone would put your photos on display in a café or a small gallery. Every once in a while you sold something, made a little money, and even came home and gave it to your father, telling him to buy something nice for your daughter with the money your art made you. He would never take it. Worse, he would throw it down on the floor in front of you, so both he and your mother would have to watch you gather the scattered bills from all over the room.

"After me nuh know where that money come from. Me nuh wan' know what someone like you have fi do to come by it."

Someone like you. He stopped short of calling you a whore for the sake of your mother. But you could feel how badly he wanted to.

You have always sensed a lie behind your parents' words, have always suspected that their Jamaica was a place that did not exist. You have always wondered why they never chose, in all these years, to return to that island so perfect. Instead it was always the right weapon to throw in your face, always the only answer to their problems, their main problem always being you.

When you were younger, you would scream back at them that if in Jamaica, the daughters were pure, saved themselves until marriage, stood by their mother's side every day in the kitchen and watched them cook, brought their father his slippers when he got home from the store, went to church every Sunday, never refused to recite the Lord's Prayer at the table before a meal, didn't proclaim themselves agnostics, wanted to be wives instead of artists, always agreed to stack canned food on the shelves of their father's store after school, didn't stand under the streetlights at night talking to boys from the block, did their own laundry and their father's too, did not jump between their parents and cuss their father out every time he raised his voice at their mother, did not promise to kill their father if he dared threaten — only threatened — to one day slap their mother in the face. If in Jamaica, daughters did not run away from home and return pregnant by a man twice their age, did not go out partying instead of staying home with their newborn child, did not walk down the street in skirts so short they barely covered their pum-pum, did not make their mother cry and waste away with worry, never did drugs and if they did, were never so weak that they would become addicted. If in Jamaica, daughters were churned out of factories without the slightest defect, why the fuck didn't they just go back there and leave you alone?

When your father tells you his secret, that he is not really Stanford Solomon, and therefore you in turn cannot be Estelle Solomon, that your family does not even exist, you will have your answer. And it is perfect.

◈

Say you are an eighteen-year-old college student named Caren who lives in a Harlem brownstone with your mother, who is a heroin addict, and your wheelchair-bound Jamaican grandfather who faked his own death, but you won't know it for a few hours.

Every morning when you wake up, you remember that your grandmother Adele, the person you loved above everyone else in this world, is gone. She worked so hard to shield you from your mother. She loved you so deep it almost rendered your mother's love supplementary—a bonus—so that the times when Estelle was lucid enough to pay attention to you felt like a holiday, a special occasion. Every child knows that holidays don't last. By the time you were eight, you had stopped being disappointed.

You don't begrudge your mother. You can see how hard she is trying. You know she hates living in your grandfather's house, but in the month since your grandma died, she no longer vanishes for days at a time, returning with no explanation. For the first time in your life, with the exception of an hour a day when she sneaks outside to score, you know exactly where you'll find her. Knowing should comfort you, but on the rare occasion when you go to the basement and stare at her, passed out on the daybed, you can't help but wish it had been her who had a heart attack instead of your grandmother. You think, *What a waste of a life*. The same words you'd overhear your grandmother mumble when she talked about Estelle. You are ashamed of your thoughts. Most of the time Estelle invokes pity in you, and you conclude that's worse than hatred, for a child to pity their mother.

Later, when your grandfather tells you that he was born Abel Paisley and not Stanford Solomon, you will understand why your grandmother was so disgusted by Estelle's addiction. Other people are so desperate to make a better life that they are willing to steal one, while your mother is fine with throwing hers away. Perhaps, a life does not belong exclusively to one person, you learn. Look how easily it can be passed from one person to the next until every bit of it is put to good use. You will wonder if there is someone out there who would wear your life better.

But before that, you notice that from the moment you wake up, your grandpa is acting strange. You had been begging him to get a home health aide for the last year because caring for him was getting to be too much for your grandmother, and now it is too much for you. All of a sudden there is one sitting with him at the kitchen table. He is giddy as he says her name to you, Irene, and you wonder if it has been too long since he's seen a woman he wasn't related to.

You are about to smile at Irene when you notice that she doesn't bother to smile at you, barely tilts her head in your direction, before she returns to reading your grandpa's newspaper. If your grandmother were here, the two of you would go upstairs and talk about this woman. For a moment, you imagine all of the things you would say about her, until you remember that your grandmother is gone. Briefly you contemplate going down to the basement and telling your mother about Irene, but that would be as exciting as talking to a corpse.

Since your grandmother left you, you've found it hard to think about anything else besides getting away from this family. So much so, you've started sleeping with one of your professors at City College. It helps the fantasy of running away. The irony that you might be following in your mother's footsteps doesn't escape you. Your father had been a professor, but your mother had been a high school girl who'd just had a bunch of college friends. Your birth cost him his marriage and his reputation, and even though he was kind the handful of times you visited him, you know he resented you. You speak to him only on holidays now, even though he just lives in Queens. But still, you want him to be proud of you. You are actually going to get a degree one day. You are actually going to leave this house.

Sometimes you imagine a scenario in which your professor leaves his wife and four children and buys a condo for the two of you in downtown Brooklyn. You are not sure what you would say if he were actually to propose this to you. He hasn't talked about leaving his wife, hasn't said he loves you. You might think less of him if he did. Besides, you have no intention of trading your dysfunctional family for another, being the reluctant stepmother to four resentful white kids. In your family, you are known as the smart one for a reason.

Now let's say that you are a dead woman, six years on the other side, whose husband let you believe he was dead. When you were alive, they called you Vera, but here there is no need for names. You did not know the truth about your husband until your own death, but the timing of the knowledge made it no less infuriating. You have analyzed all the years you spent mad with guilt, thinking you were the one who sent him to his grave.

Death is just one long therapy session. You have gone over every second of your life and divided them into the misery you caused and the misery others caused you. You have been waiting for six years for this motherfucker to die, and you know that the day has finally arrived.

You look at the elaborate theater that your former husband is producing and you laugh (or you imagine yourself laughing; you no longer have a mouth or a face). He has asked the women down to the brownstone's parlor. He has your daughter—your daughter who he barely even knew—help him move from his wheelchair to his favorite rocking chair, which he thinks makes him appear wise. Clearly, none of the women want to be there. The three of them settle side by side on a crushed-velvet settee barely listening, unaware of their blood connection.

You are there in the room with them, waiting for Abel to gather up his nerve. You have decided to choose one person in his house to be the catalyst of his death, to be briefly possessed by you long enough to get the deed done, but the question of who has stumped you. Who will hurt him the most?

You look at your own daughter, Irene, think she's owed the revenge, but you can see both the past and the future and know that giving her guilt to carry is not doing her any favors. There is a cruel impulse inside her, one that you gave her, that you do not want to feed. You know that most of her misery was brought about by you. When she dies, you will face your own reckoning, but for now you have no plans to ruin her life any further.

You look at the other two women, his daughter and granddaughter, the products of the weak woman he married after you. You have passed her in the other place, for she's dead now too. You thought you'd have harsh words for her, that her day of reckoning would come, but you mostly feel sorry for her. You can feel her pining for Abel, pleading with you to spare him, until you've recently had no choice but to shut her out.

You are so close to Abel as he tells them you can smell the Wray & Nephew rum on his breath, but he can't see or sense you. When he says the words *I was born Abel Paisley*, you see your daughter shake her head. It will take her a while to understand that her father was alive all those years and left her behind to suffer with you. After he says the words *I was born Abel Paisley*, his daughter Estelle exhales deeply, tears form in her eyes, but then she just bursts out laughing. For the first time in her life, she actually looks at her father with gratitude. She actually turns to the old man and says, "Thank you." Estelle puts her arms around her daughter, Caren, who, after he tells them, begins to cry.

Irene stands up and crosses the room, kneeling before Abel, and for a moment you worry that she will choke the life out of him before you even have a chance to. Instead she studies his face. She is thinking about the picture, the one under the mango tree, and when she recognizes him, she walks out of the room, collects her purse from the hall, and leaves for good, slamming the front door so hard it shakes you. You look at the two girls left in the room and reassure yourself that no matter which one ends him, it will actually be you. If only he could see you as he's falling. If you still had a mouth, you would be laughing. If you still had a body, you would dance.

THE LAMB OR THE LION

Kingston, 1966

ABEL

Wherever he goes, Abel drags the dead man with him. It is his first day back since the murder of his partner six weeks ago, and here is Abel in his police car, stalled in downtown Kingston traffic on his way into the station, and there is Bully haunting the passenger seat beside him, the front of his uniform stiff from the dried and caked blood, the once black color dyed a rusty brown. Bully has become an extension of Abel's imagination, a flickering light that goes on and off without notice. It's been a struggle to stay focused on the living world.

Tomorrow God comes to Jamaica. Haile Selassie, the emperor of Ethiopia, has announced that he will stop in Kingston on his Caribbean tour, and so every one of his followers on the island has migrated to the capital by any method they can manage. Rastafarians have gridlocked the roads. They arrive stuffed into the backs of chicken trucks from their mountain hamlets or on foot from the slums of West Kingston. They walk in the road and alongside it, pushing their belongings in wheelbarrows, dragging them in over-stuffed rucksacks, or holding them in their arms.

The Rastas remind Abel of the men who ambushed his partner. As he watches them snake between cars, trying to get to the other side of the street, he feels a tremor begin in his left leg that slowly builds and moves throughout his entire body. He tries to steady himself by gripping the steering wheel tighter.

Bully's acrid sweat, his living smell, is still emanating from the driver's seat. Abel wants to stick his head out of the window to escape it; he would rather inhale the saltwater air, mixed with exhaust, but he doesn't want any of the pedestrians to notice that he is shaking.

You mus' push the man outta fi yuh head, Vera tells him each night when he wakes from the same nightmare. He can't, though. The sight of his partner crumpled on the hood of their car, dying, will never leave him. His wife cannot understand or maybe she just refuses to. Vera had never liked Bully, had long harped that the man was a bad influence. Her lack of empathy is just one of the things that has pushed them apart during the first year of their marriage.

Another is the fact that Abel didn't want to return to the police force after Bully's murder; he never wanted to join in the first place, he knew he wasn't cut out, but Vera threatened to leave him if he quit, just as she insisted that he join up. There are not many options for people like him, she'd reminded him over and over. She means for the poor, the too country, the uneducated. When they argue, he stops short of blaming her for Bully's death, but a part of him does. After all, everything that Abel is now is her creation. The word that she has said the most this past year is *sacrifice*. It was she who sacrificed her family and their money to be with Abel. It was she who went from training as a bookkeeper for her father's law practice to working at a garment factory, she likes to remind him. Whereas Abel actually improved his circumstance, going from being a rich man's chauffeur to a constable. They still don't have much money, but they have a future, if he gets promoted. They have respect.

If Abel does not perform his fair share of sacrifice, he knows their marriage will end. Lately he's been worrying that she wants him to die, to get killed on duty, just to spare herself the embarrassment of divorce. Why else would she insist he keep a job so dangerous?

If that is his wife's wish, Abel is wondering if today is the day it will come true, when he hears the police dispatcher's voice through his radio: *Child stuck in tree in Harbour View*. He breathes, relieved for the easy task, hopeful that he will live to see the evening.

It was no secret that what he and Bully had for the last year was not a real partnership. Bully doled out orders and Abel obeyed them. Now he must act on his own until he's paired with someone else, but he's not sure he even knows how. The last time Bully ordered Abel to do something (*Follow me and watch the door, Abe*), Abel refused, and now his partner is dead.

Abel decides that if he can think like his partner—Bully was a thirty-year veteran of the constabulary force, after all—he has a better chance of surviving. He's tried so hard to get inside Bully's head he feels like he has come to know him better since his death. What he saw as cruelty in his partner now seems like a means of survival.

He turns on his siren and waits for the other cars to move. The cars in front of him begrudgingly ease into the next lane, but as soon as one moves, new people flood into the open space, trying to get across the street. Abel honks his horn, but the crowd ignores him. The sky, filled with a glaring sun all morning, suddenly becomes overcast, and Abel prays for rain, a reason for people to flee indoors.

He begins inching forward, pushing on the gas pedal gently. A group of women holding palm branches bang on the hood of his car, but he keeps moving, leaning on the horn, no longer timid, imagining that it is Bully's leg pressing on the gas, not his own, until they are forced to clear out of his way.

❦

Now here is Abel at the house in Harbour View, walking around to the backyard where he finds that the boy looks about nine or ten—

too old to be so cowardly. Abel, a country boy from Harold Town, grew up climbing trees, often with his friend Stanford. His mother worked as a maid in Kingston, so he barely saw her. He never knew his father. He was raised by his grandparents, who taught him to farm, how to subsist on whatever was growing around him. He is thinking someone should have already taught this boy the rules of survival, when the boy's mother puts her hand on his shoulder, wringing the fabric of his uniform with her nervous fingers.

"Lawd Jesus! Him soon drop an' bruk up himself!" she shouts.

A twenty-five-foot drop, Abel estimates. But a voice inside of him says, *Good, fall*, and he imagines the lanky body plummeting, the legs realigned at odd angles. He knows the voice is not his own; it is Bully's. People can see the boy from the road, so some have decided to use the top of a cement fence as bleachers to see what Abel will do next.

"Hurry up and get the bwai down, Red!" someone shouts when Abel takes off his hat for a moment, exposing his cinnamon-colored hair, to wipe the sweat from his brow. There are at least ten on-lookers by the time he inches up to the tree—men, women, and children—all laughing at the coward. As Abel stands surveying the backyard, an afternoon shower erupts, his prayer answered at the worst time, and he looks up at the boy, knowing he'll lose his grip on the slippery bark.

The boy's features are hard to distinguish in the distance, but Abel can see the white of his teeth as he winces in pain, struggling to hold on. He imagines Bully pulling out his gun and pointing it at the child, ordering him to come down by his own will or prepare to face God's. Abel fondles the handle of his gun, but no—he is not his partner. He doesn't have the clout to get away with breaking too many rules.

He goes to lock his holster and gun in the car. He prepares himself to climb. But what will he do when he gets to the top? This boy is almost too big to sit on his back. Abel pictures himself holding one of the child's ankles from below, tugging just hard enough until he's forced to move.

Too hard and he falls.

Fall.

Fall.

He can't stop himself from thinking it. *You mus' push the man outta fi yuh head.* He tries to concentrate on the boy and push his partner aside for the moment. Abel sees a stray cat run past him to find shelter from the downpour. He wants to do this too, to find shelter curled up inside a hollowed-out tree, safe and dry, like the saner animals, not out here doing a job no one else wants. But it is better than getting shot at, he reasons. It occurs to him that they no longer trust him to do anything more. He looks at the boy and then at the people sitting on the wall, and he knows that he cannot be the fool who let his partner get killed on his watch *and* the one who let a child fall and break his neck.

Abel starts to climb just as the rain beats down harder. He is barely five feet up the tree when he slips off, landing on his feet. The onlookers behind him erupt with laughter. He circles the area around the tree, hoping they can't see his face turning from its light brown to the color of his hair. He notices a pole in the ground with a piece of rope still tied to the bottom, probably once used to tether a goat. He asks the boy's mother if he can use the rope to make a foot strap. He takes off his shoes and socks, wraps the rope around his feet, and tries again.

The first time Abel climbed a coconut tree, he was alone. He remembers the feeling of disappointment when he got to the top, realizing there was no one there to see his triumph. But then he took in the view: he could see the zinc roofs of his neighbors' houses, the women washing their clothes down by the river, his grandfather bringing home stalks of sugarcane on the back of his mule. He felt powerful, capable, like the entire world was his and he needed no one. He tries to remember the last time he felt that way, definitely not since he joined the police force, or moved to the city, maybe not since he became an adult.

As Abel moves up the tree, he feels suddenly energized by his muscle memory kicking in. He scales about fifteen feet with ease, just as he had when he was younger. He pauses to catch his breath, sees that the boy is more attainable, though still too high. Suddenly, a bolt of lightning cracks through the sky and catches him off guard, and for a second before Abel loses his grip and falls, he sees his partner standing at the base of the tree, watching him, his skin gray, his eyes covered by a white film. Abel lands on his back, hard. The boy wails as he too slides several feet down, scraping some skin off the inside of his forearms, until the pain forces him to let go, and he lands with a thud just beside Abel.

Abel is out for a brief time; it doesn't feel like long, but when he wakes, coughing out the water that has filled his open mouth, he can hear Bully laughing. The laughter seems to surround him. He rubs the back of his head to see if he is bleeding. The boy is beside him, and Abel turns to see the child, on his back too, whimpering. The mother is kneeling over him, cradling him in her arms as if she's certain he's dying.

It invokes a slight resentment in Abel to see how this boy is babied. He thinks of how Vera doted on him when they first got together—how she showered him with a depth of affection he'd never known, how she'd stand on the veranda and wave as he drove off each morning, how she'd make sure she was there waiting as he got home. But that lasted only for a few months. Since Vera started working at the factory, she's constantly withdrawn and irritable. This life is her doing, yet she seems to hate it as much as Abel.

"Gary. Look how you get cut up so! Nuh move," the mother says to her son. "You mustn't try fi move. Make me go get some rubbing alcohol and bandage." She gets up and runs into the house.

Abel's vision is blurred, but he can see the outline of his partner, coming into focus. Bully is turned away from Abel, facing the tree that he and the boy fell from. He is standing with his face close to the bark, as if he is studying it, but Abel knows that he is letting him see his back, the deep gashes that the cutlass blade made when the men attacked him. The wounds are still open, red and raw, a reminder to Abel that all his choices so far have been the wrong ones. He closes his eyes and then opens them; the vision is gone.

Abel stands up and it feels as if a bushfire has ignited in between his temples. He sees that the onlookers have lost interest and left. The mother is dressing the boy's wounds with rubbing alcohol, and he squeals every time the cotton touches his skin.

"You alright," his mother keeps saying to her son.

Abel tries to clear his head and focus enough to walk back to his car. He wonders why he had believed this task would be simple, when nothing about his new life is. His thoughts are interrupted by the boy squealing, a sound that worms its way into his ear and makes his head pound, makes him ball his fists in frustration.

Abel bends down over the boy. "Listen to me. You too big for this foolishness," he says. He reaches for the boy's face, tries to make him look at him, but the child howls like a dog and shakes his head back and forth. Abel finds his hand pulling back and then making contact with the child's face before he realizes what's happening. The sound of the slap is as loud as the bolt of lightning.

"Wha' wrong with you?" the mother yells, pushing Abel away from them with her free hand. "You gone crazy, man? Leave fi me son alone before me report you."

Abel stands up but looks the boy in the eye. He is about to apologize when he sees that the boy has finally stopped crying. His face is absent of emotion, as if the slap has thrown him right out of his body. A part of Abel feels like he is standing at a distance, watching his own body's actions, aghast. But another part feels exhilarated. He has done this child a favor. He thinks if Bully is watching, he would be nodding his head in approval.

VERA

The last thing Vera remembers is rising from her sewing machine to get some air. Now she wakes to find two of her coworkers propping her up in a plastic chair in front of the manager's desk, as if they are staging a mannequin in a shop window. Someone puts a cup of water to her lips and raises her own hand to hold it, but she can't feel her body, let alone control it, so it falls.

Mr. Zacca nods at the floor, and she feels the girl to her left, Madge, remove her weight from Vera's left side to tackle the water. Vera's body begins to slump in the direction that Madge went until Vivian, the girl on her right, straightens her up. Mr. Zacca begins talking, but it is hard for Vera to listen, so distracted is she by the sensation of her limbs being numb.

"You know seh me cyaan have one pregnant woman in hereso. How you fi keep up? Come back when you not pregnant," he says, waving her away like dust.

Madge was the only one she told. Vera uses the little strength that has returned to her to look the woman in the eye, telling her without words that she is lucky that Vera is too weak to punish her for her betrayal. Meanwhile, Vivian offers to accompany her home, but Mr. Zacca refuses to pay her for the time, so she walks Vera to the bus stop, gives her a hug goodbye, as if she knows she will never see her again. Vivian's prediction is spot-on because Vera knows that she cannot go back, for they will ask her about the baby. She can say she lost it, true in a sense, but every time she tells the lie, she will remember how she betrayed Abel. She's pregnant by another man, and she has no intention of letting Abel or anyone else know.

And besides, Vera had told herself that the job at the factory would only be temporary. Just until she could find something better, though she's worked there for more than nine months. She planned to save up money to go back to school, but so far, she hasn't been able to make any progress. Vera's father was a barrister, so she had grown up comfortable. She never worked as hard as she should have in school, and she quit after fifth form. She had taken for granted that she would be the wife of a man with means. She knows she would have if she hadn't fallen for Abel.

It is Vera's goal to find her way back to that life again, but her choice of husband has worked against her at every turn. It never seemed to occur to Abel to want more, so she had to do the wanting for both of them. He would have been fine to continue working as a chauffeur, if she hadn't pushed him. She told him straightaway that she had no intention of making a life of hard labor part of her marriage vows. She saw how the other women at the factory had been ground down to the bone so that they looked much older than they were. She promised herself she would never be like them.

Next to the bus stop, a group of Rastafarians is congregating. Vera counts fifteen of them moving up the street and can pick out several more weaving through pedestrians to join their brethren. Most are setting up drums. They're dressed in long white tunics cinched at the waist with cords and white turbans. Some of them have dreadlocks but not all. A few carry long staffs, taller than their heads, curled at the top like a shepherd's. She's never seen Rastafarians dressed like these, and she wonders if they are wearing some special ceremonial garments in honor of Selassie's visit to Kingston.

Pages from this morning's discarded *Jamaica Gleaner* lay scattered and trampled on the ground, occasionally being picked up and transported along the sidewalk by foot traffic and the wind. Vera reads them as she waits, hoping that focusing on the words will make her feel steadier on her feet.

EMPEROR SELASSIE LANDS IN TRINIDAD

POSTAL SERVICE CRIPPLED BY STRIKE

KEEP ON POURING GORDON'S DRY GIN.

Most people are sucking their teeth and shaking their heads as they pass by, annoyed at having to go around the demonstrators. The Rastas begin beating the skin of their drums. Two of them are hoisting the Ethiopian flag, emblazoned with a golden lion. A man with his face hidden under a thick beard, his profile obscured by matted dreadlocks, holds up a photo of Haile Selassie and yells over and over, "Behold the Lamb of God!"

Which taketh away the sin of the world. Vera remembers enough to complete the verse, though she knows her pastor would be horrified to see who it is being used to describe. He would no sooner entertain the idea that Selassie is the incarnation of Christ than he would that Vera is the new Virgin Mother. What would her pastor do if he knew that she was getting rid of a child? Would he rally the congregation to chase her from the church? Would he use her as a cautionary tale, make her the Jezebel in one of his sermons?

She bows her head and asks for forgiveness, getting a head start. Takes a moment to explain it one more time to Jesus Christ himself. While she knows she's adding more sin to her soul, it is the only way to spare Abel more suffering. He's already watched his partner die. Besides, this way, if she needs to leave Abel, and that seems more of a possibility lately, this will make her load much lighter. *Well, isn't leaving your husband a sin too?* It's her mother's voice she hears. She hasn't spoken to her mother in a year, since she married Abel. Her mother did not think Abel had any drive to better himself, and it burns Vera to know she was right.

But there is no question in her mind that this Abel is not the man she married, though she had known him for just three months before he proposed. When they met, she had been the outside woman of a man twenty years her senior, Chester Brown, a friend of her father's. Her mother had always told her to find a man in the church, but those who were unmarried were still boys. She wanted a man who knew himself, someone already established like her father. She had known Chester since she was a child, so she felt at ease around him. It also helped that he bought Vera almost anything she wanted, though she wasn't after gifts. She wanted a husband, a life just like the one her parents had built. In her naivete, she thought that since this man slept with her and complained about his wife, it meant she had a chance of replacing her.

But he made it clear to Vera that she should never come by his house. He was just as afraid of Vera's father finding out about their affair as he was his wife. One day, she surprised him, when she knew that his wife had gone to visit relatives in England. He let her inside, rushed her in so the neighbors wouldn't see. They quarreled, and before she could turn to leave, he hit her. She hit him right back. He became enraged and started beating her.

She knew all the house staff heard her cries for help, but it was only Abel, Chester's driver, who did something. Abel chased the man right out of his own house and beat him in return, in his yard, as his neighbors looked on and did nothing. She had never known a man to stand up for her like that, except for her father. She thought it meant he loved her. She had never thought she would choose love over comfort, but her attraction to Abel, and her gratitude, was so strong she let everything else fall away. At first. Later, when Vera told Abel what kind of life she wanted, he promised to work to give it to her. When she asked him to become a constable, to improve his station in life, he didn't seem to hesitate.

Now he thinks that the city is not for him, and he wants to go back to his poor country life in Harold Town. He doesn't treat her like he used to. Not since they paired him with that wicked man as his partner. He's turned against her. He flinches when she touches him. She's not sure he even realizes it. Still, she knows no excuse will be good enough for her mother. *Is so you jus' go from one man bed to another? If you say vows, you mus' follow through.* If she leaves him, wherever she goes, it cannot be back to her family.

"King of Kings, Lord of Lords," one of the Rastas shouts. He holds the photo of the emperor, turning to his right, then his left, so all can see. Vera looks up from her newspaper page just as he turns to her, and their eyes meet. She looks back down at the ground.

Once the bus arrives, the teeming crowds rush it, and Vera abandons hope for a seat. She ends up standing next to the very same Rasta she'd just made eye contact with. Up close, Vera sees his eyes are a bright hazel, which stand out against his cherrywood complexion and light-brown dreaded hair. He smiles down at her, just as, to her horror, a wave of nausea hits her, and she leans over, and without thinking, she vomits into her purse. People start to groan and hold their noses. She feels light-headed, looks around with desperation for someone to give up their seat. Her knees are about to go limp when the Rasta puts his arm around her and pulls her head into his chest. "Is alright, sistah; you can lean on me," he says. Her first instinct is to push him away for acting so fresh with her, but she feels dizzy, as if she might faint. She is too sick to do anything but surrender. His head is above hers, so he can't see how red she's become. Her skin feels hot.

She wonders how she got here, leaning into this man like they are old lovers, when she had been raised to roll her eyes or curl her top lip at someone with his ragged appearance. Her mother would die if she saw her now. Vera can see her disapproving pale face in her mind vividly. Her mother, Patricia, taught her that whiteness was partly a state of mind, part manipulation of the body. Though she always told Vera her nose was too broad, her hair a little too kinky to pass as she did, if she let the relaxer sit in her hair until it burned, if she stayed out of the sun, if she displayed the right manners, the right poise, if she inserted her white grandfather in enough conversations and forgot that all of her ancestors on the other branches came from slaves, she would rise above her blackness. Jamaica was independent now; there was no need to be as lily-white as the queen—near white was white enough.

But here come these people, the Rastas like the one who held her up now, who believe that Ethiopia is the true Holy Land and that Haile Selassie is the living God. Decrying the very foundation of their colonial education, preaching instead that whites are the ones who are inferior and wicked. Embracing her blackness had become unnatural to Patricia, and subsequently to Vera, but she wondered now why it seemed more natural to put lye acid on the roots of her hair than to let it grow the way she was born. She understood why her mother carried on so when she saw Rastas walking the same streets as her, why she sometimes would call the police if she saw one near their house. They were manifestations of a truth she didn't want to face, and believed that if scorned enough could be permanently banished. Her mother didn't want to hear that more of her ancestors came from Africa than from England. That she was idolizing and mimicking the masters who raped and beat her foremothers and forefathers. That slavery was not over, and they'd never truly be free unless they rejected everything they'd been taught to value. Even the white Jesus she worshipped so feverishly. That woman would never embrace Haile Selassie, a god who looked like them, when she was taught that blackness was the opposite of everything divine.

But what if it wasn't? What if her mother was wrong? What if Marcus Garvey was right and a black king would redeem them? Save Vera from the poverty and fear she had come to know only now, but that other black people had experienced since the first white face appeared on the shores of Africa. All she knew was that her mother who had raised her had spurned her, but this stranger now held her up.

Her mother must be fuming, seeing how the prime minister is laying out the red carpet for Selassie, as they would for the queen. How his visit is invigorating a religion that people like her dismiss as nonsense and is bringing its many followers out of the shadows. Her mother will not possibly be able to call the police on everyone fast enough. *Communists*, she would spit out if she saw them. The dirtiest word she could possibly utter. She didn't think much more of Abel. While she approved of his lighter skin and red hair, 'cause it meant that somewhere in his tree, someone was white, she would never forgive his mother for having skin as black as coal and scrubbing floors.

Vera thinks of Abel as she stands on the crowded bus with her head against this man's chest. How can a man change completely in so short a time? For the entire twenty-minute bus ride home, she contemplates whether she can ever again feel as safe with Abel as she does in this stranger's arms.

When the bus reaches Vera's stop, she mumbles *thank you*, but the man insists upon helping her off the bus. She finds that she is reluctant to say goodbye; it's been so long since Abel has shown her affection and she feels starved for physical contact. Her hand is still up in the air, waving, after the bus has disappeared.

This is when she sees her neighbor Roman coming up the street, and she promptly vomits right at her front gate at the sight of the father of her child. She hasn't told him about it, and she has no intention to. She didn't choose him because she wanted to be with him. She chose him because he was there. He calls her name, but she ducks next door to Marcia Hammond's. Marcia is the one who gave her the gully root tea she's been drinking for the past week, and she will know what to do next.

The burglar bar gate around Marcia's veranda has been drawn and padlocked shut, so Vera rattles the bars and yells Marcia's name until she comes outside.

"Is wha' wrong with you, gal? You want the whole world fi know we business?"

"The tea a make me too sick," says Vera.

"Sick how?"

"You nuh see me just vomit right in front of me yard?"

Marcia nods and ushers her inside, looking past her, paranoid that somehow her neighbors will label her an abortionist from their brief exchange. Marcia had said no at first when Vera asked her for help. She'd only changed her mind when Vera begged her, refused to take no for an answer. Vera leaves her purse sitting on Marcia's veranda before she enters the house.

"Why you lookin' 'round? No one a worry 'bout me," Vera says as she crosses the threshold.

"Me nuh wan' advertise that me a try fi play doctor. Me nuh wan' fi yuh husband fi find out that is me who help you get rid of him child."

"Yuh mad? How him fi find out? Abel is the last somebody me expect fi think 'bout me today. Him no long fi talk to nobody but himself."

Marcia laughs. "Yes, me dear, that man too funny. Every time me see him me think him try fi say something to me but is himself him a talk to."

"Him not funny when you married to him, and when you the one pregnant by him."

"Him mus' did really love him partner like one bredda."

"Like slave love master," she said. "That fat man did make Abel run 'round every which way til him head nearly drop off."

"He will fix him head on straight. The man just in mournin'.'"

"Him will mourn him family one day," Vera says. "Him will mourn me 'cause if him no learn fi act right, as soon as this baby gone, me gone too."

"Stop yuh foolishness, gal. You think the man mus' run behind you every minute like pickney. Him provide fi you, right? Him no beat you, right? Then you mus' mind him. You still young. You hardly even married one year. You shoulda did see the kind of evil fi me husband do me, and me stay with that man fi twenty years. Then Jesus fix it."

Vera sucks the air between her teeth.

"After you no wish you have them twenty years back?"

Marcia pretends she doesn't hear her. She guides Vera to the back bedroom and lays her down on crisp sheets. The ceiling fan is on and the room is cool.

"You see blood yet?" Marcia asks.

"No."

"Then it nuh work yet, foo-fool gal," she says, and begins massaging Vera's abdomen, ignoring her groans. Vera envies Marcia's life. Marcia's abusive husband was killed in a bar fight. With the money she inherited upon his death, she put herself through nursing school and bought herself a house. She never had children. She does not have to wait for a man to find himself or his courage.

"Yuh belly hurt here?" Marcia asks, prodding.

"Yes," Vera says, wincing.

Marcia laughs. "Well, it right fi hurt you, you wicked woman. Me nuh know why you nuh just keep it."

Vera ignores the comment. "When yuh think it will finish?" she asks.

"Soon. Me cyaan predict exactly. Tonight or tomorrow? You fi drink more. It will make it work faster. When you feel blood, make sure you go bathroom and lock the door. Make sure Abel nuh see. Me nuh wan' that man come after me with no gun."

"You think him go bathroom with me?"

They laugh together.

"What the time?"

"Half past four," Marcia says. "So get off of me bed and go cook dinner fi yuh husband, you wutless gal."

By the time Vera makes it to her door, she's dizzy and nauseous again, but she fixes more of Marcia's tea anyway and drinks a cup. She goes into the bedroom to lie down, falls asleep for a short time, until she's woken by her stomach cramping. She turns her face into the pillow to muffle her moans of pain, just in case Abel has already gotten home. She hears footsteps.

"Abel?" she calls out, and then rises, composes herself, and goes into the living room to check. She finds the house empty. She feels another sharp cramp in her stomach that forces her to her knees. She looks at the floor and sees a spot of blood drip from her thighs, then another. She's left a thin trail from the bedroom.

"Jesus," she cries, as she feels a different kind of pain coming over her. A ripping, a tearing, as if her skin is peeling itself from her body, and then total stillness, as if her own heart has stopped. She knows that the child is gone, and she stays on the floor, letting the relief and guilt wash over her.

ABEL

After leaving the angry mother and stunned child, Abel once again has to weave through the masses—the enraged rush-hour drivers and the sojourning Rastafarians—to make it back to the station and finally clock out for the day. At the station he finds all the men gathered in a circle, cheering and laughing. The lockup is filled with Rastafarians. They have been flooded with complaints by "concerned" residents, but the police can do little about the influx of religious fervor throughout the city, except have a little fun. He thinks that they are watching a domino game, but when Abel joins the circle, he sees that they have one of the Rasta men strapped to a chair. Two rookies are at work cutting off his dreadlocks one by one with scissors. His sergeant, Singleton, has a straight razor and is working away at the man's thick beard.

"You need shave pussy?" he asks when he notices Abel. Singleton was close to Bully and doesn't hide the fact that he blames Abel for his death. *Where were you, Abel? Where were you?* How can Abel blame the man for not hiding his contempt? Abel was there and he did nothing.

"Abel, you get the bwai down yet?" Singleton asks, exchanging sly grins with the other constables in the room. The rest of the men, who all seem to share Singleton's belief that Abel is a pathetic coward, pounce.

"Me hear them will send Abe fi stake out permanently in front of the bwai primary school."

They laugh.

"You need backup, Abe? Me son will follow you 'pon him tricycle."

They laugh.

"My wife a look one work. Why we nuh jus' give her Abel job?"

He shouldn't just take this. He knows that Bully would tell him not to. *Abe, why you nuh just grab the man by him shirt neck and tump him right inna him face? Wha' wrong with you?*

If Abel were to break a nose, they would respect him. A little. He wouldn't get in trouble. Instead, they would say, *We never know you have fight in you, Abe.*

Abel tries to recall how he felt just before he beat up Chester Brown, his former employer and the man Vera had been with before they got together. Even though only a little more than a year has passed, he feels like he was someone else back then. He never thought too far into the future, so he was never afraid. He hadn't yet seen evil in the world up close. He worked for Chester to save to build his mother a bigger house in Harold Town. By then, she was the only family he had left. Yet the house wasn't something they fretted over as he did now with Vera. Money or no money, he knew they would always find a way. He had thought Vera was far too young and too pretty for Chester. The man was greedy. He had everything and yet he wanted more. When Abel had heard Vera scream, it awakened a rage in him toward his employer that he had long stifled just to keep his job. It felt good to beat him. Now he looks back on the fool he was. He could have easily ended up in jail, but luckily Chester was too afraid of his wife finding out to go to the police. Abel didn't understand then that there are forces greater than him, too big to fight, waiting to snuff him out as suddenly as they did Bully.

Besides, he doesn't want this job, sees no reason to fight for it, but looking around the room he wonders if they will leave him with no choice. Abel knows now that they only want to push him until he quits on his own.

"Why in the hell you box the bwai in him face?" Singleton demands. The tone of his voice quiets all the laughter. "We try fi make sure we send you something on fi yuh level, and you show me you lower than even I did believe."

Abel is caught off guard. He hadn't suspected that word would travel faster than he did.

"Bully woulda hit the boy," he says without thinking.

"Ah, is so it go now? You think you will be the new big man in here? Who ask you fi replace him? The man did trust you fi watch him back and you sit 'pon yuh backside inna yuh car and let him get chop up."

The word *chop* pushes him back in time. He is there sitting behind the wheel of his police car, watching the man bring the blade down on Bully's back as the other two men hold him. He tries to see their faces this time. He had told Singleton that they were Rastas, but now as he recounts the scene in his mind, he realizes he barely looked at them at all. In his dreams, they are faceless. All he saw were the blades, the blood, and his partner. In all likelihood they'll never be caught, and he knows it's his fault. In the face of a kind of violence he'd never known was even possible, Abel froze.

But what would these men do if they were faced with the same kind of bloodshed? If Abel were to take out his gun and open fire on all of them, would someone play hero? He is frightened by his own dark thoughts. The price to save face is too big, he decides. Instead, he imagines himself sliding his badge and gun across Singleton's desk. For a brief second all of the fear and pain exits his body, and he knows what he must do. He plans to tell Vera tonight. Make her understand that there's no way forward for him in this job. Some sacrifices are too much.

"Bwai, why you still in front of me?" Singleton shouts. "Matter of fact . . ." Singleton walks up to Abel and hands him a broom. "Sweep up," he says, as the rest of the men retreat to the locker room.

Abel takes the broom, hesitates before letting it drop. Singleton has already turned to walk away by the time it clatters to the floor. They have left the man strapped to the chair, crying soundlessly, and the noise from the broom causes him to look up. He's a man much younger than Abel first took him for, his youth hidden beneath all that hair. He looks at Abel and then at the hair at his feet with wet, bleary eyes filled with disbelief.

"It was nuh me who do it," Abel says, looking in the man's hazel eyes, but he gives Abel a look of such loathing that for a minute he truly feels as guilty as if he had actually snipped off the long dreads scattered on the floor.

Before going home, Abel sneaks into the evidence locker to pinch a little ganja. He had heard Vera vomiting in the bathroom before he left in the morning, and he hopes that it will help with whatever stomach virus she has caught.

When Abel arrives home, he finds his neighbor from down the street, Roman, pounding on the door to the metal grillwork, calling out his wife's name.

Abel enters the gate, stands behind him, and observes quietly.

Vera doesn't come to the door, and Abel watches Roman turn away, clearly frustrated. He jumps nervously when he sees Abel.

"Jeezam! Me never see you behind me. Why you sneak up 'pon people?"

"Why you a look fi Vera?" Abel asks, not bothering to feign concern.

"She say she will help me pick up a few things fi send to me wife over foreign," he says. He walks past Abel and leans over their fence, looking out into the street, suddenly disinterested. Too disinterested. Of late Roman has been too friendly with Vera. This is not the first time Abel's found him in his house when he wasn't home. A week ago, when he came home for his lunch, he found Roman sitting in his living room. He should have said something then.

The metal grillwork is padlocked from the inside, so he knows Vera must be home, but he doesn't say anything to Roman. He squeezes his hand through a space in the bars, uses his key to open the padlock, and fumbles with it for a few moments until he is able to pull the lock out. He goes inside the house, leaving Roman behind without a word.

He finds Vera asleep in their bedroom. He figures the same bug is still bothering her. He strips off his uniform and slides into a T-shirt and shorts, watching her, hoping she will wake, but she continues to snore. He goes into the kitchen, boils some ganja in water to make tea, and takes the steaming mug out to a chair in his front yard. Most evenings he sits here, watching like a guard on duty until the last of his neighbors arrives home from work. His squat cinder-block house is at the center of a dead-end street.

Roman is still there in his yard, to Abel's annoyance, and now he whirls around, his back leaning against the fence, stretching one of his legs out to call attention to his genuine alligator-skin shoes.

"You shoot somebody today, Abe?" he says, fingers hooked on his red genuine alligator-skin belt.

He asks Abel the same question every day.

Abel responds as usual: "Tomorrow."

"Me bet tomorrow," Roman says. He flicks his fingernail against his belt buckle to fill the silence. The sound puts Abel on edge. It feels like a taunt, a reminder of the rumors he's heard that Roman makes regular rounds with some of the women in the neighborhood, married and single alike. He should have told him to stay away from his wife. Now he feels like the moment has passed.

Abel looks down at his tea. He doesn't want to look up and see Roman's condescending smile. His teeth are gleaming white and perfectly straight. Like the belt and the shoes, they were a gift from Roman's wife in Canada.

He hears Bully in his head again: *Abe, if man wan' act fresh and show you him teet', you mus' show him them back when you pick them up off the floor.* Just a mile behind his house, their working-class housing development reverts once again into swamp and ruined cane fields. He can imagine Bully subduing Roman with his bare hands and leaving his broken body for the crocodiles. But though he carries his partner inside him, Abel knows his hands are still his own.

"Them nuh teach you fi shoot properly no more. You must make me show you sometime," Roman says.

His first and only year as a constable, Roman took a bullet in the shoulder, protecting a distant cousin of Elizabeth II from an attempted robbery. He has a medal for it, a medal that Abel is certain Roman wears to sleep at night. Now, deep in his retirement, it seems to Abel that all Roman ever does is show him how things are done. It seems ever since he moved to the city there is no shortage of men in his life eager to school him. Even Roman, who does nothing now but live off remittances from his wife.

Abel thinks about the talk he wants to have with Vera when she wakes up. Practices what he will say in his head. Does she love him enough to accept him even if he's poor? He doesn't know if he can find other work that pays as much. He's not skilled in anything else but farming.

"Going to the airport tomorrow?" Roman asks.

"The airport?"

"Them have you guardin' him?"

"Who you a talk 'bout?" Abel says, annoyed that Roman is still in his yard, interrupting his thoughts.

"Who?" Roman says, shaking his head and laughing at Abel. "Them no let you in on nuttin over there? God coming, man. Fi dem God, at least," he says, motioning off to the Rasta procession, which they can't see but can hear coming from the main road. "Selassie coming. Him plane soon land come morning. Not that me believe in that madman business, but I want to see. Fi me father was a Garveyite back in the day. Him did always say we all fi go back to Africa. Me a go leave early to get one spot. Look how Jamaican people prostrate weself every time one cousin of the white queen come down from England. The same queen whose ancestors them did put we in chains," Roman says, his voice rising. "Why we nuh make the same fuss when one black king come, when we a nation of black people?"

Abel shakes his head. He's not thinking about Selassie; he's thinking about Roman. And Vera. What if it's already too late? He thinks of his wife getting sick this morning. He'd never heard her getting sick like that before.

He looks down at his tea again, wondering if the ganja is making him paranoid. When he looks up again, it is as if time has passed without him knowing. Roman is gone; it's just past sunset, dark, but still light enough for him to feel safe. Safe enough to nod off into a dreamless sleep.

VERA

Vera somehow manages to clean the blood off the floor, careful to leave no trace, before she falls asleep. She dreams that Abel came home that day when she had Roman in the house, in their bed, and shot them both. When she wakes, she rubs the sleep out of her eyes, finds that she's shivering. She goes to wrap the sheet around her, then feels that the bed is wet beneath her. When she looks down, she sees that the sheet is drenched in blood. She remembers the way Abel's bullet passed through her in her dream and she screams.

Abel rushes into the room but stops abruptly, taken aback by the blood. His breath becomes ragged and the color drains from his face. She knows that seeing the blood has sent his mind somewhere else, back to the day Bully died.

"Abel," she says loudly, trying to bring him back. She can see the effort it takes for him to focus on her.

"Is wha' happen to you?" he says, kneeling beside her. Vera doesn't know how to answer. Abel helps her out of the bed.

"Me no feel well." A chill overtakes her, and her teeth begin chattering. "Help me to the bathroom," she says, holding on to his forearm. He touches her forehead.

"You a burn up with fever."

Vera doesn't respond. Her uterus feels as if it's trying to turn itself inside out.

"Help me to the bathroom. Me soon vomit."

Abel obeys and helps her to the toilet. She throws up violently.

"Make me bring you to the hospital," Abel says.

"Is jus' my time of the mo—" she begins to lie, but another stabbing pain catches her off guard and she curls up on the floor, whimpering.

Abel turns on the cold-water tap and begins filling the tub.

"Make me go heat up some hot water fi you to take bath. Get clean and then we go to hospital."

Her mind begins to race as soon as Abel leaves the room. Vera can't stop shivering, nor can she stop the knife that feels like it's moving in and out of her belly. Has she taken too much tea? Poisoned herself to the point of death? If he takes her to the hospital, she'll have to tell them what she took. She's scared that they might arrest her. She's even more afraid that they'll tell Abel.

Abel comes back into the room and pours the hot water he's boiled into the tub.

"It soon ready," he says, and she can hear the fear in his voice.

"Go get Marcia," Vera says quietly.

"Marcia?"

"She a nurse," she says. "Go get Marcia. Please."

He sits on the side of the tub and studies her, ignoring her pain for the moment. She can see his mind working.

"Is miscarriage you have?" he asks.

She grips the edge of the cool toilet bowl under her and grits her teeth against the cramps.

Vera is quiet as she watches Abel work out the math in his mind. It doesn't take complex calculations to conclude that the baby most likely can't be his—they haven't had sex in more than three months. He reaches over to lift her shirt to see her flat belly, but she instinctively slaps his hand away.

"Please, just go get Marcia."

He says nothing, just extends both hands and carefully raises her up. This time she doesn't resist as he helps her take her clothes off.

"Roman did a look for you when me come home," he says, too sedately, as he helps her lower herself into the tub.

"Go get Marcia," she whispers again, her throat burning from the stomach acid. She realizes she's afraid to be alone with him. She's never felt afraid of him before. She knows that her husband is not a violent man, but she thinks of the dream again, realizes that he's witnessed at least one man die in front of him. Wonders about the significance of that moment for the first time. Does that make his own violence easier? He's carried a gun for a year, though as far as she knows, hasn't had cause to use it. Now she wonders where it is. How close it is.

"Why Roman need you fi help him buy somet'ing fi him wife? Why him did come in my house when me deh a work?"

She meets his questions with silence. Will he hit her? she wonders. She never thought he was the kind of man to hit a woman, but she's not sure anymore. She never thought she was the kind of woman to cheat on a man. They don't know each other at all.

She lies back in the tub and steels herself as more sharp cramps grip her. He looks down at her and she can see that he's balled his two hands into fists as his anger grows.

Vera begins to cry. Not just because of the pain, but because she can see that Abel is now indifferent to her pain. He turns his back to her, and she can hear him mumbling to himself. He nods his head repeatedly, as if he's talking to someone else.

She closes her eyes, breathes in deeply for a few moments, trying to will herself to overpower the pain, but instead she passes out. She wakes up when her head starts to lower in the water. When she opens her eyes, Abel is gone. The cramps have calmed enough for her to sit up. She feels relieved but waits in the tub, partly to make sure the relief isn't just temporary, and partly to make sure Abel is not just outside the door. When she finally comes out of the bathroom, she is startled to find Abel sitting on the bed. She had assumed that he had stormed off in anger, hoped he'd leave her alone so she could call Marcia.

He doesn't raise his head to look at her as she enters the room, only continues staring at an empty stool in the corner.

"Me never know seh me pregnant til me start to miscarry," she says, because some lies are absolutely necessary. She puts a hand on his shoulder, kisses his forehead, but he doesn't move.

"Abel?" She slaps his face lightly. He recoils but then returns to his position, transfixed by whatever he sees on the stool, the ghost haunting him.

ABEL

The dispatcher's voice came through their radio. *Bank robbery in progress. All units in the area respond.* Bully turned the sound down. He was the only one who could ignore a dispatch.

"Bank robbery," Abel said. "We mus' go."

Bully didn't even pause; he continued eating his stew as if Abel hadn't even spoken. Abel stared at his partner's mouth moving, his nose running from the spice, the film of snot that had settled over his mustache, the bits of chewed food that dotted his shirt. Abel turned the volume back up, knowing he was risking getting cussed out by his partner, but the radio chatter had stopped. In that moment there were no sounds in the world beyond those of his partner chewing and sucking in air between swallows.

Abel rolled down the windows, desperate for some fresh air in the stifling car.

"No, Abe," Bully said.

Abel rolled the windows up.

That morning, without any explanation, Bully had driven them past their usual territory, way down Spanish Town Road, and parked on a dirt road that cut through a slum. Abel didn't ask why, because what did the why matter? Bully always seemed to do what he wanted. He regularly ignored calls, let men off without arrest or citation if they paid him a bribe, and took whatever contraband they confiscated home. No one challenged him. Abel figured they'd sweat another day away, Bully sleeping in the driver's seat and waking occasionally to tell his young protégé one of his stories from the era when he actually did honest work. Abel soon realized his mistake in rolling the windows down. The few seconds that he'd allowed air to come in had left the car smelling like a latrine.

The radio came alive again.

All units! All units!

"Them say we have fi go," Abel said, growing nervous. "Come now, man. Me no wan' get citation over this."

Bully groaned and rubbed both hands across his big stomach, which was always engaged in a fight with the steering wheel for more space. He leaned back and closed his eyes, ignoring Abel. Abel wanted to punch Bully in his sleeping face, catch him by surprise. He didn't want to get fired because of his partner's laziness.

"Come now, man. Let's go."

"Not yet. We not done yet." It was always *we* with Bully, whether Abel was clued in or not.

They sat for twenty more minutes, every one of which was torture for Abel. Then Bully sat up suddenly and put his left hand on the back of Abel's right. Abel felt the instant transfer of fluid, the unclean feeling that came from his skin being soused with Bully's sweat. If it had been any other man, he would have pulled away and told him to keep his distance, but over the last year it had seemed that part of his daily responsibilities had been to serve as Bully's hand towel. His own sweat had pooled on his lower back and was soaking through his shirt. He wanted nothing more than to see the daylight disappear and go home to where he could be clean and dry.

"You see that one, Abe?" Bully said, pointing to the figure that had grabbed his attention. "She take me fi fool." Abel looked through the window and saw a dark-skinned woman with long dreadlocks wrapped around her head like a crown. Her arms were emaciated, but somehow she was strong enough to balance a large metal wash-tub on her head. She had been walking toward them on the dirt path, but as soon as she saw them, she turned and cut through a row of junk cars. Bully drove farther along the dirt path, turned around the bend, and stopped opposite a broken clapboard fence. Half of the boards were missing, and they saw her passing by through the empty spaces. She had taken the washtub from her head and was struggling to carry it in front of her.

"She wait for me in front of me house," Bully said, putting his hand again on top of Abel's. "I come home and my wife vex. She say one woman outside lookin' for me." Abel watched as Bully took a gun out of the glove compartment.

"Is wha' you need that for?" Abel asked. Would his partner hurt a woman? Knowing Bully, it was likely. But would he kill this woman, with him just a few feet away? Abel wondered, staring at the gun. Would he make him help?

"Just listen," Bully said, putting a hand on Abel's chest. "When I go out, she say, 'You 'member me? You go bed with me once.' Me look 'pon this dry-up old gal and laugh.

"She say, 'Fifteen year now since, and we did have one son to-gether. So, go ahead and laugh.'"

The sweat had pooled under Bully's nose and balanced for a sec-ond on top of his mustache. He licked the beads as they rolled onto his lips. Abel looked out, away from the woman and his partner. He stared at a puddle of brown muck just a few feet from the car, won-dering if it was mud or something worse. He knew something was coming, and he thought about demanding that his partner let him go. Bully had a hair-trigger temper. If Abel resisted, tried to walk away from whatever Bully was planning, would he turn the gun on him?

"I tell her fi move outta me yard before I throw her out. She say, 'Our son gone bad. Everyday him in trouble with police.'

"'And you want me to fix the boy?' me say. 'Him nuh know me from Adam. If he see me coming in my uniform, all him know is his time fi run.' But she threaten me, Abe. Every day she come by me house and promise fi tell me wife. Pure headache all the time now. My wife don't know 'bout the boy. She nuh tolerate no outside pickney."

"You here to pay them?" Abel asked hopefully, naively.

Bully turned to face Abel and punched the dashboard.

"What kind of fool I look like?" he asked, slapping his hand repeatedly against his own chest for emphasis. "You think me will jus' step aside and invite trouble inna me yard? Give them a dime them will come back fi the whole house. She did get one warning already. She shoulda did listen."

Bully's anger suddenly dissipated. He looked at the steering wheel in defeat. Shook his head.

"Me too old for this, Abe," he said, as if he'd read Abel's expression. Bully got out of the car and headed over to the passenger-side door. He motioned for Abel to roll his window down, and when he did, Bully leaned in, handing him the keys. "You drive from now on."

He slapped Abel on the shoulder.

"Come. Follow me and watch the door, Abe."

Bully put the gun in his holster and walked off toward the corrugated-tin and plywood hut they'd seen the woman enter. Abel opened his door, put one foot on the ground and then reconsidered. Something didn't feel right. *Make sure that man no drag you down with him*, Vera always said.

"Me a go stay here," Abel called out as confidently as he could. Bully looked at him for a long second, as if debating whether to let Abel get away with saying no, before he said, "Fine."

Not two minutes later came the woman's cries. "Help! Jesus, help me."

Abel told himself he didn't hear them, but then they came again, louder.

"Jesus, help me! Please help me!"

He wanted to get out of the car. He wanted to help her, but he was afraid of what his partner would do to him if he got in his way.

He thought about the first time he met Vera—her scream sounded a lot like this woman's, only this time he was paralyzed.

So, when he heard yet another cry for help, he reached toward the car radio and turned on some music. He turned it up louder and louder. He didn't want to hear. Maybe he was fiddling with the radio when the three men entered the hut, or maybe they entered from a back door—Abel still wasn't sure. He heard another bloodcurdling scream. This time a man's. Then Bully came running out of the house chased by the three men, one waving a cutlass. Two of them caught him and grabbed his arms. They held him facedown against the hood of the car, mere feet away from Abel. The third one brought the cutlass blade down on his back over and over again as he screamed.

Abel was in a nightmare. That was the only way he could make sense of the scene. It wasn't really happening. He blinked and shook his head, and when the image in front of him stayed the same, he willed himself to move. He opened the car door and pointed his gun at the men. They turned and ran, but Abel didn't fire. He couldn't bring himself to. Abel had shot at paper targets before, not real people. Bully slid down to the ground once the men ran away. Abel took off his shirt and tried to apply pressure to his partner's wounds, but there were so many. Bully's eyes had rolled back in his head so that Abel could hardly see his pupils. His shirt was soaked through with blood in a matter of seconds. The blood had seeped through and covered his hands, his pants. It was everywhere. Before he called for help, Abel fired his gun in the air several times, so anyone who asked would at least think that he had tried to save his partner. He didn't want anyone to know the extent of his cowardice, but he knew.

Abel closes his eyes, opens them, and is surprised to find himself back in his bedroom. There is his wife, hovering over him, her voice distant.

"You alright, Abel? Talk to me."

There is Bully, sitting in the corner of Abel's bedroom, covered in blood. "That man lay down with fi yuh wife and get her pregnant. You cyaan stand fi that."

VERA

She decides to leave Abel sitting there, mesmerized by whatever ghost is more real to him than she is, and go to Marcia's. Marcia feels her belly, then gives her something that will help her sleep.

"It nearly kill me," Vera says, raising her voice. "Why you never tell me it will make me so sick!"

Marcia scoffs. "Well, you did look like you desperate. I say to myself, *Why a woman who married and get pregnant by her husband so desperate fi rid herself of a child?* It nuh make no sense to me. But me know if someone feel so desperate, them will try all type a foolishness to make it go 'way. Me give you somet'ing that me know will work. Me see plenty woman try worse things."

"It not Abel child," she confesses.

"Me know, gal. Me know somet'ing nuh right from the start." Marcia sighs and begins to heat up a pot of water. "Come, me will make you some fresh ginger tea."

Vera touches her belly. "God forgive me."

"This not the time fi worry 'bout God, gal. You already do the sin. Him know seh you like me. Him no mean fi us fi be nobody mother."

"Is what you a talk 'bout. Me will be mother one day," she says firmly. But she does not know where her sudden defensiveness comes from. She has never dreamed about children. The truth is she never knew that refusing to have one was a possibility until now.

"Me pray to Jesus that is not so. Some of us not born to be anybody mother."

"If my husband did treat me like him wife, it woulda been him child me was carrying."

"You cyaan judge the man so harshly. Is not right," says Marcia.

Vera's eyelids are getting heavy, but she does not want Marcia to win the argument.

"Him no understand that is him have fi be the breadwinner. We have fi do work we nuh like until we can find better."

"Not everybody cut out fi carry gun an' shoot people."

"When me firs' meet Abel, is 'cause him did stick up for me. My man back then did get rough with me and Abel protect me. Him beat the man up inna him yard where everybody can see. That's how me know say he meant fi be police officer."

"That's the kind of man you wan' fi see every day—a brute?" Marcia asks.

"Brute better than one coward," she says, but then she remembers the dream. "But no. Me was wrong fi ask him to join. Now me 'fraid he might kill me."

Marcia hands Vera the cup of tea and they walk to the bedroom and sit side by side on the bed. "Him know?"

"Think so. Me cyaan go back."

"Well, everybody have more than one person inside them. We must wait and see if the brute will come outta him again. Plenty of men know seh them child nuh fi them own and them no say nuttin 'cause them no wan' fi look like fool. You can stay here with me, though."

She looks at Marcia, opens her mouth to speak, but then lies down and buries her head in the pillow.

Marcia gets into bed beside her. "Something still a trouble you."

Vera attempts to look Marcia in the eye, but then flips on her back to stare up at the ceiling.

"Is Roman me get pregnant by."

Marcia grips her chest, as if her heart is seizing.

"Gal, is why you love fi make yuh life hard so? You pick the biggest fool God ever did make. That man not even work."

"I know! Me no tell Roman 'bout the baby. Him no need fi know."

Vera rubs her belly, remembers it is empty, and looks out at the darkness outside the bedroom window.

"The baby leave me. Me feel when it go. It walk right out the house, leave tru the door like one grown man. No reason me fi go back to Abel now."

"Of course it gone. Who wan' fi born into fi yuh madness?"

Vera finds herself halfway between sleeping and wakefulness. She's back on the bus, her head against the stranger's chest as he grips her tighter every time the driver stops short. Someone else will want her. Just as she left her family to start a new life with Abel, she can leave him too.

ABEL

God is arriving. Abel can hear the procession of Rastas moving along the main road, headed toward the airport, where Selassie's plane will soon land. Drums are beating all throughout Kingston, and now he feels like they've found a way inside his head.

The drums pound without mercy. He hears the sounds of truck horns blaring, and after an hour of imagining Roman's head in his hands, the noise is something of a call to arms. He gets dressed and walks alone to the main road, joining the procession. In plain clothes, he can blend in, and he falls in step with the bearded and dreadlocked men. He feels safe, as if he is where he belongs, among this parade of fellow outcasts.

It's so early in the morning that few other people are out to spit at them. No police around to beat them with their clubs. They continue their march, some singing, some smoking ganja, some preaching, some dancing as they walk.

"When Selassie come, Babylon will see," a man shouts.

Soon she will see, Abel thinks. To prepare himself, he plays Bully's death over and over in his mind, the moment when he held his partner as his soul left his body, until he can imagine that soul is part of him. It is as though he has stepped aside for the moment and let his partner take control. He allows Bully to wear Abel Paisley like a costume. He is being led by a force greater than himself and he won't fight it.

"Repent. Repent," a man passing in a car shouts over and over. He throws a glass bottle at the crowd, and it lands hard against Abel's hip. The sudden pain sobers him. Should he turn back? A group of Rastas surrounds him and asks if he's all right. He sees Bully's face among them. He tries to follow him, running wildly all of a sudden throughout the crowd, but his partner is gone. Regardless, Abel's eyes are open. He will not ignore this sign. He realizes that this path is inevitable, so he turns and walks back home to get his gun.

It's just after 6 a.m. Abel has returned home and retrieved his weapon. He has no idea when Roman begins his day, but he figures the earlier the better, so he puts on his uniform, walks around the corner in the light drizzle that has started to fall, and hides behind a parked car to watch the house.

Abel watches as his other neighbors leave their houses for work, none of them the wiser to his mission. It's half an hour of unbearable anxiety before Roman's door finally opens and the man shows himself. Abel prepares himself to charge at Roman but is not prepared when Roman gets in his car and drives off. He curses himself for being so slow; then he realizes that Roman is probably headed to the airport. God is coming.

Abel slips behind the wheel of his police car and catches up to Roman, sees his blue car in the distance, but then the rain gets harder, falling faster than his wipers can handle. Still, he manages to keep his eyes on the blue blur in front of him, is pleased to see the red of Roman's caution lights. Abel watches for the potholes he knows are ahead of him. He imagines the holes filled with water are tiny pools his child might one day play in. He can see the little boy's hands slapping the water in his mind's eye, moving up and down so fast his limbs blur like the wings of a hummingbird. Maybe that boy could have saved him, but that boy was never his, he reminds himself. He was Roman's. Abel leans on the gas and begins to close the space between them.

VERA

Vera wakes up in Marcia's bed, determined to begin again. Going to the airport to see God seems just as good a way to do this as any. Besides, she's not ready to go home and face Abel yet.

She convinces Marcia to join her.

When they arrive at the airport and find the soggy crowd that has amassed, she hears Marcia swear under her breath. Rastafarians line the sidewalks and block traffic. They have spilled out into the road, along with army jeeps, soldiers manning security checkpoints, and reporters. Their skin is slick from the soft drizzle as they are pressed on all sides by a never-ending crush of bodies.

The overwhelming scent of burning cannabis chokes Vera's sinuses, and her ears throb in sync with the sound of drumming. A group of uniformed soldiers plows through the crowd swinging their rifles, tipped with old-fashioned bayonets, and Vera grabs Marcia's hand and follows closely behind them as they cut through the crowds toward the tarmac.

Vera does not admit to Marcia or herself that she has come for him, until she sees him. Miraculously, in this throng of people, he is somehow there in front of her: the man from the bus. She recognizes his eyes, even though to her shock, he has shaved off his beard and his dreadlocks. She had thought it was against their religion. He is dressed in white again, shaking a pair of maracas, while his brethren drum and sing. He looks more like a boy than a man now, but she cannot turn back. When Marcia continues past him, Vera grabs her by the shoulder to stop her too forcefully, so that the woman whirls around ready to defend herself. Vera motions to him, and the man sees her and approaches. He hugs Vera as if they are old friends, while Marcia looks on with surprise quickly followed by judgment. Vera feels a rush of warmth to her head, a feeling she does not want to end. He lets Vera out of his embrace and continues shaking his maracas, then motions to a group of women who have formed a line behind the men and have begun to sing and dance. Marcia gives her a look, but Vera ignores it and joins the line, clapping in rhythm. When she felt him on the bus, a dream had formed inside of her that perhaps she had found her new life. A new man, a new family, and even a new God, one who won't make her beg for forgiveness for the choices she's had to make. And why not? If Abel leaves her, what does she have left?

But when she suddenly hears the roar of the plane overhead, she doubts herself. She breaks out of the line of women to stand next to her Rasta—she should at least ask his name first—and she is desperate to prove that this blasphemy, this pushing aside everything her mother taught her, is not in vain. He continues forward as if she isn't there. She inches closer to him as the crowd's fervor increases to a fever pitch, all eyes trained to the sky, watching as the plane descends. When she has finally pressed her body into his side, moving in sync with his flesh as if they were glued at the hip, he pauses to look at her, a new awareness in his eyes. He pulls away abruptly, as if he is sickened by her, and moves to the other end of the line.

She notices Marcia standing near to her then, knows that she is too late to stop the woman from seeing her face fall. She walks over to Marcia, who links arms with her and pulls her through the crowd, toward the barricades, suddenly desperate to get as far away from this man, and her humiliation, as possible. The sun suddenly comes out in full force, a sign from God; the people in the crowd shout, but to Vera the sudden brightness exposes her one glaring thought: *Abel is not the only one who has lost sight of what is real and what is not real in this world.*

ABEL

Abel tails behind a line of Rastas who are allowed through the gates and escorted onto the tarmac by gun-toting soldiers. He stands in front of the barricades set up to fence in the onlookers, as if he is on duty. He places his hand on his gun and feigns alertness, but he is scanning the crowd, looking for Roman. He is readying himself and rationalizing his actions as if this were Judgment Day. He is preparing himself for what comes next, even though he doesn't know what that will be. When he shoots Roman, will a soldier shoot him in return, or will he be convicted and executed later? Either way, he soon will meet his creator, for after he dispatches Roman, one way or another, he too must follow.

The drizzle ceases and in mere minutes the sun emerges in full force. People applaud as they hear the roar of the plane overhead and take the sudden shift in weather as confirmation that they are in the presence of the divine. The Rastas clap harder and beat their drums with fervor. Someone sounds the abeng. The sudden horn blast makes Abel jump. The plane descends lower and lower just above their heads, but it hovers, as if reticent to land because of the size of the crowd. Abel wants to have Roman in his sights before the people rush the tarmac. He can feel that the crowd is already surging toward the barricades. He walks along the fences, searching, and spots Roman, neck craned upward, eyes tracking the plane above.

The crowd is momentarily hushed as the plane's golden lion emblem becomes visible. As Abel pushes through the onlookers to meet Roman, he is certain that he is the only person moving. When he reaches Roman, he sees the man shows no fear; in fact, he smiles, puts a hand on Abel's shoulder, then turns his gaze back to the plane above him, mouth agape as if waiting for Abel to insert the barrel of his gun. Abel calls on God, Bully, whomever, to guide his hand and give him the strength to take a life. He puts his hand on his gun and starts to pull it out of his holster, but he feels a sudden force pushing his hand back down, stopping him. Then he feels a wave of heat concentrated on the back of his neck, so he turns to confront it, but the force is not God; it is his wife. She puts her hands together as if in prayer, pleading with him. As all eyes are on the plane continuing its descent, Abel's eyes are focused on his wife's hands, waiting for them to change shape, to spell out a new way forward for them.

GRATITUDE

Independence City, 1999

1.

There were only four bedrooms in the house, so we visitors had to triple up in beds. Those on the outer edges slept lightly, on our sides, afraid of rolling off during the night. Those in the middle slept on our backs, afraid to spoon with relatives we hadn't seen in years. We crossed our arms over our chests like dead pharaohs and tried to keep our elbows out of the way. Vera had been dead for five days by the time we arrived, and it would be four more days until her Nine Night, five until her funeral. It was Bernard, the yard boy who'd always followed behind Vera like a stray dog, who borrowed blankets from the neighbors to make the rest of us pallets on the floor.

None of us had come to see Vera in the five years she spent dying at home, but it seemed as if everyone she had ever passed on the street had flown to Jamaica in the days before her funeral. It was Bernard who borrowed Vincent's car and made a dozen trips in one day, shuttling us between Manley Airport and Independence City.

It soon became impossible to move about the house without tripping over people. Geraldine, who'd been Vera's "helper," slept on the veranda in a mosquito-net tent Bernard made her, while Vera's three dogs kept watch outside.

2.

In the aftermath of Vera's death, it had become clear to Bernard that he was property that Vera's children, Irene and Vincent, had no wish to inherit.

"You know, Bernard, in Egypt, when the pharaoh dead, the royal servant them did bury with them master," Vincent had said over breakfast, laughing. Bernard listened as Vincent shared the details of Vera's will with the visitors, while he helped Geraldine serve them food.

He noticed Vincent had started wearing a pair of oversized reading glasses, showing off because he'd sold Vera's family jewelry, before she was even dead, to enroll at the University of the West Indies. He was proud of himself for no longer being a twenty-nine-year-old man living at home with his mother, even though it was only her death that had changed that setup. The house was his now. Irene had moved with her two kids to the U.S. the year before. Vincent was free to keep the house and start his own family, or if he sold, he and Irene would split the money, and he could move to New York, as he'd always dreamed.

Vincent's words haunted Bernard. He had spent the last few days mourning Vera so deeply it had not occurred to him to have concern for himself. But that morning, after breakfast, while making his fourth trip from the airport, Bernard had driven by a skeletal man with matted dreadlocks, wading through a polluted portion of the Kingston Harbour, looking into the reddish-brown water, trying to catch fish with his bare hands. Something came over Bernard— his future, to be exact—and he had pulled off the road to get a closer look, leaving Irene and her kids sweating in the backseat of the car, spooked and confused. Exactly how he felt too.

Later that night, as he moved about the house making sure each visitor had somewhere to sleep, he wondered how Vera could have forsaken him so thoroughly. There was no mention of Bernard in her will. Though he never expected to get the house itself, of course, he thought he deserved something for building a part of it—when Vera decided a proper lady must have a guest room—with his own hands. Where would he go if Vincent sold the house? The more he thought about it, the more he could feel his throat constricting slowly, as if all of the air within the house had followed Vera. It was impossible, he decided. The woman he'd known for thirty years loved him too much to let her children cast him aside.

Bernard had spent the entire day picturing Vera using the last of her earthly strength to hide something special for him, until imagining was not enough—he decided to take matters into his own hands. Since no one would sleep in a dead woman's room, especially one not yet buried, Bernard knew he would have Vera's room to himself. If she left something for him, he would find it. He waited until the visitors and the family were asleep, lest they think he was in there to steal rather than to recover what was rightfully his.

3.

That night, as we listened from our temporary beds to the sound of the yard boy padlocking the door to the burglar bars enclosing the front of the house, we remembered why we'd left—to escape the feeling of living under siege. You had to coat your skin in repellant, hide behind a net from the mosquitoes, and lock your family inside a cage each night. No one had missed the clang of the metal grillwork or the crunch of the padlock, and the three successive snaps from the bolts on your front door. And the weather in September, a monsoon one minute, unbearably humid and hot the next. A cold breeze would deliver a sharp chill up your spine every now and then but still brought no relief. There was no way to escape the dampness, heat, and mold so bent on turning your white walls green. We fanned ourselves futilely and fell asleep longing for the air-conditioning we'd left behind.

4.

When she was alive, Vera had never let Bernard enter her room, so he didn't move at first; he stood frozen in the doorway, imagining her sitting up in her deathbed, screaming at him to get out. When Vera wanted him, she preferred he bent her over the kitchen counter when the children were at school, or they retreated to his mattress in the shed once she'd put the kids to sleep. It became trickier when they grew older, but they had managed to find places until Vera became bedridden.

But her own bed had always been off-limits, so when he walked over and ran his fingers along the white sheets, his heart raced like he was trespassing, getting away with a transgression he would not have dared attempt had she been alive. He knew these sheets weren't the ones she died on—Geraldine would have changed them by now—but he stripped them off anyway, praying to find a miracle underneath. He found only the bare mattress, not an updated copy of her will, not a note scribbled in haste on her deathbed, or a page torn from her diary—nothing that would make people believe that Vera loved him. Nothing to suggest that she'd thought of him in the end.

The sight of Vera's sheets lying in an untidy pile on the floor gave him a moment of satisfaction. She was not here to tell him that her things were too pristine for his touch. He pulled off her pillowcases and added them to the pile. He overturned her mattress and left it facedown on the floor. He almost missed the faded envelope, suddenly preoccupied with upending the too-neat room. The fragile paper inside had yellowed with age:

It is with the deepest of regrets that I inform you that on
Monday, September 14, 1970, Mr. Abel Joseph Paisley, who
was in my employ aboard the *Sovereign of the Seas II*, met
with an unfortunate accident during the execution of his
duties, rendering him deceased . . .

Enraged, Bernard tore it to pieces. He didn't want to think about
what it meant that this letter was preserved under her mattress all
those years. That she never stopped thinking about Abel, her husband almost thirty years dead. He was more to her than Abel, he
told himself; while Abel left her, then widowed her, Bernard spent
the next thirty years with his life revolving around Vera's whims.

He collapsed on the pile of linens and let himself remember their
first night together. He was sixteen and had worked for Vera for two
months; Vera was thirty-five and was drowning under the weight of
keeping a house and tending two small children. When she hired
Bernard, she let him sleep in the shed that had belonged to another
yard boy who Abel had let go just before leaving for England.

Bernard had been raised by his grandparents in Harold Town.
When his grandfather died, his grandmother sent him to look for
work in the city. He was not happy or unhappy—happiness had
never been one of his pursuits—but he found working for Vera
rather than farming with his grandfather for his own survival to be
boring. There were stretches of time where he just waited for her to
order him to do something.

Everything changed the night of the hurricane. Vera had let him
sleep in the house in the spare bed in Vincent's room, instead of the
fragile shed in the backyard where he normally slept. Vincent was
just an infant in his crib and Abel was in England, just six months
away from having a container of ship anchors fall on his head. Bernard remembered feeling colder than he had when he slept out
back. The electricity had already gone out and then the last can-

dle too. He lay in bed shivering, waiting for the storm to pass. He should have felt at rest indoors—it was the softest mattress he had ever felt—but instead he lay there in the dark night wide-awake, listening to the wind.

Suddenly, there was a pressure on his chest. He felt a person, a woman—he could tell by her smell and the feel of her legs as she settled on him—straddling his chest. He wondered at first if she was sleepwalking, but then she leaned forward, as if so that he could see that the whites of her eyes were focused on his in the dark. She ran her fingernails across his bare chest, and he felt a charge, a rush that coursed through every cell in his body. With his arousal came a sense of terror. He had never been with a woman before. He had never felt his heart beat that fast, and he both feared and welcomed what she would do next. He remembered wondering if he was in the midst of a nightmare; Vera was behaving like the witch in one of those Ol' Hige stories, getting ready to drink his blood or drain his body's last breath. But his nightmares had never brought him this kind of pleasure.

The next morning Vera behaved as if nothing had happened. At first light, she ordered him to clear the debris and the fallen branches out of her yard, later scolding him for working too slowly. He had been too distracted and upset to work, suddenly doubting that the best night of his life had really happened at all.

Vera came again four nights later. This time slinking into his shed as if she retired to such pitiable lodgings every night. From that point on, they had sex several nights a week for almost twenty-five years, until their nights together became rare as Vera's health declined. He remembers on their last night together, she had gotten so thin that as she lay beneath him he was conscious of her bones pressing into his skin. She was still and silent, and he felt so guilty as he heard a moan of pleasure erupt from his mouth that he stopped suddenly and couldn't finish.

Bernard felt as if he might now see Vera's silhouette, the phantom version of her that appeared that night, in the dark, as he got down and crawled on his belly, feeling underneath her bed for something. When he found nothing, he lay there on his back for a moment, staring at the underside of her box spring, exhausted, and wondering if this was what Vera was seeing too. Was this what Vera was feeling? But, of course, she felt nothing; she saw nothing. Vera was dead, and he would have to stop thinking about her. He must only think about how he would survive if he left this house. Bernard was so still and quiet, lying in his imaginary coffin, he could hear the chorus of outrage from the visitors.

5.

What was the yard boy doing creeping into Vera's room at this hour?

No matter if we were Vera's grandnieces or grandnephews, her uncle's cousin by marriage, her son's school friend's brother, we all had more claim to Vera's room than Bernard. Though none of us would go near it, we cringed at the thought of the yard boy with his ashy feet and thick yellow toenails desecrating the dead woman's bed.

The poor had only just begun rising up when we'd left, but now we could see that things would never go back to the way they were before. We didn't just have to fear that some glassy-eyed nobody would climb in one night through our windows, or that Melva in the kitchen was busy adding ground glass to all of our dinners, while Simone in the washroom was stealing our clothes and parading around her government yard, getting shit all over our going-out shoes. Remember the story of the yard boy cutting off the baby's head to spite his employer? It had done us in. That had been the last straw. We had liquidated our assets and left for the first country that would give us visas. Now we were vindicated; we were right. For who could live in this mad country, where servants were so shameless they would riffle through a dead woman's things before we'd had time to put her in the ground? So at last, we lay back and turned away in our beds. Let Vera's children deal with her uppity help. In ancient Egypt, the servants would be buried with their masters.

6.

They would not understand until Bernard showed them, until he gave them proof that Vera had loved him. He had to keep looking. He crawled out from underneath her bed and trained his eye on her wooden wardrobe, which was so tall it had just barely fit in her room and, in fact, had left a line scar across the ceiling where they had forced it in. Vera had bragged that it had belonged to her great-grandfather, a British lord, and had been his personal wardrobe in the master bedroom of the sugar plantation's great house. Her grandfather first inherited it and willed it to her, because of all the grandchildren from his line of illegitimate brown descendants, she was his favorite; her bone structure, if not her color, reminded him of his own mother's.

Bernard opened the wooden doors and began pulling out each dress from its hanger. They were silk and lace, dresses from another generation, a life of colonial comfort that Vera was raised in but had lost once she married Abel. She even had a fur coat in a box, which made Bernard laugh out loud as he threw it on the floor. He was quick and not gentle as he combed through everything that Vera had held valuable during her life, trying to find some trace of himself among them.

7.

Three little girls got out of their pallets and tiptoed to Vera's door. We told them not to go in there. We told them Vera was dead and had turned into a duppy until they buried her. We explained it takes nine nights for the spirit to let go, and Vera had only been dead five days. We would send Vera off in four more, on the night before the funeral, when we'd remove her mattress and her duppy would leave to find its eternal resting place. Until then, Vera's duppy still slept in her bed. But the girls noticed the man was in there with her. He wasn't afraid. We told them to move away from there and mind their business, but instead they pressed their ears to the door because they wanted to hear the duppy talk to the man. They had so many questions: Was he her husband? Would he smooch with the duppy? How did that work when her face was invisible?

8.

Outside the door, Bernard could hear little girls giggling. He had not had any children because of Vera. He had made her pregnant three times, once when he was seventeen and twice in his twenties, but each time, indifferent to his protests, she had quickly disposed of them. Was it too late? he wondered. He could start over, find a maid like Geraldine, if someone young enough to bear children would even consider a man his age. He was only in his middle age — he wasn't yet fifty, but he felt older.

Bernard wondered if any of the neighborhood women had thought of him over the years. No doubt many of them still believed he was a virgin. In all the years he had lived with Vera, he had never carried on with a girlfriend or taken a wife; no woman ever came claiming his paternity for her child. What kind of man didn't consort with women? Or even men, for that matter? Did they ever wonder? He was flattering himself, he realized. They most likely never thought about him at all.

He spent so much time alone out back that the women probably thought he was dim-witted, which is why they only spoke to him when they needed help with dirty jobs—disposing of a dead dog or slaughtering a goat. He spent a lot of time with the animals, they noticed. The young women, the ones newly married with children, didn't speak to him at all; if he stood in the vicinity of their playing children, they wouldn't go back in their houses. They would rather let their rice pots burn on the stove than take their eyes off his movements, see if he was watching their children.

Despite what others believed, Bernard had pressed many women beneath him over the years. Always on the same hard foam mattress out back. He started to seek them out when Vera took sick. They were women whose flesh smelled of Ajax and carbolic soap. They were women whose real scent, the scent that came from the pits of their arms and the folds of fat, smelled of labor. They were women like him; perhaps that's why he could never love them. Vera was so unlike him, so unlike them, touching her each time made him feel transformed. He had never thought of the future; even as he bedded the women down, he'd thought he was filling a temporary void. Even when Vera had technically become a senior citizen. People like her didn't age like people like me, he had told himself; she would want him again. He had invested his entire future in Vera, believing that somehow their arrangement would last his entire life. That somehow, if he was good to her, she would give him more. That she'd at least one day let him sleep beside her in her bedroom.

And what if he had told the neighborhood women about Vera? What if he should tell all the visitors now? Would it make a difference? He could whisper it to the visitors as they slept. Maybe they would think it was Vera sending them a message in their dreams, because they believed in that kind of obeah nonsense.

But if he were to tell them himself, in the light of day without proof, they would say he was a liar, or worse—a rapist. They would run him out of the city, the parish, right back up to the mountains and back into the hole in the bush where he had risen. A fine redbone woman like Vera, almost white, wouldn't consort with her yard boy. Bernard could picture all of the visitors nodding emphatically. If one of the visitors even woke up and found him standing over them, wouldn't they be terrified? No doubt they remembered all the yard boy murders from the '70s. Men like him turning their machetes on the families who employed them. He was that boy out back, that illiterate. Since he was a man now, he was even more frightening.

Digging in the far reaches of Vera's wardrobe, Bernard found a long gray box. It was made of a kind of metal, and his heart began to race because he believed that he had finally found the place where Vera had hidden that which was most valuable to her. He replaced her mattress so he could lay the box down on her bed. When he slid the cover off, he whimpered softly. It contained Vera's wedding dress. Yet another reminder of her love for Abel. Had she only chosen him because she needed a stand-in for Abel? They were both from Harold Town. They both came from a family of farmers. His heart seized for a moment with an emotion it took him a minute to recognize as jealousy. He was jealous of a dead man. He took the dress out of the box and laid it out carefully on her bed. He then searched the rest of the box eagerly, hoping it concealed something underneath, but it was empty. He lay on the bed next to the dress, dejected, fingering the yellowing lace. He imagined Vera as a young woman, wearing it on her wedding night. He pictured her lying in bed, waiting for her husband to remove it, as afraid as he had been on that first night when Vera had crawled on top of him.

Now the image stirred something in Bernard. He imagined himself in Abel's place, standing next to her and making vows, her legal husband. He abandoned her wardrobe and searched through her bureau drawers for her nightgowns. Which one had she worn on her wedding night? Had Bernard's fingers ever felt the same fabric as Abel's? He ran the cloth through his fingers, remembering how the fabric felt over Vera's skin. He brought one up to his nose.

9.

The three little girls tried to open the door quietly, but it creaked. They saw the man smelling the duppy's nightie, and they were in hysterics. Because why would anybody do that? The duppy must have cast a spell on him.

10.

Bernard noticed the crack in the door too late. With horror he slammed it shut, louder than he meant to. Some of the visitors stirred awake, cursing him.

He collapsed on the bed, looking around Vera's ransacked room. He had searched through every pocket and purse, every trinket box, looked between the pages of every book; she had left him nothing. He knew now that everything he thought they'd had existed only in his own mind. He'd meant nothing to her.

He was consumed by a wave of nausea and exhaustion, but he couldn't leave the room looking like this. The family would have reason to get rid of him faster. He had to fold or rehang every bit of clothing, repack every box, and close every drawer before he could sleep. It would be suspicious if he left and went back to his own bed, he figured. Then it would seem as if he had just entered to steal. But why shouldn't he steal? The thought had not occurred to him before. But now, devastated and outraged as he was, he thought to himself that if Vera had left him nothing, why shouldn't he take something, his due?

He went to her bureau to see if any of Vera's jewelry had been left behind. It wasn't stealing, he told himself, because they owed him, but he saw that there was nothing left. Vincent had taken everything.

He caught sight of his face in Vera's mirror and looked away. The mirror, like the walls of her room, was almost completely covered with photographs of Vera and her family, the visitors who now slept in the house. Just for spite, Bernard removed all of the photos from the mirror and started placing them facedown in a drawer. When he got to the last one, he saw himself, or at least he could tell it was him in the background at work; the children were in the foreground. He saw only his back, but he recognized his frame, his young shoulders as straight as a wire hanger. That was the only photo he left up.

He looked around the room and focused on Vera's bed. He decided that he would claim the thing that would have bothered Vera the most. *This room*, he thought. He would take her room. He cleared Vera's walls of her photos, her crucifixes, her portrait of the Virgin Mother and Child. He smiled, thinking that he would dare them to try to throw him out. They had never had to fight for what they had. They were too spoiled. They wouldn't know how.

So, he remade her bed and lay in it. He left her wedding dress spread out beside him, imagining her there, draping one sleeve across his chest. He hoped that it vexed Vera's duppy to see him.

11.

Bernard awoke suddenly. In the dark, he was sure he smelled rum. He felt fingers slip around his neck, thought for a second that it was Vera returned to take back her bed, but as his eyes adjusted to the light and the hands gripped tighter, he saw Vincent, angry eyed and drunk, bending over him. But when Vincent started to cut off his air, he slid the boy's fingers from his throat without much effort. Vincent wasn't a man used to hard labor, let alone violence, but he lunged at Bernard again. Vincent wore a pendant around his neck, a gold hawk with cubic zirconia eyes, and it scraped Bernard's cheek with the tip of its beak as they struggled. Bernard delivered a heavy blow to his stomach that left Vincent sprawled out on his back on the floor. He sat up with his face in his hands and shook his head. It took Bernard a moment to realize that Vincent was crying.

"Come out a me mother's room, you dutty black wretch," he said, shaking; he seemed unable to look at Bernard now, sitting in the middle of Vera's bed. Bernard looked at this man whose nappies he had changed sometimes in the early days when his mother couldn't cope, who now didn't think he was good enough to sweat one night away on Vera's sheets. Bernard wiped the blood off on his pants and tried to help Vincent stand up, but Vincent tore out of his grip and cursed at him again as he stumbled toward the door. Bernard was tempted to call Vincent back and whisper in his ear all the filthy things his mother had done to him in the dark.

12.

We couldn't help laughing at Vincent, the grown man who couldn't stop weeping like a fool, who couldn't show a servant his place without his mother by his side. We watched his wobbly legs as he left his mother's room, after he failed to throw the yard boy out. Imagine how embarrassed poor Vera would be. Vincent, drunk, stormed into his own room, forgetting some of us were in his bed. We screamed and he stormed outside to the veranda, forgetting where he'd put the key to the padlock on the burglar bars (Bernard had it), and screaming at Geraldine, who got up, fetched the key from Bernard, and opened the lock. We heard him talking to himself, just as we'd seen the yard boy do, as he stomped down the road, probably heading back to the bar. The whole family was a mess.

13.

Hours later, the singing woke him up. Three old neighborhood women—Mrs. Brown, Mrs. Pitt, and Mrs. Gold—stood on the veranda singing a sankey, a funeral hymn, for Vera. One of Vera's windows faced the veranda, so when Bernard peeked out, he was staring at the women's backs. Neighbors and visitors were spilling into the front yard to sit in chairs that Vincent and Geraldine must have set up themselves. If anyone in the neighborhood did not know of Vera's death, they now knew.

As they sang, Mrs. Brown drew her words on longer, her voice naturally higher than the others, intentionally falling out of sync and bullying the other two women into the role of backup singers. None of the women had been on speaking terms with Vera for years. It was Mrs. Brown who first spread the rumor that Abel Paisley had abandoned Vera and was living with a new wife in England. Later, she told everyone that Vera had slept with her husband and every husband in the whole neighborhood when their wives were gone. She said Vera practiced obeah and worshipped the devil. She hated Vera, and Vera hated her. Bernard thought it disgraceful that these women who had betrayed Vera feigned friendship now that she was dead. If she were able to in that moment, Bernard knew Vera would have chased all three women off her property. Bernard stood watching from the window and imagined Vera next to him, enraged, mute, and helpless. He was pleased.

Behind him, Geraldine pushed the door open with one hand wrapped in the folds of her apron as if it were contaminated. The sound the door made as it flew open and banged against the wall startled her, and she let out a low shriek. The first thing she saw inside the room was Vera's bed, the mattress stripped of its sheets.

"Bernard?"

He turned and looked at her. She would not cross the threshold.

"You alright, Bernard? Is wha' you a do in Miss Vera room?"

"What you want?"

"Vincent say you mus' go buy fish fi everyone."

He turned back to the window, ignoring her worried eyes.

"Oh, Vincent say that?" He spread the aluminum shutters apart wider and saw Vincent seated to his far right on the veranda, next to the singers. "Then me must run to market quick-quick," he muttered.

Geraldine looked at him again. She leaned her head in farther but at the same time her feet moved back.

"You alright, Bernard?"

He said nothing, and she disappeared soundlessly.

14.

We awoke and got dressed. We applied powder to our faces; on some it was several shades too light, making our skin unnatural colors, leaving us together looking like paint-dipped eggs in an Easter basket. We filed out of the house and stood in the front yard. Our high-heeled shoes poked holes into the soft, wet ground, making it hard to walk or stand, but we had to put on our best. We made sure we were wearing a little gold around our necks, in our ears, our noses. We were doing well abroad, we said without saying. No matter where we had gone, it was better than here. We had money to spare. We had even sent Vincent a little something to put toward the Nine Night and the funeral. Didn't you? *Such a shame that Irene left the man to do everything by himself*, we clucked. We noticed she had just arrived with her kids the day before and sat back with us, letting Vincent and Geraldine manage everything as if she weren't family.

We looked around us, at what they'd done, and so far, we approved. Vincent had set up chairs and tables in the yard, and we heard he was sending the girl Geraldine to buy us fish and bammy for our breakfast. We had been waiting to see if he spent the money on Vera or put some of it away for himself. How much would he spend? How much did he love his mother? You know Jamaicans save for our funerals before we save for our retirement. The worst thing he could do would be to bury Vera in a cheap coffin. We would take notice and bring the news back to everyone.

Vera's Nine Night was just three days away and we expected him to keep the liquor flowing. How many goats would he kill? Would he buy a hog, though half of us don't touch swine? The older people among us complained about Nine Nights these days, saying they had become nothing but an excuse to throw wild parties. We ignored them. What was wrong with a party? If people didn't die, we might never come back at all. This is a time for mourning, but it is also our only vacation, our only reason to come home again.

15.

Seeing everyone outside, Bernard left Vera's room. He went out the back door and circled through the yard until he was in front of the veranda, standing just behind the crowd of fifty or so people watching the women sing. He had helped with many funerals over the years. He had planned to drive into town that day and purchase cheap folding chairs for the visitors. He had planned to slaughter several of the biggest goats he had raised for Vera's Nine Night in three days. He had planned to barter goat milk and meat for crates of soda and coconut cakes, but instead he told himself he would do nothing. He would do nothing for Vera in death, as she had done nothing for him. He would do nothing for her ungrateful children, who'd forgotten that they'd been brought up by his sweat. He would rest his tired body on Vera's soft mattress while her Nine Night was done wrong, and he made himself laugh inside because he told himself that it was what she deserved for forgetting him. He knew that nothing would come together without him. By the end of it all, they would know his worth.

Passersby gathered in the yard without a word, and with the

same respectful silence, stood and listened to the singers. From his place seated on a chair behind the singers, Vincent eyed Bernard with raised eyebrows. Bernard eyed him back without blinking, and Vincent turned away. On his lap Vincent held a Polaroid camera that Irene had bought him. Every so often he snapped a photo of the singers or someone in the observing crowd.

Three little girls wandered over and stood next to Bernard. He recognized them from the night before in Vera's room and he turned away, embarrassed. They were no more than six, no younger than four. He didn't know which visitor they belonged to. The girls unconvincingly pretended to listen to the singers, but every so often they stole glances at him and giggled in unison. They locked hands with one another, played "Ring around the Rosie" and fell down, piling on top of one another. Bernard ignored them, as he had learned was the safest thing to do with children.

Irene stumbled out of the crowd toward him, momentarily blinded by her tears. Her hands reached for him and for a second he almost expected an embrace, but instead she grabbed the front of his shirt and pulled at it furiously, tearing his collar. She pointed a finger in his face and said, "Is my mother who just dead. You think you can go in and thief from her room? You nuh have no shame, Bernard?" She had to be pulled away.

And what could he answer? Should he tell this woman that her mother fucked the soul out of him and left him with nothing?

16.

When he went back to Vera's room, he found that someone had locked it with a key. Bernard had to break the lock to get back in. He found that all of Vera's photos had been put back up, and he quickly took them down again. He went out back to the toolshed and collected his things. He'd never had much—a few T-shirts, a few counterfeit pairs of brand-name jeans—but he would place his meager possessions in the room to show them that it was his now.

After he put his things away, he placed her photos in a drawer as well. He stood scanning the empty walls over and over again. He had no photos of his own to place on them. The paint was discolored where Vera's photos once hung. Their outlines tormented Bernard; they were phantoms of a life he could have had if he had never met Vera but that now was out of reach.

Since everyone was outside, eating lunch, he decided to take a shower. He could count on his hands the number of showers he'd taken in his life. He usually washed up by the standing pipe behind the shed or filled the metal basin that Geraldine used to wash clothes. When he got back, the photos had been placed again on the bureau and the crosses were up again on the wall. He checked his drawer, was relieved when he saw his things untouched. He began taking Vera's things down, one by one. He wondered if it was Vera herself, fighting him.

Outside, a goat was bleating frantically. The noise crawled closer until it was just behind the house. Bernard peeked through the metal slats and saw Vincent attaching the end of a rope to a pole. It should have been a ram, but instead Vincent had chosen a nanny goat that was much too small to feed so many people. She was quiet as she watched Vincent's hands work. He picked up the machete. Vincent moved out of Bernard's line of sight. The goat walked away from the pole until the tightening of the rope around her neck forced her back. She jumped up frantically in the air. He could hear Vincent somewhere nearby, engrossed in conversation. A man Bernard didn't recognize walked over and studied the goat. Then Vincent returned and resumed preparation, laughing every few minutes, machete in hand. The goat pulled away from the pole until her tongue lolled out of her head. Soon, she started crying. Bernard had always found it startling how humans and animals could sound the same when they were afraid.

Vincent took practice swipes at the air around him. The animal's baby-like cries filled the house. She was quiet only when she choked herself trying to escape. Bernard had taught Vincent how to slaughter a goat the right way, not to flaunt the instrument of their death in front of them. They weren't stupid creatures. They knew when they were going to die. But the arrogant boy had not listened. Perhaps because he'd thought Bernard would always be there to do it for him. Bernard did not care for animals any more than he believed that God cared for human beings. He wanted Vincent to finish quickly, only so he didn't have to hear the dying noises.

In the living room, Bernard found the three little girls huddled together on the couch. Each time the goat cried, they squeezed themselves into a smaller and tighter ball. In the moments when she quieted, they relaxed their bodies again.

The girls reminded him of when Vincent and Irene were young and scared. In the first few years after Abel died, Vera would sometimes disappear at night. He never asked her where she went. She would have told him it wasn't his place to ask, but Vincent and Irene would awaken, somehow knowing she was gone. When he heard them cry out, Bernard would come in from his shed and try to comfort them. They wouldn't sleep unless he put them back in bed, and the sounds of him moving about the house were audible.

He knew he should give up and move on. He knew that Vincent and Irene could easily call the police and have him thrown out of Vera's room, of Vera's house for good, but he hoped that they remember those nights. How, back then, when they were babies, he would have killed anyone who tried to hurt them. Maybe he could make them remember that he was family too.

Bernard looked at the frightened girls again. He knew the visitors would question why he was going near their children, but when he saw these girls, he was really seeing Irene crying under the mango tree because Vera had beaten her or spoken harshly.

He saw Irene hiding behind him when she was trying to get out of Vera's reach. He had gotten between Irene and Vera many times. Had saved that little girl from so many beatings. Didn't she remember? Bernard was thinking of Vincent wailing in his crib because Vera was asleep, consumed by a deep depression she couldn't wake from to console him, and how he would go in and pat him on the back.

He saw that Vincent had left his Polaroid camera on the coffee table. He took it up and turned it in his hands until he had figured out how to use it. He pointed it at Vera's open door and took a picture. He studied the white square with the pale-yellow center, part of him hoping that an image of Vera standing there looking back at him would develop. When the image of the empty doorway became clear, he saw that the girls were looking at him intently.

He turned to them. "Smile," he said, and focused the camera.

Bernard took a photo of the girls crunched together into a human ball. They abandoned their fear and posed for the next photo without prompting. Afterward, they begged for more, which he took, until the film finished. He gave them all but one, and the girls ran away laughing.

Back inside Vera's room, Bernard noticed the silence. He looked out the window and saw the goat's head lying on the ground, her tongue protruding. Vincent and the other man struggled to scoop up the body and carry it off, leaving a trail of blood behind them as they walked.

Bernard put the photo of the three little girls on the wall and looked at it as if it were a religious idol he hoped could grant miracles. He knew he could dig graves, slaughter livestock, clear land, become a driver—anything he had been paid for over the years—save and buy a small piece of land and build a little house in the country for his family while he worked. But he couldn't see it, any more than he could picture Vera lying in her grave. What they once had still seemed real to him. It felt more likely that he could move time backward than he could love someone else.

17.

Bernard slept in Vera's room for three more nights, undisturbed by her family. Then, once nine days had passed since Vera's death, the family held her Nine Night, her Dead Yard, her wake, her send-off into the afterlife. Whatever he had heard people call it, Bernard knew for most it was just an excuse to get drunk. He watched it all unfold from a window in Vera's room, burning with resentment that Vincent had pulled everything together without him. He had planned to stay in the room, awake all night, guarding it, because he knew her family would want to enter. Besides, he did not want to celebrate her death. He wondered if anyone noticed his absence.

The music began around five in the evening. Earsplitting dance-hall music blasted from six-foot-high speakers. The man who had helped Vincent with the goat now acted as DJ. Crates of soda lay stacked on either side of the chicken coop like the pillars of a grand house. The old women of the neighborhood covered their ears pointedly and stood by the food table. Though he had been to many Nine Nights before, Bernard couldn't help feeling the celebration seemed perverse. He thought of Vera lying in the mortuary while her family and neighbors danced.

Around six, someone knocked on Vera's door. When Bernard made no sound, they tried the knob. Bernard had locked the door from the inside, and he prayed they didn't have a key.

"Bernard," he heard Geraldine shout. "Bernard, you in there?"

"What?"

"Bernard, time fi you come outta Miss Vera room now. You know them wan' fi send her off properly. Them wan' fi turn up Miss Vera mattress."

"Who wan' fi send her off? Where them did deh when she lay in here a dead? All of them is nuttin but hypocrite. Tell them me nuh intend fi move. Vera say me fi stay in this room."

"Stop tell lie, Bernard. Me nuh wan' Vera people send them man fi drag you outta the room. That's why me come tell you first."

"If them wan' me fi come out, then them have fi come take me out," he said. He waited for her to speak again, and when he heard nothing but the music from outside, he decided to move the dresser in front of the door. He knew the older women wanted to gather in Vera's room and say prayers, read scripture, and sing songs. That was the old way. They wanted to lean her mattress against the wall and draw a cross above her doorframe, so Vera's spirit would have to leave. They would cleanse the room by spreading salt on the floor. He knew these were just rituals, symbolic and not real, but he found that the only comfort he had was to think that Vera was with him, that somehow part of her still remained. They would stay in this room together. He wouldn't move, and he would not let her go.

About five minutes later, he heard a furious banging, and then what sounded like someone throwing their weight against the door. He began to pray. If Vera wanted him to have this room, if she had ever loved him, wouldn't she stop them?

"After everything my mother do for you, this is how you do we, Bernard?"

This time it was Irene's voice coming through the door.

"After you not even take care of your mother when she take sick! You run off to America. Is me who take care of her!" he yelled back at her.

"You mus' not let them move me," he whispered to himself, to Vera.

"What this crazy man a do?" He heard Irene speaking to someone on the other side of the door. Soon he could hear the sound of a key being inserted. The door opened a crack, but the dresser stopped it from opening farther.

"Him block the door."

"You never really know fi yuh mother," Bernard shouted. "Is she who tell me fi take this room." He found it easier to lie than to tell the truth. No one would believe him.

Vera, he thought, *tell them they cyaan move me*.

"Bernard," Irene shouted. "After the funeral you need fi find somewhere else fi live. You hear me, Bernard? We will give you a severance, but you need fi move on. My mother gone."

He heard the sound of hammering. He got down on his knees, full of desperation, and said another silent prayer to Vera. If she had ever loved him, she would let him remain in this room. With her.

18.

In the end we had to take Vera's door off the hinges. Three of us came in and pushed the dresser out of the way. We could have grabbed him, punched him, thrown him out violently, but instead we stood in front of him with a look of pity in our eyes, the look you give a raving lunatic. He kept shouting, "You cyaan move me!" But we did. We held him as gently as we could, but we had to drag him. He wrenched out of our grip and clawed the floor. We had to grab him by his feet and pull him across the threshold. He stood up once he was on the other side of the doorway, with the posture of a dejected man, as he watched as the rest of us entered the room. Irene stood outside the room with her arms crossed over her chest, so filled with rage she couldn't speak. We told the girl Geraldine to take Bernard out back, to pour him a glass of rum to keep him calm because we saw real grief there. As we turned away and opened our Bibles, some of us immediately began wetting the pages with our tears. We could not let the yard boy mourn our relations harder than us.

19.

Bernard refused the curried goat meat that was offered to him and stood alone by the chicken coop. The music made his head throb. The lights that Vincent had strung around the trees hurt his eyes. He stood outside of Vera's room and peeked in the window through the metal slats. The trio of women was gathered around her empty bed, holding candles and singing. Unlike the music outside, their songs were slow and somber. Women wept. Someone had spread salt all over the floor. People started to enter the room to watch Vera's send-off, and he heard the salt crunching under the weight of their shoes. Two men lifted Vera's mattress and leaned it against the wall. This time, Mrs. Brown held back and the women sang in unison, emoting a single pure voice. The voice pushed back the shadow of superstition, and soon the visitors came in droves until there was no more space left inside the room. Bernard knew that the room was lost; both he and Vera had been exorcised from it.

Instead of going to bed that night back in his shed, Bernard downed glass after glass of the 100 proof rum ritually laid out for guests; he demonstrated his best interpretation of dancing to Geraldine, and tried to grab her wrists and lead her behind the chicken coop. He tried to eat Vera's last meal, which had been left under the silk-cotton tree for her duppy and was not to be touched until after midnight. He was soon restrained by Vincent and his friends. He woke up alone in the makeshift DJ booth. His face burned where Geraldine had slapped him.

20.

The next morning, Bernard found his things piled beside him. He walked by Vera's room, seeing if he could retake it, but Vincent's DJ moved the door aside—it was still off its hinges—and passed by wearing only a towel on his way to the bathroom. Bernard snuck into the room once he heard the water running to take his photo of the three little girls off the wall and to take a last fleeting look.

On his way out back, he found Vincent standing by the gate, yelling at Irene.

"Is you mus' go. Is only right," he said.

Irene had told the morticians that she would dress her mother before her burial, a family tradition, but had backed out once she'd glimpsed her corpse. The morticians had warned them that Vera's condition was extreme, but she had not understood, since she was in Brooklyn when Vera died. Vera hadn't been able to take food in the end, and she was already in a frightening state when they had arrived to take her away. They had embalmed her, but there was barely anything left for them to preserve; she had wasted away to nothing.

Vincent wouldn't yield, fearing what the neighborhood women would say if family didn't attend to Vera but not volunteering himself, as if dressing a corpse was suddenly women's work. They both stopped and looked at Bernard, waiting for him to say something as he walked by. But he said nothing to them as he returned to his shed to lie down. Only when the task was unpleasant could he stand in for family. *No more*, he said to himself.

Vincent and Irene decided to send Geraldine over to the mortuary with a white dress, a box filled with pushpins, and a needle and thread. Vera had made it clear before she died that there mustn't be any buttons on her burial dress. If so much as one of them was unfastened she had heard that it would result in her spirit being earthbound.

Geraldine came out to the shed and begged Bernard to accompany her, saying that he wouldn't need to work, just stay with her in the room. She held his hand and wouldn't let go, insisting that he follow her. She reminded him of how drunk and rough he'd been with her the night before. It was the guilt that got him to agree. Also, he couldn't help wondering, hoping, looking at her hand clasping his as they walked to Vincent's car to drive to the mortuary, if there was a chance that when this was all over, and it was time for him to leave, he could convince her to come with him. That he would not be cast out alone.

The next day, a hearse would drive her body to the countryside, to the church in the mountains of Saint Elizabeth, where she'd be buried in the same graveyard as her parents. As soon as Geraldine saw Vera, she retreated to the farthest corner of the room and sat down on the floor, facing the wall. She covered her nose and mouth with her hands and shut her eyes, rocking back and forth as if she could shake the image out of her mind. But Bernard needed to look at her. Perhaps then he could move on.

So it was Bernard who slid Vera into her dress and pinned it in place. He tried to put a comb through her silver hair, but it had receded so much that it was barely visible. Even as he stared at what remained of Vera, as the smell of death filled his nostrils, he could only think of the feel of his hands on her breasts, or her breath against the nape of his neck. If she were to arise now, as monstrous as she looked, he would have her. She had ruined him; he knew it then.

21.

Bernard got dressed for the funeral early. He borrowed some of Vincent's cologne while he was in the shower, borrowed polish from Geraldine to brighten up his old shoes. Then he climbed into one of the long buses that came to take the family to the church. Vincent had paid two young boys, barely out of their teens, to dig Vera's grave, once he realized that Bernard would not help. Bernard wanted to be in the church with the rest of the family. He wanted to see Vera's casket closed and loaded into the hearse. Perhaps then it would feel real. He told himself that then he'd be ready to move on.

In the church the family inched up to the front pew reluctantly. At the sight of Vera's skeletal body, Irene and Vincent broke out into hysterical sobbing. They hugged each other and cowered together in the front row. They did not protest when Bernard took his place beside them. Geraldine sat with the neighborhood women, several rows back. When the service came to the portion where people viewed the body, the line advanced at a pace quicker than at any funeral Bernard had ever seen. Irene in front of him turned away from her mother and tugged at Bernard's arm as she had done often as a little girl; she nodded through her tears at the casket, as if she expected Bernard to do something about what had become of her mother. He was the only one who lingered over her body. He told himself that he needed one last look.

Bernard walked out of the church just as Vincent prepared to speak into the microphone. He went ahead to the graveyard and found Vera's plot. The gravediggers were to arrive before dawn to dig Vera's grave in time for the burial. When Bernard arrived to find they had barely made a dent in the ground, their shovels bringing up insignificant piles of dirt and depositing them on the side of the plot as if their arms would give out at any moment, he was enraged. He grabbed one boy by his shirt neck and tried to pull him up. The shirt ripped and the boy scrambled to climb quickly out of the hole to minimize the damage. Bernard let go of his shirt and snatched the shovel from his hand. He took off his suit jacket and his shirt and set them aside and then jumped down into the hole and began to furiously dig.

The two young men stood feebly above him, not knowing whether to assist or run away. Bernard's pace quickened every few minutes, but he panted heavily. The funeral party made its way out of the church, led by the coffin bearers hoisting Vera on their shoulders, and even though Bernard could not see outside his hole, he could hear the women singing and the people chattering, so he dug even faster. His black pants and white T-shirt were covered in brown stains. Blades of grass and bits of leaves stuck to his hair. His shoes were filled with dirt.

The three little girls somehow burst out and ran ahead of everyone. Like all of the girls, they wore long white dresses with satin belts. As they ran, the belts came undone and trailed behind them on the ground. Meanwhile, Bernard dug and dug, throwing dirt out of the hole furiously, where it slid right back down, forming symmetrical piles on either side of him.

22.

The boys struggled to pull Bernard out of the hole, and when they finally got him back to the surface by use of a rope, Bernard looked at Vincent and Irene and the rest of the visitors shaking their heads at him with disgust instead of gratitude. What more could he do for them?

The coffin bearers came and rested the coffin on the platform. The preacher read Psalm 23. Bernard looked on as Vera's coffin was lowered into the ground. The tears running down his face were from the dirt in his eyes, he told himself; his hands were filthy, so he couldn't wipe them. He didn't want anyone to see him crying for Vera—she didn't deserve any more of his tears—but he couldn't stop. He felt a hand on his shoulder, and he saw it was Vincent's.

He leaned in close to Bernard and whispered: "That foolishness you did have with me mother nuh mean nuttin. You nuh family." His breath was still hot in Bernard's ear as Vincent walked away.

So they had always known. They knew, and yet they still hated him. Perhaps that was why they hated him.

Bernard looked at Irene looking down at her mother's casket. Did she know too? Was it shame in her eyes he saw? Did they hate him because he reminded them of who their mother really was?

The boys began slowly filling in the hole with dirt. It started to rain softly, just as they began, and some visitors ran off to get a tarp so Vera's coffin wouldn't be covered in mud.

Bernard concentrated on the hole, the mud. He remembered a night, decades ago, when he'd had Vera pressed down beneath him in the mud. It was her idea not to bother with his mattress in the shed. She said she wanted to be like the animals. And so she let him pin her down, completely naked in the wet dirt; he felt her wriggling beneath him, like a pig.

When Vera was well, the night was a time for mischief, where everything was reversed. It was like there were two Veras—who she was in the day and who she became when they were alone at night. Bernard rolled off her, and Bad Vera rose up damp and filthy, like someone who'd just clawed her way out of a grave, a trail of leaves and slime wedged between her buttocks. She looked so small underneath the canopy of coconut and breadfruit trees; she washed her mosquito-bitten body by the standing pipe without fuss. Shivering in the darkness, Vera ran back to the house, suddenly covering herself with her hands, embarrassed, which meant that their time was up.

Bernard remembers seeing the whites of Vincent's and Irene's eyes, watching from the kitchen window. He could hear Vera yelling at them as she ordered them to bed. They were so young then that he had assumed they wouldn't remember. Vera wasn't worried. If they asked about it in the morning, she said, she'd simply tell them they'd been dreaming.

He looked at the mourners and wondered who would bury him when he died or bother to give him a funeral. Would they put him in a sack and dump his body in the Riverton landfill as he used to do with stray dogs that had been struck by cars?

23.

We were angry that we had to soil our good funeral clothes, lifting the yard boy who had just thrown himself like a fool on Vera's coffin.

He was heavy, and it didn't help that he was lying back in her grave as if it were the most comfortable place in all of Jamaica. It gave us a bad feeling.

When we had finally gotten him out and left him lying in the church cellar, yelling the words, "They know. They know," over and over, we joked that we should have just buried him with Vera. It was because of people like him that we'd had to leave in the first place, abandoning our education, our almost-white, brown, and high-yellow privilege, and spend all of our money on visas and plane tickets and American clothes, and now we were nothing. The next day we'd go back to our real lives in New York, Miami, Toronto, London. We blamed the yard boy for that too. Over foreign, we were the Bernards—we were the underclass; we were home health aides, janitors, and nannies. We would think of him and spit the next time we helped elderly women wipe themselves over toilets. We would think that it was all his fault. If people like him would have stayed in their place, then we could have stayed too.

Just as we were being corralled back into the buses, preparing to descend back down the mountain, a woman broke off from our group and ran screaming over every inch of the graveyard, bumping into grave markers until she fell down and just wailed where she sat, clutching a brightly colored silk ribbon. We thought she looked quite the fool until we heard what she was screaming. "My babies, my babies. Them gone!"

24.

As he led them through the bush, Bernard told the girls that Vera would fly above them, whispering to God, and get them everything they ever wanted. He told them that they belonged to Vera now, just as he did. He told them not to be afraid to walk into the bush; Vera had promised him, as he was lying in her grave, that she would protect them always. He told them not to pity their mothers and fathers because they were fools; they were probably still standing there, looking at that rectangle of upturned ground with sad eyes, believing that Vera was still that thing that they had just covered with dirt.

25.

We searched the church cellar and found only the yard boy's suit jacket and a Polaroid of the three little girls in the pocket. When had he taken it? Some of us had seen him walking away from the graveyard and into the bush. None of us had been sorry to see him go. We knew he was a madman; we had hoped he wouldn't be back, and we had said to ourselves, *Good riddance*, as he disappeared. We had sworn he walked away alone. But the three girls had been there too, Irene said, playing with her children behind the buses. She had heard them laughing. No one suspected anything was wrong. Where were the yard boy's people from? Where would he take them? Not a soul knew. We had thought the man was no one to know or remember. We had expected him to disappear with Vera, to fade away with her ghost. But we were left searching for him well into the night and the next morning, calling his name into the bush, imploring him to bring our girls back. Now we find ourselves whispering his name in our beds at night, reciting it like a prayer, hoping one day he will forgive and have mercy on us.

PAST LIVES

Brooklyn, 1999

Irene decided not to mention her mother's death to Betty when she went into work that morning. For one thing, Betty already had no regard for professional boundaries, as Irene had learned over a year working as her home health aide. And for another, Betty was obsessed with the dead; she had undergone past life regression therapy on a weekly basis for the last ten years. The old woman was scheduled for a session that day, in fact, and Irene was afraid that if she mentioned her mother, Betty would insist on conducting a séance or putting her into a hypnotic trance so she could speak to Vera's ghost. As soon as Irene heard Bill Davidson's car pull into the driveway, she told Betty she needed to go upstairs to dust.

"But I need you, Irene," Betty said. "I need you to make sure my guys don't get me in trouble." That was what she called the people Bill convinced her she used to be and could become again for an afternoon—"her guys."

"Make Mr. Bill earn him money," Irene said, and turned and hurried upstairs. A month ago, she'd found a check made out to Bill that Betty had left on the coffee table. She paid him $120 an hour for his sessions, while Irene made $8.50. That morning, $8.50 was not nearly enough for Irene to listen to all of Betty's made-up stories about the lives and deaths of strangers.

Irene was eager to busy her mind with her work. Most of the time, she approached domestic work for Betty and her own family with visible resentment. In Jamaica she'd always had servants, after all, helpers who took care of her more diligently than her own mother. It was the servants who made sure that she and her little brother were fed every day and walked to school. Though she was grateful to them, she had never once aspired to become them. No one had told her that in America, "home health aide," to many people, was just another way to say "maid." But that day, she filled her mind by making a list of every chore she could possibly accomplish within the next seven and a half hours.

While straightening up the rooms upstairs, she thought about how there was really no need for therapy to help Betty remember her past life, when she had a shrine right here. Betty had painstakingly preserved the bedroom that once belonged to her first daughter, Lucy, who passed away when she was five. The room was a museum for Lucy's childhood artifacts—ancient toys had been stowed in every closet and corner. Porcelain and plastic dolls sat on the shelves of a glass display case. Betty had kept every one of her daughter's baby dolls, with their cracked heads and torn-out hair, their filthy crayon-stained faces, as if she thought that one day that abusive child might come back for them.

Looking at the dolls made Irene need a cigarette, a habit that she'd managed to cut down to only a few times a month. She'd smoked heavily during her first six months in America. Growing up, Irene had never seen a woman smoke before. Her mother had always told her that smoking was only for "bar women and bulldaggers." But Irene now kept an emergency pack hidden in Lucy's room, behind a ratty brown teddy bear with one black button eye missing. The bear was an alien among the bedroom's plastic- and porcelain-doll society.

She knelt with her head out the window, elbows resting on the windowsill as she smoked. It wasn't to hide the smell. Since her knee surgery, Betty rarely went up to the second floor of the house anymore. Her kids had to convert the den into a bedroom for her. It was that Irene couldn't stand the thought of all those vacant little eyes staring at her. If she accidentally met a pair, she couldn't keep her gaze for more than a few seconds.

Irene inhaled and exhaled deeply so that she coughed; she did so on purpose, as if hoping the smoke could stir and expel something she could feel blocked within her. She could not yet feel her mother's absence from the world. She hadn't seen Vera in a year; Irene had moved farther and farther from Jamaica—first to Miami and then to Brooklyn—exactly so that she wouldn't have to. She had been running away from her mother her whole life, and in the end it was her mother who left her.

The only thing she felt now was that somehow, she'd been cheated. She would never get to look Vera in the eye and tell her what a bad mother she'd been. She doubted her mother would have admitted to ever hurting her, even if she had lived to be one hundred. When Irene came back to see Vera at twenty-four, married and carrying her first child—after running away to Kingston at seventeen without saying goodbye to Vera—her mother behaved as if nothing bad had ever transpired between the two of them. She would never apologize, and Irene would never forgive her. But still she wondered if crying for Vera would release the thing she'd felt trapped within her for years, like a tapeworm feeding off her.

Vera had cried uncontrollably at her own mother's funeral. They had been estranged since before she was born, so the first time twelve-year-old Irene had seen her grandmother, she was in a casket. Irene still remembered the sound of Vera's body hitting the floor when they walked up to the coffin. She had never seen her mother that way, heaving and sobbing, curled up on the floor in a protective pose, like an animal. She had to be picked up and carried out of the church. Irene would not cry like that for Vera. She was sure she couldn't. She wanted to feel sad about her mother, but she was more worried about where she would get the money for the plane ticket to attend her funeral next week.

Irene looked at her watch and realized that Betty's session was almost over by now. At each one, Bill set up a recorder in the dining room while his assistant, Roy, simultaneously transcribed on a laptop. Irene usually helped Roy, who was actually just Bill's teenage son, pack up the equipment when it was all over and then a few times had listened from a distance as Roy mocked Betty's impressions of the dead.

"Them take you for fool, Betty," Irene said after each session, but Betty paid no attention to Irene's assessment. Whenever Betty found Irene reading a book during her lunch break, she always said, "Oh, look at you, Irene," in the same tone that she used to speak to her cat, Ruffles, when he fell asleep on his back, exposing his furry belly, almost like a person.

Usually, right after one of the sessions, Betty wouldn't respond to her own name. She walked around the house studying her keepsakes, as if seeing them for the first time. She believed she was channeling a personality from one of her past lives.

Bill let Betty believe that in one life, she'd been an Incan girl ritually sacrificed at the top of a volcano, in order to appease the gods. In another she had been a little boy who walked ten miles home alone after getting struck by lightning, just to say goodbye to his mother. Betty could describe their last moments in excruciating detail.

When Irene saw Bill and Roy exit the house and walk to their car, she withdrew into the room. She groaned because she did not feel like talking to Betty, but she knew she had to go check on her. She threw her cigarette butt against the display case glass in frustration, watching with satisfaction as it bounced off, its ashes scattering all over the floor. This was not the day for her to look after a dead girl's toys or pretend to care about the lives that Betty invented, not until she could process how she felt about her mother. But it was too late to call out sick and almost time for Betty to eat lunch, so Irene slowly made her way downstairs.

As Irene trudged down the staircase as slowly as possible, her fingers trailing along the banister, she felt a passing chill, as if someone had blown on the back of her neck, and wondered, not for the first time, if Lucy's ghost still haunted the house. It seemed that no matter how thoroughly she cleaned each day, she inexplicably returned to a mess only a child could make—Cheerios spilled on the floor and crushed underfoot, marker-stained walls, and wads of dirty, wet paper towels left in the middle of the living room. They weren't messes she could see Betty making. Except for the days when she had her therapy, the woman spent 90 percent of her time asleep, like Ruffles.

Irene found Betty in the living room, rubbing her liver-spotted hands across the television screen, trying to touch the people on the other side. Irene stood and watched her silently from the hallway for a moment, wondering why this kind of role-play gave the old woman so much satisfaction. Was it just the kind of game that bored people with money liked to play? Betty lived off her late husband's pension, alone in a house that she had once shared with her family, two daughters aside from Lucy, who were grown now with kids of their own and who rarely came to visit. Seeing how hard Betty worked to convince her that past life regression was real filled Irene with sanctimonious pity. She didn't have sense enough to be content with what she had, so she was easy prey for Mr. Bill and his stories.

"Who are you this time?" Irene asked, walking into the living room. Betty was too busy pretending to be in awe of the television to answer. "Tell me your name," Irene said again, louder.

Betty cringed at the sound of her voice and crouched behind the love seat. Irene walked over to her and knelt on the couch cushions, looking down at the top of Betty's head, the sparse white fluff that barely covered her pink scalp. Her empathy fell away, and she found that she was just annoyed. Usually, when Bill left and Irene ignored her, Betty would return to herself within an hour at most. But Irene wanted to get Betty's lunch out of the way, so she could go into the basement and start the laundry. She couldn't seem to stop herself from shouting.

"Come now, me have work to do," Irene said. "I can't play with you for too long, Betty. You don't pay me enough. Let we get through this." She put her hand under Betty's chin and made her look up at her. "Now, what is your name?"

"Elias."

"Well, Elias, you want a tuna-fish sandwich or chicken soup for lunch?"

"I want you to take your bloody hands off me," she said. "You're hurting my neck."

Irene thought it was a decent attempt at a British accent. Betty had even managed to sound younger, somehow removing a bit of the gravel from her voice. She let go of Betty's chin.

Irene hadn't meant to hurt her neck. She worried that Betty might call the agency on her. She couldn't afford to lose this job, not now when there would be so many expenses surrounding her mother's funeral. She figured Betty probably wouldn't tell on her, because then she'd have to admit she was just pretending. When Betty was through playing a character, she rarely admitted any memories.

"Me will get back to my work, then. You can finish playing your game. If I don't see you again, it was nice to meet you, Elias," she said, trying to make Betty forget how harsh she'd been just a minute ago.

Elias went back to discovering the TV, and Irene went down to the basement. The light bulb had blown out, but Irene wasn't in the mood to replace it. It was overcast outside, so she was in the near dark loading the laundry—the only light coming from a tiny rectangular window and a flashlight—when she heard feet on the stairs.

"You Betty now?" Irene shouted.

Neither Betty nor Elias replied. She listened as the feet moved across the basement's concrete floor. Betty dragged her right foot, the one with the bad knee, behind her when she walked. These footsteps seemed more pronounced.

"Whose house is this?" Betty demanded in a British accent, her voice a few octaves lower than usual. "Where's the cook?"

Irene could only see the white of Betty's eyes and her hair, so bright compared to the rest of her body they made it look like her head was floating.

"Is what you need the cook for?" Irene said, kissing her teeth. "You did have your chance for lunch, madame, and now it gone."

"I've got to turn the roast. The cook will butcher *me* if I let the roast burn," she said.

"Ah, so you one servant this time!"

"What time is it?" Betty asked.

"If you are a servant, you need to help me with this laundry."

"I've got to turn the roast."

"The cook, him find someone else. Come help me with these clothes. You look like strong man," Irene said. "How old are you, Elias?"

"Fourteen."

"Good. Elias, you have work to do. Pass me that basket full of clothes," she said, pointing down at Betty's feet. "It should be easy for a strong boy like you."

She knew the basket was too heavy for Betty to lift, not without hurting her knee or back, but she wanted to see Betty break character. She was surprised Betty even came down to the basement. That must have been at least a little painful for her.

Irene watched as Betty struggled to lift the basket. She managed to pick it up a few inches off the ground before her knees buckled and she had to let it fall out of her arms.

"I'm weak," Betty said, staring at her two hands. "I must be sick."

"More true-true words never been spoken," Irene said, but she wondered how Betty had found the strength to lift the basket for as long as she did. Irene didn't know why Betty felt suddenly determined to make her believe she was really possessed by someone else, so determined she would hurt herself in the process.

Irene bent down and started transferring the laundry from the floor to the washing machine.

"What's that smell?" Betty asked.

"Piss. Them no piss where you come from?"

Betty covered her nose with her hand.

"Our missus can't hold her pee pee, and she too proud to wear grown-up Pampers, so is me who have to wash for her every single day."

Betty didn't reply. Irene couldn't see her expression, but she hoped that her words had cut Betty. She hoped that the woman was finally through for the day and would eat and take a long nap.

"You back to being Betty now?" Irene asked.

"The roast . . . If I get in trouble, I'll tell them it was you . . . you black bitch!"

Irene let the clothes in her hands fall to the basement floor. She pointed a finger in Betty's face, close enough so the woman could see it in the dark.

"Listen to me, you crazy old woman. Don't play with me. If you ever talk to me like that again, me will slap you right in your face. You hear me? This likkle money you paying me is not enough for you to talk to me any old way. Me a warn you." Irene stepped back and took a breath, trying to calm down.

Betty had never insulted her before, no matter who she was pretending to be. She wondered if she was paying Irene back for the basket or for her neck. She was tempted to run upstairs and close the door, leaving Betty alone in the cold, dark basement, but she grabbed Betty's hand and started to lead her toward the stairs.

"Matter of fact, I need you to get out of my way, Betty."

"I told you to take your hands off me," said Betty.

Irene ignored her, pulling Betty along; she knew she was being rougher than usual. When they got to the foot of the stairs, Betty suddenly turned and bit Irene on the arm. Irene yelped and let go. She rubbed the spot that Betty had bitten, trying to feel if her dentures had left a mark on her skin. Betty scurried away and hid like a mouse as soon as Irene let go. It had gotten even darker in the basement, so it was hard to see where the woman had gone.

"Alright, me did warn you," Irene said. She started walking around the room with her hands extended, feeling for Betty. She thought she saw a shadowy figure in the right corner of the room, just behind the stairs. She tried to sprint over to grab it but tripped over a box that had been left in the middle of the floor. The pain that shot through her as she banged her left knee against the concrete floor caused Irene to scream out loud. With her good leg, she kicked at the box while cussing loudly. She closed her eyes, waiting for the pain in her knee to pass. She heard the sound of footsteps, moving across the room toward her.

She studied the dark shape as it drew closer, and then she stood up and grabbed Betty by each of her forearms.

"Get your hands off of me!" Betty shouted, still maintaining a British accent.

As she held on to the struggling woman, Irene latched on to a theory for why the old lady wanted to erase herself so desperately, why she needed to pretend to be somebody else. In this life, she would always be the woman who went to take a phone call for five minutes at a pool party and let her little girl drown in a swimming pool. Those five minutes would be the entire duration of her real life.

This gave Irene ammunition. "Go ahead and pretend you don't remember you let her die," Irene said, squeezing Betty tighter. The cruelty was a release, and she instantly craved more.

"Stop playing. Say that you are Betty now. Your daughter was Lucy. You wan' me fi get one of her dolls for you? From her room? Her shrine? You remember! You remember what you did!"

"I don't play with no bloody dolls!" Betty shouted as Elias, trying harder to wrench her bony arm out of Irene's grip.

Irene shook the old woman. She thought of Vera. Once, when Irene was six, Vera had been in bed, catatonic for nearly a week. After shouting at Vera for hours brought no response, Irene became so frustrated that she poured the contents of Vera's chimmy—her chamber pot—over her mother's head. It had taken both Bernard, their yard boy, and Claudette, their helper at the time, to pry Vera's hands from around Irene's neck. The marks took weeks to fade, but still when she thought about them now, she knew that Vera's anger had never matched her own.

"Say you was a bad mother," she said to Betty, shaking her again, this time harder. "Say it! Say you are sorry!"

Betty shook her head back and forth and thrashed even more wildly, nipping at Irene's arms with her teeth. Irene had trouble keeping her grip, so she finally let go.

"Animal," Betty said. "I'm gonna get the law on you."

Betty collapsed on the cold floor.

Emboldened, Irene stepped closer and continued, this time her voice deadly calm: "It was you. You should have been watching her. You should have been a better mother."

"I don't have to listen to you, you damn witch," Betty said, covering her ears and swallowing a sob quickly.

Irene knew she had won—she just didn't know how she felt about that, both triumphant and ashamed of herself.

Now she would prepare Betty's lunch. If the woman didn't eat it, they couldn't say it was Irene's fault. But as she was arranging sweating deli meat on bread, Irene felt a panic come over her. What if Betty called one of her daughters? How would she explain? She kept looking behind her as if someone was watching her, someone who had seen her lose control.

When Irene went into the living room with the sandwich, Betty was lying on the sofa with her back to her. She moved closer and peered over Betty's shoulder. Her knees were drawn up, tucked into her stomach, a position that Irene knew must have been painful for her. She was sucking her thumb noisily, a streak of dried tears and snot still visible on her face. Seeing that she had one of Lucy's dolls clutched against her chest, Irene knew that she had gone way too far. But how had she gotten it? Betty couldn't have gone upstairs and taken it so quickly. Irene stepped back and looked around the room. She felt a chill, as if the room had gotten a few degrees colder all of a sudden.

She put the plate with the sandwich on the coffee table and sat down in an armchair next to the sofa. Betty lay back and closed her eyes, and Irene watched her until she began to snore. She thought about how when Betty passed, it would be her, not Betty's children, who found her lifeless body.

When she woke up, as Betty and not someone else, Irene knew that she would look around the room, frightened, and call out to her. Irene made up her mind to apologize. Maybe she would tell her that her mother was dead and that she wished she could cry—that she feared that she couldn't.

But for now, she'd let Betty sleep.

Later, when Irene was in the kitchen chopping vegetables, she swore she heard the sound of a little girl laughing. She put down the knife and listened. After a few seconds she heard it again. She followed the sound back into the living room, but all she found was Betty, still asleep in the same position. The old woman was mum-

bling softly, but in her own voice, having a conversation with someone in her dream.

Irene couldn't hear the little girl's voice anymore, but the sound
had shaken her so much that she went into the kitchen and got a
container of salt. Her mother had told her that salt could cleanse a
house of spirits. She spread it on the carpet in the shape of a circle
around Betty. She reminded herself to vacuum before she left.

When Irene went to return the salt to the kitchen, she looked
out the window by the sink and saw that it was raining. She watched,
momentarily mesmerized as the rain started to fill Betty's stone
birdbath she kept in the backyard, next to the patch of ground
where the swimming pool had been filled in.

As she watched the rain, Irene thought about how the same
year that she had poured the chamber pot on Vera, she had awoken
weeks before in the middle of the night to the sound of laughter.
It had just finished raining. She had looked out the kitchen window and had seen her mother running naked, Vera's wet body il-
luminated every few moments by the light of a lantern, then fading
away into the darkness. Their yard boy, Bernard, had been chasing
her, and when he finally caught her, he pushed her body down into
the mud, and Irene watched, wide-eyed with shock, as they ground
their naked bodies against each other by the lantern light.

To Irene, seeing them together like that was almost worse than
the times her mother hit her. It was the reason she couldn't take
care of Vera when she became old and sick. Every day she would
have wanted to shake Vera with all her strength and demand to
know why. *Why did you love everyone more than me?* Irene had never
heard her mother laugh the way she had that night with the yard
boy in her presence, and she never would again.

But that is how Betty found Irene when she woke up—standing
in her backyard during a rainstorm, completely naked, barefoot,
alone, and laughing.

"Irene! What's wrong with you, Irene?" Betty kept shouting.

"You were sleepwalking," Betty told her later, standing in the doorway to the bathroom as Irene sat on the edge of the tub drying herself off. "Let's hope you don't catch pneumonia." She didn't say anything about Irene's behavior earlier; she seemed not to remember. Yet Betty seemed both afraid to leave Irene alone and afraid to come any closer.

"My mother died this morning," Irene said. And stopped there because how could she explain? How could she tell Betty that she'd been awake the whole time—as she tried to imagine her mother lying in her coffin, as she peeled off her clothes, as she stood feeling the cold drops of rain on her skin and the mud between her toes, and as the loud fits of laughter exploded from her, puncturing the serenity of the night like shrapnel. How could she describe that she'd felt like someone else was taking over her body? How could she capture the exquisite freedom of that?

ATONEMENT

Brooklyn, 2010

12 June 1813: Caught Maddie stealing honey from the kitchen this morning so I bade Ezra hold her before she could flee and then had her put in the stocks. I could hear her calling for me during the hottest part of the day as I inspected the cane fields. "Massa Fowler. Massa Fowler. Me will behave meself." I passed her on my way to the mill. Her sweat had formed a puddle below her head. I listened to her whimpering. "You'll learn," I said. "How many times do I have to teach you?" "I already learn, Massa Fowler," she begged. I had the honey in my hand, and I poured the entire jar over her bare feet. "There, now you can have it," I said. "No, Massa Fowler," she screamed, as I walked away. As I sit in my study and write this, I can hear her screams. If I cannot teach her, then the mosquitoes, the rats, the fire ants swarming her feet will.

It only took Debbie reading one passage of Harold Fowler's diary to have her first nightmare. She couldn't see him, but she could hear his voice shouting, "You'll learn." She screamed as the red ants streamed across her feet until they were completely covered. Even though it was a dream, she could feel her skin burning. She struggled to get free, but her neck and wrists were clamped steady by the wood.

Debbie suffered from sleep paralysis, a condition where her brain started waking from dreams before her body. She was awake, technically, but she found that she couldn't move. As much as she wanted to jump out of bed and flip on the lights, she was helpless. She told herself the voice was not there, just an aftereffect of her dream, but as she struggled to revive her limbs, she could feel her heart pounding in her chest, and if she were capable of moving her mouth, she knew that she would still be screaming. Finally, after struggling for a while—she was never quite sure how much time had passed—she sat up and promised herself she wouldn't read Harold's journal again. She put it in the archival storage box she'd bought for it, covered it with tissue paper, and hid it on the top of her closet behind some sweaters she didn't wear anymore.

ᴥ

It had never occurred to her that someone in her family had once owned slaves. Debbie knew that the first of her ancestors to come to America on her mother's side had immigrated decades after the Civil War. Her father had come from England in his twenties. She had grown up in Atlanta and attended schools where many of her classmates were black. When it was time to learn about the history of slavery in school, she'd always felt relief because she thought it had nothing to do with her. Many of her white classmates, however, had deep roots in the South. Some of their families still owned the land that belonged to their slaveholding ancestors. Most were apologetic, while some were openly hostile when anyone suggested that they had something to apologize for. She remembers a boy who liked to brag that he was descended from Robert E. Lee jumping up from his seat during a class discussion about reparations, pounding on the desk, and shouting, *Look, did I enslave anybody? Did my parents? My grandparents?* Debbie always thought getting defensive was the worst reaction a white person could have. *Just admit it and say sorry,* she'd thought.

But then one day at a staff meeting, the director of development at the SoHo Museum of Art, where Debbie interned, handed out free DNA kits from a new corporate sponsor, a genetic testing company. She explained that the kits would soon be widely available in drug stores, but the sponsor had been giving them away for free in order to build up their DNA database. She noticed everyone else in her department tear open the box with excitement, so she followed suit. She spit in the tiny cup that came with the kit and let them mail hers in with the others.

When an email arrived to notify her that her DNA breakdown was available, she logged into the company's website and found that she was white, 100 percent. She was a little disappointed, but not surprised. Most of that was British and Scandinavian, which made sense because her mom's family emigrated from Sweden. She was also 5 percent Italian and 1 percent Portuguese. The website offered the option of allowing your DNA to be cross-referenced with other people who had registered for the site. Debbie had opted in, thinking she could use it to find cousins on her father's side. He'd had a falling out with his siblings after his parents died, and he had never returned or invited them to visit since. She didn't find anyone closely related to her, but she noticed that she had about a hundred fourth to sixth cousins. While they started out white like her, as she scrolled farther down the list of usernames and profile photos, she saw that the rest were predominantly black.

"How can we be so genetically white and yet have so many black cousins?" she asked her father a week later when she flew from Brooklyn to Atlanta for the weekend to visit her dad for his birthday. She assumed it meant someone in their family had owned slaves, but her dad obviously knew more about his family than she did.

Her dad put down his fork and wiped his mouth with his napkin. He had a habit of building suspense when he spoke, as if he were going to make some grand announcement. His wife, Eliza, a flight attendant who was forty years his junior, also put down her fork. Debbie had been so sickened when she heard that her dad planned to marry a woman that young, barely ten years older than Debbie herself, she hadn't gone to their wedding.

"Well, my two cousins Ralph and Spencer married women from India. No relation to each other," he said, wagging his finger in the air like he was ticking off boxes in his mind. "I believe that my oldest brother, Drew, is married to a woman who is a quarter Nigerian, but I hear you can't really tell." He shrugged and picked up his fork.

"Well, Indian and Nigerian—that's very diverse! You've got a diverse family. Isn't that a good thing?" Eliza said, looking back and forth between Debbie and her father as if she was desperate to keep the peace.

"For them to be our fifth and sixth cousins, it means the mixing had to have happened generations ago." She looked at him, but he kept eating, concentrating on his food. "It meant that someone owned slaves. Do you know of anyone in your background who owned slaves, David?" She knew it set him off when she called him by his first name. Out of all his eight children, she was the only one who he still supported financially, and she was the one who visited him the most, but they'd also always had the worst fights.

"I don't know what difference it makes," he said, still not looking up from his plate. "People mixed. That's how. Did we raise you that sheltered, dear? I told you I don't talk to my family. We had a falling out over money years ago."

"I'm not asking about your family now, David. I'm asking about your family back then. Can you stop being so cagey and just answer the question?" Debbie started tapping the table with her knuckles, signaling her growing impatience. Eliza stood up and started to clear away dishes.

"You are such a brat. I don't know how I let you get this way. It's my greatest regret . . ."

Eliza started to take his plate away, but he held on to it.

"Sit down, Eliza. Don't let Debbie put you off your dinner. Debbie's always this dramatic. Okay, if it matters, some of our ancestors settled in Jamaica. It was a British colony back in the—"

"I know that, Dad."

"Well, if you know everything, why are we even having this conversation?"

He lifted his fork and seemed determined to focus only on his plate. They ate in silence.

When dinner was over and her father reached for his cane nearby, both Debbie and Eliza bolted up from their chairs to be the first one to help him up.

"Do you mind if I spend a little time with my dad?" she said to Eliza, forcing a smile.

"Of course," Eliza said as she turned to clear the table. What Debbie found most unnerving about Eliza was how much she looked like her. They both had strawberry-blond hair and green eyes. They both had petite builds, and Debbie was only about one inch taller than Eliza at five foot four. At twenty-nine, Debbie was David's baby, his last child, much younger than her other seven siblings. She was closest in age only to her older brother Rob, who was fifteen years older. There were four different mothers between them all, but she was the only one born out of wedlock, so to them, she wasn't a real Fowler. She had her mother's last name, Norgood. Her mother had been David's secretary, and though they never married, they were together for five years, and after their affair ended, he made sure they always lived well. He felt guilty for Debbie's alienation from her siblings, so as she grew up, he became overly indulgent with her. He blamed himself for her not finishing college, he'd often said. He hadn't taught her how to have any grit. He had been too afraid to put his foot down.

Nothing had changed about the house since she'd last visited six months ago, but after living in a studio apartment in Brooklyn for twelve years, the size of the house still always seemed absurd. It had six bedrooms and seven bathrooms. The living room, which she now tried to help her father walk across, had thirty-foot-high ceilings. It was a mansion. She would stay here with her dad one weekend a month growing up. Her mother's house, just a few miles away, was much smaller. "It's a really old house," she'd say, when her friends from school would visit on those weekends and commented on how big it was. "There are a lot of structural problems, so my dad got it for cheap." Eventually she stopped bringing her friends over. They came from middle- or working-class families. She didn't want them to think that she was trying to flaunt her money. But now that she was older, she realized that it was worse to hide her privilege. Her father still paid part of her rent in Brooklyn, and she felt guilty for never admitting it to anyone, even when one of her recent boyfriends asked how she paid for her own apartment in Fort Greene on a museum intern's stipend.

She worried about David in this big house. He had finally retired from the real estate company he had founded. Now it was just him and Eliza, and his housekeeper, Nadine, who only worked until six. Though she wanted to hate Eliza, for she was absolutely nothing but a gold digger, she couldn't help noticing how the woman seemed lonely and overwhelmed at dinner. How disappointed she looked when the two of them left her in the dining room alone.

In the cavernous master suite, decked out in various shades of beige, David sat on the edge of the bed as Debbie removed his shoes and pulled a pair of pajamas out of a drawer. She thought about how strange it was to have finally come full circle. She was caring for her dad, like he had cared for her. But then she thought about it again and realized that was a lie. Her dad had never helped her get ready for bed. On the weekends she visited, it was always Nadine, a baby-sitter, or whatever girlfriend he'd had at the time.

She noticed that the walk-in closet was still filled with only men's clothes.

"Eliza doesn't sleep in here, does she?"

"I snore."

She scoffed.

"Why did you marry her?"

"I'm an old man," he said. "Who else is gonna take care of me?"

Debbie knew better than to offer.

She watched as her father unbuttoned his linen shirt on his own. She sucked in her breath when she saw how thin he'd become; his chest was concave, his ribs prominent.

"Daddy, are you eating?" she asked calmly, trying not to reveal her alarm.

"Debbie, I'm eighty-five. Wait, shit—eighty-six as of tomorrow. This is it."

"Don't say that."

He slipped on a loose-fitting T-shirt. He motioned for her to help him with his pants. She helped him up, let him lean on her, as he stepped out of his linen pants.

She had never seen her father stripped down before. Her friends growing up always referred to her dad as an old man, because he was older than their parents, but now it was actually true. She saw that he was even wearing adult diapers. They were black and obviously designed to imitate underwear, but she could see the extra padding.

"Don't stare, honey," he said.

"Sorry."

He sat on the bed while she slid his pajama bottoms around his legs. Once he was dressed, he reached over and squeezed her hand. "You seem surprised to see me like this. I'm not going to live for-ever, you know."

"Dad, stop . . ." She couldn't bear the thought of either of her parents dying. When she thought of her life without her father, she imagined everything going to shambles. Though he had never been the most hands-on father, he was reliable. He was the one she called first when she had a problem because she knew he would fix it. How would she manage without him? At the same time, she wondered who she would be if he wasn't constantly babying her, if she didn't have him to use as a crutch.

"No, no, I want you to have the peace of mind of knowing everything's been arranged."

"Do we have to talk about this now?" she said.

"Do you want to wait another six months? What if I don't have another six months? It's time, honey." He looked at her with desperation.

"Okay, okay. What do you need me to do?"

"Moneywise, you'll get your fair share."

"Oh, Dad, I'm not worried about that." Though the truth was, she was.

"You should be. I remember how nasty it got when my parents died. I still don't talk to my brother Darren, and we were full siblings."

"What does Eliza get?" Debbie resented the idea that her own mother would inherit nothing while Eliza, who'd been married to David for barely a minute, could possibly take half.

"We have a prenup. I'm not stupid. I just want you to know that I set up a trust for you. You can draw the money for your rent from there. And there's enough if you need to go back to school and finish college."

"Daddy, please don't start this again." She wanted to say that soon she'd be paying her rent on her own, but she wasn't sure. She'd gone from internship to internship for years, mainly because she knew she could. She was currently working as a curatorial intern at the SoHo museum for a whopping $12 an hour; life would be impossible without her dad's check arriving like clockwork every month.

"I just wanted to let you know. I'm not trying to argue. But also, there are some family items I want you to have. Open that box," he said, gesturing to a tiny lockbox on his dresser. She brought it over to the bed and put it between them. "I didn't want to talk about it in front of Eliza."

She let her father open it.

"First, I want you to take this ring. It was my grandmother's."

The ring was a gold band that had a large ruby with three diamonds on each side. She had never seen a stone that large, and she wondered if it was costume jewelry. Her dad had always bragged that he was self-made because he came to the U.S. on his own, but for the first time she realized that he came from money. She put the ring on but didn't think she would ever have an occasion to wear something so opulent. He took out a book with a battered leather cover.

"This is what I wanted to give you. I was actually going to leave it to my sister in England in my will, but since you have this sudden interest in learning about our family, I've decided to give it to you."

She took the book and ran her fingers over the cracked leather cover and quickly fanned the yellowing pages.

"No, no," he said, holding her hands still. "Please—it's fragile. It's too valuable for you to be flipping through it like it's a phone book. It belonged to one of our ancestors."

She opened the book again, this time more carefully, and focused on the delicate pages. The script was faded and so ornate it was hard for her to decipher the letters, and most of the ink had faded over time, making some pages illegible.

"Who did it belong to?"

"Your great-great-great-great-grandfather Harold Fowler. He owned a plantation in Jamaica in the eighteen hundreds."

She placed the book on the bed between them.

"So you lied?"

"It's not good dinner conversation. Harold and his brother had slaves. Their father and grandfather owned the plantation before, but they were absentee landlords. Harold was the first to actually live in Jamaica, to make a life there. It was a sugar plantation. It was the eighteen hundreds; that's how those places functioned. They used slaves. It's not pretty, dear, but it's history. That's how people lived back then. Don't let the PC police shame you."

"You're the one who's ashamed. You lied."

"It's not something to be proud of. I'm proud that we come from a family of industrious folks. Of course, though, I'm not proud of the slaves part. It's not something we need to go talking about. Especially, well . . . you never know in this day and age. All this talk about reparations. What if someone tries to sue us one day? I wish you hadn't put your DNA on some website. I would have told you not to if I'd known."

"We have hundreds of cousins who are black, and those are just the ones who registered for the site. Do you know what that means?"

"Don't be crass. I meant what I said. Things didn't work in the West Indies like in the South. There weren't a lot of white women. People mixed over there. They had arrangements. Some of the planters took up with black women while they were away from their families. Don't make assumptions."

"David, I'm not making assumptions. If they were slaves, then it was rape."

He looked at the journal. She saw a look of concern appear on his face.

"Yes. It happened in some cases. You'll read things in this that will disturb you, but it's important. You always insist that I don't treat you like full family. I'm giving you this because I think you're the best qualified. You can be the historian. You can be the one to know everything. It's the oldest heirloom in our family, and I'm giving it to you."

"Why don't you give it to Graham? He'd like this." Though she knew that she was the child her dad fawned over the most, she felt her oldest brother, Graham, was the one he truly respected. While Debbie called her dad when she needed help, her father called Graham when he needed an opinion he could trust.

"I want to keep it for us. Graham would sell it. He reminds me of my older brother. I don't want a bunch of strangers scrutinizing our history. They'd pick it apart, make it something shameful. I just want you to keep this for your children, so they know where we came from."

"I'm not having children, David." She wasn't sure if she meant it, but she had a habit now of resisting any expectations he placed on her. He'd just assumed that she would finish college, get married, and start having children. Debbie had seen how sad he'd been when she'd dropped out of college. Maybe she just wanted him to get his disappointment over with now rather than further down the line.

He rolled his eyes and continued. "They should know that we helped build a country. Bad and good, it's ours and we should know about it, but I don't want the name Fowler to become synonymous with slavery. We did more than that. You'll promise to keep it in the family, won't you?"

"Are you sure you want me to have it? I'm not even a Fowler."

"Don't start that again. You don't need my last name to be my daughter. It's about blood, not last names."

"If it's about blood, aren't all our black relatives Fowlers too?"

"Don't argue just to argue," he said, and got under the covers.

Debbie contemplated saying no. She didn't have the Fowler name, he never offered to give it to her, and though she found taking a man's name an archaic convention, it still made her feel a little less than. It was a fact that allowed her siblings to dismiss her, helped them rationalize always keeping her at arm's length.

As she thought about them, there was a piece of Debbie that wanted revenge. To throw it back in her father's face and say, *Give it to the ones you think are worthy enough to have your name*, but she could see how earnest he was when he held it. He seemed certain that it had to be her. It turned out to be one of the last things he'd ever ask of her. When she pushed him the next morning, he finally admitted that he had been diagnosed with prostate cancer and though it had a high recovery rate, he wouldn't be getting treatment. He had six months to a year to live. When she left that afternoon, she thanked him for the journal, tucked it deep in her bag, and held her father's frail body until he pulled away.

⁂

As soon as she returned home to her apartment that night, she sat down to read Harold's diary. She was surprised at her own excitement. It was a piece of history, the likes of which she was used to seeing in an archive or a museum; she felt greedy, like she was breaking some unspoken rule, keeping it all for herself and handling it without gloved hands or an archivist peering over her shoulder. Her goal was to one day become a museum curator, so handling something rare had special meaning for her. Though her specialty was outsider art, she found many other areas fascinating. Debbie hadn't dropped out of school because she hated learning. It was the opposite. She found college too restrictive. She wanted to study everything. She couldn't choose.

But when she read Harold's first entry, where he delighted in torturing a slave over a jar of honey, she wondered if history was easier to digest when you were disconnected from it. When you stared at it through a glass display case. She didn't want to acknowledge

Harold as a part of her personal history. Sometimes knowledge was overrated.

⚜

The next morning, Debbie had a lunch date set up with Jane Smallwood, a black woman who was a curator in the African art department of the SoHo museum. Debbie's intern coordinator had assigned her to decorative arts, though that hadn't been on her list of preferences. She had hoped to be assigned to modern American painting and sculpture, or else African or Asian art. Debbie still hadn't gotten comfortable with these kinds of informational meetings over the years, asking more experienced people around her how they had found full-time jobs and what she could do to make herself a stronger candidate. Though they were a good way to network in the field, they never seemed to lead to a full-time job. But it was something you were supposed to do, so she did, however reluctantly. And since a new assistant curator position had just opened up, she realized it was important to make sure as many senior staff members knew her name and face as possible.

She met Jane at the museum entrance, and they walked to a Vietnamese restaurant a few blocks away. Over steaming bowls of pho, Debbie talked to Jane about her past internships and where she planned to apply for full-time positions.

"I'm looking in a lot of places, but I am also interested in the assistant curator position at SoHo."

"You should really finish your degree in art history," Jane said. "You won't be competitive without it. With your experience, you would have already found something if you had the degree."

"School didn't work out for me," she said, demoralized that Jane had so quickly dismissed her as a candidate.

Jane nodded, but Debbie saw the judgment in her eyes. Jane looked impeccable in her bright-yellow dress and shocking red lipstick that made her dark-brown skin seem to glow. She herself was basically a piece of art. Which made Debbie wonder if she would have found a job already if she didn't dress so plainly. She wore the same blue, black, or brown blazer, button-down shirt, and jeans with flats combo every day.

"And are you working somewhere else?" Jane asked.

"No. Just here," she said.

"And you live in Fort Greene?" she said.

"Yes. What about you?"

"I live in Bushwick," she said. There was a moment of silence, and Debbie could feel Jane's unspoken resentment.

"My father pays for my studio," she said, hoping her honesty would diminish any class resentment. "You know, we millennials are kids until thirty-five now, technically. Hopefully, I'll be settled in the next few years."

Jane chuckled. "It took me more than a few years to find a decent-paying job, and I'm older. These rents are crazy now. Things were much cheaper when I first moved here. I don't know how you would do it without parents. I highly recommend you finish your degree, if you don't want your dad supporting you forever."

Debbie regretted telling Jane about the help from her dad that quickly. Once people knew you had a leg up, they found a way to use it to take little jabs at you forever. At least, that was how it had been in Debbie's experience. When she'd refused to help her last boyfriend, Roy, with a security deposit for a new apartment, he'd said bitterly, *Well, it's not like you had to work for that money.* She'd broken up with him afterward.

For the first time it dawned on her that Jane was the only black curator at the museum. She was the only black curator that Debbie had met at any of the museums where she'd worked. Debbie feared that Jane now saw her as just another trust-fund baby, one who was trying to take positions away from hard-working minorities like herself without even having a degree. Jane would never want to put in a good word for the assistant curator job now. Debbie had to win her over somehow, she thought. She didn't want to do another internship—she was almost thirty.

So, she told her about Harold's diary. She didn't want her to think that she was one of those white people who were in denial about their white privilege. Besides, she knew that it was the kind of primary source that anyone in the museum world would drool over.

"That's so fascinating," Jane said. It seemed like an oversimplified response, but Debbie could tell that Jane was sincere.

"I read one entry, and it gave me nightmares. I couldn't read any more," Debbie said.

"Would you mind if I took a look at it?"

"I'm not sure," she said, pretending to consider it. She sipped her soup quietly for a moment. "My dad asked me to keep it close. It's supposed to be for our family's eyes only."

"I totally understand. But I really would love to look at it," Jane said.

Debbie smiled slightly and put her hand on Jane's. "Okay, I'll let you look at it. I'll bring it tomorrow, but please, please don't share it with anyone else," she said. "You're the only person I'm letting see it."

She did hope that Jane wouldn't share it. Her dad would kill her if he knew that she was giving it to someone outside the family, but Debbie wanted to let Jane feel as if she were granting her a special favor. In exchange, maybe she would do the same if Debbie's résumé should pass through her fingers.

Debbie gave Harold's journal to Jane and said she could borrow it until next week. On the following Monday, they met for lunch in the museum café to make the exchange.

"How was it?" Debbie asked.

Jane just shook her head back and forth. She squeezed her lips together tightly, looked Debbie in the eyes, and shook her head again like she was trying to clear her head.

"Was it that bad? Worse than the fire ants?"

Jane slid her hand across the table and placed it on top of Debbie's.

"It would be really brave of you to make this public," she said.

Debbie heard the shift in her voice. It was suddenly too gentle, slightly condescending. "I know, but my father would be upset. He's very elderly. He has cancer. I really don't want to stress him out. Maybe after he dies, I'll revisit the option," she said, hoping Jane would let it go.

"Well, you really need to read this for yourself," she said, closing her eyes and pausing, reliving something, searching for the right word. "It was astonishing. No . . . it was devastating. But in a really profound way."

"Profound how?"

"It is a very vivid picture of Caribbean plantation life. Like, I literally had no idea, and my grandmother is from Trinidad," she said, shaking her head again. "The women. The poor women."

"You're making me not want to know more."

"Oh, no, no, Debbie. You need to know. This is *your* past too. You have to acknowledge it. You can't hide from it."

"It's not my past. I didn't enslave anyone," Debbie interjected. She knew she had slipped into defensive mode. She had sworn she'd never be one of those people.

"But we all have to know our history, Debbie. Even if you come from the bad guys."

Debbie focused on keeping quiet. *The bad guys* line had triggered something in her. She didn't want to get more defensive, but she so badly wanted to say that she wasn't a bad guy.

"Think how valuable this could be to a genealogist. For black people, finding our ancestors who were slaves is almost impossible. There are names in this. This could be part of a larger puzzle. This is so, so valuable, Debbie. I can't stress it enough. I charge you to face it. Be brave." Jane cupped Debbie's hands in hers and squeezed. She stared into Debbie's eyes without saying anything more, her face affixed with an expression Debbie couldn't exactly pinpoint but that definitely contained pity. And maybe something like scorn too.

Debbie left the meeting with a sudden dislike for Jane. Who was she to charge Debbie to do anything? It was her family, her personal business, and she could face it or not face it any way she liked. But she remembered her General Lee–loving classmate and how red his face had gotten that day, just because people were talking about the facts of history. She didn't want to be one of those white people.

⚘

That night, Debbie found herself trying to imagine what a Caribbean plantation looked like. It had never occurred to her to look. She found a website online that had photographs of the last intact great houses in Jamaica, what they called the main house on the plantation where the masters lived. As she scrolled through the photos, she found herself picturing herself there, standing in a dining room below a crystal chandelier in a lace dress as servants set a long table. Then she caught herself. Slaves. As slaves set the table. She was embarrassed, even though no one else could read her thoughts. She wondered if she was no different from the people who still hung up the Confederate flag. Did all white people secretly have some strange antebellum or colonial fantasy? Was there a part of her that would have gotten off on the idea of being a mistress of a big house? If she were alive back then, would she have gone along with it or would she have been brave enough to resist? Would she have married someone who owned slaves?

Her Fort Greene neighborhood had gotten much whiter in the

years since she'd moved there. Initially, it had been filled with black people—West Indians, specifically. Her landlady was from Trinidad or Jamaica—she wasn't sure. She and her husband lived on the first floor of the brownstone, and Debbie rented the upstairs apartment. She had never before taken much interest in her landlady or her grandchildren, who often played in the backyard. But that night she noticed her landlords had their grandchildren over and were grilling outside for dinner, after dark. She watched the two children, a boy and girl about eight and nine, chasing each other through the grass as they waited for dinner. She wondered if there was a chance that they all had Harold as their common ancestor. How many children had he fathered with his slaves? How many of them were here now, walking on the same Brooklyn streets? She could contact them through the DNA website, but should she? It didn't seem like a welcomed email. *Hey, I think my ancestor raped yours and exploited their labor at the same time* . . . Did they have a right to read Harold's journal too? How many of them had grown up poor and still struggled to get by, while she lived in a brownstone apartment paid for by her father?

The questions plagued her. Of course, there would be no reckoning like her father feared. She was far from the only white person whose family had profited off of slavery, but she knew the least she could do, as Jane said, was face the truth. Still, she dreaded reading it, so she put off taking the book out of the closet that night. The next day, she called in sick. She planned to spend the day doing different things that she thought would help prepare her to be transported once again into the world of Harold's diary.

This is how she found herself walking forty minutes the next afternoon to a well-reviewed Jamaican restaurant a few neighborhoods over for lunch. She had never had any interest in Jamaican cuisine before—she hated spicy food—but she figured that it was, in a way, her culture now too. After looking over the menu, she ordered only a vegetable patty and then walked to Prospect Park to eat it. She sat under the shade of a tree and ate her patty. It was still too spicy for her, and even though she was forced to guzzle water to keep from coughing, she made herself finish it. She had the journal in her bag. She carefully applied hand sanitizer before she took the book out, along with a pencil, a notepad, and her magnifying glass. She imagined it might be easier if she treated it like research, a homework assignment. She would write down the names of the slaves as Jane suggested. She didn't know what she would do with the list, but it was somewhere to begin.

15 November 1815: Father returned today with girl of fourteen from Iceland named Katrin. Very pretty and fair. Does not speak a word of English. Offered her first to my brother, Enoch. He refused, forever the bachelor, though he has taken up with mulatto Bertha, much to father's dismay. I accepted. In exchange, Warm Manor will be transferred to me, not Enoch. An act of spite by Father, punishment for Enoch being so hardheaded.

22 November 1815: Married now. Katrin fares poorly. Bullheaded and childish. Hired a tutor to teach her English, but she refuses to speak. Also, very sickly and melancholy. Tried to visit her chambers but she cried and fought. Sent Florence to attend and nurse Katrin.

1 December 1815: Enoch says, "A married man is a miserable man." He laughs at my condition. Wife has malaria and is hysterical. Never seen Negroes and has been afraid. Fights when they try to feed her, clean her. Fights me. They in turn are afraid of her. "What tongue she speak, Massa?" Joab asked me. Malaria spreading through slave quarters. They think she's casting

*incantations, as if malaria did not exist in Jamaica before she
arrived. Madness. Heard Joab whisper the word "witch" to
London in the kitchen, who was making a compress for Katrin,
and had them both flogged. Must put an end to this foolishness
before it spreads like wildfire.*

*9 December 1815: Flogged Florence for talking back, not coming
to my room in the night when summoned.*

*12 December 1815: Wife's condition improved. Doctor Evans
has provided a potion to make her more docile. Finally submit-
ted. Learning English. Knows the word "husband."*

༄

That night, Debbie had her second nightmare. She was locked in
a room of a strange house, banging on the windows. She got one
window open. A man was outside the door, fumbling with the key,
and she knew she didn't have long. He was coming. In the distance
she could see little huts. Smoke rising off fires. Finally, desperate,
she looked down at the earth. Below her there were bushes. It was a
long drop, and though she didn't know whether she would survive,
she decided it was worth it. She held on to the window frame and
started to slide her legs over the sill. Just as she was about to jump,
she felt a sharp pain on her scalp, and before she knew it, she was on
the floor, looking up at an older white man with a red face. He had
yanked her back inside by her hair. She could see a few strands, still
sticking out between the fingers of his balled fist. He put his foot
on top of her chest and started to press down, crushing her rib cage
until she cried and begged him to stop.

It was a dream, she said when she awoke. It was just a dream, but
she was panting, trying to catch her breath. In the morning her dia-

phragm hurt. That angry red face looking down at her kept flashing in her mind throughout the day as she tried to work. Every time she saw it, she felt the pain in her chest, remembered the weight of the boot. She was so distracted she nearly dropped a Fabergé egg, but her coworker Devon caught it before it hit the floor.

❧

Reading the journal was a chore that she came to dread each night, but she promised herself that she wouldn't stop until she finished. When she told Jane that she was reading the journal a few days later, Jane hugged her. It did make Debbie feel like she was doing something brave. She wouldn't know what to do with it until she finished. All she knew was that she was always thinking about Harold, from the time she woke up in the morning to the time she went to bed at night. One day she experimented with reading it before work instead of before bed, hoping it could stop the nightmares.

3 August 1816: Katrin has given birth to a girl. Not expected. Old Margaret had taken a look at her and said boy. Old Negroes and their foolishness. I let cousin Alma name her. She named her Peta-Gay. Wife won't nurse, looks at the babe like she's something from the devil. Have given her to Maddie to wet nurse.

10 August 1816: Profits increasing. Father pleased. Wife has been holding the child. Recovered from her fear of Negroes, but now too friendly. Found her laughing with Florence, Maddie, and Ruth as if they were girls at school. Had the slaves flogged for cavorting when they should have been working. A sugar estate is no place for a white woman. Looking to purchase property in Spanish Town. Once there she can learn proper social graces and refinement.

15 August 1816: Maddie told wife about her child, but Katrin still has no command of English. She told Alma to tell Katrin that her bastard is mine to punish me for having her flogged. Alma came to me straightaway to tell me about the slander one of my slaves is spreading. I found Maddie washing clothes by the river. I crept behind her and pushed her under the water. Let her thrash until her body became still. Took her on the bank and revived her. Told her that was the last piece of gossip I expect to hear she's spread. Mr. Paisley came asking to buy Florence. I told him that he is not the only one who has taken a shine to her. She has a rare beauty. I pulled her from the fields myself. For now, I prefer to keep her near me. But when I am ready to see her sold, he shall be the first to know. I told him that I would sell him Maddie and her babe for one price in the meantime. He went away sulking.

17 August 1816: New overseer, MacDaniel. Lazy Scotsman. Too easy on field Negroes. Caught Muriel, Cleo, and Moses sitting in the cane fields, resting while the others worked. Claim permission was granted from MacDaniel. Ordered all flogged with the cat. Cleo ran away the next day. Second time this month. Had her branded. Caught MacDaniel in the smokehouse with Muriel. Told him if I found him again fornicating during work hours, he would be dismissed. Saw Mary entering his quarters after hours as I was riding back from Hughes Plantation. Caught Florence leaving his quarters the next night. Had her flogged. Told him Mr. Paisley has offered to buy Florence for a good price and keep her. Reminded that unwashed crude scoundrel MacDaniel to keep his eyes and hands off the niggers in the house and keep himself to the ones in the field as he was hired to do.

23 August 1816: Florence and Cleo ran away. Cleo came back the next day. Had her branded on her forehead. She does not have much clean flesh left. Found Florence three days later. Received a flogging and time in the stocks.

1 September 1816: Florence pregnant. This may be why she ran. Suspect MacDaniel but he denies it. We will see what color the child is.

1 November 1816: Katrin behaving like an animal again. Tried to visit chambers at night but was clawed at and bitten. I told her it is imperative that we have an heir. She bit my ear until it bled. Told Maddie to keep door locked. Katrin not permitted out of room until she learns to behave.

2 November 1816: Told Maddie she'd be put in stocks for letting Katrin out unless she visited my room in the night. She came and I had her instead.

12 May 1817: Magistrate hung Florence for poisoning my food. I still cannot believe she was so bold and that I was so reckless. She was spiteful, I suppose, because I sold her babe to Mr. Paisley. Did not plead or make a sound as they put the hood over her head. The quietest hanging I'd ever witnessed.

Debbie couldn't eat for the rest of the day, and she still had trouble concentrating at work. When Jane saw Debbie in the elevator, she took one look at her and gave her another hug.

"Are you okay?"

"I've been reading it," said Debbie. "I'm almost done."

"Do you know what you're going to do with it?" asked Jane. "I know a few people who would be interested. I have a cousin who's a professor at the University of the West Indies. I told him about it. I hope you don't mind. He'd like to take a look at it. He'd even fly up here."

"I'll think about it," she said. The thought of handing it off was tempting. She didn't want all the horrors contained in the book living in her house. Even though they were just words, they built a world that she couldn't stop thinking about, that she felt trapped inside every night.

❧

Reading Harold's diary made Debbie think often about whether evil was passed down. She used to think that she was a good person. She'd never led a lavish life. Even though she had a seemingly never-ending stream of money from her dad, she only took enough to pay her bills and go out to eat once in a while. She wasn't greedy. She didn't act like someone who came from money. But now she thought about the fact that she never really did anything to make the world better. She did nothing for other people, for humanity. She wasn't evil, but she wasn't particularly good either. She'd started to wonder whether, since Harold had put so much evil in the world, she could afford to be neutral. She had to atone. She had no choice. If there was such a thing as hell, she was certain that Harold had tipped the scales so deeply toward eternal damnation he must have tainted the souls of his descendants too.

She borrowed books from the library on the history of Jamaica. She combed the internet. That was how she discovered that there was a town named after Harold, simply called Harold Town, where the plantation once stood. She looked for other mentions of Harold Town, but she could barely find it anywhere. The little she did find on the internet just mentioned how poor it was. Residents basically existed as subsistence farmers, scrounging whatever they could off the land. She knew that her dad was leaving her money. She hadn't thought about how much before, but she figured now that it was probably significant. Maybe she could build a little school or a library. If her dad didn't leave her enough, she could fundraise for donations. Maybe if she offered college scholarships, it would make a difference. There were real steps she could take—concrete actions—to offset some of the evil that Harold had done. On the last day of her internship, she asked Jane for the professor's contact.

❧

Debbie decided to fly to Jamaica without telling her father. When she called him, he claimed that he was still doing well, but she worried that he was just trying to protect her. Professor Gregory taught classes on slavery and plantation life, and he said she could audit his class in exchange for allowing him to take a look at the journal. He had a room she could rent, and he promised that on her first weekend in Jamaica, he would drive her to Harold Town. He said he would take her on a tour of the ruins of Harold's plantation himself.

On the flight over, Debbie fell asleep. She dreamed that she was on the bank of a river, beating white clothes against a rock. She felt two hands grab her. One clenched her shoulder and one held firmly onto her hair and then plunged her head forward into the water, smashing her head against a stone on the way down. Her nose and windpipe started to burn as she struggled to hold her breath. Her lungs were on fire. At some point she passed out, and when she came to, she was spitting out water. She saw Harold's face; she always pictured a broad white face, as expansive as the moon, with two inflamed ruddy cheeks, his features dimmed by the wide brim of his hat. His eyes hateful. He lifted up his foot, pulled it back, and just before he kicked her in the face, she woke up screaming.

"Are you all right?" the man next to her asked.

Two flight attendants came over.

"I'm fine. I'm fine. Can I just have some ice water?" she asked, just to make them go away.

When their plane landed, there was a smattering of applause. Debbie made it out of the airport and was ambushed by a throng of darting eyes, Jamaican people looking for loved ones. Most of the white people had gotten off when the plane made a stopover at Montego Bay, so Debbie felt self-conscious. She saw a sign with her last name. The man who held the sign wore a red mesh tank top, denim shorts, and thick-strapped leather sandals; a white visor shaded his eyes but left his slightly thinning hairline exposed to the sun. His face was light and covered with freckles; his buzzed hair had a reddish tinge.

"Debbie?"

"Yes," she said.

"Professor Gregory send me to pick you up," he said. "I'm Vincent."

One of his front teeth was twisted around, giving his smile a childlike quality, which contrasted with his bullish frame. Debbie had never seen a black redhead before. She did not mean to treat him as if he were some medical oddity, but she found herself sneaking glances at him as she got into his white pickup truck. She thought the ride would be uncomfortable, that they would drive in silence, but Vincent wouldn't stop talking. He asked her where she lived, and when she told him Brooklyn, he bombarded her with questions. He asked her about the weather, the stores she liked, the movies, what food she ate. Finally, he asked why she wanted to go to Harold Town.

"It's named after my great-great-great-great-grandfather," she said, not wanting to go into too much detail.

"Ah. Him the one who did run the plantation?" he asked.

"Yes. Are you from there?"

"My father from there. He died when I was born, but when I take Professor Gregory class, he help me do research. I never get to finish my degree, but we stay in touch. He a good man. I do work for him from time to time. He ask me to drive you two there tomorrow."

She wanted to say something. Did Harold own his great-great-

great-great-grandfather? Did Harold rape his ancestor? Was it sick that she felt attracted to him? She wanted to apologize, but she didn't know how to bring it up. He didn't seem upset or angry with her. He turned on the radio and started singing along to the music, a song about chasing the devil away.

"Who's this?" she asked.

"Max Romeo," he said, and continued to sing along to the radio the entire way.

Professor Gregory was younger than expected. He had dark, smooth skin like Jane's and a direct stare. Once he showed her to her room, he didn't waste any time asking for the journal. He took it back to his room to read immediately, and shortly after, his housekeeper, an older Jamaican woman, fixed Debbie a chicken sandwich. She didn't see him again until Vincent arrived to pick them up the next morning, when he handed the journal back to her.

"We need to talk about what you plan on doing with this," he said. "Let's do the tour today and then we can discuss next steps at dinner."

It was hot outside, in the nineties. The palm fronds seemed to spasm in the wind as they drove along the shoreline, past the seaside factories billowing clouds of clay-colored smoke. It took them an hour to leave the city and begin the trek into the mountains. When they did, they passed through town after town made up of houses that looked like they had been pieced together with scraps. They saw goats wandering around aimlessly with greater frequency than she saw rats on the subway tracks in New York. The higher they climbed, it seemed, the narrower the roads became. Whenever they were going around a bend, Vincent had to honk his horn so the drivers coming in the opposite direction knew to slow down. One of them had to stop and let the other pass or else they would have smashed into each other and perhaps dived over the side of the road, plunging into the deep valley below.

The professor had talked for most of the trip, explaining to Vincent and Debbie that he was writing a book on the sexual exploitation of slaves in Jamaica. He talked about the narratives he'd read so far and the other scholars whose research he'd explored. She wanted to ask him to stop. The thought of the rapes that Harold had committed along with the bumpiness of the roads was making her nauseous. But Vincent seemed interested, so she said nothing. Vincent turned on the radio later, cutting the professor off, signaling that he had spoken enough. She met his eyes gratefully in the rearview mirror. After about four hours of driving, Debbie fell asleep. She dreamed she was under the river again. This time she wasn't in pain. She was in the water looking up at the sky, and she realized her body was floating with the current. She was dead, yet it was the most peaceful dream she'd had in weeks.

"You can read me a little bit of the book?" Vincent asked when she woke up.

"It's very graphic," she said.

"Me a big boy, you know," he said, giving her a grin.

She flipped to the page she knew she had just dreamed about.

6 June 1823: Katrin gave birth to a boy! Harold Fowler II.
Wife and baby in good health. Peta-Gay is a beautiful child,
nearly seven and already growing tall, but she is not a son. I
will sleep deeply tonight and ever more with the knowledge
that I have an heir.

7 June 1823: Katrin drowned in the river. Do not know how
she got out and walked all the way in her weakened state.
Slaves swear even after flogging that none of them aided her.
Alma has told Peta-Gay that her mother died of dengue fever.

"Jesus Christ," Vincent said. Debbie didn't want to tell them how she'd been Katrin in her dream, how she'd known that she was happy that she drowned. They'd think she was crazy.

They rode in silence for about half an hour. Finally, Professor Gregory announced that they were approaching Harold Town.

"You can see the river he spoke of in the journal below."

She looked down at the valley, saw a few people wading through a river that looked half dried up. She could see houses with corrugated-tin ceilings or brightly painted concrete roofs spread out across the dense green landscape.

"You excited?" Vincent asked, looking back at her.

She nodded, but seeing the river filled her with dread. In another thirty minutes, they had managed to wind down into the valley.

"You in Harold Town now," Vincent said. She didn't know how she would feel once she set foot in the world of the diary in real life, but as they got out to take a picture in front of the WELCOME TO HAROLD TOWN sign, she had a strong urge to run. She felt a heavy boulder in the pit of her stomach the deeper they walked into town. She didn't know how much more she could take.

Debbie didn't even realize that she still had the journal in her hand. She could ask Vincent to hold it. Maybe that was why she felt so afraid. She could feel its dark energy flowing through her. She saw that Vincent was walking away from them, toward the river. He took off his shoes and walked into the water, bending down and splashing his face with water to cool off.

"Let's sit by the bank for a minute and talk about where we should go first," Professor Gregory said. He walked toward Vincent. There were rocks to climb over before you could stand on the bank, and Professor Gregory offered her his hand. She was still a few feet away and felt like her feet were anchored into the dirt like the roots of a tree. Everything inside her said, *Stay away*.

"Are you okay?" he said. "Come on—I'll help you climb over."

Debbie looked at Vincent, who was sitting on the bank. He stopped to take his T-shirt off and laid it out next to him. He saw Debbie and gestured for her to sit down. His wave eased her anxiety for a moment, enough for her to walk toward the professor's open hand. But as she approached, she felt heat on the back of her neck; she was paranoid that at any moment Harold would emerge and force her head under the water. She could hear Harold's voice in her head saying, *You'll learn! You'll learn!* When she looked at the surface of the river, she thought of all the women who Harold had probably held down beneath him. She settled down between the professor and Vincent, but she felt like she was coming out of her skin. Harold was dead, she told herself. He wasn't some boogeyman who was going to rise from the bottom of the river and pull her down.

"Are you okay?" Professor Gregory asked. "You look a bit sunburned. Are you too hot?"

She felt like she was having a panic attack, but she didn't want to concern them. She didn't want to explain why. Vincent studied her for the first time since she had sat down, took in her ragged breathing, her panicked red face. He held her hand.

"Come," he said, rising and then trying to pull her up.

"What are you doing?" she said.

"You mus' cool off. You look like you a get heatstroke."

"I just need to drink some water," she said.

"Come," he said. "You 'fraid a water?"

"No," she began, but she was afraid. She was terrified.

"It hot today. Your clothes will dry fast." He gently tugged at the bottom of her T-shirt, beckoning her to follow him into the water. Debbie took off her sandals. She was wearing shorts so it was easy for her to at least dip her feet in and see how the water felt. Vincent kept his eyes on hers while he backed slowly into the river.

"Come," he said again.

"If you're going to wade in, let me hold the journal," Professor Gregory said behind her.

She felt it again, in her hand. Harold's voice. The source of all her fear. She stepped toward Vincent and he stepped back. He motioned her forward until she was up to her ankles in the river. The water was cold, giving her a sudden chill.

"Good," Vincent said. "You need fi cool off."

She thought of the terror Maddie had felt, the pain, as Harold held her head under the cold water. Then she thought of herself as Katrin in her dream, how serene she had felt floating under its surface. She felt pulled in two different directions.

"Let me hold the journal," Professor Gregory called after her again. She ignored him and kept wading toward Vincent until she was up to her knees. Vincent was splashing his arms and chest with water, cooling himself off. He didn't notice as she walked past him, deeper into the river.

She heard Professor Gregory calling her from the riverbank.

"You alright? Is wha' wrong with you?" Vincent said, sloshing after her.

"Nothing," she said, now up to her waist in water. She held the book above the surface.

"Make the professor hold the book," said Vincent, for the first time realizing that something was wrong. He kept looking back at Professor Gregory with concern.

Debbie shook her head. His voice was too alive. In this book. In her head. All the women were in there with him, she thought, like prisoners. She didn't know how to make a difference until she stepped into the water.

She opened the book and tore a page out, letting it get carried away downstream by the current. Then she tore several out together, let the wind pull them out of her hand and scatter them along the surface of the river.

"Jesus! Is wha' you a do?" Vincent yelled.

"Killing him," she said, keeping her eyes on the floating pages. She heard the professor sloshing through the water toward her.

"What?" Vincent said. "Me nuh understand what you a say."

"Debbie!" Professor Gregory called. "Debbie, try not to get them wet. Let me hold it for you!" When he came closer and saw that she'd torn out the pages, he screamed, "Fuck!"

But when Professor Gregory tried to grab Debbie, Vincent stepped in front of him and started to push him back. She could hear the professor begging her to stop as she tore each page out, one by one. With each submerged page, Debbie could hear Harold's voice in her head saying, *You'll learn, you'll learn, you'll* . . . until she heard only gurgling, the sound of his throat filling with water as he drowned.

FORGIVE ME

Brooklyn, 2011

Vincent didn't think he'd be so eager to see someone from back home. He'd only been in New York for two months, but when he saw Ernie Pitt on the Q train, he raced down the aisle with such an aggressive determination that the other passengers hurried to get out of his way without him having to say a word. He still hadn't even bothered to look up his sister, Irene, or even to tell her that he'd left Jamaica and was now living in the same city as her. He still had not bothered to tell her that he was married to a white American woman he'd met last year through one of his old professors at UWI. Debbie came to Jamaica to conduct some research into her family's history, and Vincent had acted as both her guide and driver. She was older than the average student, which was why she believed they gravitated toward each other. In reality, Vincent had always gravitated toward anything American. The food, the music, movies, clothes, the women. He had pictured himself in New York for as long as he could remember, and so he didn't have the nerve to tell anyone or even himself that he hated it.

Age had not been kind to Ernie. It had made his most awkward features more pronounced—his slouching gait, his oversized Adam's apple, his question mark–curved spine. Ernie was six foot six, so he was not difficult to spot across a train car. Everyone had teased him when they were kids, nicknaming him String Bean, even Vincent, who was ten years younger.

Ernie held a small sleeping child in his arms, a girl in a denim jumper dress, white stockings, and red patent-leather shoes.

When Vincent was a few feet away, he called out. "Ernie?"

Ernie looked Vincent over for what felt like a long time before nodding. He didn't smile.

"Is me . . . Vincent Paisley. You the first person I run into from back home," Vincent said.

"When you come 'ere?" Ernie asked.

"Last year," Vincent lied. For some reason he was too embarrassed to admit how green he was, how overwhelmed and lost.

The little girl in Ernie's arms stirred.

"And who's this sweetheart?"

"This me daughter. Rebecca Ann."

The girl opened one eye and peeked out at Vincent with the same look of pure ice that her daddy had given him. She closed it immediately and pressed her face back into Ernie's neck, as if she'd judged him unworthy of her time.

"How your mother?" Vincent asked.

"She good, man. She good. She over here too." Vincent had seen Ernie's mother, Marva Pitt, at his own mother's funeral twelve years ago. The old woman had sung hymns, told stories, and even produced a few contrived tears as if she and his mother, Vera, had been close friends. In reality, the neighborhood women had long shunned Vera for a number of perceived transgressions. Vincent did not remember Mrs. Pitt calling on his mother or even waving hello throughout his childhood. Vera's old friend Marcia, who lived in Kingston, was the only one who came to see her when she was dying. She was a retired nurse, and she took time to show Vincent different ways to relieve some of Vera's pain. But a few days before Vera's funeral service, there were Mrs. Pitt and a few other neighborhood women standing on his veranda, singing hymns for Vera. There was something about their voices, singing in unison, that had brought back a memory of one of the last times he had ever seen Ernie, decades before. He remembered that Ernie was wearing a priest's collar and he was praying over Vera with the neighborhood women. But he had doubted the memories that came back since then; he was only a boy when it happened, and he knew how easy it was for a child to confuse reality with dreams. He had dreamed about Ernie often since his mother's funeral. He wanted to ask him how much of what he remembered was true and how much was the memory distilled through a child's overactive imagination, but it didn't feel right to bring it up just then. How could he look at a man he hadn't seen in more than three decades and confess that he'd been dreaming about him for years?

Vincent waited for Ernie to ask after his family, so he could tell him his mother had died, though he was almost certain that Ernie's own mother must have told him about Vera. Ernie didn't ask. They were crossing the waters between Manhattan and Brooklyn, and Ernie turned away from Vincent to stare at the water as if he were seeing the view from the Manhattan Bridge for the first time. He wondered if this unfriendliness was a by-product of living in America, a disease that you caught. He had seen it everywhere he went. He'd known so many Jamaicans who'd claimed family in Brooklyn over the years, so Vincent had been surprised to find it filled with so many white people. They were everywhere and all seemed determined not to meet his eye, so he became determined not to meet theirs either, and he was disappointed that America passed this reticence back and forth like a contagion. When he saw Americans on TV, their presence was big and loud, and they were always smiling. He saw none of that in the people he came across day to day.

Vincent braced himself to try again to spark the conversation. "What stop you a get off at?"

"Newkirk Avenue," Ernie said. "You?"

"Seventh Avenue. West Indian down there, by Newkirk?"

"Yea, man," Ernie said, and it was the first bit of light that he beamed in Vincent's direction. "Pure West Indian live over there."

Vincent didn't ask Ernie if he could follow him to his stop, for he was afraid that he'd reject him. He simply bypassed Seventh Avenue. Ernie said nothing, but as they drew closer to Newkirk, Ernie kept looking at Vincent, trying to meet his eye. Vincent turned away from Ernie and pretended to be intently studying a subway map. When their stop arrived, Ernie looked to Vincent, who made a motion for Ernie to exit.

"Me live with me wife in the white part of Brooklyn. Me wan' fi see where the real West Indian live. Show me," he said, hoping that he could find the right moment to ask Ernie about what he remembered.

Ernie sighed but gave Vincent a smile. When they were on the street, Ernie put his daughter on the ground, and she made a big show of pretending to sleep standing up.

"You mus' walk today, gal," Ernie said sternly. To her credit, the girl stood up straight, held Ernie's hand, and walked quietly for the rest of the way.

The street outside was busy with vendors and people moving in and out of discount stores and fruit markets.

"Make me take you to one Jamaican spot," Ernie said.

In the restaurant, Vincent ordered a large plate of oxtails with butter beans, rice and peas, and plantains. Plus, a small bowl of mannish water soup that was so spicy he coughed until he was forced to take a pump from his asthma inhaler.

"It feel like one long time since me eat food that season right," he said, his voice raspy.

They ate without making conversation, Ernie taking longer because he had to coax Rebecca Ann to eat.

When they were done, they both sat, watching Rebecca Ann

make a poor effort of coloring within the boundaries of a Teletubby outlined on a paper place mat.

Vincent knew there would be no better time. "You hear seh my mother dead?"

Ernie nodded. "Me did run into your sister 'bout one year ago, and she tell me. Me never even know seh my mother gone a the funeral. Me woulda fly down if she did tell me."

"Diabetes," Vincent said, and he looked into Ernie's eyes to see if he already knew.

Ernie took out his phone and looked at the time for longer than seemed necessary.

"Is only Jamaica where diabetes still kill you," Ernie said, without looking up. "People have it 'nough over here but them live long time with it."

Vincent thought about the priest's collar. The image was clear in his mind, but as he watched Rebecca Ann, he doubted the world his mind had filled in around the picture.

Unlike his sister, Irene, Vincent always tried to keep the good memories and let the bad ones go. So when he thought of his childhood, he remembered only the tenderness of his mother, the way she doted on him when he was little and barely scolded him when he misbehaved. He remembered the backyard in Independence City as the Garden of Eden. Even though he had lived there his whole life, and he would eventually grow to feel trapped by it in the years he took care of his ailing mother, as a little boy it seemed like he had a forest just out back that he spent hours exploring. He remembered always being the littlest boy in the neighborhood and Ernie lifting him on his shoulders when they played with the other kids, so that they wouldn't trample him.

But he and his sister had very different versions of their childhood. Irene remembered only the times their mother was abusive and volatile. Vincent told her once, screamed at her into the phone actually, when she knew their mother was dying but still refused to fly home, that it was her memory that was the problem.

"You try too hard fi remember bad t'ings. You try so hard you make up t'ings that never even happen!"

He wanted to call his sister now and ask her what she remembered about that day, if it even happened, Ernie in the priest's collar, in their mother's bedroom, for he knew she had been there too, but calling her, admitting that for once they remembered their life together the same way, seemed impossible.

Instead he asked Ernie: "When you quit the seminary again?"

Something inside him told him not to ask, but he had to know. He also did not feel like going back home to Debbie. She was having friends over, and he knew he'd have nothing to say. They'd all just end up telling him about the time they climbed Dunn's River Falls. There was something about the way she was constantly showing him off to her friends that made him uneasy. He felt like just another figurine she'd picked up on her travels. When they'd met, she'd had ambitions of one day getting hired as a curator at a museum or gallery, but now she'd abandoned those dreams and decided to stay home to make and sell jewelry. It wasn't that he didn't think she had talent, but until her new business took off, his mother's house sold, or his immigration paperwork came through and he could work, they were stuck in the apartment together all day, living off the trust fund her deceased father had left her. He didn't like the idea of living off a white man's money, especially one he'd never even met.

Ernie chuckled.

"Me did only stay in seminary school fi t'ree months. Priest life not for me."

"Me remember one time when I was little, you did inna your white collar and yuh black shirt, and you was in our house," Vincent said. He was thinking out loud. "Me remember you was reading scripture to us." The more he spoke, the clearer the memory became, the more he realized that it couldn't all have been a dream.

"You remember? You did young, man. Probably six or seven. Fi you mother take sick, and so me did come fi pray fi her," Ernie said.

It was then that Vincent noticed the look on his face and how his Adam's apple seemed to twitch erratically as he swallowed. He realized that Ernie had been thinking of that day from the moment he first saw him.

⚬⚬⚬

Vincent did not have a name for what they did to his mother back then. He was too young, but now he understood what they had tried to do to Vera: an exorcism.

There were seven of them in the house that day. Ernie, his mother—Mrs. Pitt—Mrs. Brown, Mrs. Gold, Claudette, who was their helper back then, Vincent himself, who stood with his arms curled around Claudette's left leg, and Irene, who hugged Claudette's right side. Eight if you counted Bernard, Vera's yard boy, who the adults had to barricade in the toolshed out back when he'd tried to stop them. Nine if you counted his mother, though he noticed that the adults had ceased treating his mother like a person. They'd tied her hands to her headboard, and Vincent could hear her cursing at them from behind the bedroom door. Secretly, he had a plan to cut her loose as soon as he was alone, but the adults had been deliberating what to do about his mother for hours and it didn't seem like they'd ever leave.

⚬⚬⚬

Plates cleared, Ernie abruptly stood, so Vincent did too. Ernie brushed the rice grains off Rebecca Ann's dress and led them both outside.

"You need me fi walk you back to the train?" he asked Vincent. Vincent shrugged and looked back in the direction of the subway.

"Let me walk with you. Me nuh wan' go back jus' yet. Me will walk you home." Now that he knew that Ernie remembered that day too, he couldn't leave. The truth seemed so implausible, but some of it had actually happened. Now that he had Ernie here, he had to know.

"Me have fi take Rebecca Ann to the playground."

As if on cue, Rebecca Ann started bouncing up and down in place.

Vincent nodded. "Me will walk wit' you."

They walked in silence for a while, Vincent pretending to be interested in looking at the houses and the stores.

"Me remember that my mother hands did tie," he said, without turning his head to face Ernie. "That day when you did read scripture. She did tie up 'pon the bed."

Ernie stopped in his tracks.

"Is not me tie her up. Me never believe in them somet'ing. Is me mother and the other women who tie her up. You know seh Jamaican woman believe in all type of foolishness. Them did think Vera have somet'ing wrong with her. She did a act too strange."

"Them think she possess?" Vincent said.

Ernie nodded.

"Why them think that?"

Ernie opened his mouth but hesitated. He began walking faster. Vincent matched his pace.

As they walked Ernie explained: His mother had seen red eyes staring at her from the darkness one night as she stood in her front yard. She'd thought it was some kind of animal, a stray dog, watching her from the road, but it was Vera who stepped out of the shadows and walked toward her. She was so frightened she ran inside her house and locked the door.

Vincent laughed. "What kind of foolishness that? Grown people believe her?"

"You know them old-time people believe in all a them foolishness."

"Did you?" Vincent asked.

"Me was what? Seventeen? Me do what my mother tell me. And . . ."

"And what?"

"Me cyaan tell another man this about him mother," Ernie said, looking away from Vincent, following a passing car with his eyes instead.

"Me know all 'bout me mother. Me wan' know what them did say about her fi do them crazy thing to her."

"Mrs. Brown catch Vera in bed with her husband."

"No, man. My mother never the type fi do that."

"She say she catch her," Ernie said.

"My mother never behave like that. Since my father die, she jus' keep to herself. That woman did always jealous of my mother. Me nuh know why."

"That jus' what she tell everyone. And then Mrs. Gold say she see Vera walk down the street naked in the middle of the night. When she call to her, she notice Vera feet did nuh touch the ground."

"Stop," Vincent said. "Quiet for one second."

They walked a block without speaking, while Vincent calmed himself down. Irene would have delighted in hearing all the gossip about their mother. She had told him when they were teenagers that their mother slept with Bernard, the yard boy, whenever they weren't home. He had fought with her then. They had wrestled on the floor, until Irene got the better of him and punched him in the face, nearly breaking his nose. Vincent refused to believe it was true, but he avoided Bernard as much as he could after that day.

"Them did always make up pure lie 'bout me mother. From the

time my father die, them make up lie. Them mus' did 'fraid that 'cause she so pretty, fi them husband would leave them fi her. Me remember one time when we walk down street with her, and Mrs. Brown see my mother coming, she make her husband cross the street."

"That don't support what she said happen between her husband and Vera?"

"Nuh, man. Is jus' jealous; she jealous. You nuh know her husband did run 'round with w'ole heap a women and get some young girl pregnant when him inna him sixties?"

"Me never hear that 'cause me did over here long time by then."

"Mrs. Brown jus' did wan' fi find someone fi blame 'cause she never know how fi control fi her husband."

They arrived at the park. Vincent sat on a bench as Ernie waited at the bottom of the slide to catch Rebecca Ann. He lifted her so she could pretend to climb across the monkey bars. She soon joined a group of other girls doing chalk drawings on the ground. Ernie joined Vincent on the bench.

"Me nuh know, man . . . people now would never believe the crazy t'ings them did get inna back then," Ernie said.

❧

Vincent was quiet for a moment, thinking about how tightly he'd hugged Claudette that day. How his hands had cramped from clenching the fabric of her dress.

"Me no wan' the pickney fi see them mother like this," he remembered Claudette saying.

Mrs. Pitt stepped forward as if to scrutinize the children. She grabbed Irene's arm without warning.

"No tell me say you cyaan see the bruise 'pon this gal pickney arm. We know who put it there. Or is you put it there?" She let the arm go, and Irene pulled it back and hid it farther behind Claudette.

"Is not yuh mommy who do them singting to you, girl. Is the demon. Is the devil. Yuh wan' we fi fix yuh mommy, right? Make her treat you nice?" Mrs. Pitt said.

Irene nodded at Mrs. Pitt and began to cry.

"See? Is good fi them fi see that them mother is not one whore or one madwoman. Is jus' the devil take set 'pon her."

It was his sister's fault, Vincent had wanted to explain then, and even now to Ernie. But now he was a grown man, and he realized you could not blame a little girl for provoking a grown woman to beat on her. But still, he had always blamed Irene for everything that happened.

Vincent understood, when he was younger, that when his mother raised her voice suddenly or didn't smile at him in the morning, he had to go out back and play by himself until it was time for bed. But Irene wouldn't listen. When his mother slept for days, Irene was insistent that she wake up. She would talk back to her mother when she was clearly not herself, even though she knew what would happen to her.

"It was Claudette, the helper," Ernie said, watching his daughter who was now on the swings. "She the one who tell them somet'ing nuh right with Vera. She said she start fi beat yuh sister too much. Every day she find reason fi beat that girl. Them never wan' fi call the police 'pon her. Them try fi help her. Fi help all of you. Them did mean well, you know?"

"Me no believe that," Vincent said. "Them nuh see how my sister did provoke her. And is true, my mother did get depressed after my father pass away, something did wrong with her, but we never know about them t'ings back then. When she sick, when her mood turn dark, she try fi stay by herself, but Irene always did wan' fi provoke her and act out."

∽

While sitting on the bench next to Ernie, Vincent could feel the outlines of that day becoming sharper, crystallizing in his mind. Vincent remembered that when the group finally entered his mother's room, Vera cackled in a voice he had never heard before.

His real mother was gentle and contemplative. She liked to take walks alone at night around the neighborhood. During the day, she liked to pick a tree in her backyard to sit under with her eyes closed. Sometimes she'd read a book, and when Vincent sat beside her, she'd scratch his hair or his back gently until he fell asleep with his head in her lap. It was true that at one point in their childhood, her strange moods had become her, all of her. That day, part of him had hoped that the neighborhood women could cure her. He had wanted to believe that they wished his mother well.

Vincent had watched as Ernie opened a small bottle, dabbed his fingers, and approached Vera, making the sign of the cross on her forehead. But Vera caught his fingers with her teeth when he went to pull away and wouldn't let go. Mrs. Pitt had to slap Vera to make her let go. Vincent remembers now that he cried out when he saw her hit Vera. Ernie looked from his bleeding finger to Vera's face in disbelief.

"She bite me!" he shouted. "Me finger a bleed!"

"Ernie," Mrs. Pitt said. "Remember the demon will do anyt'ing fi stop you. You mus' not let it."

Ernie let out a frustrated sigh.

"I cast you out, unclean spirit . . ." he said.

"Ernie! We not at that part yet! You mus' start with the litany," his mother said.

Ernie sighed again. He gave his mother an exasperated look and flipped through the book he held in his hands.

"Me know none of you is Catholic," Mrs. Pitt said. "So me will repeat after Ernie, and you mus' follow me."

"Since when you Catholic?" Mrs. Brown said. "After me and you nuh go Pentecostal church fi years?"

"Repeat," Mrs. Pitt said, paying her no mind. "Go ahead, Ernie."

"Lord, have mercy."

"Lord, have mercy," Mrs. Pitt said.

"Lord, have mercy," they said in unison.

"Christ, have mercy," Ernie read.

"Christ, have mercy," Mrs. Pitt said.

"Christ, have mercy," the group repeated, except for Vincent.

Vincent looked at his mother to see if something stirred inside her, but Vera seemed to be writhing back and forth in a way that signaled she needed to go to the bathroom more than demonic possession. She had been tied to the bed since early that morning, and for the first time it occurred to Vincent to bring his mother a chimmy to use. He slipped out from under Claudette's grip and left the room. Claudette didn't protest, and Vincent knew she wanted him to see no part of it. She was always protective of them, even putting herself in between Irene and Vera when things got out of control; Claudette had taken a few hard blows meant for his sister.

He went to the bathroom cupboard and got a chimmy for Vera. He slipped back into the room quietly.

"Holy Mary, pray for us."

"Pray for us," Mrs. Pitt said.

"Pray for us," they said in unison.

He brought the pot to his mother. He picked a sheet off the floor so he could cover her while she did her business. He remembers she met his eyes with a look of pure gratitude, before Mrs. Brown grabbed his arm and pulled him back.

"You musn't get too close, bwai. Is not yuh mummy."

"She have fi pee pee," Vincent tried to tell her.

"Take yuh hand off my son. As soon as me get up from this bed, me swear me will tump you straight inna yuh mouth," Vera yelled.

Mrs. Brown kept looking at Vincent as if she'd heard nothing.

"You mus' not help the devil." She snatched the pot out of his hands.

A few minutes later, Vincent could smell that his mother had soiled herself. He felt such shame that he hadn't helped her and avoided meeting her eyes again. He looked to his sister. He had hoped that his sister would do something, but she simply stood reciting the prayer along with everyone else.

"Saint Jude," Ernie said.

"Pray for us," said Mrs. Pitt.

Vera cackled again. "Look 'pon this bighead bwai a play priest. Yuh balls not even drop yet; you t'ink you can wrestle with the devil?"

Ernie looked down at his Bible, his embarrassment plain across his face, but he soldiered on, his mother tapping the page with her finger.

"All you holy disciples of the Lord," Mrs. Pitt read.

"All you holy disciples of the Lord," Ernie said.

"Pray for us," said the women.

"Who will pray fi all a you! Mabel, who will pray fi you and yuh old dry-up pum-pum?" Vera said, looking at Mrs. Brown with a cruel smirk. "Is nuh my fault yuh husband stray. Him get tired a you!"

"All holy innocents," Ernie said.

"Pray for us," Mrs. Pitt said.

"Innocent? Who in here is innocent except fi me baby bwai? Ernie, you know say fi yuh mother did already pregnant when she meet fi yuh father? She tell me herself!" his mother screamed.

Mrs. Pitt stepped out of line, ready to shake the hell out of Vera.

"The devil is a liar!" Mrs. Brown hissed. "You mus' not give in to him provocation."

Mrs. Pitt snorted and got back in line.

"And you, Marie?" she said to Mrs. Gold. "Who will pray fi you? You jealous 'cause me have freedom, while you have to live with man who knock you 'pon yuh head whenever the mood strike him. No man tell me whe' me can go, who me can talk to. You nuh know what free woman look like, so you say is demon. You wish demon could jump into you too!"

❦

Ernie looked at his watch. Vincent knew he was becoming impatient.

"All me know back then fi do was read the Bible. Exorcist have fi be trained. We never do nuttin but pray," said Ernie.

He seemed to be waiting for Vincent to lay an accusation at his feet, for his mood to change, but Vincent was still lost in his recollection of that day. Ernie stood up to get Rebecca Ann.

"Them hurt her," Vincent said as Ernie walked away. "Them make me help them."

"Me no know nuttin 'bout that," Ernie said over his shoulder. He called to Rebecca Ann, who ran to him. He scooped her up in his arms, and she buried her head in his neck again. He walked over to Vincent and held out his hand.

"Well, is good fi see yuh, man. Take care." After they shook, he turned and walked away without looking back. Vincent waited until Ernie had rounded the corner before he started following him.

He thought about the women who were there that day. He had seen them all at his mother's funeral. Most of them, unlike his mother, were still alive. Claudette had been fired and banished from their house days later, as soon as Vera recovered. He didn't know what became of her. He remembered how she cried and hugged him before she left. He remembered how his sister had cried and refused to let go of Claudette's T-shirt. Bernard had had to pry her away. He noticed a change in how his mother treated Bernard after that day. Every now and then he would catch the two of them leaning close together and whispering, as if he were a friend, not just an employee.

So much of that day had flashed through his mind over the years, but the details had seemed improbable, confusing. He returned to the picture in his mind, feeling his brain churning to make sense of it all. Ernie was right. Most of the time, all they had done was pray for Vera. Then Mrs. Brown stepped out of the line.

"What kind of foolishness we a talk?" Mrs. Brown said suddenly. "The demon jus' a laugh after we."

"Since when you start seminary school?" Mrs. Pitt said.

"Me nuh have fi play priest fi cast out demon. God give power to all him righteous. We need to purge the wicked outta this gal, now. Gimme the holy water, Ernie."

Ernie looked to his mother.

"Ernie! Me seh gimme the holy water! No make me tell you again," Mrs. Brown insisted.

Ernie handed it over.

"Gal," she said, motioning at Irene, "go get me a bucket of clean water and cup."

Vera had a smile on her face, pleased that she'd disrupted their ritual. She herself seemed mostly entertained and sat rapt at what they'd try next.

Irene left the room and returned with the water. Mrs. Brown took the bucket, bent down next to Vera's bed. For years, she and Vera had been close, and Vincent was used to seeing the two of them sitting at their kitchen table, talking well into the night. But Vincent hadn't seen Mrs. Brown get so close to their mother in months. Vincent had not known why then, but it must have been because of the rumors Mrs. Brown spread about catching Vera with her husband. The same thought must have occurred to Vera, for she took the opportunity to spit in the woman's face.

"No!" Irene shouted at her mother too late. But to Mrs. Brown's credit, she simply wiped the spit off with the hem of her dress and continued. She ladled the water from the bucket with the cup and topped it off with a single drop of holy water.

"I cast you out, unclean spirit. In the name of the Father, the Son, and the Holy Ghost." She went to hold the back of Vera's head, but she fought. "Hold her," she commanded them.

Ernie and Mrs. Pitt held Vera's feet as she tried to kick. Claudette and Mrs. Gold both held her head back.

"Miss Vera, everyt'ing will be alright. You jus' need to drink, Miss Vera," Claudette said, trying to be soothing.

Mrs. Brown forced the water into Vera's mouth, and though she tried to spit it out, Mrs. Brown wouldn't stop pouring. Vera was gasping for air.

"Me a choke," Vera cried. "Let me up."

"Mrs. Brown," Irene said diminutively. "She say she a choke."

Hearing his sister speak up for their mother filled him with dread. He believed his sister hated their mother even back then. If she was concerned about Vera, then something must be wrong.

"We mus' flush the demon out," Mrs. Brown said.

She fixed another cup and poured it into Vera's mouth. One after another until he noticed that Irene was looking up at the ceiling instead of at Mrs. Brown and Vera. Vincent moved to the back of the room and sat on the floor against the wall. It seemed like no one remembered that he was there. He couldn't find a moment to untie his mother, and as he listened to her cough and plead, he felt more and more guilty.

He watched his mother vomit water on herself, again and again, which only caused Mrs. Brown to pause for a few moments. As soon as Vera finished, Mrs. Brown poured more water into her mouth. She poured until the bucket was empty. The women let go of Vera's head, finally, and she rose up as much as she could and vomited a foul-smelling brown liquid beside her.

"Everyone, look. It workin'. Is the demon poison a leave 'er body."

When his mother was finished, Vincent watched Vera's head fall back in exhaustion. She closed her eyes, and he noticed her breathing had become so shallow it was hardly detectable.

"Moomie?" he called. The room was quiet as they waited for Vera to show signs of life. Claudette put her hand under Vera's nose. "Moomie jus' asleep, Vincent," she called.

Mrs. Brown grabbed the Bible from Ernie and raised it above her head; without warning, she slammed it down on Vera's forehead. Vera screamed and started thrashing around, trying to free herself from the ropes.

"We mus' not let the demon rest. No rest fi di wicked," Mrs. Brown said, with a renewed vigor. "Me cast you out, unclean spirit!" She brought the Bible down on Vera's chest. She raised it up to do it again, but both Ernie and Claudette tackled her and managed to wrest the Bible away.

Vincent began to sob from his place in the corner. Irene went to him and pulled his face into her chest. It was one of the few times they had ever hugged each other.

Ernie and Claudette held Mrs. Brown against the wall until she calmed down. Mrs. Gold got a wet rag and began wiping Vera's forehead.

"Enough, Mabel!" Mrs. Pitt said. "Make Ernie finish this."

Mrs. Brown wriggled out of their grip and looked down at Vera, who was lying back again with her eyes closed.

"After me nuh already do most of the work? The demon gone," Mrs. Brown announced, and with her nose raised so high in the air that Vincent had wondered how she could see in front of her, she walked out of the house.

Irene and Vincent approached their mother, who still hadn't opened her eyes. Mrs. Pitt put her hand up to stop them.

"Ernie!" She motioned for him to hurry.

"Deliver our souls from eternal damnation," Ernie began. "And the souls of our brethren, relatives, and benefactors."

"Lord, hear our prayer," Mrs. Pitt said, but no one repeated her words. The whole room was looking at Vera.

Her eyes remained closed, and her skin was turning an odd gray color.

"Alright, make we go outside and leave Ernie fi finish," Mrs. Pitt said.

Vincent had not wanted to leave his mother alone, but Claudette clenched his hand firmly and led him and his sister out. She closed the door behind them. They all sat on chairs on the veranda while Claudette made tea for the women, sliced bun and cheese for Vincent and Irene. When he looked at the yellow cheese, he thought of the liquid that had come out of his mother. He couldn't eat.

He decided to slip away from the others and see if Ernie had finally untied her.

When he went around the side of the house, he had to drag the metal basin Claudette used to wash their clothes to the window. Only by standing on top was he tall enough to see inside. What he saw didn't make sense to him then, he remembers. It did not make sense until he sat beside Ernie on the park bench. If it had only come to him in his dreams, he would have said that it was impossible, but as he walked behind Ernie, saw how quickly the man moved, how eager he was to put distance between the two of them, he knew he was not confusing a dream with reality. It happened.

Vincent had peeked through the metal slats and had seen Ernie sitting on the bed next to his mother. Vera was still asleep. Ernie was not holding his Bible; instead, he had one hand up her dress, and Vincent could see it moving under the fabric slowly. Ernie's other hand was between his own legs.

That day, Vincent had climbed down from the metal washtub,

thinking that maybe it was just part of the cure, but now he understood.

☙

Vincent tried to keep at least a block's distance between himself and Ernie. He was lucky the man still carried his daughter so it wasn't easy for him to look behind him. After about six blocks, Ernie stopped at a small white house with a green chain-link fence. Vincent stood across the street staring at the door after Ernie had closed it behind him. He did not exactly have a plan. He hoped that Ernie would come outside by himself eventually, which he did, two hours later, to take out his garbage. Vincent ran toward the man, readying himself to strike Ernie, though he'd only had the nerve to hit another man in the face one time before in his life.

When Ernie spotted Vincent running toward him, he dropped to his knees on the sidewalk. Vincent stopped suddenly, confused by the surrender, almost stumbling forward. He balanced himself and looked down at Ernie, who started to cry. He could hear that Ernie was mumbling something, reciting what sounded like a prayer—*Please forgive me, please forgive me, please forgive me.* Vincent looked up and saw Rebecca Ann's face appear in the doorway. Her eyes widened at seeing her father on his knees, crying. Ernie shouted for her to go inside, and she too started to cry, though she obeyed him.

Vincent punched Ernie only once, as hard as he could. Ernie's body wobbled, but it wasn't hard enough to knock him over. He shook his head a few times, making small drops of blood fly out of his nose, and then Ernie went back to mumbling his prayer. Vincent looked down on him, and every time he heard the word *forgive*, he quietly said *no*.

REPLACEMENT

Brooklyn/Harlem, 2003

Ruthie met her father for the first time at a soul food restaurant in Fort Greene when she was seventeen. She never thought she'd find the courage to call him, but at the time she was desperate for money. She'd found his address and phone number a few years before, while she was flipping through one of her mother's old day planners when she was in middle school. She realized her mom had been lying to her ever since she was little, pretending that she didn't know how to make contact with him. As soon as she put the address into Google, she found out that it belonged to a West Indian grocery store in Harlem—Solomon's Caribbean Market—that he owned. Later, when Ruthie confronted her mom about what she'd found, she told her that she'd met him while shopping in his store. That was the first time she knew that she couldn't trust everything her mom told her. If you'd asked Ruthie before that day who her best friend was, she would have said her mother, but after that things were never the same.

By seventeen, Ruthie had gotten used to keeping secrets from her mom too. She didn't tell her she was meeting her father. She didn't tell her mom she hated the fancy boarding school she had begged to go to. She hadn't told her that when her roommate at school died, Ruthie had been the one who found her. She didn't tell her that the image kept her up at night and stopped her from eating or studying. And she didn't tell her when she came home for summer break a few weeks ago that she'd been asked not to return the following year. A letter had been sent home, but Ruthie had intercepted it.

When she called her father on the phone and they talked a little, he hadn't seemed surprised to hear from her. He mentioned that he also owned a vegan Jamaican restaurant along with the grocery store, not far from the cramped studio apartment Ruthie and her mom had shared near East Harlem before they moved to New Jersey. She wanted to ask why he couldn't be bothered in those first eleven years to walk twelve blocks from where he worked to go see her, but she bit her tongue. She didn't want to scare him away, not before she asked him for money.

She offered to meet him at his restaurant, but he insisted they meet in Brooklyn, as if he needed a neutral space, a place where neither of them had ever lived. It didn't occur to her just then that he was probably still trying to hide her existence from his wife.

He was going on thirty-five minutes late, and while she waited, she had three cups of coffee. She started to feel jittery. Ruthie wanted to order a mimosa to calm herself down, but she decided she should meet him before she had alcohol. Her mom would have killed her if she knew that she drank, but everybody in her school did it. They all had fake IDs they used when they went into town on weekends. Her roommate, Grace, had had one made for her too. Their school was in such a small town, in the middle of nowhere in New Hampshire, it was pretty obvious who the boarding school girls were, but the townies didn't seem to care. They served them anyway. Besides alcohol, her friends had introduced her to Xanax, cocaine, Adderall, and Molly. Her mother would have pulled her out right away if she'd known. Ruthie had only done each a few times. Ultimately, she realized drugs like that were for people with money, and she didn't have any. She'd take them when they were offered to her at parties, but she was too self-conscious about being poor to ask for anything for free. Grace had a bunch of prescriptions that she'd been tempted by: Percocet, Klonopin, Vicodin—drugs she'd never heard of. But she never touched them; everyone knew she was on scholarship. She didn't want to develop a reputation for mooching or stealing.

She didn't feel bad about lying to her mother anymore. Her mother was so good at lying to her. But she decided that her drinking was not a secret she wanted to share with her father, just in case he and her mother ever ended up on speaking terms again.

She looked up every time a man entered the restaurant, trying to recall her father's face. The one picture she had of him, stolen from her mom's computer, was older than her. In it he looked kind of sleazy. He wore a shiny silver silk shirt unbuttoned enough to show off his patchy chest hair. He had a long thick gold chain around his neck and was wearing a matching gray fedora. Her mom was twenty-five years younger than her dad, and the age difference was obvious in the picture. Even apart from being old, he didn't look like the kind of guy she'd go for. He had his arm around her and behind them was a pair of slot machines. They must have been in Atlantic City. The two of them were mugging for the camera like they'd just won a big jackpot, but she didn't see any money or chips. Her mom always said that their affair was short and didn't mean anything to them, but after she found that photo, she started to think she'd caught her in another lie. Ruthie always swore that she had vague memories of him being around when she was very small, even though her mother claimed that he never spoke to her after she was born. He hadn't wanted her to have Ruthie; he was married. Maybe the man she remembered was an uncle or a cousin, she often wondered. Maybe it was one of her mother's old boyfriends, or maybe her mother just never told the truth when it came to her father.

When he finally appeared in the restaurant, she was surprised at how quickly she recognized him. She'd only seen that one photo, and he'd aged so much since then, but she knew him right away because he had her face. He really did. She didn't expect to see herself so clearly in this strange man walking up to her. Growing up, she was used to people asking, *What are you?* She had freckles and nappy, light-brown hair that sprouted red highlights in the summer. She would always say she was half–African American and half-Jamaican, but she wasn't quite sure what Jamaica had to do with her red hair and freckles. But she saw where she got it from now. He was much older than she'd expected, maybe in his late sixties or early seventies. People around them probably thought that she was meeting her grandfather. He walked hunched over, his weight resting on a metal cane. He wore loose denim shorts, and his legs seemed too skinny for his body.

He approached the table. "Ruthie?" he said. He pronounced it like *Roo-tee*. He still had a thick Jamaican accent.

She nodded.

"Yuh pretty," he said. He sat down and took a long, awkward look at her. She nodded again. He seemed nervous too. She didn't know what kind of compliment she should give him, if one was even necessary. He was wearing a gray Members Only jacket and a matching gray Kangol hat. He looked like one of the older Caribbean men who stayed in the park near her house 24-7, leaning on their canes, playing dominoes or chess. His hair was thin, but even though it was cut close to his scalp, she could see that it had gone white. He was light skinned, and his face was covered with freckles, just like hers. Still, she looked at this old guy and wondered how he could have tricked her mother into having an affair. She wondered how he even got her to give him a minute of her time. Her mom was good-looking. Usually when she and her mom walked down the street together, at least one guy would say, "Hello, beautiful," or try to talk to her.

"How you feelin'?" he said.

"I'm okay," she said.

Ruthie pretended to study the menu, while she planned what to say next. She'd already gone over it several times while waiting for him. She remembered his vegan restaurant just then. When she asked him why he picked a soul food restaurant to meet when everything on the menu had meat in it, he confessed that he wasn't vegan. He'd bought the business from a friend, a Rastafarian, who'd been deported back to Jamaica. He explained he was going to sell it soon.

Ruthie had figured that he was better off than her and her mom, but she hadn't known he had so much money to throw around that he could buy and sell businesses whenever he felt like it. She was right for asking him to help her get her own apartment, even if her mom wouldn't have wanted her to. What she didn't know wouldn't hurt her.

She asked him where he lived.

"My wife and I did buy a brownstone in Harlem long time ago. Lucky thing. It woulda cost too much money now."

She knew he was just making conversation, but she felt a sting when she pictured him and his wife and their massive house, even though she'd never seen it.

She tried to let go of the image and focus back on her game plan. She'd planned to get all of her bitterness out of the way. She thought she'd first shame him for being such a deadbeat dad all of these years. She'd tell him about all the terrible places they'd lived in because he'd left her mother to bring her up alone. She would tell him how they once lived in a basement where the sewage system would back up and overflow after really bad rainstorms. How they couldn't afford to throw away most of their furniture, even though it technically had been drenched in shit water. How her mother had withheld rent to cover the damage and the landlord had shut off the lights and water on them. How they'd ended up just moving all their stuff out in the dark, in the middle of the night. How they'd gotten bed bugs once and instead of throwing away their furniture, her mother had lined everything with double-sided tape to catch the bugs. It had worked, but that wasn't the point. He wasn't there through any of it.

And where was he? Working in his store, buying restaurants, living in a whole house with his wife. She bet he drove a flashy car—a Benz or a Jaguar. She realized that he was talking and talking, but she was not fully listening. She was just getting more pissed off.

"Me see seh you go one good school. White people school," he said, beaming at her. She wondered how he knew. Probably Facebook.

"They kicked me out," she said flatly, and was glad when the smile disappeared from his face. She didn't want him to think that she was okay. She didn't want him to have a reason to feel proud. She was messed up, and she wanted him to know it was his fault. She knew her mother bragged about her school to her friends. But her mother worked hard, and though she wasn't perfect, Ruthie wanted her to feel as if she had raised her right. Eventually, Ruthie would have to shatter that illusion by confessing she got kicked out of school.

When she had suggested boarding school to her mom, she'd said no at first. The two of them had never been apart for more than one night. Her mom had boyfriends regularly ever since Ruthie was small, but she didn't start spending nights at their houses until Ruthie entered the eighth grade. Still, she had a rule that she would never stay away from her two nights in a row. But then her mom met Kofi, and he was the reason Ruthie wanted to go away. He was the first of her mom's boyfriends to move in with them, into their one-bedroom basement apartment in Newark. They'd always lived in attics or basement apartments, the only places her mom could afford, places where there was barely any light and definitely not enough room for her mom to move her boyfriend and his gym equipment in with her teenage daughter.

Her mom met Kofi at the gym where she worked. Kofi was one of the trainers; her mom worked the front desk. Even though he already had a girlfriend, they started seeing each other. He was only twenty-five, fifteen years younger than her mom—actually closer to Ruthie's age. His girlfriend kicked him out once she found out about them, and all of Kofi's family was in Ghana, so he had nowhere else to go. Her mother had always said that she'd never let a man move in unless she thought they were going to get married, but Kofi left her no choice.

Once he moved in, things just didn't feel right. He never did anything creepy or made any weird moves on Ruthie. It was just that she felt trapped, like the three of them were stuck together, living in a little cage. The apartment had already felt too small for just the two of them, and now suddenly her mother's bedroom was off-limits. She couldn't just walk in whenever she felt like it—she had to knock first.

Kofi was just starting out as a trainer, so he didn't have that many clients. He did a few sessions a week, but mostly he just watched soccer on their couch in his bathrobe or did pull-ups on the bar he'd installed in their bedroom doorframe. Her mom had partitioned the living room using two big moving screens so that Ruthie had some privacy. No one could see her change or anything, but with Kofi there, she felt self-conscious. She would want to sleep in late when she had off from school, but Kofi would come into the living room, and she'd have to listen to whatever he was watching, usually soccer.

Her mom expected her to change her behavior to work around him, but never vice versa. Ruthie started to make smart comments to him: *Aren't Nigerians usually really hardworking?* she'd say. *I'm from*

Ghana, he'd reply, without smiling. After that he stopped trying to be her friend and only spoke to her when necessary. It got even more uncomfortable to live with a strange man who wouldn't even speak to her. Her mom stuck up for him, told her that Kofi was right to feel insulted and that she'd just have to wait for him to get over it in his own time. She felt like she didn't know her own mother anymore. She had always criticized women on TV who put their boyfriends over their children. So much for not throwing stones.

Kofi didn't seem stressed about their estrangement at all. He ignored Ruthie and went about his business as if she weren't there. If anything, not having to pay attention to her made him feel even more comfortable. He stopped wearing a robe during the day. He just started walking around in basketball shorts and no shirt.

She could see his body: his perfectly sculpted arms, his toned legs, his eight-pack—she didn't even know an eight-pack was possible until she saw it on him. She understood why her mother was so quick to let him move in. He was very good at pretending that he had no idea how he looked, like he was oblivious to the effect he had on people.

One night, about three weeks after Kofi stopped talking to Ruthie, she had a dream about the two of them. They were together in her mother's bed. When she woke up, she felt like she'd betrayed her mother, even though the dream was involuntary. What's worse was she found that her attraction to Kofi did not end with her dream. In the mornings, she started to realize that she wanted him to come into the living room and watch soccer. She began to think of reasons to walk out of her screened-off room and pass him in the apartment. Eventually she started sitting in the armchair next to the couch, filing her nails and pretending she'd just developed a half-assed interest in soccer. She started to ask him questions about the game, and to her surprise, he began to answer. She would talk to him all day, and then when her mom came home, she would feel guilty.

When she realized that her feelings for Kofi were only getting stronger, it was worse than when she'd hated him. She didn't want to betray her mother, even if the betrayal only existed in her mind. She didn't think he would make a move on her, but being stuck in such a small space with him had gotten even more torturous. So she applied to a program that gave inner-city kids like her scholarships to elite East Coast boarding schools, and then she suddenly found herself in a different world. Then she promptly got herself kicked out of that world.

"I was depressed," she explained to the man across from her, her father. "So I stopped going to class. I failed every subject." This was the first time she had ever admitted it to anyone.

Ruthie couldn't go back to her old high school. She couldn't face her friends. They had already thrown her a goodbye party; some of her teachers had cried. They told her how lucky she was to have such an amazing opportunity. She couldn't tell them all that she failed. Plus, being home with Kofi again had made her realize that her feelings for him hadn't faded over the nine months she'd been away. He seemed oblivious. In fact, he was excited to have her home. He treated her like his little soccer buddy. When she returned, he even tried to convince her to follow him to the park to play with him and his friends.

Ruthie thought the best alternative was for her to move out on her own. She knew that she was running away; she was doing it so she wouldn't have to face anybody. She was going to find a job as soon as she told her mom. She just needed money for the first month's rent and the security deposit.

"Me was depressed before too. When me did live in Jamaica and later when me go a England," her father said. She was surprised that he was being so open with her.

"Why were you depressed?"

"I did somet'ing that me shouldn't have done."

"Like have an affair?" she asked.

"Worse."

The waitress came again, so Ruthie ordered a mimosa, and instead of stopping her, her father ordered a screwdriver. That felt like bonding to her, maybe not in a paternal way, but something about him felt safe.

When his drink came, he took a sip and a deep breath, and he told her his story. He told her about how he hated his life in Jamaica. How he had a wife who he could never seem to make happy. How he'd once been a cop, and when he failed at that, he went to England and started working on a dock. His friend died in a work accident, and he decided to let his wife back home think he was the one who had died. He abandoned her and his two children and never went back.

When he finished his story, there were so many questions she wanted to ask him that she felt like she was getting a headache just trying to process them all. She had thought that her father did a bad thing when he left her, that it was an isolated incident, and maybe that he still had some good in him. She had never expected him to turn out to be a kind of con man.

"Why are you telling me this?" she said.

"You need fi know that you nuh miss out on nuttin. You did better off without me. The one daughta who me raise meself turn out the worse out of all a you."

"How would you know how the rest of us turned out? You left us."

He shrugged. "Me check up 'pon you. Me make sure you alright."

For some reason she found that response even creepier. She pictured him standing across from her schoolyard when she was in elementary school, spying on her with a pair of binoculars. It made her shudder.

"Tell me about them," Ruthie said to change the subject.

"Who?"

"My sisters." She had always wanted siblings, especially a sister. She had fantasized about it when she was younger. Her mother had told her that her father had been married when they met, but she never said anything about other children. Now that she knew that her father had made a family three times and abandoned two of them, she didn't think she could meet him again. She would get what she needed from him and then fall out of touch. He was a bad person. Maybe even evil, but it didn't mean she couldn't try to meet her sisters.

He sipped his drink and stared at a napkin on the table for a minute, lost in his memories.

"Me can only tell you 'bout the one who me raise. Estelle." He sighed. "She nuh too right in the head. You know?"

She nodded, but she in fact didn't know.

"Are you trying to say that she's crazy?"

He nodded.

"She always been crazy. Since she was one likkle gal." He drained the rest of his screwdriver.

She felt sorry for Estelle. Maybe it was worse for her, having a father who would describe her that way to a stranger. She wanted to change the subject, and she might as well get the pressing question pinging around her mind right out in the open, especially since her father seemed in the mood to confess.

"Why did you choose my mother? Why'd you cheat on your wife?"

"Me never plan for it. Yuh mother come in my store every day fi long time. You know seh your mother pretty. We get to talkin' and it happen. Me buy her nice things. It jus' last for a few months, then me nuh see her fi some months. Me run into her when her belly get big. Then when you born, she tell me she nuh wan' me in your life."

Ruthie didn't want to accept that her mother had told another lie.

"If you checked on us, then you knew we were poor. Why didn't you send us some money? How did you expect my mom to pay for everything on her own?"

"She ask me fi money every once in a while. Every time she ask me, me send it to her. But she never wan' have too much fi do with me."

She wanted to make it through brunch without crying. She felt her eyes get moist, so she pretended to be looking at something on her phone so he wouldn't see her tearing up. She and her mother had been so close once, and now she felt as if she were losing the only family she'd ever had.

"I need some money," she said when she'd composed herself. "So I can move out by myself."

He looked at her unblinking for a moment, like he was disappointed in her for asking, but he didn't argue. He took out his wallet.

"How much do you need?" he said.

"At least eight hundred dollars," she said. "For me to rent a room. But I'd rather get my own apartment."

He laughed and raised his eyebrows.

"You think me rich?" He took $150 out of his wallet and slid it across the table to her.

"Me can give you something once a month, help you out. But you too young fi live by yuhself. Your mother give you permission?"

"Since when do you care?" she said.

"Me nuh want she fi call me on the phone and yell."

Ruthie found it frustrating how calm he was. Nothing seemed to faze him. He didn't feel bad about leaving her; perhaps he was incapable of feeling at all.

He looked at his watch, grabbed the handle of his cane, and stood up.

"Me have fi get back to the store. But me want fi see you again. Come meet me here next month and me will give you some more money."

Ruthie stood up, but she didn't reach over to hug him; she just nodded. She stayed standing as she watched him slowly limp out of the restaurant.

She realized that he'd left her to pay the check with the money he'd given her.

She didn't know what to feel toward him. He wanted to see her again, and that gave her some comfort. At least he didn't reject her. At least he gave her money. She'd have someone to turn to if her mother got so mad that she kicked her out before she had time to get her own place. Yet it bothered her that he hadn't shown a trace of guilt. It felt almost like he got more out of their meeting than she did. As if he got some closure by unloading his secrets on her. She supposed if he was telling the truth, her mother had been partly to blame. She had told him to stay away. Then again there were laws. If he had wanted her, there was no way her mother could have kept him away. He must have been too afraid of his wife. It seemed that above all, keeping her from his wife was of the utmost importance. She thought it was strange that he had shared secrets that she hadn't asked for with her but only said a few things about the family he'd spent most of his life with. She didn't know his wife's name. He hadn't bothered to show her a picture of her sister. If he was telling the truth, then he had seen her at different points in her life without her seeing him. Why did she have to ask his permission to enter his life?

When she left the restaurant, it was only 2:00 p.m. She looked up directions to her father's store on her phone. She window-shopped near the subway for twenty minutes, just to make sure she wouldn't end up on the same train as her father. It took her more than an hour to get to Harlem, the C train slowly snaking from under the East River and then from one tip of the island to the other. When she got above ground, she recognized St. Nicholas Park, so she walked along Frederick Douglass Boulevard until she arrived at 137th Street. She stood on the corner across the street looking at her father's store, not sure whether to wait for him to come out or to go in.

It was a busy Sunday, and she watched the patrons shopping, digging in the fruit bins outside. Ruthie wasn't ready to go in, so she circled the block a few times and came back. If he kept her a secret from his wife, then she would possibly think that she was just another patron. But what if she did know? What if his wife screamed at her? What if she struck her? She'd never been yelled at by a grown woman, other than her own mother. But she didn't want to be her father's dirty little secret. It wasn't fair that he knew her life but she didn't know his. She braced herself and crossed the street. As she entered the store, she thought for the first time that he might be the one to scream at her, or worse—pretend he didn't know her.

He wasn't at the register when she went in. Instead, there was a woman there, slightly younger than him but older than her mother. At first, she smiled as Ruthie walked toward her, and then Ruthie watched the woman's smile disappear. She was only going to ask if she knew where Stanford was, but she saw that the woman was studying her. She could see the moment when she had fully taken in the light-brown face full of freckles, her reddish hair. She stepped out from behind the counter and looked Ruthie up and down. Ruthie was afraid. She worried that the woman would suddenly slap her across the face.

"Did he tell you about me?" she asked, because now it was obvious the woman had figured out who she was.

She scoffed. "You t'ink them tell them wife anyt'ing before we catch them?"

She stepped back and gave Ruthie a final once-over. Her father came out of a back room then, carrying a plastic jug filled to the brim with tamarind candies.

"Yuh daughta is here," the woman said, and walked past him into the back. He followed without saying anything to Ruthie. She didn't know what to do, so she walked around the store, pretending to look at the fruit in the bins, all the while waiting for someone to emerge from the back. Soon she could hear them yelling. The whole store could.

"You nuh have any morals!" the woman was yelling. Ruthie could hear her father's raised voice, but she couldn't make out his response.

A line of customers started forming at the register. She counted twelve people waiting impatiently. After five minutes of waiting, the man at the front of the line pounded his fist against the counter.

"Hey, you have a line out here! Why don't you argue at home!"

Her father emerged from the back, looking flustered. He started ringing the man up.

"Just a moment, folks," he said to the line.

Shortly after, his wife burst through the plastic curtain, walking fast toward the door.

"Adele!" he called after her, but she ignored him and left. Ruthie circled the store until her father finished with the last customer. He motioned her over.

"Is she all right?" Ruthie asked.

"She will be, me dear," he said, but he looked worried.

"Maybe you should go after her."

"Too many people in the store."

He didn't offer any more than that, and she regretted coming. She didn't know the woman, and she had no reason to want to mess up her life. She felt terrible. More customers began to line up. There was a small card table next to the counter, and he motioned for her to sit. Between customers, he looked over at her and smiled apologetically and said, "Soon come." She watched as people bought foods she'd never seen before. She got bored with just watching, so she walked around the store as she waited, trying to identify them—breadfruit, guinep, star apple. She wondered if one day she'd know how they tasted. Eventually the line slowed again, and he called her over. "You know how to work a register?"

She shook her head.

"Come make me show you," he said.

It didn't take long—a few transactions—for her to figure it out. He stepped aside and let her do a few on her own. This could be her life, she thought. Maybe he could give her a job. At boarding school, she saw how the other kids used their connections to get internships and summer jobs. Why couldn't she do the same? Why couldn't anything just be easy for her?

The phone rang and her father moved to the end of the counter to answer it. A woman came up to the register. She looked about her mother's age, or perhaps she was in her late thirties. Ruthie noticed something familiar about her. She didn't have any groceries to ring up. She looked sloppy. She had clear brown skin, the kind that Ruthie envied—perfectly smooth and poreless—but at the same time she looked greasy, like she'd left the house without washing her face. She wore a wig, a plastic-looking ponytail with bangs, but it seemed like it wasn't fastened straight. It looked as if it hadn't been combed since she bought it.

"Can I help you, miss?" Ruthie asked, because the woman wasn't saying anything.

She didn't respond. Her eyes seemed like they were looking at Ruthie, but they were unfocused, sleepy. She smiled and Ruthie saw that she was missing one of her canines. Ruthie recognized that look. It was the look her roommate, Grace, had had, whenever she'd taken too many Vicodin. At the beginning of the semester, she'd only seen her that way on weekends or a few nights a week, but by the end she started going to class like that.

"Do you need help?" she said, trying again.

"Caren?" The woman looked confused as her eyes scanned Ruthie's face.

"I dunno who that is," she said, hoping the woman would leave.

The woman's eyes slowly moved from Ruthie to her father, who was still on the phone, back and forth, back and forth, like she was trying to make a connection but her brain didn't compute.

"Do you need help?" Ruthie asked again. The woman stared at Ruthie with a half smile that made her uneasy. She made eye contact with her dad, who noticed the woman and quickly placed the receiver down. Her father put a hand on Ruthie's waist and nudged her aside.

"Me tell you nuh fi come in here, Estelle."

"I need the money you promised to let me hold," she said finally, but it was as if she were talking to both of them.

"Me never promise to give you nuh money, Estelle. Me already tell you never fi ask me. It must be yuh mother who promise you," he said impatiently.

"It was you," she said. "Please, it's an emergency."

"I can only imagine what kind of emergency someone like you have."

An old lady in line behind Estelle cleared her throat impatiently. Ruthie's father raised his hand in front of Estelle and made a stop motion. "You a hold up the line, Estelle. Come outta me store."

Estelle didn't move. She seemed to be trying to engage in some kind of staring contest with her father, trying to intimidate him, but after a minute her eyelids began to droop. Her father came from behind the counter and put his arm around Estelle. He led her out of the store and onto the sidewalk. She saw Estelle try to grab his arm when he turned to leave her, but he tore out of her grip and reentered the store without looking back at her.

"You know who that was, right?" he asked, as he rang up the next customer.

"That was my sister. What did you do to her?" she demanded, looking at her father.

"Me tell you Estelle crazy."

Ruthie thought about the end of her first semester, when she woke up and started getting ready for class, not noticing Grace was still under the covers. She knew Grace had an 8 a.m. class, and it was already 8:15. When she realized Grace was still in bed, Ruthie pulled back the covers ready to shake her awake. Grace's eyes were open and milky. Ruthie shook her, but she didn't blink. She screamed for help, and slowly girls from her floor began to stream in. Ruthie had stayed up late studying in Jesse's room the night before. When she had come in in the middle of the night, she had left the lights off because she hadn't wanted to wake Grace. She wasn't sure how long she'd been lying there dead and if there had been any way she could have helped her. The school had made her spend a few sessions with a grief counselor. They had notified her mother, but when she had talked to her on the phone, she had lied and said that she wasn't the one who found her. She'd been afraid her mother would have made her come home. She'd stopped seeing the counselor and started taking Grace's Xanax she'd saved to help her get to sleep. She was always too tired or restless after that to do any work.

Ruthie burst from behind the counter and ran out of the store after Estelle. She heard her father call her name, but she was already out the door. She had so many questions for her. She wanted to ask if her father was right and she'd been better off without him. She wanted to ask her if their father had been kind to her at least. Mostly she wanted to help.

She found her sister around the corner, on 137th Street. She'd stopped and was stooped over. At first, she thought Estelle was leaning over to pick up something off the ground. But as she got closer, she saw her eyes were closed, and realized that she was nodding out in the middle of the sidewalk.

"Estelle," she called. "I need to talk to you."

Estelle perked up, her eyes opened, and slowly she righted herself, apparently startled upon realizing where she was. She looked at Ruthie as if she'd never seen her before.

"What do you want?" she barked. They didn't look alike at all, Ruthie thought as she looked at her. Estelle had the face of the woman she had seen earlier.

"I'm your sister," she said. Then she told her how their father met her mother in the store. How he had abandoned her. How she and her mother lived in Newark. How they'd struggled all those years and the only thing that she held on to was the idea of finally meeting him. Estelle started nodding out again, her eyes closing. Ruthie saw that she was incapable of listening in this state, incapable of having a reaction. Her head was almost to her knees again. It looked like she was trying to do a yoga pose. She wasn't sure if Estelle had heard a word she'd said. Ruthie began to back away slowly. She'd try again another day. Suddenly there was a loud noise in the distance, a pop; it woke Estelle, and almost as if in pursuit of the sound, she turned and ran into the middle of 137th Street.

"Wait!" Ruthie yelled. Cars were coming fast. She followed on the sidewalk as Estelle made her way toward Frederick Douglass Boulevard. Cars jammed on their brakes, and drivers cursed at her. Estelle seemed confused by the sudden flood of sounds, so she stopped in the middle of the intersection, spinning around as if figuring out which way to go. Ruthie started to run toward her to get her out of the intersection, but then she felt hands squeeze her shoulders and pull her back, just as she was about to get clipped by a Prius. A man who'd been waiting to cross Frederick Douglass Boulevard walked to Estelle in the intersection and led her out onto the sidewalk across the street.

"You almost get hit!" her father shouted, angry at her. Ruthie felt embarrassed by his anger. Small in a way she hadn't felt in a long time, like a little girl. She looked at her feet.

"Leave her," he said. "Nobody can do anything for Estelle. She long gone. Come back to the store." He rubbed his hand gently across her back, soothing her, a gesture that made her uncomfortable.

He turned and began walking away, and she didn't know what else to do besides trail after him. They didn't even know each other that well. As Ruthie followed two steps behind, she thought about why he was so interested in her all of a sudden. He wasn't even mad that she'd barged into his life. Maybe his wife was in his house right now, throwing away all his stuff. Maybe Estelle would never get clean and would overdose at any moment. She didn't understand how he could remain so calm, so focused on her. She thought he was just fascinated with her because he didn't know her. With her, he could start over. She was his little replacement daughter, he must have been thinking. He could start fresh, make up for the others who he'd fucked up. Nothing bad that he'd done made a difference, because he still had someone to stand between him and dying alone.

As she looked at his back, she listened to the sound of cars whizzing by, and it crossed her mind how easy it would be to suddenly push him into the street. Just then, he turned and waited for her to catch up. She had never wanted her mother so badly. When she got close to him, he put his arm around her shoulder and started walking again toward the store. Ruthie broke out of his arms and ran back toward Estelle as fast as she could. She was not going to leave her behind.

ESTELLE'S BLACK EYE

Harlem, 2020

I gave her a key to my house so that she could always come back and rob me. I figured it was better Estelle take from me than from a pharmacy or a convenience store. Who wants to walk into a Walgreens and see her mother's Polaroid on the Shoplifter's Wall of Shame behind the register?

I was terrified of seeing Estelle's face among a gallery of teenagers who could be one of the high school students I taught. I imagined my mother standing against a dirty white wall, shriveling under the fluorescent lights, as she waited for a security guard to snap her picture, forcing her to flaunt the pathetic tub of Vaseline that she'd tried so hard to pinch.

That day, when I came home from school and found my apartment door unlocked, I turned and ran back downstairs. I knew instantly that it was her. This wasn't the old Harlem, the one that she and I knew; an unlocked door didn't always equal trouble. I knew it was Estelle—I swore I heard her mumbling to herself inside—and I suppose I wanted nothing but for her to take what she needed and go. I hadn't seen her in two years. It was the longest she'd ever stayed away. The last time, she'd spent the night, and in the morning I found she'd disappeared with some of my clothes and a laptop.

I stood by the gate, waiting it out. I thought that she'd soon be finishing up and any minute would emerge, her body slouching under the weight of my belongings. I pretended to be busy pulling out the store circulars and Chinese food menus stuck between the gate's wrought iron spears. But she didn't come outside, so I busied myself by examining the recycling bins and saw that my new tenants hadn't washed their jars clean before throwing them out. Spaghetti sauce had spilled everywhere. I picked up the jar and thought about knocking on their door.

Just then I saw one of them coming up the block. It was the woman, Bergitte; she and her partner, Erik, were from Denmark. I waved to her and held the gate open as she pushed her twins into the yard in their double stroller. They rented the garden apartment, but I knew little about them except that Erik was doing his PhD in art history at Columbia. We had hardly spoken since they moved in last year, though we were both around the same age, our early thirties. But I so desperately wanted to talk—not about Estelle . . . about anything but Estelle. I hoped that Bergitte would invite me in. I stood there waiting for her to say something to me as she put her key in the lock and flung open the door, but she was oblivious to my presence, busy as she was wrangling the stroller and her tow-headed children over the threshold.

I watched, still holding the jar, as she shut the door behind her, leaving me to wait for Estelle alone. I threw the jar back in the bin, too hard—I heard it break. What if Estelle had already come and gone? What if she was never in there at all? I felt like a fool, standing out in the cold because I didn't want to spend time with my mother. I had a sudden desire to see her, just for a second, to confirm that she was still alive and doing as well as someone like her could. I pulled the recycling to the curb and turned and looked back at my house, taking a moment to prepare myself to see her again.

Inside, the creaking of the timeworn staircase under my feet seemed louder than ever. When I inherited the house after my grandfather died, I asked Estelle to leave and had it converted into three separate apartments. I should have fixed the stairs, but putting up walls had been so expensive. When the renovations were done, I decided to live on the top floor because it was harder for her to reach.

At my door I saw that she'd taken off her shoes and left them on the rack. How considerate. They were scuffed loafers, two sizes too big, Goodwill castoffs. She had dumped a shopping bag full of black umbrellas in front of the door. A few had spilled out onto the welcome mat. It was supposed to rain the next morning. Estelle must have spent the morning and afternoon going from store to store, taking umbrellas: easy to sell in a storm, standing by the mouth of the subway. Just like bottles of water in the summer. Estelle was nothing if not enterprising.

I didn't see her in the living room, but she'd taken off her coat— a mottled white mink that belonged to my grandmother—and left it on the floor. Grandpa had bought it to placate her; Grandma had always complained about New York winters. They had both been born in Jamaica, and though they'd met when they were working in London, she had always thought they'd move back to Jamaica someday. I wish that she'd gotten her way, that they had gone back, and Estelle had grown up there. Maybe she would have been different. Maybe I would have been different. Or maybe I wouldn't exist at all.

I picked up the coat and placed it on a hook, wondering again how Estelle resisted pawning it all these years. I could hear her moving around in the kitchen, but I noticed that the picture I'd hung over the fireplace in the living room was missing. I searched around the room. She had hidden it as she always did when she came back, to remind me that it was I who had first stolen from her.

I found it behind the couch. To Estelle, it was a terrible print, I knew. She turned her nose up at anything mass-produced and smarmy. It was a photo of a baby in a ladybug costume, perched on the petal of an enormous flower. I put it there because I knew she'd hate it, like putting up a crucifix to ward off a vampire. I had always dreamed of the day when my mother would stop calling herself an artist.

I know the story so well now. She'd been telling it to me forever: Before my father's first wife, Yvonne, divorced him—just weeks after I was born—Yvonne ambushed Estelle as she was leaving the house and punched her in the face. That became her first good photo, her first self-portrait: *Estelle's Black Eye*. June 1987. It hung over my grandfather's fireplace for twenty years, until I sold it. I'd always hated it. When I was still a kid and Estelle would disappear for weeks at a time, the portrait would remind me that she was out there somewhere, hurting herself. But as I got older, its meaning changed. When I looked at it, I knew that despite everything she'd put my grandparents through, me through, she could never see anyone's suffering but her own. My mother is a narcissist. Not only did I sell the photograph, but I threw away the negatives too. She never forgave me for that either.

I can still remember how Estelle and my grandfather battled whenever he tried to take it down. She always accused my grandparents of loving me more than they ever did her. I thought she loved that photo more than me. To her, it was the piece of art that got her started. She became a hit among a certain crowd of people, people who wanted to see but didn't want to know.

For a time she gained some local notoriety with her photographs of Harlem at its lowest, its burned-out shell: the vials on the playground, buildings on fire, pregnant junkies nodding out on park benches. She took a picture of her best friend, Kenneth Rudolph, after he'd been electrocuted, his hands fried to a crisp. He'd been trying to tap into a power line because his lights had been cut. Estelle took a lot of heat for that. No pun. Our neighbors wouldn't talk to her. No galleries would show it.

After that she went back to self-portraits: *Estelle's Track Marks*, 1989. *Estelle with John*, 1990. *Estelle Begs for Change*, 1991. She didn't have an original story to tell, so she started using and retold a familiar one.

I found her sitting on the stool by the kitchen counter, digging through an oversized white patent-leather handbag. She had already taken out a rubber strap and placed it on the counter. She was cursing to herself and didn't hear me come in. She was still wearing the same ugly wig I'd seen her in two years before. The wig was raven black, short at the ends, with a collapsed bouffant—a cheap imitation of Diana Ross from her days with the Supremes.

Estelle sucked the air through her teeth as she searched. Her bare feet were dirty, almost as black as her wig. She took some objects out of her bag: her old Canon film camera, a model they hadn't made since the '80s (deep down, I was proud of her for never going digital); a Polaroid camera; Scotch tape; Vaseline; a few lighters. She found the needle and was so pleased with herself she smiled as she slammed it down on the counter. She rolled up the sleeve of her billowy gray dress, picked up the strap, and then she saw me.

"I'll do it in the bathroom," she said by way of greeting. She swept the objects back in her bag with one arm, dropped it on the floor, held the stool steady with both hands until her feet touched the floor, and slid off. I wondered if she'd always been that small, or if her age was catching up to her.

I waited until I heard her close the door and turn the lock. I was determined to show Estelle that she couldn't disrupt my life whenever she wanted. I wouldn't fawn over her and beg her to go to treatment. Those days were over. I would carry on as if she weren't there. I sat down at the kitchen table and took out seating charts for my classes. I had to move Natasha Rodriguez and Stanley Jones far away from each other. They gave each other back rubs and pecked each other's necks in class. I felt like I was the one being rude, like my teaching was intruding on their intimate moments; I couldn't get through a whole lesson anymore.

When I was done, I took out the quizzes I had given that day and started grading. Meanwhile, she stayed in the bathroom for an hour shooting up. Despite Estelle being a drug addict my whole life, I'd never seen her with a needle in her arm. I have to give her credit; she always protected me from that at least. Of course, I'd seen her after she injected the drugs, got used to seeing her high before I knew how to speak. But for a long while, I just thought that was who she was, a little strange, hazy, eccentric, prone to falling asleep in the middle of doing things.

Once, during the year when Estelle and I moved out of my grandparents' house and lived on our own in a studio apartment in Spanish Harlem, she was high while she was trying to cook me dinner. We had a gas stove, and she nodded off while the burner was on. Her head dipped forward, toward the stove, and a strand of her hair caught on fire. I was at the table doing my homework. It happened in a split second, but somehow, even though I was only ten, I found the reflexes to grab some kitchen towels and blot out the flames before they burned her entire scalp. Her hair was singed on one side, with scattered red welts on her scalp. That was when she started wearing wigs. I got a nasty burn on my hand when I was putting out the flames. When my grandfather came to the hospital, he called CPS, and that was the last time I was ever allowed to live alone with my mother.

I was running my finger over the smooth skin of the burn scar on the back of my hand when Estelle came into the kitchen. She dragged her feet over to the counter and climbed on a stool.

"How are things?" she said.

I told her about my lessons and let her help me practice my demonstration for my classes the next day. We counted out twenty-six spoonfuls of sugar. I added each to a bottle of seltzer, then a few drops of red and yellow food coloring. She watched the color change with her eyes half-closed.

"To show kids how much sugar is in a bottle of soda," I told her.

"How did I make someone so boring?" she said.

She fell asleep, head collapsing on the counter, still holding the bag of sugar. When it fell out of her hand, some of the sugar fell into her lap; most of it spilled on the floor. I thought about picking her up, brushing off her clothes, and tucking her into bed. I could have; she was that small. But I left her there to sleep on the stool.

That night I woke up over and over again, swearing I had finally heard the thud of Estelle falling off the stool.

The next morning, by the time I got up, Estelle had moved to the couch. I went out and brought back coffee from Starbucks, an egg-and-cheese for her from Jimbo's. When I returned, I found her awake, standing by the door to the spare bedroom in her underwear, with a drill in her hand, some screws in her mouth.

"What the hell are you doing, Estelle?" I asked.

"Look at this," she said, pointing at the door, as if she'd had nothing to do with it. She'd added a spare dead-bolt latch I'd kept in my utility closet. "You can lock the door from the outside now."

"Why?"

"I want to stay here with you and get clean," she said. Her eyes looked at the greasy bag in my hand. "I can't eat that."

I threw her sandwich in the garbage without asking why not.

"You can't stay here," I said, looking at the latch, not at her. I wanted to shake her, to slam her body against the door.

"I want you to help me get clean."

"We can go by the clinic later," I said, getting impatient.

"No. I want to do it here. Look," she said, jiggling the handle. "Just don't let me out."

"You want me to imprison you?"

She gestured at the coffee, and I handed it to her. She took a long sip, looking up at me over the cup.

"I'll start when you get home from work. Then we'll have the whole weekend together," she said. Estelle had only been clean for a few scattered years since I was a kid, though at times she could trick us into believing she was okay—until she couldn't anymore.

"There are cameras in my bag and film," she said. "Take pictures. I know it might be hard to look at me when I get sick. But take as many as you can manage. I know you're busy, but I need to document this."

I said nothing. I just stared at her dirty little feet as she walked into the room to get dressed, wondered when she would wash them again. She came back out in a different wig, auburn with pigtails, and offered to walk me to school.

Outside, it was raining. We walked down Frederick Douglass Boulevard; some bums had taken shelter under the scaffolding covering the steps of a church. She took a picture, and then we stopped for more coffee.

A group of Nigerian women wearing long mud-cloth dresses sat on crates, guarded from the rain by the canopy of a hair salon. One woman, her dress different shades of green with a matching head wrap, broke from the group and approached us.

"You want your hair braided?" she asked.

Estelle lifted her wig slightly off her head to show her baldness and then refastened it. The woman started to walk away, but then Estelle grabbed her. I was embarrassed, just as I had been when she'd walk me to school as a little kid. I stared at her small fingers, urgently pressing into this stranger's forearm.

"I'm an artist," she said. "I know this is a personal question, but have you, or any of those girls over there, been the victim of female circumcision? I'd like to take your picture."

I'll always remember the way the woman moved away from us—

the way she floated backward and twirled around gracefully, in that green outfit, like a leaf suddenly picked up by the wind.

When I got home that night, I saw that someone had defaced the façade of the house. They had drawn a small penis in black marker above the doorbell. I could suspect no one else but Estelle. She would never say I stole her house, her inheritance, but I know she thought it. Though she hated living there when my grandparents were alive, she expected them to leave it to her, but they left it to me instead because of her addiction. They raised me, so in a way, I became more their daughter than she was. She was jealous of how they doted on me. I was grateful to them for keeping me safe, but I understood now how they sometimes used me to control and punish my mother.

I didn't mention the vandalism when I found her in bed, under the covers, her wig on the floor. I made her tea. I placed it by her bedside, and she held my arm.

"Why didn't you go to your father's funeral?" she asked.

"That was eight years ago."

She pulled the covers up over her nose. I had never seen her shaved head without the wig. She looked pathetic with her bald head and her beady black eyes.

I knew that didn't count as an answer, but it bought me some time so I could figure out what to say. The truth was even though Estelle was just a kid when my father got her pregnant, for some reason he was the one who was always mad. At her. At me. Whenever I spoke to him, I'd have to listen to him complain about his life, how unfair everything was. So I stopped messing with him, stopped trying to pretend that he was a better person than he was years ago. I should have said that I didn't go because he'd hurt her—that was what she wanted to hear, no doubt—but instead I said, "Because I didn't care." I didn't want to give her anything just then, even the impression that I loved her.

Estelle shook her head, as if she was disgusted by me. I wanted to ask her when it first dawned on her that she would never be anybody's wife. I didn't think I'd be one either. I'd gotten so used to living in the house alone. But instead I said, "You're just mad you weren't invited."

"You should probably bring me a bucket and some paper towels."

I brought them to her and closed the door. I heard her getting sick throughout the night. Soon, I could even smell it, but I didn't feel like rushing in with the camera. A part of me liked the idea of locking her in. I could think of nothing better than keeping Estelle in a room where I'd never have to worry about what she was doing to herself out there. But that would make her more of a pet; she'd still never be my mother. So I never padlocked the door at all. I thought if I left it unlocked, she'd get the message and leave again.

Instead of filming her, I stayed awake and looked at the work of other artists online: a photo of a crucifix submerged in a jar of the artist's piss; a dead woman's hollowed-out head filled with flowers like a vase. I knew Estelle would be angry if I didn't help her; she thought if she didn't make every experience into a perverse joke, she'd have no career, and in her mind, she could make up for her entire wasted life with the right piece of art. But I knew it was too late; she'd never leave anything anyone but me would remember, regardless.

In the morning, I found that she'd overdosed in the night, that she'd left the room, only to die on my living room couch. As if to make it up to her, before I called the ambulance, I took a Polaroid of her and placed it in her hand.

When they took Estelle away, I sat on the royal blue velvet sofa. It smelled of her, of drugs, of death. I had inherited it from my grandparents too. Except when they were alive, my grandmother kept it completely covered in plastic.

I paid two teen boys who lived next door to help me move it. We left it on the curb, and I hoped someone would take it before the next morning. Before going to bed, I looked out the window and saw Bergitte and Erik, small in the distance, like little elves, their blond hair looking icy in the moonlight, moving the couch back in through the gate, and into their apartment.

ANCESTORS

Spanish Town, 1831–1832

Yesterday, Louise Paisley, who previously resided as a ward in the home of Henry Paisley, bookkeeper of Warm Manor Estate and resident of Spanish Town, was tried for arson, murder, and attempted murder for setting fire to the home of Mr. Harold Fowler, who was then Mr. Paisley's employer. The fire was set as Mr. Fowler, his daughter, and eighteen other guests dined in celebration of his daughter's engagement. The defendant was found guilty of all crimes except murder, and the judge, considering the crime an act of rebellion intended to inspire further uprisings among local slaves, sentenced the prisoner to be hanged by the neck until dead. The sentence is to be carried out in three weeks' time.

— *Spanish Town Chronicle*, April 1832

From *The Written Confession of Louise Marie Paisley*, Spanish Town, Jamaica, April 1832

Every Saturday, the white penal gang was marched up McKinney Road, bonded together by chains and iron shackles on their legs, their coarse brown uniforms cut from the same cloth as the rice bags in our kitchen. We could hear the jangle of the metal as they started up the base of the hill. Peta-Gay and I always ran to the window to watch. The sound progressed as they drew closer, reaching its crescendo at the gate of Mr. Fowler, Peta-Gay's father, and then resounded throughout the day as they built a stone wall around his property. His brother, Enoch Fowler, was warden of the Gaol and House of Corrections in Spanish Town, which I have come to know all too well.

In truth, at least half of the convicts were colored, but so rare was the sight of white men in chains that both the free Negroes and the Spanish Town slaves would find excuses to pass by Mr. Fowler's gate so that they could point and laugh. What egregious crime could a white man have committed to leave him humiliated this way? When too many onlookers gathered, they were shooed off by Mr. Fowler's valet.

Because Mr. Fowler spent most of his time working up at the family's plantation in Clarendon, he dedicated his time at his Spanish Town residence purely to socializing and leisure. The Fowler brothers spent those Saturday mornings into the late afternoon sitting on the veranda playing dominoes and drinking bottles of Warm Manor rum, which their family had distilled in Jamaica for nearly three generations. All the while, two prison guards stood with muskets, acting as barriers between the masters and their convict chattel, while the gang driver barked his commands.

Though the Fowler family had owned hundreds of slaves over the years, Peta-Gay and I knew that her father took special pleasure in temporarily lording over these men—the white men, especially. Their novelty—white men in chains—seemed to give him perverse pleasure. At some point in the recent past, these white convicts had been accustomed to giving orders, and that made them all the more dangerous. In their minds, perhaps they were still those men who sat upon high horses shouting at Negroes; they had yet to be broken, but Mr. Fowler and Enoch seemed gleeful to take on the task.

Often, Enoch would become so intoxicated that he would pause his game, stumble as he tried to climb off the veranda, and stay seated for a few minutes where he fell on the grass, amid the circle of men at work. In order to give off the impression that landing in this place was his intention, he would shout out his own new commands, which were usually contrary to those given by the driver.

"Dig up the hibiscus! Pull it out!" he'd order, after they'd just finished moving the flower beds to accommodate the expansion of the wall.

Peta-Gay and I loved to stand in the window and laugh at her uncle Enoch, but she had nothing but pity for the men in chains. I myself never pitied men. They had the world to explore. What did we have? There were few places that we were allowed to visit unchaperoned, and we were so terribly bored. Which was why Peta-Gay was always seeking out new adventures for us and how my misfortune began. She was the one who taught me that asking permission was not always the wisest course of action, and that God would not actually strike you dead for telling lies. When I first lied to my guardian, Mr. Paisley, it was at the instruction of Peta-Gay; when I first left the house without permission, under the cover of darkness, it was to meet Peta-Gay; and when I once jumped off Cast Iron Bridge and almost drowned in the Rio Cobre, it was because I had been dared to by Peta-Gay. Our houses were right next door to each other, so we saw each other every day.

We had always been forbidden to pass through the front gardens while the prisoners were there. Or rather, Peta-Gay was forbidden. I was an afterthought. Neither of us had mothers, but she had her father, while I was left under the care of Mr. Henry Paisley, who had taken me on as a ward when I was a babe. When I was a little girl, I was his reflection. He could go nowhere without finding my face peeking out of corners back at him. But as I grew older, I found that he was becoming more and more distant, claiming to be constantly occupied at Warm Manor, Mr. Fowler's plantation, a day's ride away, where he was the bookkeeper. The last time he returned home, three weeks before, he stayed in his study for most of the day, then had drinks in the afternoon with Mr. Fowler. He had our maid bring his food to his room, not even bothering to dine with me. I wondered if he had tired of playing father to me.

I was a doorstep child, as Peta-Gay liked to refer to me—my origins were a mystery. Mr. Paisley told me that I had simply been left in a basket on his veranda, and he felt it was his duty to care for me. Peta-Gay suggested that my mother must have been someone of a high social standing who had disgraced herself. Why else would a mother abandon a child? We had seen women of low birth—mostly the free colored women—rear children out of wedlock without the slightest hint of shame. I reasoned that my mother came from a good creole or English family and had the kind of social profile that would have been scandalized by acknowledging me. Though it hurt me to think that I was brought into this world a bastard, I was comforted by the belief that the woman had no choice. She had at least possessed enough sentiment for me to leave me on the doorstep of Mr. Paisley, who had always been kind and who earned a decent living. That he was somewhat distracted gave me a sense of freedom that Peta-Gay did not enjoy, under the iron rule of her father as she was. However, since we were always together anyway, I took on her limitations as mine. In fact, I felt it was my duty to protect her. Often from herself.

After all, Peta-Gay was the Fowler heiress, and that made her more precious than me. Peta-Gay's grandfather had come across her mother, Katrin, during his travels and had transported her all the way from Iceland to marry Mr. Fowler. She was only fourteen when she arrived, a year younger than we were when the events I describe took place. I have few memories of her, for she died when we were quite young, but one in particular always comes to mind. I remember Katrin leaning far out of one of the attic windows of their house with her arms spread as if she were preparing to fly, and then Mr. Fowler yanking her back inside by her hair. Sometimes when I looked at Peta-Gay's strange gray-blue eyes, I recalled that unhappy woman. But everyone regarded Peta-Gay as beautiful because she had the fairest skin of anyone we knew and had inherited her mother's icy-blond hair.

No matter how many times Mr. Fowler commanded that Peta-Gay use a parasol or not venture outside at all to keep her skin pale, she spent hours in the sun each day. Yet her skin remained inexorably pale, barely sun kissed. That day, I recall, was especially hot, but Peta-Gay, as always, was energized, not depleted by the heat like other white people, so she suggested we take a stroll through the garden.

"We can go to the back gardens, but you know the convicts are in the front," I said, though I knew my words bore no effect. She had her intentions set. It was just a courtesy to pretend she was making a suggestion. If Peta-Gay wanted to walk through the garden, we would walk through the garden. Though I spent much of my time trying to dissuade her from foolish ideas, in the end I always ended up relenting. You see, back then, she was all I had, my only friend. I can say it now without feeling the sting: no one else liked me.

We were in the sunroom, looking out of the enormous bay windows. We could see the convicts were engaged in their work, and it would be hours until they took their leave. The gang driver had no pity for them, though the heat was unconscionable. Their routine had been firmly established, and any deviation might result in more punishment for them, and perhaps for us too, but Peta-Gay liked to provoke people, especially her father. And because she was a Fowler, she got away with it.

"I want to speak with them . . . the convicts," she said, looking over at me, obviously formulating a plan.

"Speak with convicts? Are you mad?" I said, but she had already turned to walk outside. I attempted at first to keep a wide berth between us as I followed her out the rear door. It had to be the rear because her father and uncle were sitting on the front veranda. This way they would not see us coming until it was too late. We were behind the house and were making our way around when she turned to smile at me, reached over, clasped my hand tightly, and pulled me close so that we walked arm in arm. Before us, I could see the men working with their heads bowed, breaking and hauling stone. The driver was shouting at them: "I see you moving as if I have nailed your feet to the cross. Move those feet now or else you'll lose them on the treadmill!"

The men groaned as they attempted to move faster, but it was not a day fit for any human to toil. When we approached, one man spotted us and paused the pickaxe he was about to drive into the ground midair. Others saw us and stood still, as if they were a pack of rabbits listening for a predator. Even the gang driver grew quiet. Peta-Gay tightened her grip on my arm. She suddenly paused and turned away from the men. I thought she had lost her nerve and we would go back the way we came, but she stood with her back to them, pretending to admire a bush of pink bougainvillea in front of her.

"Girl!" I heard Mr. Fowler shout. He was addressing me. "Girl! Why have you brought her into the gardens?"

Since I was Mr. Paisley's ward, Mr. Fowler seemed to presume that I too was in his employ by association and he could order me about. He treated Peta-Gay as if she were still a small child or perhaps an idiot. The rest of us were her minders. She could never possibly be at fault for her actions. The blame for his daughter's indiscretion would fall on me, as it always did, and she would keep the sacred place in his heart.

"Pretend that you don't hear him. Pay him no mind," Peta-Gay commanded me, talking directly into the flowers.

"Girl, come to me," he said. Peta-Gay tightened her hold on my arm. I tried to loosen myself from her grasp. I didn't want to be summoned by her father. He had no right to, but I feared him too much to show him open defiance, lest he tell Mr. Paisley. I tried to grab her wrist and force her to unhand me, but she only clenched me tighter.

Then we turned, against my will, to face the audience of men.

"These conditions are . . . are . . ." Peta-Gay stammered briefly before she picked up steam and spoke with a loud, clear voice laced with righteousness. "These conditions . . . are not fit for a donkey to toil under, let alone a man."

She let go of my arm and stepped forward, balling her hand into a fist for emphasis. She looked from face to face, but the men seemed all to be frozen in the same tableau, as if her words had bewitched them. They stood with mouths agape, not a muscle twitching, watching her.

I looked behind us at Mr. Fowler. Her father stood up and walked to the edge of the veranda. I had no idea if this was her intention from the beginning, but a slight smile developed as she stood looking at Mr. Fowler's red face, knowing she had embarrassed him completely. Then, to make matters worse for Mr. Fowler, the men awoke from their spell. They all looked at one another, seemed to reach a consensus, then each and every one began to clap!

Peta-Gay reveled in their attention. Oh, her face was so proud and smug; her cheeks were flushed from the exhilaration of having done something so forbidden. Mr. Fowler had gone from mortified to catatonic with rage. Though he looked at his daughter like he wanted to tear her limb from limb, he seemed to have lost the ability to speak.

If I knew anything about her, I knew she was thrilled to have finally left her father speechless. She backed closer to me and went to reach for my arm again, satisfied that her mission had been success-

ful, and it was now time for us to make our retreat. But she under-
estimated the power of her words. She did not expect one convict
to be so overcome with the spirit of rebellion that he would lay his
hands on her. I was so stunned by Peta-Gay's act I did not even see
him approach. Before she could firmly clasp me, he wrapped both
arms around her waist and pulled her away, lifting her body off the
ground in an enthusiastic embrace.

The convict had the brightest red hair I'd ever seen. Once he
had her suspended in the air, he twirled her almost completely
around, making her dress skirts fan; that red hair blurring looked
like a fire spreading. He couldn't turn her in another full circle, else
she would have been tangled in his chains, so he put her down and
took her hand so that he could bow like a gentleman and bestow a
delicate kiss upon it. He seemed to do this for the pure exhilaration of the act, in the same spirit as she had just performed her own
grand gesture.

All of the convicts looked on in shock, mouths agape. Then they
remembered themselves and looked at the ground or pretended to
resume their work, terrified that they would all be punished for this
man's transgressions. Peta-Gay herself had turned paler than I had
thought possible. I looked to the veranda. Enoch made a motion, a
mere wave of his hand, and the guards began beating the man with
the butts of their muskets. I, for one, was surprised when they didn't
shoot the wretch the moment he reached for her. After all, we knew
nothing about these men and had no idea what they were capable of.

Peta-Gay buried her face into my shoulder as they beat him,
and cried. I thought that a more decent action would have been to
watch the suffering her childish impetuousness had wrought. For
my part, I didn't turn away, even though I feared the beating would
never end—it seemed their goal was total obliteration of his person. The man was a mound of bloody clothing and pulp by the time
they were done; I could barely make him out beneath the gore. The

other convicts had turned their backs on him and tried to appear as though diligently working, the rigidness of their movements exposing their terror. I thought the man was dead, but once a period of time had passed without another blow, he sat up very slowly. He looked right at Peta-Gay, and to my surprise, he smiled. Somehow, though he had been subjected to a terrible beating, his smile managed to still be that of a shameless rascal. The sight was hideous—some of his teeth had been broken, and a steady stream of blood flowed out of his mouth.

Can you imagine? As if she needed any more flattery, I thought at the time. Was touching Peta-Gay so delightful that this man found it worth the risk of his life? But Peta-Gay screamed at the sight of the blood and turned away. One of the guards gave the man another sound knock on the back of the head, which rendered him unconscious. Then they unlocked him from the chains and dragged him around the back of the house, his body hanging like flayed skin.

That is how Mr. MacDaniel first made our acquaintance.

"Take her away," Mr. Fowler commanded me, having found his voice. "Into the house—into the house now, girl!" he yelled.

I led the hysterical Peta-Gay away to my house right next door, which was a miniature version of hers—the two houses were separated only by grass and a long hedge, which ran parallel between them. The home we lived in was technically Mr. Fowler's guesthouse. He was our landlord, our home a part of Mr. Paisley's compensation. In that way, Peta-Gay's father lorded over every aspect of our lives.

I made her sit beside me on the veranda.

"Louise," she said in a barely audible whisper. "Louise, do you think he's . . . dead?"

"If he is, it would serve him right."

"That's an evil thing to say," she said, suddenly pinching my upper arm. "Take that back."

I could see the thought troubled her deeply, so I said, "Yes, I do take it back. I'm sorry. He was alive when they moved him. I am sure he will recover." Though I doubted anyone could recover from such a beating.

I have to confess that seeing her so shaken for the first time left me feeling a little self-satisfied. My instincts were correct: it was at her own peril that she chose not to listen to me. She always found the most pleasure in breaking rules, but it was because she faced no consequences. I often tried to make her understand that it was she alone who held this privilege. She had grown up never fearing a slap in the face, a lash to the back, or the blades of the treadmill like her father's slaves did. No one would put a mark on her pretty white face or risk a crook in her upturned nose. Not here, not where she was such a rare bird. And though I had nothing to fear—after all, I was a white girl with a caring, if sometimes preoccupied, guardian—Maddie, my nanny and maid since birth who was previously a slave at Warm Manor, though she was free now, had told me stories of the horrors that still consumed her and haunted me.

Maddie often wore gloves to hide the *HF* initials that were branded into the backs of both her hands after she once tried to run away.

But Peta-Gay was never allowed to visit the family's plantation, and I doubted she ever took the time to listen to the stories of the poor masses, unless she could use them to frustrate her father in some way. She acted as if she were the anointed and no harm could ever come to her. She didn't understand what cruelty existed in the world. After her mother died of dengue fever while staying at Warm Manor when we were little, Mr. Fowler purchased the house in Spanish Town as if to quarantine Peta-Gay from catching the same illness that had consumed Katrin.

I saw that there was a spot of blood on her cheek that had splashed on her during the beating, so I took out my kerchief and wiped it. She was still so pale; I thought she might faint. She had her eyes closed for what felt like an eternity, but when she finally opened them and looked at me, I saw their look had shifted from fear to outrage. Her breathing calmed, and she said, "We must do something."

She grabbed my arm and yanked me out of my chair; I had no idea how strong she really was until I felt her anger, and I was too embarrassed to admit to her that she had hurt me. I followed her to the line of hedges that divided the Fowler gardens from ours.

"Crouch down," Peta-Gay whispered. I watched her get on her hands and knees, but I was puzzled as to why, so I didn't follow. She reached for the back of my dress and pulled me down so forcefully that I hit my left knee on a small stone. I sat back and lifted up my dress to see that a small bead of blood had appeared.

"Why are you being so impossible today!" I yelled, pounding my fist against the ground.

Peta-Gay put a hand over my mouth.

"Please, we have to help him. It's because of me that he has been so poorly treated. It's my fault," she said, her eyes filling fast with tears. I couldn't say no to her when she cried, and I could see the thought of causing another's suffering troubled her so.

So we crawled like infants, slowly and clumsily through the grass, hiding behind the hedges along the side of my house. When we knew we were close to the back and the work gang could no longer see us, we ran through a gap in the hedge onto the Fowler property. We found the man there, still unconscious. His face was covered with blood, and his eyes were swelling shut.

"What exactly do you intend to do here?" I asked Peta-Gay, unable to turn away from the horrendous sight in front of us.

"We must free him. You see that they have just left the poor man here to die."

"He's already half-dead. How can we free him? Does he look like a man with the energy to run away?"

You see, with her, I was always the voice of reason, but she never considered a word of what I said, perhaps because she truly thought me inferior. I folded my arms over my chest, determined to go no further along in this plot.

She lifted one of the man's limp hands, which were tied with rope to a metal ring firmly staked in the ground. Peta-Gay ignored me and began untying them.

"We must hurry," she said once she'd freed him. She held the man's leg and tried to pull him with all of her strength, but it proved fruitless. He barely moved an inch. She looked at me with those sad eyes, and reluctantly I grabbed the other leg and pulled. Eventually, very slowly, we were able to drag the man to the gardener's shed behind my house. The gardener had been dismissed weeks before for thievery, so we knew no one would be coming and going that day. How easily we could have been found in the act before we reached the shed! I thought then that it was by God's grace that none of the guards came to check on the prisoner. Now I know that it was by the grace of that other.

"This is the first place that they will look," I said, once I'd closed the door behind us.

"We'll move him," she said. "But first we must wake him. Go and get some water for him and clean rags." I obeyed her and cursed myself all the while as I did so. I came back and she cleaned the man as best she could. She insisted that I keep a lookout periodically.

I could hear the driver screaming at the prisoners to move faster. I knew how their routine would unfold for the remainder of the day, for I had observed it often from the window. During the hours they spent in the sun, there were no pauses or breaks; no one even dared ask for water. Sweat dripped from their foreheads and the beads rolled into their eyes, but no man lifted his hands from the soil to even wipe them. They worked without ceasing, usually until Enoch and Mr. Fowler were overcome by their heavy consumption of rum and went inside for their afternoon nap. Then the convicts were allowed to sit in the shade for a spell and rest.

"They will finish soon," I warned her.

"They have already forgotten this one," she said, her voice revealing an edge of irritation. "He is not a man to them."

"Don't be an imbecile," I said. "They can't just forget a convict."

Just then I noticed that the man's eyes were open. I was so startled I cried out. Peta-Gay shot me a hateful look, and I caught myself. He was lying on the floor of the shed looking up at us. His face was so twisted and bruised it is hard to recall a human face when I think of him now. Only one eye could open, and that eye was a shocking green, more like those of the lizards we often found creeping along our walls. It frightened me to see that eye darting back and forth between us. His red hair appeared dull, rust colored, stained as it was by his own blood. I could tell he wanted us to move first, that he wanted to know our intentions with him before he reacted. It was Peta-Gay who broke the silence.

"You are safe with us," she said. "We won't let them harm you anymore."

She bent down, cradled the back of his head in her hand, and slowly helped him raise his head to drink water. The man sipped briefly, which resulted in a long fit of coughing. Then he sat up on his own and began spitting out a great deal of blood. He took the bottle from her, this time using it to rinse his mouth, and intentionally spit another wretched mouthful onto the floor.

He sat straight up now and carefully tested his arms before putting weight on them. Then he looked us up and down again. This was the first time I noticed his hands. How the width of them appeared thrice as wide as Peta-Gay's neck. He could have easily lunged at her and broken her in two. I held on to her arm and started to pull her back.

"Stop your nonsense," she whispered to me before turning back to the man. "Sir, I do not mean to rush you after all that you have been through because of my transgression, but you are not safe here. We must find you a more secure hiding place."

Again, he obeyed us, carefully rising to his feet but saying nothing. I wondered if he was mute or dim. I went out to make sure no one was searching for us. I could hear pickaxes digging into the earth. The day had cooled, and the sunlight seemed to be fading. They would finish soon. We couldn't afford to wait.

Peta-Gay and I exchanged glances, and without speaking we knew where we would take him. The widow Garnett's house, a half kilometer away. It had stood empty since she'd died ten months ago. She had passed on without any family by her side, with only her house help around her. After, the family came from England and had taken what they liked; then the servants stripped the rest bare, and now the house was left abandoned. Mr. Paisley had promised her eldest son to keep an eye on it until he came back to see it sold, but he was too preoccupied with Mr. Fowler's business to remember. Peta-Gay and I had begun using it as our hideaway from the rest of the world. We had spent hours exploring each and every room, and we knew all of its secrets. And now it would be a shelter for ours.

Peta-Gay handed him the gardener's work clothes to wear. Much to our horror, he began stripping off his clothes without warning. We both ran outside before we observed anything indecent.

"Sir, are you finished?" Peta-Gay whispered through the door after we noticed it was taking him a long time to change. We were pressed for time. The sound of tools had ceased. In response, the man opened the door wordlessly. We saw that he had managed to pull on the pants but seemed exasperated with the shirt. He tried again to get his arms through the sleeves and then stopped and sighed, looking at us.

"Oh, you must be in terrible pain!" Peta-Gay cooed, and helped him raise his arms and guide them through the sleeves as he groaned.

"We must go now," I insisted.

We moved as quickly as we could, cutting a path through different yards filled with lush bushes and trees to provide cover until we finally were able to hobble across the threshold of the back door into Mrs. Garnett's house. Not so much as a crumb left in the cupboards. It had been stripped of everything except for a dingy settee whose upholstery seemed to have been destroyed by a pack of rambunctious cats.

Mercifully, the curtains still remained too. I immediately went to the pantry, which we had restocked with matches and candles. I did not want to be in the dark with this man.

"Ladies . . ." he said, and then mumbled something incomprehensible. His voice was breathless, his speech slurred. The sound of it startled me, but I attempted to keep my fear concealed. I had almost convinced myself that he was mute, which somehow allowed me to believe he was not as dangerous. He paused and clutched his jaw, as it clearly pained him to speak. He gave up his attempt and seemed to instead be working on forcing air into his lungs.

We watched him limp over to the settee and lay on his back. In a matter of minutes, he was snoring. We watched him sleep. We didn't know what else to do.

"What will we do with him?" I asked Peta-Gay.

"I do not know."

"What will we do if they come to search the house?" I asked.

"I do not know," she said more harshly. I was growing angry at her recklessness.

"We must simply pretend as if nothing is amiss."

We decided to go home and return at nightfall. I prayed that he would be discovered while we were gone, and we could forget him. It was excruciating waiting those hours alone in my room. My heart raced as I was forced to listen to the search party frantically combing our yards to try to find him. But I knew they wouldn't question us. We were just girls, after all. By the time they noticed he was gone, we were both safely in our rooms. They might have assumed he would head to the river, to make a quick escape out of Spanish Town.

I returned to the widow's house around midnight, after I checked that Maddie was fast asleep. I waited until I was safely inside before lighting a candle. I could hear voices coming from the parlor, low and incomprehensible. Peta-Gay was already there, and I wondered for how long. My heart skipped to think of her alone with this man, though in his damaged state there wasn't much he could do to her. Still, I did not know what to expect from a criminal, so I grabbed a poker next to the iron stove and brought it with me as I went to meet them.

When I entered the parlor, the man was sitting up, and he and Peta-Gay were facing each other without speaking. I sensed that I was interrupting something. They were surrounded by lit candles. He looked as if he were putting her into a trance. I struck the floor with the poker, startling them both. Then I walked over to them with the poker drawn in front of me like a sword.

"Well, well . . . one of you at least has a bit of sense," he said. He had clearly recovered his ability to speak, though his speech was slow and deliberate. I did not need to look at Peta to know that his words had stung her. "But let me ease your mind, pretty girl."

His voice was more refined than I expected from a convict, but he still had a distinguishable Scottish brogue.

"Mr. MacDaniel," he said, extending a hand as if he expected me to shake it. "Come closer." He beckoned. I shook my head, rooted in place.

"I was just about . . . to tell your friend the cause . . . for my incarceration," he began. It was clear that speaking was taking enormous energy. Peta-Gay implored me to come near, so I finally did. When I saw his face in the light, I gasped. It was swollen to twice a normal man's size and was turning purple. I did not know how anyone could have survived such a beating, let alone continue to speak as much as he did. He placed a hand over his jaw, as if to steady it as he spoke.

"Perhaps you will come to fear me less if I tell you my story," he said.

I nodded, though I knew he expected no answer. But it was true—I saw no reason we should give him safe harbor. I needed to be persuaded, and I could tell that, like Mr. Fowler, this was a man who needed to hear himself speak no matter the consequences.

"Why, you see, not too long ago, I worked as an overseer at Warm Manor. Your father's plantation, girl," he said to Peta-Gay, as if she did not know the source of her family's fortune. "Some of the slaves were planning to rebel, and I gave them arms."

"Why? Why would you turn traitor?" I asked, for I could not believe that it was because this man had affection for Negroes. I could see that this man had affection for no one at all. Somehow, with his single reptilian eye, he managed to look at us with amusement and mockery, and I supposed it was how he looked upon the whole world.

"You will have your answer soon if you just listen. I was once the overseer at Warm Manor. If a slave would not work, if he did not harvest enough cane to our master's liking, then it was I who had to make sure he was subject to a flogging with the cat-o'-nine or sent to run the treadmill. But one night I came to blows with Mr. Fowler's brother, Enoch. Whenever he came to Warm Manor, he became too drunk and reckless. Once he knocked a Negro girl, Sabina, about the head so many times that she could never work, speak, or even feed herself again. I complained to Mr. Fowler about letting his brother mishandle his property so, but he blamed me instead for standing idly by. So, the next time he attempted to take a girl from the slave huts while drunk off spirits, I so badly injured Enoch he went the next day to the magistrate. I was flogged on the plantation right where the slaves could see and given only one day to remove myself from Warm Manor.

"Yet I did not remove myself right away. I skulked about the property seeking revenge. The slaves knew I had been dismissed, and I overheard two discussing their plot to rebel. By then I was done with Warm Manor and was not sorry to see it burn. I gave them the key to the closet where I stored my arms; then I departed. Their plot was quickly thwarted, but some of the Negroes spoke against me—trying to save their own lives or simply take me down with them, I don't know—but the magistrate was unwilling to hang a white man upon the word of a Negro, so they put me on the chain gang instead. It is no accident that Enoch is the warden over me."

He was drained by his monologue and collapsed back down on the settee.

"So, you are here because you helped men in an attempt to earn their freedom?" Peta-Gay said.

"For certain," he said.

She seemed pleased and looked from him to me for my approval. I shook my head at her in disbelief. I did not know why she was so willfully playing the fool. It was clear this man only helped out of spite.

"If your story is true, then you turned on your employer just for your own personal revenge." I looked to Peta-Gay. "What if they had succeeded because of his aid? What if your father had been subject to harm?" I knew she enjoyed creating mischief before her father, but I did not believe before then that she truly held ill will toward him.

"But it is the rebels who suffered in the end. Not my father. It is this man who was forced onto the chain gang and then cruelly beaten. My father remains unharmed."

I was speechless for a moment.

Mr. MacDaniel laughed briefly while lying on his back, which caused another violent coughing fit. He sat up again and coughed up more blood, staining the settee. He did not display any shame at this but instead resumed his foul laughter as soon as he could. I had to turn away.

"But I thought that you especially would be pleased by my story," he said to me.

"Why would I be pleased by your treason? I have no time for games. They'll come looking for you soon. What will we tell them?" I said, ignoring him now and looking to Peta-Gay.

"You may call me a traitor," he interrupted. "But I am still alive. It is my plan above all to remain alive." He slowly sat up again, wincing against the pain. "Besides, this day has shown me that I have been chosen for a higher purpose. Tell me something: What is the name of your mother and father?"

"My mother and father are no concern of yours," I said, disconcerted that somehow he managed to guess the mystery that consumed me.

"Will you tell me?" he said, asking Peta-Gay. "What is the name of her mother and father?"

"She has no mother and father. Louise was left in a basket for her guardian, Mr. Henry Paisley, to raise."

"Aha!" He clapped his hands together gleefully.

"Does my early misfortune make you happy?" I asked.

"No, girl. It's just that when I saw you, you reminded me of someone. Someone who died years ago. But now that I know you have no mother, then indeed, you are her child."

"Ridiculous. You don't know me or where I come from."

"Of course I do," he said. "You come from Warm Manor. You must. You are the spitting image of her. Why, when I first laid eyes on you, it was just like seeing a ghost."

"I have never even been to Warm Manor," I said, pulling away from him and standing behind Peta-Gay, using her as a shield between us. I knew that I could not be sure, but I thought if I displayed the slightest doubt, then he would continue to tease me.

"These matters are of no consequence to us now. We must find a new hiding place for him," Peta-Gay said, moving away from me and leaving me exposed.

"Oh, but it is of the utmost importance," he said, looking me up and down. "You must have wondered about your true origins. You come from Warm Manor. I knew your mother."

I shook my head. I tried to recall some mention of a white woman living at Warm Manor, other than Peta-Gay's mother. There hadn't been for years, according to Mr. Paisley, not since Katrin died.

"I will say this politely, but only once more, sir. You are mistaken," I said.

"Florence. Her name was Florence. I will never forget her," he said. "Why, she was the most beautiful slave ever to be reared at Warm Manor."

"I have no time for your teasing. You like to play games even though today they were almost the death of you," I hissed. "We saved you today, and this is how you treat me. We should have let them beat you to death."

With much effort, he rose from the settee and stood, limping toward me, reaching out a hand as if to touch me. I stepped farther back.

"I play no game. Your mother . . . you owe me no ill will, for I never flogged a pretty thing like her with the cat, not even when Mr. Fowler himself told me to. Seeing your face, her face again makes me gleeful. Oh, Florence. Beautiful, Florence," he said, growling at the sky. "Look at your beautiful daughter. Why, she passes for white!"

"Stop trying to torment me!" I yelled, running at him and pushing him hard in the chest so that he fell back on the settee. He cried out in pain. I had aggravated his numerous injuries, and I was glad to teach him a lesson. I had never lashed out at anyone that way, but I showed him that I would not tolerate his prodding. I stood panting, looking at him eyeing me with a half frown from the settee. He would surely retaliate. I contemplated whether to turn around and run alone or to grab Peta-Gay's hand and force her to follow.

Peta-Gay stepped between us to keep the peace.

"You know she is white, sir," Peta-Gay said. "Louise does not do well with jokes."

"Her father was a white man, but she is not white. Close," he said, looking me up and down most wantonly. "But not white." He put a hand on his chin as if he were deciphering a complicated puzzle. "If she should have a child with a white man, then that child has a child with a white man, then I believe in the eyes of the law that offspring will be white. But now, she is a quadroon, I believe. Though Florence was brought to Warm Manor as a babe alone, so there is no way to validate her true admixture. She could have been a quadroon, and you could be an octoroon. If you worry about the fate of your offspring, I can help make you a child with a white father. Just give me leave."

"If you ever touch me, I promise you will feel fire—" I said, picking up the poker and moving to lunge at him again, but Peta-Gay held me back.

"Eh-eh!" he said, imitating the old Negro women. "White father or not. A girl born to a mulatto slave and a white man is still the property of him who owns her mother. You once belonged to her father," he said, pointing to Peta-Gay.

In that moment, I could think of nothing but gouging his eyes out with my fingers. I was sure his mission was only to torture me. If I were not white, would I have not seen it every time I looked in the mirror? It was absurd. Why would Mr. Paisley consent to raising a child of a slave? I thought his words were ridiculous, yet I felt shame, incomprehensible shame. I had always wondered if, upon my birth, there was something my mother and father found so objectionable about me they saw fit to leave me on the doorstep of a stranger. But then again, I was not naive; I saw how some of the white men in Mr. Fowler's circle were rumored to have children with colored women. I knew it to be true of Mr. Fowler himself. I had never considered that Mr. Paisley might be my father. Under different circumstances I would have felt joy, but then I felt only shame at the thought that my birth was so disgraceful he could not even claim me.

"You know nothing. My mother was not a slave, and if you continue to try to spread slander, I will tell the authorities exactly where you are," I said, but my voice was shaking and cracked midsentence. I was exhausted and my head was spinning. I had been pushed too much that day and wanted to be away from that man.

"Oh, will you?" he said mockingly. "And will you tell them how I came to dwell here? Will you?"

I looked at Peta-Gay, who said nothing while this man spoke to me this way. She had a slight smile on her face, in fact.

"Go ahead and smile while he attempts to slander my family name."

She just laughed. "Oh, Louise, we are the only ones here to listen to him. What harm has he done?"

I turned and stormed out. It was only when I was almost to my house that she caught up to me in the dark.

"Promise me you won't tell," Peta-Gay said.

"Why would you spend another moment alone with that animal?"

She grabbed me and squeezed me roughly. "Promise me! I need him."

I was not in my right mind, swirling as it was with this man's accusations and the surreal events of the day; I did not have the wherewithal to deny Peta-Gay—I so rarely did. So I promised her.

But I planned to go to Mr. Fowler and tell him of Mr. MacDaniel if he wasn't discovered soon.

When I arrived near home, I could see Enoch was on Mr. Fowler's veranda, talking to two constables. I could not let them see that I was out alone, unchaperoned at that hour of the night. And I thought of how viciously Enoch had beaten a woman on the head in Mr. MacDaniel's tale. What would he do to me if he had known I'd helped? I bent down low and crept quietly toward the line of hedges so that I could hear if they suspected Mr. MacDaniel's true hiding place. I heard that the search party had found his clothes in our shed, but they had searched the house thoroughly and there was no sign of him. The policeman said that a fisherman had reported a stolen boat just a few hours after MacDaniel went missing. Police were following the river. The officer said that he suspected that MacDaniel was probably long gone. If only that were true.

From *The Written Confession of Peta-Gay Fowler,* York, England, April 1832

Oh, the measures we take to feed our hunger for attention! I am expecting my firstborn in a few short months and have since had to shed my own childish appetites, but let me make one thing clear: It was Mr. MacDaniel's idea to set both fires. We would not have thought of it ourselves. How could we have? We were just girls. Louise was not even present at the ignition of the first, but I was naive enough then so that it took little convincing for me to agree to become his enthusiastic accomplice. In the end, as she no doubt has told you, his guile did seduce her too.

But I will be truthful: I sought out mischief then. Growing up in Jamaica, I was often treated as something more fit for a curio cabinet than for the world. And the fact that I was forced to remain there alone, without a mother, created a quiet anger. I was such a terror to my father back then! The poor soul! He is so dear to me now; though but a short time has passed, he has graciously offered me his forgiveness. I assure him that I am not worthy.

What I confess to you now about the events in question I reveal with great shame, but I do it to remove some of the stain from the name of my dear friend Louise Marie Paisley.

The fire at the deceased Mrs. Garnett's house broke out during the night, while poor Louise lay sleeping in her bed. I stood watching outside as it spread through every room, eventually burning so hot it blew the glass out of her bedroom windows. The flames awoke something primal inside me, previously hidden before. I grabbed Mr. MacDaniel's hands, and the two of us attempted to dance, pretending to be savages before a bonfire. Then I ran as fast as I could, pulling Mr. MacDaniel, still injured, along behind me as fast as he could go, before the neighbors came.

I pictured the neighbors gathered, looking on with expressions that revealed their confusion. Was it the slaves? Was it an act of rebellion? But I knew. I felt pride. I had made a mark that no one could ignore. Me, a girl of fifteen. This was just the beginning, I swore then.

I know that it is widely believed that Mr. MacDaniel, the escaped convict, lit the blaze alone and then perished in it. It is of the utmost importance that you come to understand that he did not perish. Because even now, you make plans to hang my dear Louise for that man's crimes. I can even hear you laughing as you read this because you believe we are just desperate girls concocting silly stories. But I assure you I am not telling ghost stories. MacDaniel is very much alive and out wreaking havoc somewhere in the world, though at the time, I needed you so desperately to think that he was dead. My plan worked brilliantly, but how we have all suffered for my deception!

The widow's house had for a time been a refuge for Louise and me, so you see, I knew every piece of it. Louise thought she did too, but there is a secret about the house that I never told her, and it has been to her great detriment now. I did not trust her with it, so quick was she to nag and whine and run to her maid, Maddie, to tell on me when she thought I would do something that would get us in trouble. When Louise and I first searched the cellar of the widow's house, emptied of every last jar of preserves, we found it to be a dank and cold place, as cellars are. There was a kind of darkness there that felt alive. As if it peeled itself off the walls of the room and somehow seeped into your heart, your soul, whenever you were down there. You'd have to feel it to understand. Louise said it was the perfect place for a duppy or an Ol' Hige to live in, and she would have no part of that room after our first explorations. But I loved dark places. My mother died when I was six, old enough for me to remember her light. I have always believed that she watches over me and will protect me from whatever horrors stalk the night.

One night, months before meeting Mr. MacDaniel, not long after Mrs. Garnett died, I had crept out of my house, determined to hide at the widow's until dawn to make my father worry himself to pieces. He had refused to let me go to the Negro craft market in town with Louise, and I wanted to teach him a lesson. Mrs. Garnett's husband had been a captain who had sailed all over the world, and to pass the time that night, I resolved to search the entire house in case he had hidden some precious or exotic treasure. I wandered through the cellar and found an old steamer trunk beneath a pile of empty crates. I thought it held treasure. When I opened the trunk, I found a dead man.

I screamed, but I did not run. I was fascinated by him. His flesh was so desiccated that it was hard to tell his true identity, but I knew it was Mr. Garnett because he wore a captain's uniform. Also, because the corpse, like Mr. Garnett, was missing a hand. He liked to tell us children that it had been bitten off by a shark, but my father said it was just an accident during a campaign. The widow told us that her beloved Captain Garnett had been lost at sea on a scouting mission to the Pacific. Now you know that story is a lie because I swear to you: she left him to rot in that old box in the cellar.

After Louise stormed off toward home, I thought of Captain Garnett's body as I went back to the widow's house to rejoin Mr. MacDaniel. He had fallen asleep on the settee, but I woke him and bid him to follow me down to the cellar. I knew it was the perfect plan. Though the body was decayed, if we burned it, they would believe it was MacDaniel. I have to confess I was proud of my ingenuity, devious as it may have been.

"All events have converged in our favor to create this one perfect moment," I said, popping open the trunk. "For here lie the remains of that poor escaped convict, Mr. MacDaniel!"

He stared at the contents for a long time before he spoke. "Perhaps I am on a divine mission. Perhaps God has sent me here for a purpose," he said.

"Of course," I said, and could not help embracing him impulsively, though I regretted it immediately, for he clung to me much too tight. "We were meant to meet under such circumstances. I have liberated you, and soon you will return the favor." That night we lifted the body out of the trunk and brought the stores of kerosene from the cellars to spread throughout the house.

The next morning, Louise came over, abuzz like everyone else about the fire, which was still smoldering and smoking in the distance. Her eyes were so large with fear I thought if they bulged any farther they might fly from their sockets and strike me in the face. I could not tell her all of what I had done; I knew the truth would prove too much for her.

"Where is he?" she asked.

I couldn't stifle my laughter.

"It's the funniest thing," I said. I grabbed her by the arm and pulled her to the kitchen, where we stole from a pan of cooling dumplings. Then I brought her to the rooms in the attic floor of the house. Two London cousins of mine had died from smallpox while visiting the prior year, and the room they had occupied had remained abandoned since. The maids would not go near it. And there were so many rooms I knew my father wouldn't notice. It was very dark when I entered and even worse when I closed the door behind me. The curtains were draped, and there was a mustiness in the air that made one expect to find one of my cousins' corpses still covered with a sheet, but the bed was empty.

I whispered, "It is safe, Mr. MacDaniel."

He crawled out very slowly from beneath the bed. He still suffered tremendously from his injuries and was heavily bandaged, so his moving shape was a lumbering and featureless phantom.

"Look who it is!" I said, a little too loudly. I thought I was the cleverest thing, but Louise was mortified. I had to cup a hand over her mouth to prevent her from crying out. Oh, how I did love terrifying Louise. I wish I had lit a candle first, so I could have better seen the look on her face.

"If anyone comes in, I've instructed him to hide under the bed." I lit a candle then, so we could see one another as we conversed.

The bandage I'd placed over Mr. MacDaniel's eye was slipping down his face. I had done a poor job of it the night before. I had never played nursemaid to anyone.

"Those savages had damaged it so badly that it had swollen and filled with pus," I explained to Louise. She stared at Mr. MacDaniel silently, so I felt it up to me to make polite conversation.

I gave him the biscuits, which he devoured without so much as a thank-you. Once he had had his fill, he gave her that look again. He had the most vulgar smile on his face. We were so alike, he and I. Oh, he took pleasure in getting her riled up too.

"Do not look at me, you pile of rags," she said, not bothering to mask her distaste.

"How can I not look at you? I've never seen such a pretty quadroon."

I could tell from how Louise suddenly looked a shade too embarrassed that the night before she had probably spent hours studying her reflection. I thought it silly of her to fret about something that could not be confirmed and seemed unlikely. Did she have Negro blood? I had never asked my father about the identity of Louise's mother or father. I had never had cause to. We all accepted Mr. Paisley's story of finding her on his doorstep.

So, was it possible? Perhaps. Her eyes were not as pale as mine, her skin not as fair, but whose is on this sweltering island? I studied her then and saw a white girl, as I'd always seen, looking back at me. I was not bothered by the fact that none of the other girls in town would keep company with me when I was with her. They told me that it was because she was always so sour, but it could have been because somehow they all knew. Hypocrites, all of them. Most of the whites here have both legs so deep in the pit of slavery, how can they think they can come out pure? I embrace the truth in these matters. I know my father has fathered many bastards, though I only know the names of one or two. But other girls are not as morally developed as me. Anyway, let us avoid the political.

"Did you like the fire?" he asked her. "Was it not the most majestic thing you have ever seen?"

"You should have remained and burned in it," Louise said.

"Louise Marie, what an awful thing to say."

"He's an awful man, and you're a fool for helping him."

I was not used to her being so harsh with me. I thought it was a terrible overreaction on her part. After all, Mr. MacDaniel had done nothing to her.

"Don't blame her, dear. She has been taught to believe a lie. Waking up can be difficult," he said. His broken teeth made him look so pathetic that I felt a deep sympathy for him. He seemed to look like a kind old man far beyond his years. The eye that was not bandaged was bright green and appeared all the more beautiful, contrasted against the gruesome background that was his face. I did not think he meant us any harm. I was still a foolish child then.

I went on, undeterred by Louise's disapproval. "They will think that he has perished in the fire and stop the manhunt. We left scraps of his clothes, his chain." I did not tell her about the corpse. "We must find another hiding place for him, in case they uncover our deception."

"If God is merciful, he will hang."

"Oh, Louise. You are being just awful. If you cannot be nice, then I think that you should go home . . ."

She turned to leave then, to my surprise. I stopped her. "Will you slip outside at midnight and meet me in the path between our houses?"

Louise did not even answer. Instead, she gave me a look of horror and left us. I trusted she would be there. She always resisted at first but eventually obeyed me. I found myself once again left alone with Mr. MacDaniel. You may wonder if I was afraid in these moments, but I assure you I was not. He played quite the gentleman with me.

Louise did not know what plans I had for Mr. MacDaniel. Before I confess, let me swear in my defense that since having left my life of crime long behind me at the conception of my child, I have spoken no evil since.

Let me also add, though it might be hard for you to understand, that all of the bad deeds I did back then, or planned to do, I did for my mother. They were my homage to her. My revenge for her suffering.

She had met my father only once before their wedding day. My grandfather had come across her while doing business in Iceland. He was concerned that both his sons were still unmarried, and though she was of little means, he knew that her beauty would entice one of them into abandoning life as a bachelor. My grandfather feared that if he did not act quickly, his sons would decide to legitimize some octoroon concubine and her bastards, as was becoming more common fashion among some of the less-pedigreed Creole planters. The fact that she was the unwanted ward of a man who he was attempting to purchase a sizable parcel of land from only made the match more convenient. He received a substantial discount, and his son received a young wife who could bear him genuinely white heirs.

My mother was fourteen when she was sent to the island. According to my father, she spoke not a word of English and, knowing only country life in colder climates, upon her arrival was immediately struck with malaria and was so afraid upon seeing Negroes for the first time in her life, and of course they were everywhere, that she barricaded herself in the bedroom for nearly a fortnight, only opening for occasional water and food (unbeknownst to her, prepared and left at her door by the same Negroes she cowered from).

Louise's maid, Maddie, knew her personally. Once my mother had gotten over her fear, Maddie was one of the slaves who attended to her in Warm Manor. According to Maddie, she never quite understood life in the West Indies, shut up in that big house, no work to do except to hope to bear children for a man she only occasionally saw and would never truly know. She missed her home, her language. I was always told that she died of dengue fever. But when I turned fifteen, Maddie told me I was old enough to know the truth: she'd killed herself. Maddie said that after my brother was born, she became ill and even more despondent, eventually drowning herself in the river near the plantation. Though my father had been forewarned that she was too sickly to care for another child,

Maddie told me he insisted on a male heir. The boy himself died six months after. I remember him well. He was a good-natured child. Though I believe my mother was relieved to be free of this place, I could not deny her suffering. Can you understand why I believed my father a tyrant back then? Why I didn't find it surprising that Mr. MacDaniel had wished him harm? I wanted him to feel at least a fraction of my mother's pain and helplessness, and I wanted to ensure that I did not suffer her same fate.

My mother was just a dog to him. We women are all dogs to men, as I saw it back then. Some of us were treated better because of our pedigree. If we were pure breeds, rare breeds, we could be married at least, but we were all raised for breeding nonetheless.

Already he was beginning to look at prospects for me. They often came to the house, and he would make me go on walks with them through the garden or around Spanish Town Square. He looked at only other planters, and most of them were so terribly old. I resented being used to close business transactions and increase his profits. I was sure he would marry me off to the owner of the Burgess Plantation, who had recently become a widower. He was twenty years my senior and bore a striking resemblance to the bull-frogs we found bathing in the puddles in our gardens. I did not want to be traded to this man, to become a prisoner in his great house.

As I grew older, I became aware of all of the hours I spent in the company of my father without him having asked me a single question. Of course, he believed I was beautiful, but he did not know that I could be bright, let alone devious. He was proud of me, but proud as if I were an ornate chair that he had carved himself. He didn't think that there was anything else to me.

So, I hope you can imagine my state of mind at the time, as I say flat out that I gave Mr. MacDaniel bidding to do my father harm. I did not say where or when or ask him to inflict a specific punishment. I left it up to him to take his revenge for the beating he had received in our garden and whatever other slights my father had done him while he was overseer at Warm Manor. Of course, I did not want my father dead. Rather, I wanted him to be rendered just as helpless as I felt, or as my mother had. I do not think that you can understand. (You reading this—you are a man, no doubt. People think that you were meant for more in this world than to lie on your back and suckle babies.)

I wanted him to hurt my father, not to kill him. Simply to incapacitate him in some way, so that he could no longer exert so much power over my life, our home, and the people who slaved away at our plantation. I thought this plan would ease the suffering of hundreds. (Though I am the mistress of a grand sugar estate, I have always been for emancipation. We've heard that the sun will soon set on that foul practice, and my husband and father have already begun to mourn. My father so loves being a Big Man! I have told him he can still be one, only in time, he will have to pay the men after he orders them about. But he is arranging a trip to India, looking to save expenses with coolie labor! Forgive me for this brief digression. I could not help myself.)

As I said, at the time, my plan was to render my father lame. I would be by his side during his recovery. I imagined reading to him by his bedside, reporting on all the activities that transpired each day at Warm Manor. I believed he'd come to enjoy our time alone, and, forced to rely on me, temporarily exiled from the world of men in his invalid state, he would come to trust me and know that I was more than my face. That I could be as valuable as he had hoped my brother, God rest his soul, might have been. Maybe then, he would let me choose the path for my own life—who I wanted to marry and where I would and would not go. Maybe I could finally walk down the street alone without an escort, for goodness' sake.

Mr. MacDaniel seemed pleased with my plan and promised to play his part.

But I knew that using him as my tool made things all the more complicated. I assumed the authorities thought that he was dead and had perished in the fire at the widow's house, but if he were discovered in our home, I would lose what little freedom I had. My father would ship me off to a convent school in England. I lived in fear as I waited for the right moment.

Louise did not meet us that night after all, so I realized I could not include her in our plot any further. The next day, when I met her, I told her that I had paid a boatman with sympathy for the plight of the abolitionists to take Mr. MacDaniel to Cuba. I claimed that I told the man that MacDaniel was a Baptist missionary who'd been caught teaching the Negroes their God-given rights. Louise readily believed all of this—she was that gullible, or maybe it didn't occur to her that I would lie to her. In any case, I could see her relief upon learning that Mr. MacDaniel was gone.

Yet, he still remained in my house. I knew I'd soon indeed have to find a place for him, but the truth was it pleased me to keep him close. He called me his savior and pledged his fealty to me, like a knight to his queen.

Several days passed without me seeing Louise. Before him, she was my shadow, but since we'd met Mr. MacDaniel, I could feel her slowly pulling herself away from me. She didn't trust me anymore. Each day she would find a new excuse to remain indoors. And I did not appreciate Mr. MacDaniel's constant mention of her. *Where has your pretty friend gone? When will she come again?* As if anyone else ever referred to her as the pretty one.

I did not expect Mr. MacDaniel's strange obsession with her to become so intense that he would creep out of my house one night to stand before her window. Louise sensed his presence, she claimed, so deep was her fear and detestation of him. She saw his figure standing in her yard one night, and the next day she burst into my room and practically attacked me.

"How dare you lie to me and protect that monster!"

"How do you even know it was him?" I said, feigning ignorance.

"I would know that creature's silhouette anywhere," she said. "I am going to tell."

"For heaven's sake! What has he done to you except call you a quadroon?"

"He is a twisted, violent man! Why can't you see?"

"What violence has he committed? We have only witnessed him being brutalized."

"He burned down a house."

I didn't mean to laugh at this. It was only that Louise was always so naive.

"I did most of the burning. He merely told me how."

"I don't believe you," she said. She was always so cautious and careful. She knew few people and was practically neglected by her guardian. She knew little about the world and the deceit that humans are inherently capable of. Even as I told her the truth, she refused to believe me. Instead, she reached out and embraced me. Louise was much smaller than me in stature and rather bird boned and frail, so it felt more as if she clung to me then as a desperate baby who feared being separated from her mother.

"I do not know how he has brainwashed you into saying those terrible things, but I must tell Mr. Paisley. We have to be rid of him," she said.

I pushed her away. I knew if things were to proceed as planned, I would have to get Louise to be silent. I saw the concern in her face, and I thought about what she feared the most.

"My father told me about you," I said. "He confessed that you were born of one of his slaves! Mr. Paisley felt pity for you because you came out so white. He couldn't see you for what you are. He begged my father for you. No one else knows but my father and me, and if you tell about Mr. MacDaniel, I'll tell everyone."

Oh, how her face lost its color! She was speechless. It was as if I'd just plunged a knife in her belly. She turned and ran out of my house. Of course, I made all of this up. I knew nothing of her true parentage then, other than what she herself had been told. It was an empty threat. She was my friend! My one true friend. But in that moment, I needed her to heed me. It was cruel of me. I'll never forgive myself for the way I tortured her. And in the end it was all for nothing.

Each night I went to visit Mr. MacDaniel, and I would ask him, *When will you act? When?*

He kept saying, *Soon, my girl, soon.* But as we know now, he could not have had more dreadful timing. My father was home from Warm Manor for the Christmas holiday, but after no more than a day or two of celebration had passed, he received news of what would come to be known as the Christmas Rebellion that was ravaging the countryside. The slaves, riled up by the Baptist missionaries and the slave preachers, had tried to strike for better conditions, but eventually chaos ensued and they set Warm Manor and the surrounding estates on fire. It was an uprising much worse than the one Mr. MacDaniel had aided, the likes of which not even my father had ever seen. He rode off to the country to fight with the militia that was trying to quell the rebellion, before I had even slammed the door to Mr. MacDaniel's room behind me for the last time. A few hours later, my father's cousin, the spinster Ms. Alma Fowler, came to stay with me while my father was away. She arrived in a covered carriage and declared she had made arrangements to take me close to Kingston Harbour. I refused to go at first.

"There is no need to go to Kingston, when they are fighting in the countryside, not here," I said, plotting that I could lock myself in my room.

"He has entrusted me to keep you safe, and for us women there is safety in numbers. What if that darkie over there," Alma said, pointing to Gerard, our butler, who immediately turned and bolted the other way, "should find sympathy for those field slaves and take a cutlass to your throat while you are sleeping? Who will protect you?"

I knew Gerard was scared of his own shadow. I doubted he would ever lay a hand on me. I wanted to say that Mr. MacDaniel would protect me, but I was not sure. He could choose the side with the better odds, as he had before.

"What about Louise?" I asked.

"Her maid is getting her ready," Alma explained. I took some comfort in the fact that at least Louise and I would be together in our exile.

As soon as Alma was busying herself by supervising the maids who were packing my bags, I went to see Mr. MacDaniel and suggested he hide away in Mr. Paisley's gardener's shed until I returned. When I bid him good night, I said I would be back to see him soon, but things did not unfold as I intended.

From *The Written Confession of Louise Marie Paisley,* Spanish Town, Jamaica, April 1832

I was devastated when I left Peta-Gay's room. If what Mr. MacDaniel said was true . . . well, it was hard for me to reconcile the thought. But I could not so easily dismiss my dearest friend as a liar. Of course, we were sometimes associated with half-castes and quadroons—it is unavoidable, living on as small an island as this one where there are so few whites. But I often found them too cloying, so eager to ingratiate themselves—to Peta-Gay especially—when we patronized their stores or agreed to attend a function in which one was the host. (Neither Mr. Paisley nor Mr. Fowler would attend a function if there would be more than a few in attendance.) They may be invited for tea at our houses, but they would never be invited to stay and dine at our tables.

Mrs. DeSouza, a quadroon who ran our favorite perfumery, always gave Peta-Gay and me the newest scents to sample for free and had homemade coconut drops waiting for us. But if a Negro girl tried to enter, oh my—she was practically chased out with a broom. When Maddie accompanied us, Mrs. DeSouza would behave as if she weren't there, never even laying eyes on her directly. I never understood the shopkeeper's cruelty. Were they not kin? I had reasoned. But now that I could be their kin, I felt as though I had suddenly stepped into a pit of quicksand and was struggling to keep from sinking to the bottom. I could see Peta-Gay above me on solid ground with a pleased expression on her face as I sank. We had to step on one another to get to the top. Didn't we? Those of us who were colored and free. For it was sinking in that Peta-Gay must have heard the truth from Mr. Fowler, that perhaps I was a colored girl now, and I looked at behavior that once puzzled me with a new understanding. No one wanted to sink to the bottom with the slaves. That wretched existence. I thought of Maddie's hands, how I had kissed the seared flesh on the back that bore Mr. Fowler's initials when I was still a child because I thought it could ease her pain. But I never wanted those hands to be mine.

Peta-Gay had shown me with her threats that it was only if I did her bidding that she would reach down and pull me back up to stand on level ground with her. Otherwise, she would let me sink. The girl I once thought of as a sister would let me sink. I had thought that Peta-Gay belittled me because of wealth, but just then I wondered if it had been due to my color all along.

I decided I must confront Mr. Paisley that very night. I needed to know if I had been the only one living in ignorance. I feared that he would laugh at me and tell me I was being ridiculous, which would bring both relief and embarrassment. But worse was the fear he would confirm it was true.

Still, I swore that night that even if Mr. Paisley did tell me I was colored, I would never pander to the likes of Mr. Fowler or Peta-Gay. I would rather drown. I feared Mr. Fowler, indeed, but you would never find me kissing his shoe, no matter what color Mr. Paisley told me I was.

As fate would have it, though, I would not find the answer that night. Rebellions had broken out on estates in almost every parish. All able-bodied white men were rounded up to serve in militias. Mr. Paisley and Mr. Fowler were gone in haste. Before my guardian could leave, I told him I had a question to ask him, but his only reply was, *What is so important it cannot wait?*

Maddie would not let me even go to the window once he was gone.

"They are fighting at the country estates, not in Spanish Town," I said.

"You mus' keep your white face from the light, tonight of all nights."

I wondered what would become of Peta-Gay's pet. Morose as I was, I went to bed early while it was even still light out and was tormented by feverish dreams that Mr. MacDaniel was slicing off pieces of me, handing them to Peta-Gay, who was wrapping them in wax paper and selling them to customers, my room and bed transformed into a butcher's counter.

I woke with a start from one of the dreams, aware that someone was standing over me. I saw a hand reach toward me in the dark, and still dizzy with sleep, I feared it held the same carving knife as the one in my dream. I thought it was him. I struck first, not willing to give him the satisfaction of taking me without a fight.

Maddie yelped. In the lantern light, I could see her standing over me, clutching her face.

"You dream you turn into a cat?" she shouted.

"I'm so, so sorry, Maddie. Forgive me!"

"We mus' go," she said. "Or you wan' stay here and burn?"

"Go?" I said.

"All white people mus' stay close to harbor."

"What about Peta-Gay?" I asked.

"Mr. Fowler's cousin bring a carriage to take you to Kingston. We will meet the Fowler girl outside."

I should have been afraid, but I found comfort. Perhaps Peta-Gay had been playing a trick on me. I was being sent to safety with those of my own kind until the reinforcements came. Mr. MacDaniel's lies had not passed far beyond his own vulgar lips. I was still white.

We met Peta-Gay and her cousin Alma in the carriage and rode to a home in Kingston where we could look out and see the ships waiting to steal us away, should the rebellion spread outside the plantations. At first, we would not look at each other. We rode in silence even though we sat side by side. I could tell that she knew she'd wronged me, and so I refused to speak first. It was up to her to win back my affection. Her demeanor had changed. She looked small and timid. Had she ever had cause to fear for her life before? And to make matters worse, I knew it plagued her with worry to be away from Mr. MacDaniel. Just before we arrived, as I was looking at the ocean in our view, I felt her clammy hand slip into mine and squeeze it affectionately. I squeezed hers back.

We were the guests of the Bradfords. I had no idea who they were, but they had taken it upon themselves to take in some of the white refugees who had fled from all over the island.

Mrs. Bradford was quite kind to Maddie, but two of her other guests were uncomfortable having any Negroes in the house.

"What you wan' me fi do? Sleep with the horse?" Maddie said, insulted.

Mrs. Bradford gave Maddie directions to the home of one of her housemaids. *If the blacks should come for us tonight, then they have increased their number by one,* I thought.

Maddie was a proud woman. She liked to speak to me harshly,

as if she were my own mother, but pride alone could not change her color. She had been my confidant in my younger years. She had held me when I cried because I wished I had a mother like normal girls. It shames me now to think that in that moment, the thought that she and I could suddenly be kin had made me at first want to throw myself against the waves. She would feel betrayed. Today, as I sit waiting for the executioner to carry out my fate, she is my only confidant. My only true family, and I am grateful for her.

I could see the ocean from my room. That night the tide was high and the waves were especially rough, as if God himself was against the idea of the white people getting off this island alive.

Soon after we arrived, Peta-Gay came to my room. Even after our tentative peace in the carriage, I still had an urge to strangle her for the torment she had caused me. Despite myself I gave her an embrace. The world around me was shattering, and it felt good to hold on to someone familiar. Someone I had known all my life. Besides, we were both afraid. We had never heard of a rebellion being so big that there was fear it might spread to the city. We stayed up all night together fretting.

"What will Mr. MacDaniel do left alone on the property? What if someone should discover him? Will he harm them? How will he eat?" Peta-Gay wrung her hands with worry.

"I have no doubt that he shall prove very resourceful," I said to reassure her, but I couldn't help imagining him wringing the neck of a chambermaid as we spoke.

Peta-Gay seemed grateful to me, for she knew that my words were meant to calm her. We decided to sleep together that night, and when she reached for me, I lay beside her and we held each other. She looked into my eyes.

"I know nothing of your mother or father—whether they were born free or slave. I only told lies to stop you from telling on me," she said.

Though I had suspected she was being deceitful, it angered me to hear her confession.

I rose from the bed and went to sleep in her room without uttering a word to her. Otherwise, I was afraid I would have done her harm. I had never felt so much anger, and I swore I would never speak to her again. But the fact that we were trapped in our quarters in Kingston for another two weeks made this difficult. Mrs. Bradford would not release us until she was certain the rebellions had been extinguished and white people were no longer under threat. And even then we heard that they had not ceased completely, for new slaves were being emboldened by the stories, and smaller insurrections continued to pop up. It felt like the country would never quiet. The slaves and the planters would be at war until emancipation was declared. I had heard nothing from Mr. Paisley for weeks, and I feared for his life. Where would I be without him? I had no one else to talk to to soothe my fears besides Peta-Gay. At first, I refused to be in the same room with her, but as the days passed, I needed someone to confide in. I grew lonely, and eventually my iciness toward her thawed.

Mr. Paisley eventually arrived in Kingston, remained as Mrs. Bradford's guest for two days, and then escorted Peta-Gay and me back to Spanish Town. He told us that Mr. Fowler intended to remain up in the country until every single one of the three hundred rebels still alive were hanged.

The damage to Warm Manor was devastating, he told us on the ride back. He was not sure if anything could be salvaged. He was afraid he'd be released from employment when all was said and done. I could tell his morale was low; he wept on my shoulder for part of the ride back and slept the rest. He was so fragile Maddie and I had to help him upstairs to his room and tuck him into bed. I had never seen him so vulnerable. Maddie left to prepare dinner, and I sat with him, watching his eyelids flutter through an obvious nightmare. His eyes flew open suddenly, and he sat up coughing. I remembered the question I had planned to ask him all along. Was this the right time? Though Peta-Gay admitted that she had lied, I wanted to be certain once and for all. I wasn't sure, seeing him in his distressed state, if that was the appropriate moment, but then he put his hand on mine to settle himself, seemingly relieved to still find me there. I decided to ask before I lost my nerve.

"Was my mother a slave?"

He looked at me with shock. Then his face turned a deep red.

"What . . . what? Who has told you something so absurd?"

"It was a girl from church. She said her father told her." I made up the lie quickly, realizing that there was no way the truth would be a wise explanation. He looked at me as if he were pondering who it could be. Then he shook his head with finality.

"Why, my dear, it is just a foolish girl trying to tease you." He lay back on the pillow, and I took that as the end of our conversation. I could sense something unspoken, but I had no reason then to distrust him, especially as he was telling me what I most wanted to hear. I went back to my room, trying to find peace from the explanation I'd been given, but as I paced around and thought about all that MacDaniel had put me through, I had the urge to find him just to spit in his wicked face. I thought of a better revenge. I sat at my desk and began composing a letter, anonymously, of course, informing Mr. Fowler that the escaped convict had lived and had since taken residence on his property. I thought there was a chance that Peta-Gay would get in trouble, but I still felt the need for justice. The whole ordeal was her idea, after all, and so it was only right that she should receive some form of punishment. Mr. Fowler would lie to the authorities or bribe them for her, of course—he would not let his little girl be punished for harboring a fugitive. I was sure she would not receive much more punishment than being confined to her room. I thought that perhaps I would face some consequences, but in that moment I only saw red. As soon as I got to the end of the letter, I noticed Mr. Paisley standing in the doorway, watching me.

Our eyes met, and he approached me hesitantly. I quickly folded and sealed my letter. When he reached me, he just stood there, looking down at me. Then he sat on the bed next to me, studying his nails, as if I could not see him.

"Is something the matter?"

He reached for me then and squeezed my arm, too hard.

"I have always loved you. My first instinct was that of a father, to lie to protect you. But you are old enough," he said, giving me a reassuring smile. I knew what was coming and wanted to shout, *No, no—I am not old enough. Please continue to lie.* He could not hear the words in my head, so he continued.

"It *was* a house slave who birthed you. I don't know your father—a white man, obviously—but it's impossible to know more. Your mother was colored, but she was so beautiful. Like you. Everyone admired her. I could not bear to see you raised in bondage. I knew you would grow to be beautiful, and you are even more so than your mother."

I began to cry. Instead of comforting me, he hardened.

"You already knew that I was not your father, and we both know that you are not a child anymore. You have turned into a woman."

"Is she alive?"

"No, no; she was hanged when you were just a babe . . . an act of rebellion."

I let out a loud sob. I don't know if it was for my dead mother or for me.

"Why are you crying? You have never known her. She is no more dead to you than she was before; nothing is different. And who your mother is does not change anything. No one has to know. Only Mr. Fowler and a few Warm Manor slaves know about you," he said, dismissing them all with a wave of his hand.

"It was easy to see you as my own child when you were small.

Every helpless babe brings out the fatherly instinct in a man. But as you age, I know that I will never see my face reflected in yours. You are not my child. We are not blood, and that is a fact. You have always known this too."

He stood up then and started nervously pacing before me, looking at the floor and then the ceiling, clearly working something over in his mind. Then he stopped and knelt before me, took my hand.

"I will most likely return to England. There is nothing left here for me now. Now that you know your true birthright . . . if you come with me . . ."

He moved his face closer to mine and stared into my eyes in a way he had never done before.

". . . as my wife, no one will have to know about you. They will only know you as my wife, a Creole from the West Indies."

He leaned in and kissed me suddenly. I pushed him off me. I covered my mouth, shocked and sickened.

"I have never thought of you as anything but a father," I said. He reached out and held my hand and then leaned over and kissed it. I felt an instant corruption. He could no longer touch me without me thinking of his ulterior intentions. I ran from the room.

My stomach swirled with nausea and contempt. My guardian had told me he no longer loved me as a father, and then he had proposed to me. I wanted to tear off my own skin. As soon as I stood outside, I vomited off the side of the veranda.

I spent the next few hours crouching behind a bush, crying and digging my nails into my own flesh. I went back to the house later but circumvented him for as long as I could that night. Whenever he knocked on my door, I did not respond; eventually, he grew tired and went to sleep.

When I was certain he was asleep, I crept down the stairs again and out the kitchen door. I had to tell Peta-Gay. I somehow believed she was the only one who could save me.

From *The Written Confession of Peta-Gay Fowler,* York, England, April 1832

As soon as we returned from Kingston, I went to search for Mr. MacDaniel, but he was nowhere to be found. I saw that he had left the clothing I'd given him behind, but I wondered where he had acquired new clothes. I had been back for five days before Father returned from rounding up as many of the rebels and slaves who had fled from Warm Manor into the bush as he could find. When I saw him again, a bandage covered his forehead, where someone had struck him with a stone. The wound had reopened, and I could see a large spot of blood seeping through the cloth. I did not pity him then. Instead, I grew excited, for that was when I knew that it was possible to strike down a tyrant; it was like toppling an elephant. It might take many blows, but it can be done.

I kept imagining that any moment Mr. MacDaniel would creep into my father's room as he slept and deliver justice, but of course I now wondered if I was merely indulging in childish fantasies. Mr. MacDaniel, no doubt, was getting comfortable in his new life as a ghost. I thought that was the end of him, that he had indeed escaped by boat to another island.

My father was exhausted, so after regaling me of all the finer details of how he "had made the niggers pay," he slept well into the next day. I had no idea that he had been merely putting on a brave face or was perhaps still riding high on the violence and retribution he sowed, for the next day when he came down to breakfast, before he could sit in his chair, he collapsed at my feet and wept. I had never seen him without that arrogant look on his face, not for a moment. This man was a stranger to me, and so I felt great pity for him.

"We are ruined," he cried. "They burned all of the cane fields. They've burned down the mill. Half the slaves have disappeared into the bush." He said more, but he blubbered and wept so fiercely I could scarcely make out any of his words.

"Ruined?" I said.

"Do I need to provide you with the definition?" he barked. "Has that expensive tutor taught you nothing?" He picked himself off the floor, wiped the tears, and composed himself. He returned to being the father I knew.

"It's impossible," I said.

"Well, I suppose we will have to wait and see. Maybe you will believe me when you are sleeping in a gutter."

"There must be something . . ."

He grabbed me under my chin. His eyes bored into mine. While I did not believe we would suddenly be out in the street, living like gutter rats, I didn't doubt my inheritance was greatly diminished. I had read the account of the damage the rebellion had caused in the papers.

He didn't have to say the words. I knew what I needed to do.

I nodded.

I would have to make a match, quickly. You may think my father won in the end, but such is not the case. For I had leverage. He needed me, and therefore he had to find a match that pleased me. I was glad to have something to hold over his head. His future rested on me, and besides, who wants to be poor?

That very night, I went to bed dreaming of my future husband. I felt almost as if I could dream him into reality. In my dreams I saw a man, handsome, fair, kind, valiant, but when I woke up, I found myself staring directly into the eyes of a monster. Mr. MacDaniel had his large hand over my nose and mouth. I couldn't breathe. All I could see were those two glinting green eyes (the other had healed by then) smiling down at me with perfect amusement. I started hitting him.

"Will you be quiet?" he said.

I nodded. He released me.

I lit the lantern by my bedside. I did not recognize the man who stood before me. Somehow, since we had been gone, he had acquired the clothes of a gentleman. He had abandoned the gardener's uniform and had now acquired a pair of cotton twill trousers and a clean white linen shirt with matching neck cloth, over which he wore a beautiful blue silk waistcoat with the most delicately embroidered red flowers. He had received a clean shave and his hair was washed and combed. I could only speculate how he had come by the means to change his appearance. It was obvious he must have stolen these items, but did he use cunning or violence? For the first time, I felt guilty. Had I put innocent lives in danger by freeing this man? Well, we know now that I did.

His disguise was effective. Though there was still a misshapen and abused look about his face, if I did not know the truth, I would still have believed that he was a man of decency and means.

"Where have you been?" I asked.

He cackled. Obviously proud of the way he'd come by his clothes. I braced myself for quite a yarn, for I knew he was always the hero in his own story.

"Why, this rebellion could not have arrived with greater timing. If you hear that the niggers are rebelling and you come across a white man lying in the road badly beaten, his teeth broken, his eye swollen shut, what would you presume?"

"That it was the rebels?"

"Precisely. I met two fine English matrons. Sisters. They could not think of a nobler endeavor than to nurse a victim of the Negro insurrection back to health."

I shook my head. "But they did not even rebel in Spanish Town."

"Well, that was thanks to me. I told them I came upon a gang of murderous house slaves, plotting to take machetes to the throats of their mistresses in the middle of the night. I fought them off before they could turn on all of the innocent city women who had been left alone and vulnerable after their men rode off to the country to fight with the militias."

"It seems that you are indeed more clever than all of us. May I ask why you have even returned?"

"Because I'm ready, my dear," he said.

"Ready for what?" Though I knew.

He balled his hand into a fist and struck the inside of the opposite palm with it.

"To enact my revenge and yours too. I keep my word."

I felt like a fool. I had believed that I might control this demon, but now I realized how easily he could obliterate me, all of us, while I slept unaware.

"May I ask that you wait until you receive word from me? My father is working on a matter of the utmost importance to the future of this family. I only ask that you allow him time to finish."

The pleasure drained from his face instantly.

"Why, of course, missus," he said, imitating the voice of the Negro and bowing. He backed out of the room without taking his eyes off of me.

"I shall return tomorrow night," he said before closing the door.

"Wait—" I tried to whisper, but he was gone.

As soon as morning came, I went to look for Louise, but when I opened the door, I found her waiting on my veranda with a look as if she'd just witnessed a death.

I forgot about myself for the moment.

"Oh, Louise, has something bad happened? You look exhausted! How long have you been waiting outside my door?"

She pulled me inside, looking behind her as if she were being followed.

"Has Mr. MacDaniel been to see you?" I asked her.

I was worried that he had stolen himself into her bedroom too. I knew whatever she was dealing with must truly be horrible because she didn't bat an eye that Mr. MacDaniel was still lingering in our midst. She insisted we go upstairs to my bedroom before she would reveal what troubled her. When she told me all that she had learned, that she was in fact, as Mr. MacDaniel said, a quadroon, I admit I allowed my face to slip into a faint mask of disgust. I tried to look at Louise more carefully. I wondered how I could not have known.

"You hate me now, don't you?" she said.

"Oh, by no means!" I declared, putting my arms around her.

Then she told me the rest as I held her in my arms, how Mr. Paisley had proposed that they marry.

"Well, that's wonderful! Isn't it?"

I ignored the look of pure horror on her face.

"I simply mean that it is perhaps the best road ahead of you, is it not? No one will know about you if you marry him, yet at the same time, he knows, so there is no need to deceive him. What other choice do you have? White men do not marry colored girls. They keep them as outside women. If you refuse, what better match can you possibly make unless you deceive people? Don't tell me that is your plan. I have always thought of you as an honest person. You could, of course, marry a colored man now. There are many colored men with property these days. The wealthier ones do tend to prefer to marry white women, to clean up their lineage a bit, but I'm sure you can make a decent match. A civil servant, perhaps?"

She pulled away and put her head in her hands. I felt sorry for her. I had only meant to talk reason into her. It occurred to me, then, a way to solve both of our problems.

"Perhaps Mr. MacDaniel can be of service?"

She shot me a look of disgust.

"Well, perhaps he can persuade Mr. Paisley to allow things to remain as they are."

"Persuade?"

I told her we would meet in the gardener's shed at midnight and I would explain. Later, when MacDaniel reappeared in my room, I told him that Louise was under great distress. He wanted to go to her instantly, but I told him to wait for the rendezvous time.

Perhaps Mr. Paisley needed to meet with a bit of an accident, I thought, that would leave him bedridden for some time (callous, I know—I was terrible back then, but it was a fast solution to Louise's problem and would keep MacDaniel occupied).

So you see, even I bear some fault in the fate of poor Mr. Paisley. Though I did not in any way imply that they should murder him, I did encourage Louise to use MacDaniel to free herself of her guardian.

When the three of us met that night, Louise broke out into furious weeping, so distressed was she by Mr. Paisley's unwanted advances. I had to help her! Mr. MacDaniel actually stepped forward to comfort her, but she quickly backed away.

It was in that moment, when I saw the two of them together again, side by side in the shed, with Mr. MacDaniel's face no longer bruised and swollen from his attack, that I could see the resemblance between them. What I had mistaken for lust toward Louise and just general lewdness was actually something else entirely. I never told her, but let me tell you now of my personal theory.

We know that Louise's background is somewhat of a mystery. We know that Louise's mother was a slave but her father, her color leaves no doubt, was a white man. When she first confirmed her origins, I confess I feared that perhaps she was conceived by my own father. I was sickened by the thought, though Louise and I were like sisters, because it meant that she was a living sign of my father's profligacy. But looking at MacDaniel then, I did not know why I did not see the obvious resemblance. He is her father! Don't you see? Why, they had similar coloring, the light freckles, the red hair, though Louise's appeared brown until she stood in sunlight. I can think of no other reason this MacDaniel was so concerned with her, and why he didn't clear off when he had the chance. I was so overcome with giddiness by my sudden revelation I was concerned that I couldn't hide it. I had to get away.

I claimed that I heard footsteps outside and promised that I would go out and distract whoever was creeping around so that the two of them would not be discovered. I ran back to my room laughing, thinking I could never tell Louise he was her father. She would absolutely die!

I wish now that I had told her. Perhaps she would have indeed considered Mr. Paisley's proposal as I had initially suggested. With a pedigree like that, being born of a convict and a slave, what right did she have to be so picky? Mr. Paisley had done her a great kindness if he knew and was still offering to make her his wife. Or perhaps learning about Mr. MacDaniel being her father might have driven her even more mad. Alas, we will never know.

For the next two weeks, my father and his cousin Alma did nothing but extend dinner invitations to suitable prospects. I needed a handsome, kind, young man, and I swore that I would not rest until I found someone. I have to admit I neglected Louise during this time. She came to visit, attempted to talk, but each time, we were not alone. Alma took her role as chaperone very seriously. While young men came calling, she had to vigilantly keep watch to protect my honor. Poor Louise was a bit lost in the shuffle. She was uncomfortable around these strange gentlemen in our sitting room, and Alma was rude in her presence, for she found Louise a bit unkempt and below my station.

And then once I decided on my future husband, I was distracted and overwhelmed with joy at the prospect of becoming a bride. I have to say we made me a good match in the end. I was to marry the heir to the Singleton Plantation. He was only a few years older than me and quite shy and pleasant to look upon.

I still harbored some great dislike for my father, but out of necessity, we had come to an accord. I thought that Mr. MacDaniel had abandoned our plan or else I would have told him I'd had a change of heart. My future husband's father pledged to rebuild Warm Manor, and thanks to this partnership, our fortunes would not be lost.

But let me change directions here. It is not me you want to hear about, is it? It is Louise. So, let me move to the night of my engagement feast, just a week later. My father had decided to put on airs and had planned a tastelessly ornate engagement dinner—fine linen, ten courses, only the best. Eighteen guests were in attendance. Louise and Mr. Paisley came. She had a pained look on her face as she wished us congratulations. I knew it was because she longed to escape Mr. Paisley's grip. I wanted to pull her aside to ask if Mr. MacDaniel was planning to act, but Mr. Paisley would not leave her side. And my betrothed wouldn't leave my side. He followed me around like a puppy.

Later, at dinner, Louise was sitting so far away, and though I ached to speak to her, it was not the time. My future husband had no intention of living the life of a Creole planter. He planned to take us back to England, leave my father and his brother in charge of his plantation, and live off the profits. I felt like I was finally breaking free, oceans away from my father and his rules.

I didn't smell the smoke. Later, a few guests mentioned it, but my father blamed it on the new cook. A small kitchen fire, he said. But then we saw that smoke had started filling the room. Some of the guests were coughing, so we agreed to step out for some air. My father tried the door, but he could not move it, and the knob was so hot it singed his hand. The servants tried too, and the other men. It was barricaded from the outside. We all started screaming for help. We realized the smoke was coming from outside the house, not inside. The door itself was on fire. The gardens. When we looked out of the windows, all we saw were flames and black smoke. So you see, Louise could not have had anything to do with the fire, for she was inside with us at the time of its ignition.

I knew that MacDaniel was behind this. I had let a demon loose upon this earth, and for that I am sorry. I looked for Louise, but she was nowhere in sight. I found her walking away from the other guests, who were desperately smashing windows, which only allowed more smoke to come in. I followed her through the kitchen. The door to the cellar was open. I had forgotten that the cellar led to a wooden door in the garden. Only the cooks used it. I noticed the kitchen staff was gone. I presumed that they had already escaped through the cellar but hadn't bothered to come back for us. Just as Louise was about to go down into the cellar, I called her name. She looked at me, we locked eyes, and then she proceeded without saying anything. I followed after her. That is when I realized that she had some foreknowledge of what was happening. He had influenced her. She could not have thought of a cruel plan like that herself, not my cautious, sweet, fretful Louise.

I ran down the stairs after her, and she started running too. When she got to the other side of the cellar and pushed open the door, I caught her by the hem of her dress just before she could climb out. I could see that the fire hadn't spread as far back as the cellar door. So it was indeed a safe means of escape.

"Louise," I begged, "don't leave me behind!" She glanced over her shoulder but didn't pause to look me in the eye. She continued through the door, even as I tore the end of her dress. She was in a trance. I am convinced now that somehow she had been brainwashed or bewitched. She slammed the cellar door shut. I tried to push it open, but I couldn't move it. It seemed as if Louise had put her weight against or was using something to quickly barricade it. How could this be the Louise I knew? She had spent our childhood trying to keep me safe from myself.

I ran back upstairs and showed the other guests the route to escape. The men began banging on the door, trying to force it open. Alas, I had inhaled too much smoke by then, so eventually I fainted. The last thing I remember was my father squeezing my hand as we both screamed for help. Perhaps I should have perished there—it was my action that set all of these events in motion. But then I remember waking in that very same garden where it all began. Except now it was a garden of ashes. My betrothed was shaking me. Everyone was looking down at me with concern, but my first words when I awoke were, "How is Louise?"

I searched for her, but she was gone. I knew Mr. MacDaniel had set the fire. I wondered if Louise had gone to him after. Nevertheless, I stand by my claim. Only he was capable of being so vindictive. Not my sweet Louise. I will not rest until I clear her name.

I know you believe that we are telling lies, that this Mr. MacDaniel is a figment of our imagination, a ghost who perished in the fire at the widow Garnett's house. All this sounds fantastical, but I swear on my mother's grave that it is all true. The court even tried to blame Louise for the death of Mr. Paisley. How could a little thing like her have broken a grown man's neck? You must admit there had to have been a male culprit.

I have built a new life here in England. As I mentioned, I am currently awaiting the birth of my child. I pray that it is born a boy. But the thought of Louise sitting in gaol in Jamaica is too much for me to bear. The thought of her being hanged makes me sick inside. The guilt keeps me up at night. I have told my husband that we must return to Jamaica one day. I cannot abandon that island, for it is a part of me. I cannot abandon Louise, for she is a part of me. I hope that this confession will alleviate the severity of her punishment. I pray every night that one day the two of us will be reunited, and we will be as thick as thieves once again.

**From *The Written Confession of Louise Marie Paisley*,
Spanish Town Gaol, April 1832**

When I told Peta-Gay that I wasn't white, I saw her affection for
me leave her body. She tried to hide it, but I knew then that I
was alone. She seemed determined to convince me that only Mr.
MacDaniel could find a solution to all my problems. That was absurd, I thought at first. I had no doubt that he had never done
a good deed for anyone in his life, but I feared going home and
being alone with Mr. Paisley more than I feared MacDaniel. And
now that I knew that he had been telling the truth all along, I was
curious to hear the full story. I had dismissed him when he said
the name of my mother, but now that I knew that she was indeed
the woman who birthed me, slave or not, I wanted to know her.
I waited in the shed, and when the two of them entered, I didn't
recognize him. He had somehow stolen fine garments from some
poor gentleman and was masquerading around the island, pretending to be a decent man.

He had transformed himself. He had even changed his voice.

"Oh, my dear, you must tell me what has transpired!"

He could perfectly imitate the inflection of an English gentleman. I wondered if he were even human. Who else could transform
so easily except for the devil himself?

I confess I no longer had concern for my safety around him.
What did it matter if he snapped my neck? It was better than being
wed to the only man who I had ever looked upon as a father. I didn't
know what other road was before me. Peta-Gay no longer loved me.
Though she denied it, something had changed. I could feel it. She
did not even have enough concern for me to stay at the meeting
that she had arranged. Though I felt alone and dejected, she looked
at the two of us with amusement and then promptly made up an
excuse and left. She could think of nothing but finding a suitor to

marry, and then she'd quickly leave me behind. We stayed standing, he and I, in the shed, scrutinizing each other in silence.

"Have you learned the truth?" he asked me.

"Yes," I said.

"Good," he said. "The truth is always better."

"How so?" I said, for I saw little benefit in my recent awakening.

"Now you know who your enemies are," he said. He sat down on the bare floor in his good trousers, and I wondered if he planned to fall asleep right there.

He patted the floor beside him.

"Will you tell me about my mother?"

"Anything you wish," he said.

I had never been so close to imagining the face of my mother before. I had tried to but had no clues to follow. But now, though she was not the mother who I wanted, she was real. I had to know her. I sat beside him.

First, he told me about life on the plantation, how it would be for girls like me. How men compete to be the first to break in the girls. I didn't quite understand the phrase. I was used to hearing it only applied to horses, but he explained it to me. It was nothing but a game to them. I shuddered to think of it.

"Did you?" I asked.

"What, dear?"

"Did you do that to my mother? Break her in?" He thought for a moment, as if he could not remember. It took everything not to shout at him for being so monstrous that he would forget.

"Not her," he said.

I was relieved. "Who did it, then?"

"I know others tried. I cannot attest to how many succeeded.

"I know your Mr. Paisley tried many times, but each time, she fought him viciously or ran away, and took a flogging for it instead. When she became pregnant, she thought he would stop his pursuit of her, but he continued. When you were born, when you were a babe still weaning, he tried to buy you from Mr. Fowler. It was only to punish her, you see. I advised Mr. Fowler against the sale. She had run away too many times, and she would continue once you were gone. A weaning babe would keep her obedient, I told him. But after I was banished from the plantation, the sale went through. She became so angry that she poisoned Mr. Paisley's food, poisoned Fowler. They became sick but neither, of course, died. She had to hang for that. I could not save her. I heard from those who witnessed it that she didn't cry. She only cursed Paisley and Fowler."

I couldn't bear to hear any more. Not another word. I got up and fled from the shed. In that moment I hated Mr. MacDaniel, yet I hated Mr. Paisley even more, more than I thought possible. He had expressed the same depravity toward my mother as he had to me, and after she had refused to fall into his trap, he had preyed on me. Though I had not understood Mr. Paisley's intentions for me until now, it was clear he had known them all along.

After I had returned to my room and lay my head on the pillow, the door opened and Mr. Paisley entered. I feigned sleep, hoping he would leave me. Instead, he bent over my bed, and I felt him pulling back the sheet. My heart was racing. I could feel the cool air on my body, and then I felt his hand on my shoulder. I sprang upon him immediately, and I swear I nearly succeeded in clawing his eyes right out of their sockets. He screamed and Maddie came in holding a candle. I ran to her and held her as tightly as I could.

"You dream you turn into a cat again?" she asked.

Mr. Paisley stood panting, dumbstruck. I could see the thin red lines beginning to form on his face.

"Yes . . . she had a night terror," he said, and left the room so fast I was surprised he didn't trip. I begged Maddie to stay with me that night and she did. She slept in my bed and held me until I fell asleep.

When I woke up, she had gone back to her room, and I wanted to go find her because I hoped she could keep me safe. The thought of her and I being kin no longer alarmed me. In fact, I wanted desperately for her to promise to be my mother and to take me out of Mr. Paisley's house. Forgive me for repeating gossip, but it is well-known that Mr. Fowler is the father of my maid Maddie's daughter, Helga. Helga attended a convent school just for colored girls up in Westmoreland. It was Mr. Fowler who made the arrangements. She very rarely came to town, but it was on account of her birth that Mr. Fowler had Maddie manumitted and brought to Spanish Town to work as a paid maid for us. I had pitied Maddie before for her scars. Now I knew that her pain ran deeper, for she must know what it is to be forced to submit to a man who you despise. I wanted Maddie to take me out of Mr. Paisley's house and tuck me safely away in the convent where Mr. Fowler had stowed Helga, away from these men. But ultimately, I knew she could not. It was Mr. Fowler who decided who was safe and not safe. I had thought the Christmas Rebellion an act of treason; now I saw that for those in bondage, violence was the only choice.

I went to see Mr. MacDaniel the next night. "Would you like me to kill him?" he asked me plainly. I hesitated to give him an answer at first. But just then I knew that the only way I would be free was if Mr. Paisley were dead. If they were all dead.

Though I still found him revolting, I knew if I was going to make them pay, I would need to use his strength. Revenge would be more plausible if we worked together. I told him that I would accept his help. He told me he would help me only if I let him steal an embrace. The thought of him touching me sickened me, but I had no choice. I stepped closer, and I found he smelled of sour milk and blood. His breath was hot on my face as he leaned in and swept me into his arms. Though he only held me for a moment, I felt defiled. And I thought now that I have been defiled twice—once by him and once by Mr. Paisley—I know my mother, how she thought. I felt closer to her. I was ready to make them pay.

I met him every night for the next two weeks to plan the best time to strike. We couldn't think of a way at first to bring everyone together, but when I received Peta-Gay's invitation to her engagement feast, I knew there would be no better moment. For another week, I sat with Mr. MacDaniel in the shed for hours as he formulated our plan. I cannot tell you all that was said. I was in a trance. I know he told me what to do. How to play my part, which was rather simple: First, I had to go to Peta-Gay's dinner with Mr. Paisley and pretend not only that I did not hate him, but that I was learning to think of him as a potential husband. I had to make sure he stayed there until Mr. MacDaniel set the fire, which he promised would occur during the first course of dinner. So, the next day, when Mr. Paisley came out onto the veranda, I let him wrap his arm in mine. As he escorted me across the yard, I turned one last time and looked back at our house.

"Is something wrong?"

"I'm hoping to turn to salt," I said. He just laughed; he thought I was joking.

Then I had to walk into the dinner as if I believed that I was still white. I had to smile at these people who would have withdrawn my invitation; some would have even recoiled from me in public had they known. I embraced Peta-Gay, and she introduced me to her future husband. She told me about their wedding plans and how they would eventually move back to England. "Back," she said, as if she had ever set foot in that place. I had to pretend to be happy for her. I cried, and then she cried, and we embraced again.

"I'm glad that you are happy for me," she said. "Will you go back to England with Mr. Paisley?" she asked. I did not respond. I only cried, and she embraced me again. It did not occur to her that I cried for myself.

Just before dinner was served, I was supposed to pretend to

have forgotten something, a present for Peta-Gay. I was to assure Mr. Paisley that I could manage on my own to run just next door to fetch it. It would take me just a moment, I was supposed to say. I was to slip out the front door, find Mr. MacDaniel hiding in the hedges, and make the signal for him to barricade the doors and light the match. He would have already drenched the property, the lawns, the verandas, all the doors with kerosene. But Mr. Paisley would not leave me alone. It was like he sensed that I wanted nothing more than to run away. When I tried to go get the gift, he insisted that he come with me. So, I told him that I'd give it to her at the end of dinner. I had to wait until he was distracted by the fire to slip away. Mr. MacDaniel had planned for everything. If for some reason I couldn't get away, he would wait until half past six, and he would light the fire anyway. He would make sure the fire did not spread as far as the cellar door, which was dug into the ground in Mr. Fowler's backyard gardens. He would make sure the door was open so I would have a means of escape.

Mr. Fowler made a speech at dinner. I could not hear it, for as I watched him, I only grew angrier. It felt as if that anger muted my other senses. I thought about what he had done to my mother, and it made me almost want to remain there, just to see him lit on fire.

It was vile, after all. Mr. Fowler had watched as hundreds of Negro and colored men and women, my own mother, were hanged and let the John Crows pick at their flesh. Yet he would no doubt tire of this place and follow behind Peta-Gay one day. He would live the life of an English gentleman and tell his grandchildren wild stories about his time as a Big Man in Jamaica.

Though I still had love for Peta-Gay, I told myself her fate was her own fault. If she had never freed MacDaniel, I would have never asked Mr. Paisley of my true origins. Now that I knew who I was, how could the child of a slave ever trust the mistress of a plantation? We were natural enemies. It was just that before, I hadn't known.

She had changed the course of my life in a way that was irrevocable, yet she was going off to England to forget this place. I could see how easy it was for them to slip into new lives, shed their skin and grow new ones like snakes. I knew I could change my mind, go with Mr. Paisley and continue to be white, but really, I was becoming a true slave, like my mother, for I had no choice in the matter. And how could I be with a man who had tortured my mother as he did?

When the smoke began filling the room and all of the guests ran to the doors, I was still at the table, sipping wine and drinking my soup. I was not afraid. Fire is a painful way to die, but I thought most would be taken by the smoke first. I imagined all of the townspeople gathered around their ashes the next morning, and I felt at peace. I did not want Peta-Gay to feel any pain. I only wanted her to disappear from this earth. I thought Peta-Gay would understand why I could not be on her side anymore. Instead, I had chosen the side of my mother. All our lives we'd both longed for our mothers. When she tried to follow me out the cellar door, I swung it closed quickly and held it shut with all my weight. She had always taken so much pleasure in tormenting me. I was pleased that it was my turn to see her squirm. I had tried so hard and for so long to be good, in the way they taught me, and I had grown weary.

Mr. MacDaniel appeared. He pressed his weight against the door and then told me to run. I had assumed he barricaded it and vanished, but he must have remained and watched, saw that they had all escaped, and decided to put an end to Mr. Paisley with his own hands. I took no joy upon hearing of his death. Yet I can't mourn. It is simply the most just outcome. Judge me however you will. It does not matter. My solicitor and Maddie, my only visitor, the poor dear, have asked me to write this, hoping these words might spare me the noose. There is not a lie that can save me, so I will tell the truth. If I could do it again, I would have put poison in their food. I would have made sure that we succeeded. I caught a glimpse of Peta-Gay before I ran. I looked over my shoulder, and she gave me such a look of complete disbelief. I should have explained, but by then I knew I was pressed for time, and I couldn't get it out. I wanted to say to my friend, as I will end by saying to you now, that I have no wish to look upon a world that will not let you people sink down, and stay down, like the rest of us.

Interview with Enoch Fowler, recorded by Inspector Jeffrey Preener, April 1832

PREENER: You said a ghost?

ENOCH: I said he was cold as a ghost. I got a chill when he touched me.

PREENER: And you are saying it was him? MacDaniel? How do you know?

ENOCH: Who do you think put him on that penal gang? I'm the warden, you idiot! I know every man who passes under my charge.

PREENER: You will refrain from abuse, sir, else I will put it on the record.

ENOCH: How far could he have gone? You are standing here with your questions while he makes off again. Go out and search for him!

PREENER: The boys are out there looking for him. Now, what did he want?

ENOCH: Look at me, you fool. He wanted to beat me over the head with his shoe, the lamp, a broom. He wanted to hit me with anything he could get his hands on. He wanted revenge.

PREENER: Yes, I can see he beat you, but did he say anything, sir, while he was beating you? Or before or after? I need to know everything he said.

ENOCH: He said, "I should have burned the lot of you while I had the chance, but I couldn't see the girl burn."

PREENER: So he confessed to starting the fire? Do you know of which girl he speaks?

ENOCH: Who do you think, you simpleton? Your mother? The Holy Virgin? The Paisley girl. The Paisley girl. She's the one you nabbed for the fire.

PREENER: Did he say that she was involved? Did you ask him?

ENOCH: I'm sorry. I forgot to think of it while my brains were getting bashed in.

PREENER: Sir, I know that you are in pain, but I need you to cooperate. What did he say next?

ENOCH: He said, "Tell her that the devil can make a better father than the good lord. He does not leave his children behind to be martyrs."

PREENER: Father? Is he her father?

ENOCH: He's out there! You're letting him escape!

PREENER: Mr. Fowler, please stay focused. Was he calling himself the girl's father?

ENOCH: I'm sure that bastard is someone's father. You seem more interested in scandal than you are in preventing crime.

PREENER: All right, sir. Where do you think he will go next? Do you have any idea? Did he confess to the murder of Mr. Paisley?

ENOCH: He went back to hell, I suppose. But he said he wasn't done with me. He said he wasn't done with any of us. He'd do us all in as he did Paisley. He said he would finish what he started.

PREENER: Do you think he'll attempt another fire? Do you think he will set fire to your brother's home again?

ENOCH: Well, since he has given us a clearing warning, if we

allow him to do it again, then we deserve to die, don't we?
And you with us?

PREENER: All right, all right, sir. That's enough. I will see that
someone tends to your wounds.

Louise Paisley, the colored woman convicted of arson and attempted murder and scheduled to be executed in one week's
time, has been resentenced, following the arrest and confession of the convict William MacDaniel. However, while the
court previously had due cause to believe Paisley was a free
quadroon woman, new evidence presented by Harold Fowler,
owner of Warm Manor Estate, has shown she was never properly manumitted and therefore should have been treated as
a slave when tried previously before the court. As Mr. Henry
Paisley was murdered by Mr. MacDaniel shortly after the
fire, there was no one who could rebuke the claim. The court
has ruled that Louise must serve twenty-four months hard
labor, following which she should be considered property of
Mr. Fowler and returned to his custody.

—*Spanish Town Chronicle*, May 1832

ANCESTOR WORSHIP

Queens, 2020

FLORENCE

The story is short: it begins with a woman getting fed up; it ends
with her dying. The year is 1817. The woman is a slave named Florence. She has just been sentenced to death for attempting to poison
her master, Harold Fowler, and another unnamed man. Why did
she poison Harold? What pushed her to the brink? Abe has asked
himself that question too. No one knows, or at least the answer
isn't significant enough to be included in the court digest. But
they do note, after the verdict, in parentheses, that as she is being
transported back to the jail to await her fate, she escapes briefly by
throwing herself from the moving wagon. Her escape is short-lived.
She injures herself badly in the fall, and with her hands and legs
chained and cuffed, and with her newly acquired limp, she barely
makes any headway at all before she's apprehended. Two days later,
she's hung. There is no record of her final words, so Abe imagines
them.

PURGATORY

This is how Abe passes the time in the hospital with his mother,
Irene, as they wait for his sister to wake up: he writes about Florence. He wants to tell his mother what he's found, but he knows she

doesn't want to think about dead family at that moment. His sister, Chloe, got into a car accident two days ago and the doctors have put her in a medically induced coma to deal with her brain swelling. She is in critical condition; the doctor who came this morning put it in blunt terms that made Irene wail but that Abe appreciated for the brutal honesty. "She has a fifty-fifty chance." So there it was—either his sister dies or she doesn't. Fifty-fifty. The police officer said that she was probably texting while driving, didn't see the stalled car on the shoulder of the highway, and swerved too late, into the path of a passing truck. *No time for any last words,* Abe thinks, followed by a wave of guilt.

Abe plans to use Florence in his master's thesis, due in a month, so as he waits, he types feverishly on his laptop. He's in graduate school to be a librarian, a career goal that still makes Irene roll her eyes. For his final project, he's evaluating the best electronic resources for studying Caribbean genealogy, using his own family as the subjects. While he feels remorseful for staring at his computer screen while his mother obsessively watches his sister's lifeless body for the slightest sign of improvement, the only way he can keep his composure is by distracting himself with his work. He's combed database after database of scanned newspapers, slave registers, wills, and letters, getting a picture of life on the plantation, and now the summary he's writing about Florence has become longer than the original article he read about her.

Abe hides behind his laptop, and his mother stares at Chloe with her face like stone. They do not talk about their feelings as they wait; they do not talk about their fears. He and his mother are both naturally laconic. His sister is the one who they can count on to talk and talk until it forces them to overcome their own awkwardness. The silence is unbearable without her. Both he and Chloe still live at home even though they're both well into their twenties. He complains about his mother and sister to friends, to his uncle

Vincent, but he admits that their relationship is strangely codependent. It's always been just the three of them against the world. He often compares their little family to a three-legged dog—obviously deformed but still able to function.

As they sit in this dark, suffocating hospital room, he and Irene exchange words only to convey information or when his mother wants to give him an order. For example, every twenty minutes or so, Irene says, *Tell me when the clock reach six o'clock.* She says this despite the fact that the clock is in full view of both of their eyes. Despite the fact that he knows she has her cell phone in her purse. At six, she's going to take the bus to work. She has an overnight home health aide job in Forest Hills. He wants to ask her to stay. He wants to offer to call the agency for her and let them know why she can't go. But he knows she'll snap at him if he offers. *If me nuh work, who will pay the rent? You?* It's strange how adamant she was all their lives that they study and get good grades, even going as far as giving him a brutal spanking when he got an "unsatisfactory" on his second-grade report card. He never got a bad grade again. But now, here he is, an Ivy League graduate, and now a master's student, and she still can't seem to stop herself from taking digs. He wonders if it's her working the graveyard shift that's made her so mean, even meaner than when they were kids.

ALL THE THINGS ABE DOES NOT KNOW ACCORDING TO HIS MOTHER

Abe does not know what a real beating feels like.

(*You think you a cry now, one day me will show you what real beatin' feel like.*)

He does not know what struggle is, or what a real day's work does to your bones.

(*The two a you jus' take and take, while me a work myself to death.*

You nuh know what real struggle feel like. Wait til you have fi yuh own pickney.)

He doesn't know his father. He talks to him once a month on the phone, he's visited him three times in Jamaica in twenty years, and they are cordial, but he doesn't know know him.

(Make sure you nuh trust that man. Never send him money. Him one ginnal. Look how him jus' go back to Jamaica and leave we here fi struggle and then every month him have some nerve fi call me and beg me fi send him money. Is suh Jamaican man stay.)

He didn't know his grandfather Abel Paisley, the man he was named after. He had always believed he died when his mother was a baby, until one day, at age twelve, when he was home alone, the mailman delivered a box marked "cremated remains."

(—Yuh grandfather never dead. Him jus' abandon we and go make one new family. Is suh Jamaican man stay.

—Then why are they sending him to us?

—No one want him. Him American daughta Estelle, the one him raise, mus' did cremate him outta spite. Is so American people treat them family. She call me and say if me want to bury him, me can send him back home. Me say me nuh want him but she send him anyway.)

Later that night, in bed, Abe heard the toilet repeatedly flushing, and in the morning the box with his grandfather was gone. He doesn't know for certain that she flushed him—she'd deny it if he asked her—but he has always just assumed.

The only Jamaican man Abe really knows is his uncle Vincent. He lives in Brooklyn with his wife, Debbie. They don't have children—his wife never wanted them—and so Abe has felt that his uncle has used him to fill that void, and vice versa. Abe is closer to Vincent than Irene, though Vincent came to the U.S. years after them. Vincent gives him hope that he can become a good man, that there isn't some genetic predisposition as his mother seems to believe that will make him one day turn into a piece of shit like his father.

It was Vincent and Debbie who led Abe to his thesis topic. His aunt and uncle had met when Debbie traveled to Jamaica to visit Harold Town. Harold Fowler, Florence's brutal master, was Debbie's ancestor, though neither she nor Vincent knew if he was, in fact, related to Harold too. But Jamaica being a small country, it was both shocking and expected.

One night, when Abe went to Vincent and Debbie's for dinner, she'd told him about Harold's journal. That it had once been in her possession, a family heirloom, lost years ago, though she never told him how. She'd taken brief notes as she'd read the journal, she explained, and asked if he wanted to see. She was sheepish when she handed him her notebook but nodded with satisfaction as she stood over him, watching him read as if she were doing something selfless, giving food to a starving child. The names of the slaves she had jotted down were a boon for beginning his project. That was where he first saw the name Florence, next to a date, 1817, a date that made no sense at the time but that he now knows is the year she was hanged.

Before beginning his research, Abe had asked his uncle if he wanted to know if there was a connection between him and Debbie. If by chance Abe uncovered bad blood between their two lines that went back generations. Would he want to know? Would it change anything? They'd known since they first met that it was a possibility. Vincent had laughed and said of course he wanted to know but warned Abe to let him break the news to Debbie.

Later, after he told Vincent about Florence, his uncle had joked that maybe God had brought them together so he could avenge his ancestors by getting close enough to wring Debbie's neck. He laughed, but it gave Abe a chill.

Abe is limping around the cramped little hospital room, attempting to awaken his right leg, completely numb from the hours of sitting on a small wooden chair, when the machine attached to his sister starts beeping rapidly. Nurses and doctors rush in. He and his mother are forced to press their backs against the wall while people prod and poke his sister, inject fluids into her IV, and shout terms that are wholly unfamiliar to him, back and forth.

Abe has declared himself an atheist since he was in high school, but he does not know what else to do but pray. He studied religion in college, and he thinks now about a class he took—African Myths and Rituals. He learned about how many African tribes practiced ancestor worship, believed the dead still remained among them, influencing their lives. He repeats Florence's name, quietly under his breath, until the beeping machine slows.

RECKONINGS

He doesn't understand why he wants it so badly, for Florence to be his ancestor, his great-grandmother many times over. He feels an inexplicable connection to this woman, even if he can't prove that they are related. He tries to imagine what she looked like, and in the image she has a grim expression and bright eyes, smooth honey-brown skin. In his mind's eye, she is beautiful.

Abe has been drawing a family tree, and Florence is at the top; next to her is a question mark. There is no information about anyone before Florence. The dead end frustrates Abe. She has no last name in records, and there were no birth certificates for slaves. In an inventory of property, dated 1817, he finds mention of Louise Marie, daughter of Florence. Age ten months.

He has found John Paisley, born in 1854 in Harold Town, whose mother was listed as Louise Marie Paisley. Abe continues to dig for deeper roots.

He'd felt an irrational sense of triumph when he came to the death certificate for Harold Fowler. The cause of death is listed as sleeping sickness. Sleeping sickness, he learns later, is more commonly found in sub-Saharan Africa. It's caused by a parasite most usually carried by the tsetse fly. He likes to think that Florence was that fly.

WORSHIP

Another day passes without his sister making any progress. Abe needs more ancestors to worship. Maybe if he knew which country his ancestors came from, he'd know which gods to pray to; maybe the spirits of his long-dead family could find him now and save his sister's life. He's desperate for a sign that she'll recover. He's never taken one of those mail-in DNA tests, but he wishes he had now. He was paranoid about giving the government access to his genetic material. But it wasn't just Africans who prayed to ancestors, he remembers. They did it in Jamaica too. When Columbus first encountered the Arawaks in Xaymaca, as they called it, he found that they kept the skulls and bones of their ancestors in baskets in their homes.

When his sister flatlines again and the machine starts beeping rapidly, like a heart about to explode, he holds his mother's hands, and as the doctors work on her, he repeats all the names he can remember. Florence, Louise, John, Vera, Abel. Even Abel. If Chloe lives, he swears, he'll go home and comb every inch of their apartment for that cardboard box or any remnants. If anything is left of the real Abel Paisley, even a thimbleful of ash, he'll wear him proudly around his neck as a poultice. He'll exalt him, like the rest of his ancestors, even if he isn't worthy.

HOW WE ARE BORN

Harold Town, 1999–2010

BIRTH

In Harold Town, they tell their children the story of the three little girls who followed a man into the bush. He had no children of his own, so he promised that he would grant their every wish if they would be his daughters. The girls agreed to leave their mothers, and they walked for a few days with the man. When they stopped, they found that there was no one around for miles. Just grass, flowers, and trees. They had to build a little hut themselves. The man had nothing to give them; they were tricked, they'd realized.

When he fell asleep, they tried to go back home to their mothers, but they only got lost in the dark. The man found them again, told them they would never find their way out of the bush on their own, and he would never show them. So, the girls gave up and lived together with the man peacefully for a short time, pretending he was their father. Then the girls became very sick. The man loved them so much he couldn't stand the thought that his three little girls might die.

One special night, when the moon glowed red, he said he would show them a cure that his grandmother had taught him. He gave them something to drink. *It tastes like blood*, they said. He told them to drink it all, for he had to leave soon, but not to worry—in the end his leaving would only make them stronger. In the morning people from the town found his body at the bottom of a ravine. They had thought he was just another weak-minded man driven mad by the blood moon. No one knew his name, so they buried him quietly.

NORMA MONTAGUE

I left Jamaica when I was fourteen and moved to Toronto to be with my mother. My years out in the bush with my crazy grandfather are a nightmare that I'm still trying to suppress, but if you think it will help the families move on from what happened to the girls, I'll tell you what I know. You must understand, though: I haven't seen those girls in years. Not since we were children.

Here's what I remember: They were three girls with no names. They weren't triplets, but they were always together. I assumed that they were sisters. Now I know that that made no sense. They were the same age, but not triplets. How could they be sisters? Unless they were half. It wasn't so uncommon for men to have outside children. My father had a wife and family, so he denied me, and then he died. But where were their mothers? Their fathers? America? Canada? England? My own mother had left me with my grandfather and had gone to work in Canada. I never thought too deeply about these things back then. They were all the same age and they called themselves sisters. I didn't care because I finally had other children to play with.

My grandfather was a hermit who only talked to people when he had to. Even me he ignored, except twice a day he'd shove food at me like I was some barnyard animal. I only saw other children when I walked down to Harold Town. But that was seven miles away from where I lived, so I rarely went. I was so lonely before I met the girls.

One night I went to bed, the sole child for miles, and when I woke up and went to the stream to bathe, three girls came out of the trees on top of the hill in white dresses. The last time I'd worn a white dress was to my own father's funeral. I was only nine, and so I thought that they were ghosts. Duppies, I would have said then. I wanted to run away screaming, but I was so scared that I froze. And there was something beautiful about them. Three brown girls came out from behind the line of trees in long white dresses, hair plaited in two long braids each. They had even stuck a few bright-pink flowers in one another's hair. When they came closer, I saw that they were younger than me, maybe only six. At first, they advanced slowly, cautiously; then when they saw me, saw that I too was a girl, they threw off their dresses all at once and ran into the water naked. Splashing at one another, splashing at me, getting my hair wet, like we were old friends.

INFANCY

The little girls were hungry. During those early days without the man, they had to find food on their own. They walked for miles scavenging and scrounging. For days they ate nothing but fruit and only a single mongoose that they'd managed to catch. It didn't fill them. They were ravenous. One day they found a little girl, Norma, bathing in a stream by herself. She was the only person they'd seen for miles. They joined her in the water. After, they told her they were hungry. Norma showed them where to find cocoa beans to make hot chocolate, as well as ackee, green bananas, and breadfruit. She brought them back to the hut she shared with her grandfather, and she showed them how to cook and eat all they'd found. They ate everything, but afterward they felt even hungrier. They lay on the floor holding their stomachs. Cramps, Norma told them. You eat too fast, she said. They threw up all the food she'd given them. Meat, they begged. Meat. Everything else tasted like dirt in their mouths.

So Norma killed one of her grandfather's chickens, even though she knew she'd get a beating for it later. She cut off the head and was sitting outside on a tree stump, plucking its feathers, when the girls emerged from the house. I'll show you how fi cook it, she said. The girls grabbed the chicken from Norma's hands and ran, each taking turns holding the chicken like a pack of dogs fighting over a kill. Wait, Norma shouted, but they were already gone.

They came back the next day. Norma opened her eyes, and there they were, standing around her bed. She was lying on her stomach because her grandfather had beaten her with a switch when he found out about the chicken. The three of them patted her head and stroked her hair.

We're hungry, they said.

Go to Harold Town, she told them. My gran'father say we fi stay away from him chicken.

She showed them the way. When the girls entered Harold Town, they found the market women were set up behind their stalls, and they begged for food. No one could resist three little girls. *Look how them pretty white dress stain*, the women said. *And look how them ribbon tear up to shreds! Them have no shoes, and my God, even them foot-bottom cut up from all the walkin' them have fi do. Where yuh mothers deh?* they asked. The girls could only shrug.

They soon found themselves being lifted and carried, cradled, nursed, and tucked into beds, into new homes, where the women took turns mothering them, promising to be their new family.

AUGUSTUS MONROE

Me live me w'ole life in Harold Town. Everybody know me 'round here from the day me drop outta fi me mooma, and me know every somebody who ever set foot or born in this place. But me tell you me never see them t'ree pickney before, and me never see the man who bring them before til me find him mash up at the bottom of the ravine.

Me know seh them gals no have no relations in town, and no one journey up here 'less them have relations. This likkle town no deh 'pon no map. But few miles from town, white people did once have a plantation that slave them burn down during Christmas Rebellion.

The man who own it did name Harold. That how come them name this Harold Town. But w'ole heap a time pass since everyt'ing gone to ruin. But me did know seh them still have some good cocoa tree grow there. So one day me walk up to the ruin from town to collect the cocoa bean. Nothing left from the old days 'cept one stone vault where them did keep Harold and him family coffin.

Now, the vault deh underground and you have fi walk down stone step fi go inside. Them seal it shut when them bury the last Harold coffin, but of course that grave did long since break open and rob and so one of him descendent come back and recover them family bone and bring them dead fi bury in England, where them shoulda did stay in the firs' place.

Me know seh most country people too 'fraid a duppy fi fool 'round in graveyard, so me nearly drop dead when me did walk past the vault and see one likkle gal walk out and up the stairs. That 'bout ten year ago. Me was fifty years old back then and me think I already did see many things. Me even see duppy before. But me tell you, me never see one walk outta grave in broad daylight. And the gal walk up to me and hold me hand like me and she friend. When she touch me, then me know seh she real. Me say, Pickney, you nuh know you nuh fi play 'round in graveyard? You nuh know duppy will follow you home?

But the girl jus' look 'pon me like me fool. She say, Poppa, you have any food for me? And me notice the gal accent, not from country, not from city, not even from Jamaica. It have likkle bit a patois, but it sound put on. Me figure she just one American or English gal who outta school fi summer, so them send her come country fi stay with cousin.

Me say, Likkle gal, you nuh know not fi beg nuttin from stranger? Fi you mooma no teach you that? But then me feel two hand dig up in me pocket. Me did still a hold the gal hand so me surprise, wonder again if she really one duppy.

Me look behind me and me see two other likkle gal. Where you come from? Them no answer me. When them realize me pocket empty, the two gal look at them sister, and then the three of them put them mouth 'pon me arm and bite me. Them break me skin and nearly draw blood. Me knock them off a me, and the three of them hiss at me like cat, then them get up and run gone.

CHILDHOOD

The three little girls had no intention of hurting their new mothers, but they knew that the food that the women cooked would never fill them. When they stayed with Birdie Wimberley, they snuck into her chicken coop and bit the heads off all of the hens and drank their blood. In the morning they heard Birdie screaming.

Dog get in me coop and kill every last one a me chicken!

Not the rooster, Birdie! We would never eat the rooster, they said, but she was so busy surveying the damage and wailing, so she didn't hear them.

The next time the three little girls ate Birdie's hens, she came out in the middle of the night, dressed in her nightie, swinging a machete blindly in the dark coop. They didn't know what to do, so they hastily turned themselves into kittens. It was the first animal they could think of. It was the first time they'd ever transformed.

When Birdie turned the flashlight on them, she saw three little kittens looking up at her from the straw floor. She went inside to get a bucket of water to drown them. They may be too small to kill a hen now, but one day, she reasoned.

When she came back in, the kittens were gone, but the girls were standing there. Me never mean fi wake you girls, Birdie said. When she held the flashlight up, she saw their lips were covered with blood. She gasped and stepped back. The girls ran around her and barricaded the door shut. She was shut in there for three days, with only raw eggs for sustenance until Augustus found her.

ASTOR GRAHAM

I was hired by the families to recover the girls. Two of them were sisters; one was a distant cousin to the others. I had a feeling they were dead, but nothing can ever prepare you. You never know with kidnappings. Especially those done by someone so peripheral to the families. The girls had been missing for just over eight years, after being led away from a funeral by their cousins' gardener. A man they called Bernard. I say *called* because we later found that the man had no birth certificate, no record he'd ever been born; he was a ghost. I assumed the worst for them. So, when I found out that they'd stayed alive so long, I became deeply depressed. How could we have failed them so perfectly?

People had seen them, knew exactly the girls I came asking about. I found it hard to believe that it took so long for someone to get as far into the investigation as I did. The family had hired three—yes, three—white PIs before me who all hit a brick wall and returned home empty-handed. You think, *This will be easy*. Jamaica is a small island, it will be easy, but you can get lost in those mountains. It helped that I was black; I don't know how it will be for you. Harold Town is a small, insular place, built around the ruins of an old sugar-and-rum plantation. I told them that my father was from Jamaica, which was true, but left out the fact that I never knew him.

They let me in. In fact, the more time I spent with the people of Harold Town, the more at home I felt. They welcomed me precisely because I was an insider/outsider. They were hungry for news of the places I had lived—America, Canada, Australia—and in exchange they tried to teach me a little bit about myself. This is how good PIs work. You earn trust. This old woman, Birdie, practically adopted me. She had known the girls well. When they were ten, she said, they had locked her in her own chicken coop for seventy-two hours.

The way they spoke about these girls . . . boy, they were strange. But any young child kidnapped by an unstable individual is bound to display some abnormal behavior. I pressed on. It didn't matter how damaged these girls were. Their parents wanted them back. But Birdie warned me. I won't lie and say she didn't. She said, Asta—she couldn't quite pronounce the *r*.

She said, Asta, you nuh wan' know the true true story. You from over foreign. Is no way you will believe what we country people a deal wit'.

But I said, Birdie, I've been paid to bring these people relief. I'm doing God's work.

I knew all I had to do was mention God, and she couldn't deny me.

Alright, Mista Graham, I will show you where them deh, but you will not believe me.

We waited until dawn and then we set off. We drove farther up the mountain and took a side road that wasn't paved. Then the road stopped altogether. Trees had grown in its path, and Birdie said we'd have to go the rest of the way on foot. I was worried about Birdie. She was ancient, hunchbacked. She had two thick tree branches that she used as walking poles. Still, once I helped

her out of the car, she didn't hesitate. She disappeared between
the trees like some forest sprite. I had to hurry to keep up. I didn't
know how she knew where she was going. There was no longer
any path. Every direction looked the same, but somehow, she
found the clearing. She pointed to the middle of the dirt field.
I walked the perimeter over and over until I had the courage to
stand in the middle. I could feel it. I can't explain, but I knew that
I was standing on their grave. I bent down, and I saw that mixed
in with the grass and weeds and tropical flowers were bits of de-
tritus and ash.

Him go mad, Birdie began, and him kill them. Him bury them
and burn down the w'ole house with the three gal inside. Augustus
see him do it. Him see the fire, but it did too late.

I knew that Bernard, the man who had kidnapped the girls, had
long since thrown himself into the ravine and been buried by members of the town, but if he was the one who killed them before he
died, why cover it up? I didn't quite believe her. Maybe I couldn't
imagine a crime so gruesome. I was a PI, not a cop. I was used to
tailing cheating spouses, embezzlers, staking out hotels, following
money trails. But I went back to my car to get a shovel anyway, because a job is a job. I didn't think about getting lost this time. I
moved as if guided by a scent.

I made it back alone and started digging, while Birdie sat off to
the side on a tree stump and shook her head at me. I had never had
to dig a grave before, or, rather, dig bodies out of a grave. It took me
the whole day. The sun was setting by the time I finished. He buried
them properly, as if it wasn't done in haste. I went down the full six
feet before I found them.

I wish I could say they were all bleached bones, grinning white
skulls, but there was hair, gray flesh, the residue of the faces of once-
perfect little girls. I think I was screaming the whole time. I don't
know if the screaming was in my head or Birdie could hear me—

when I found them, she turned her back to me. But regardless of how I felt, I worked until all three were free.

PUBERTY

The three little girls really did not want to hurt their new mothers and fathers, but they were hungry, and they didn't know how to make it stop. They sometimes ate chickens, goats, cows, and even lately had taken to dogs. They would feel full for a little while but soon would be even hungrier than they had been before. They needed answers. The people in Harold Town treated them like little girls, but they were starting to realize that they were different. Sometimes they would leave town to visit Norma. She seemed to be the only one who understood. She let them feed off her, which helped, but even that would only make them full for a short time.

If they could understand what they were, maybe they could find the answer. Why could they drink Norma's blood and feel wonderful, but when Norma drank theirs, she had to go behind a bush to retch? Why did Norma keep getting taller, but they never seemed to grow? Why could they change into animals, little kittens or birds, but Norma was always Norma? Norma tried to warn them, to put fear in them, because it was clear that they had none. Norma would say what her mother told her: fear is what keeps little girls alive. What about blood? they asked Norma.

When the girls turned twelve, they noticed a change in their bodies. While other girls had grown taller, developed breasts, hips, filled out their clothes more, none of those things happened to them. Instead, their skin began to itch. At first it was just a minor irritation, but soon it became a kind of burning. The hunger was no longer their only worry. They started scratching at their skins, clawing at themselves, as if they could somehow peel a layer off. Norma began making them poultices each night made of mud and honey.

NORMA MONTAGUE

As they grew up, they changed. Not physically, though, which was very hard to hide. Some sensible people from the town argued they must have been malnourished before they found them, which stunted their growth. I was their friend, so I tried to warn them. I said, Stop stealing all the animals or they'll lock you in jail. That thing you did to Birdie was really evil, I told them. But they'd always just look at me and laugh. Then they'd do something worse.

One time, Augustus got mad at them for stealing his goat. They had tried to drink from him years ago, before they knew better, but no one believed him. The goat made him furious. All he found was its head. They'd eaten the whole thing. He told everyone that they hadn't even cooked it first, that they'd eaten it raw, but they just called him an old rum head.

I said, Girls, at least tell anyone who asks you that you cooked it first. That you're not out there drinking blood. But they just laughed again. Blood taste nice, they said, and ran away. People started to notice all the dead hens. At first, they blamed it on the dogs, but by then all the dogs were missing too. And then all these cats appeared. People would wake up to find a little cat sitting on their chest, watching them sleep. You can't fool around with these country people. Superstition spreads. Then the three girls took the baby. They stole a fucking baby. No one knows for sure what they planned to do with it, but I couldn't help them after that.

ADOLESCENCE

In Harold Town, the girls learned, children their age made themselves useful. The women were giving them more responsibility. They wanted them to watch the younger children in exchange for food. They had to earn their keep. They had never paid much attention to the other children. They were older now and were no longer interested in childish games. But once their babysitting jobs began, they noticed that the children had the most unusual smell. They were sweet. The smell grew stronger daily. The younger the child, the sweeter the smell. Whenever the three little girls heard a baby cry, it seemed to call out to them. They couldn't decipher its message, but they tried and they tried. What was it trying to tell them? Should they eat it? They knew that there were some lines that even they couldn't cross. It haunted them, not knowing.

ASTOR GRAHAM

I uncovered the bodies but had to leave them there in the clearing. I didn't want to disturb the scene too much. Whatever investigation had to happen I wanted to happen fast so that I could take the girls home. What happened next was my fault. I shouldn't have left them. I didn't stop to ask myself why everyone knew where they were and did nothing. What did I think going to the police would accomplish? If you were thinking of working with local police, do not. They will laugh in your face.

When I had the three all laid out side by side, I started to cry. Birdie finally got off her tree stump, walked over with her sticks, looked at them, unfazed, and said, Now, Asta, you mus' put them back.

What do you mean? I have to take them home to their families. We have to go get the police.

This is not fi police. Put them back.

I ignored her. I left them exposed while I drove to the police station. She drove back with me, but I didn't ask why she was so silent. Why she wouldn't look at me. When I walked into that little hovel of a police station, the only constable on desk was asleep with his feet up, his hand slipped down the front of his pants. I cleared my throat. He didn't stir. I rang the little bell on the front desk. He sputtered awake.

Wha' gwan? he said, yawning.

I found them. The girls. They're all dead, I said. Come with me.

He just stared. What gal you a talk 'bout?

They're dead, I shouted. Don't you hear me? They're dead.

Here's something I knew as a kid but seem to have forgotten since becoming a PI. Never shout at a cop. He got up, suddenly awake, approaching me with one hand on his baton, and I swear I thought he was going to crack me across the face, but then Birdie came back with that man, Augustus, and started pulling me away.

Is alright, Asta, she said.

No, Birdie, we have to file a report. They won't let me fly the bodies back without the paperwork.

Is alright, Asta, she said again, and nodded to Augustus, who proceeded to pull me forcibly away while that useless constable looked on, shaking his head like he was long bored by the madman. Augustus looks like an old man, but he has a vise grip. He wouldn't let me go until we were outside the station. Outside, Birdie looked me in the eyes and said, Is we who kill them, Asta. Not that man.

She wasn't making sense. Who, Birdie? Who killed them?

All of we! All of we! she screamed. The whole town kill them.

PHILOMENA RANDOLPH

One day them gal thief my baby right from under my nose. I put her down in her crib and say to myself, Let me just wash up while the pickney asleep. Me go outside to where the stream pass through my land and wade in. Is not even ten minute since I gone, but when I come back to see if the baby wake, my pickney is nowhere to be found. Augustus did a pass by same time and hear me scream. Him come inside my house. She gone! My baby gone! Them thief me pickney!

I know it was them 'cause I did catch them peepin' tru my window night before. I have to chase them down with a broom. I did give one gal a lick with the broom right 'cross her back. Them thief my pickney, Gus, I scream again. Them three girls is Ol' Hige. Them will drink the blood from my child!

AUGUSTUS MONROE

Me never believe pickney could turn wicked so. T'ief baby right from crib without regret. Me go look fi them, but me just did plan to beat them and take the baby back. Me take Philly to the bush fi find them, 'cause me know whe' them stay, sometimes when we nuh see them in town. Them stay with that gal Norma, seven mile out. When we arrive, we see Norma grandfather a skin one goat. Him not even say howdy, but is so him stay. Me ask after the three gal and him point to the trees. Me think of fi me goat whe' them pickney t'ief and eat by themselves. We find the three gal them in the woods. Them just sit cross a fallen tree. The baby deh 'pon the ground. Them not even put sheet under the pickney. It deh 'pon the groun', and them three jus' a look 'pon it like them never see nuttin like baby before.

NORMA MONTAGUE

Word about the baby spread fast. I wasn't with them when they took it. I found out about it too late. Augustus had already found the baby unharmed by the time the townspeople came. But it didn't matter. People were too angry. They'd been putting up with them for years. When we came, Philomena was holding her baby, and Augustus had one of the girls across his knees and was spanking her.

They were too big for that. I think they were eleven or twelve by then because I was fourteen, though they still looked exactly the same as they had when they were six.

The other two were pulling at Augustus, trying to get him to stop. Then they both picked up stones. They threw them simultaneously from either side of Gus. One missed him, but the other hit him right in the forehead. He let go, and the girl slid off his lap. She scrambled toward her sisters and picked up another rock. She threw it at him, at his chest. It hit him right in his heart. He stood up and began staggering, gripping his forehead with one hand and his chest with the other. The girls didn't stop. They never knew when to stop.

I screamed, No!

I knew what was coming. I think it was Philomena, baby in one arm, who was the first townsperson to pick up a stone. She threw it at them. I think she just did it in defense of Augustus, or maybe it was revenge. But then others picked up rocks.

Run! I shouted. Run! But they stood their ground. They threw stones right back at her. She turned just in time, and they bounced off her back.

Them throw rock after woman with pickney in her hands! I don't know who shouted it.

More people picked up stones and branches. The mob moved in closer.

Run! I screamed again. But they stood their ground. I don't know how many people picked up stones. There must have been forty people there. The girls were getting hit. I could see they were bleeding. I had always told them not to change in front of other people, but then I don't think they could help it. They were scared. By the time we had all blinked, we were looking at these tiny kittens. I ran to scoop them up, but I couldn't get through the crowd. The kittens tried to run in different directions, but the people moved too fast for them.

Them can transform, people shouted.

Them is Ol' Hige fi true! Philomena yelled.

How can them be Ol' Hige when them jus' likkle pickney? Them not even old, someone else said.

Ol' Hige no born old, another townsperson reasoned.

Give them to me, I shouted, but I was still a child, so no one listened. Augustus, still bleeding from the head and furious, grabbed a kitten and snapped its neck. Two other men followed suit. It was hard to kill a demon in the body of a child—much easier to kill a cat. Without a word, Augustus got a shovel and started to dig a grave.

DEATH

In the ground they found that they could speak to their mothers. All the women who had ever been transformed under a blood moon. They were not alone. Somehow, though they were trapped in that grave, they were everywhere, with everyone at the same time. The women told the three little girls how to blaze across the night sky. How to shed their skin. How to make people forget after you fed on them, and, most important, how to get older, and when they were old, how to get younger.

BIRDIE WIMBERLEY

Hm-mm. So that was how all a we damn our fool selves to hell. We know is wrong. That night I did pray for forgiveness. Then I wake up in the middle of the night. Me hear like someone did a whisper, Birdie, Birdie, Birdie. I turn on the light but nuh see nobody. But me recognize them voice. I say, Me see when Gus bury you.

Me cyaan see them, but is like the girls still talk to me in my head. Them say, Birdie, you mus' dig us up. Set us free. But me say, No, you too wicked; you mus' stay where you is.

God say you mus' dig we up, Birdie.

Me jus' kiss me teeth and roll over and go back sleep.

In the mornin' when I wake up and go wash my face in bathroom, me see the scratch mark. Them deh 'pon me neck, arm, my face, my breast. Blood spot up my nightie. I know the three gal them do it to me. Me nuh know how them do it, but I know is them. I raise them like them my own family, and then I betray them. I turn myself into them enemy. It was Sunday so me get dressed to go pray. As me walkin' down street, everyone who see me stop and ask, Is who hurt you so, Birdie? I want to tell them. I want to warn them, but every time I try is like my tongue twist up in my mouth and make me cough. I can hear the girls in my head, saying, No, Birdie. They will see. Them visit me every night for one year, but still I never dig them up, no matter what trick them play 'pon me. Them dangerous, I tell myself. Them finally did give up and leave me in peace, but Asta come and let them loose again.

ASTOR GRAHAM

I didn't know what to label this. A mass hallucination. I'm a PI, not a psychiatrist. I went back for the bodies, looked all over for them, but they were gone. I suspected Augustus hid them. But I couldn't work out why.

Look, he said. You nuh see footprint? Look, them nuh tiny foot, like three likkle gal leave them when them walk away? Count them: two, four, six.

I told him that if he was trying to imply that those three corpses got up and walked away, then he and I were gonna have a fight. I simply wouldn't stand there and allow him to insult my intelligence.

You hid them. I'll call the police, I said.

He just scoffed and walked away from me. Who could blame him? I'd seen the police in this town. The fact of the matter was they were gone, and I didn't know where, so I followed the footprints. They led out of the clearing, but I lost them when they started moving between trees. They disappeared and were replaced by smaller prints, like those of little animals.

Back in town, none of the people I talked to seemed a bit surprised. The thing is, though, they really believed. The whole town believed. You're not from here, but you will have to learn the folklore to really understand these people. This case. You have to learn about the Ol' Hige. It's a Caribbean version of a vampire story. She's an old lady who sheds her skin like a snake and drains the blood from newborn babies. Or sometimes she steals their breath, makes mothers believe their babies died of natural causes.

No one ever claimed to have seen these girls do any of these things. They did say they stole a woman's baby but left it unharmed. Don't listen to the crazy stories people will tell you about them. How does that story even apply to them? They were little girls. But it still didn't stop all the talk. In reality, they were just a little bit feral. I understood. They were isolated and left to fend for themselves for a while before they found this town. And even then, they were never formally adopted. They bounced from house to house in Harold Town, taking scraps like stray dogs. I understood why it would make them angry. If I had been through what they'd been through, I'd want to hurt things too. The girls had just needed more time to learn to become part of a normal family.

REBIRTH

It was hard for the three little girls at first, having to feel the sun on their skin after so much time. At first it burned. Their bodies were stiff, petrified. The man who dug them up left them alone for hours. After a time, their limbs loosened, their flesh softened, and they arose. They remembered what the townspeople did, but they weren't angry; they were glad, for they had learned that for girls like them, dying was part of growing up. The three walked into the woods and when they came to a stream, they shed their skins for the first time. They did not fly across the sky, though they knew they could. They also knew now why Norma had warned them to be careful. Instead they washed their skins in the stream and laid them out in the sun to dry. When they put them back on, they found that they were older. They wanted to find Norma and show her that they were as big as she was now, but when they went to see her grandfather, who looked like he'd seen three ghosts, he told them that Norma had gone abroad to live with her mother.

That night they went to find the man who had freed them, to tell him that they were grateful. He was sleeping in Birdie's back room. He opened his eyes, saw the three standing on one side of his bed in a row, looking down at him. I am dreaming. I am still asleep, he said.

They were wiser now, so they said, Yes, you are asleep.

I will take you home, girls, he said. I promise. I'll make sure you see your mothers again.

We are home.

This is not your home, he said. This is the place you were stolen away to. This is your prison, he said.

This is our home, the three girls said. These people are our family.

They killed you . . . I'll take you home soon. He turned over onto his stomach and buried his head in the pillow, a signal that the conversation was over. They had not intended to bite him, but they decided that this man needed to learn that sometimes a little fear can help keep men alive too.

BIRDIE WIMBERLEY

Let me tell you somet'ing. If you pass through Harold Town and you see one young gal walkin' roadside, her skin cover with blood, do not stop. Her sisters a lay wait you. Is not her blood on her. Is fi yuh blood. You jus' cyaan feel it yet. Is that kind of power them have. Bring a hen. Leave it at the boundary line before you drive on. One hen is enough. Them three girl is older now. Them learn restraint. Them will let you pass through.

ACKNOWLEDGMENTS

My deepest thanks to:

My agent, Monica Odom, without whose intervention I would have kept rewriting the same five chapters of this book forever, and my editor, Christine Pride, for her extraordinary vision and for pushing me to make this book better. The wonderfully supportive team at Simon & Schuster, especially Dawn Davis, Lashanda Anakwah, Heidi Meier, and Carina Guiterman.

Meryl Branch-McTiernan, Betsy Narvaez, and Ledia Xhoga for always being available to read whatever I was working on over the last decade. My partner, Karl Schwartz, for reading drafts of this book whether he was in the mood to or not, and Dawn Ryan for her honest criticism and support. My Brooklyn writing group—Diana Yin, Wendy Holmes, Liz Humphreys, and Farah Miller.

Joshua Henkin, Michael Cunningham, Meera Nair, Amy Hempel, Ernesto Mestre-Reed, and my peers from the Brooklyn College MFA in Fiction program.

Lisa Ko and Victor LaValle, whose workshops were invaluable sources of feedback and inspiration.

The editors of the following journals, where portions of this book first appeared:

Ampersand Review: "Estelle's Black Eye"
Sycamore Review: "Gratitude"
AGNI: "The True Death of Abel Paisley"
Liars' League NYC: "Past Lives"

Acknowledgments

Kaitlyn Greenidge and Julia Fierro for their generosity and support throughout my career. Kiese Laymon, Michele Filgate, Helen Phillips, and Alexia Arthurs for their kind words about the completed manuscript. Trevor Burnard for his book *Mastery, Tyranny, and Desire: Thomas Thistlewood and His Slaves in the Anglo-Jamaican World*.

Elizabeth Bobrick at Wesleyan University, whose creative nonfiction class helped create the seeds of this book.

Thanks to the Queens Public Library and my middle/high school teachers (especially Nancy Gannon, Kip Zegers, Janice Warner, Lois Refkin, and Dr. Rembert Herbert) for making me both a reader and a writer.

The Newark Public Library for allowing me to take a leave to complete revisions on this book.

My mother and father, my brothers, my sister, and the rest of my family, living and dead.

ABOUT THE AUTHOR

Maisy Card's fiction has appeared in *AGNI*, *Sycamore Review*, *Liars' League NYC*, and the *Ampersand Review*. Her nonfiction has been featured in *School Library Journal* and *Lenny Letter*. She is a graduate of the Brooklyn College MFA in Fiction program and earned her MLIS from Rutgers University. Maisy lives in Newark, New Jersey, where she works as a teen services librarian at the Newark Public Library. This is her first book.

BOOK
CLUB
FAVORITES

READER'S
GUIDE

THESE GHOSTS ARE FAMILY

BY MAISY CARD

This reading group guide for *These Ghosts Are Family* includes an introduction, discussion questions, ideas for enhancing your book club, and a Q&A with author Maisy Card. The suggested questions are intended to help your reading group find new and interesting angles and topics for your discussion. We hope that these ideas will enrich your conversation and increase your enjoyment of the book.

Stanford Solomon has a shocking thirty-five-year-old secret. And it's about to change the lives of everyone around him. Stanford Solomon is actually Abel Paisley, a man who faked his own death and stole the identity of his best friend.

And now, nearing the end of his life, Stanford is about to meet his firstborn daughter, Irene Paisley, a home health aide who has unwittingly shown up for her first day of work to tend to the father she thought was dead.

These Ghosts Are Family revolves around the consequences of Abel's decision and tells the story of the Paisley family from colonial Jamaica to present-day Harlem. There is Vera, whose widowhood forced her into the role of single mother. There are two daughters and a granddaughter who have never known they are related. And there are others, like the houseboy who loved Vera, whose lives might have taken different courses if not for Abel Paisley's actions.

These Ghosts Are Family explores the ways each character wrestles with their ghosts and struggles to forge independent identities outside of the family and their trauma. The result is an engrossing portrait of a family and individuals caught in the sweep of history, slavery, migration, and the more personal dramas of infidelity, lost love, and regret. This electric and luminous family saga announces the arrival of a new American talent.

TOPICS & QUESTIONS FOR DISCUSSION

1. In *These Ghosts Are Family*, two families are created by an unexpected accident when Abel Paisley decides to fake his own death and assume the identity of his friend Stanford Solomon. How do you think the two families would have been different if Abel hadn't faked his death, moved to New York, and started a second family? Would Irene have been protected from her mother's wrath? Would Vera have been protected from the condemnation of her neighbors? Was Abel justified in running away from his life in Jamaica?

2. Describe Abel. How does the captain in England see him, which is the cause for his new life? How do the women in his life see him, his wives and his daughters? How does Vera see him? How does Estelle see him? Are these judgments of him fair?

3. Consider the title of the book. Why do you think the author chose it? Who—or what—do you think are the ghosts that the title refers to?

4. The book flips between life in Jamaica and New York, with a short stint in London. How important is place and that place's history to the experiences of its characters? Why do Irene and Victor move to New York? Why does Debbie decide to visit Jamaica? What binds these places together—the people currently living? Or the painful history that connects the three places?

5. What do the Rastafarians represent in the context of the book? And what does their ideology threaten—especially in regards to women, like Vera's mother, who value whiteness and believe that it is "partly a state of mind, part manipulation of the body" (p. 26)?

6. At the beginning of the book, Caren thinks that "Perhaps, a life does not belong exclusively to one person" (p. 10). What do you think of this statement, in light of all the lives represented in the novel? Does considering slavery impact your interpretation? And what does it mean in the case of the present-day characters (Abel, Estelle, Irene) distancing themselves from their familial obligations?

7. Abel and Vera's marriage is a key relationship in the book, though their marriage devolves quickly into infighting and infidelity. Abel says that he loves Adele, his second wife, because she did not try to "remake and mold" him as Vera tried to. What are some of the ways that Vera prods Abel into change? What is the result of this prodding? Early on in Vera and Abel's marriage, Vera thinks "She never thought he was the kind of man to hit a woman, but she's not sure anymore. She never thought she was the kind of woman to cheat on a man. They don't know each other at all" (p. 39). How much do you think a married couple can ever really know each other?

8. While Abel is the patriarch of the two modern families in the book, the early family history is traced through its mothers. Discuss how this shaped the storytelling. What does the book have to say about the role that women play in a family? What brings women in these families together? What drives them apart?

9. Irene works as a home health aide and one of her patients, Betty, is "obsessed with the dead" (p. 85). What do you think of Betty's desire to commune with the dead and to inhabit past lives? Irene seems to think it's foolish, but in what ways does her family history affect her life in the present? To what extent do the past events in our lives affect our present?

10. There's a dramatic scene in the middle of the book where Debbie decides to destroy the journal of her ancestor, Harold Fowler, in order to drown out his voice in her head. What did you make of Debbie's decision?

11. Louise grows up thinking that she's white, and is shocked when she learns that her mother, Florence, was a slave. How does this knowledge change how she sees herself? How does it change how others see her?

12. In the same chapter as above, Peta-Gay says "[Louise] knew little about the world and the deceit that humans are inherently capable of" (p. 214). What are some of the other secrets kept by the Fowler and Paisley families? Why do they lie (or omit the truth)? What effect do these secrets have on the generations that succeed them?

13. When Vincent and Irene are children, the women of the neighborhood perform an exorcism on their mother, Vera. In response, Vera says "You nuh know what free woman look like, so you say is demon" (p. 144). Discuss the things that happen to Vera during this exorcism. How do these echo the traumas undergone by Abel's ancestors on the plantation at Warm Manor? Are any of the women in Abel's family truly free? What does it mean to be free under the law versus acting like it? What are the repercussions for women who pursue their freedom in this book?

14. When Abe, Irene's son, is in the hospital, hoping his sister will emerge from a coma, he recites the names of his ancestors like an incantation. He says "If anything is left of the real Abel Paisley, even a thimbleful of ash, he'll wear him proudly around his neck as a poultice. He'll exalt him, like the rest of his ancestors, even if he isn't worthy" (p. 251). What does Abe mean by "worthy" and how is it valued? How much should we own of our ancestors successes or failures? How do we determine if they're worthy of our praise or our scorn?

15. Why do you think the novel ends with the story of the three girls who were kidnapped at Vera's funeral? What are these girls hungry for? How does this fit into the other themes throughout the novel?

1. Debbie learns about her family history from taking an online DNA test. DNA tests have become very popular in recent years, but there are inherent risks in the information they provide, like learning about family history you or other family members would rather not know. Discuss if anyone in your group has taken a DNA test. What did you learn about yourself? If you haven't yet, would you? Why or why not?

2. Though slavery was abolished in Jamaica over one hundred and eighty years ago and in the United States over a hundred and fifty years ago, slavery is more of a pressing global issue than ever before. It is estimated that there are currently at least 40 million men, women, and children in slavery around the world. As a group, look into the work being done by the International Justice Mission (www.ijm.org/our-work) and consider supporting their efforts.

3. If you're curious for another multigenerational novel for your next book club, consider picking *Red at the Bone* by Jacqueline Woodson or *Homegoing* by Yaa Gyasi. Compare and contrast the families in these stories with *These Ghosts Are Family* and discuss the intergenerational effects of the various characters' decisions. Also discuss how black characters are able to function in the different spaces they find themselves, depending on their country of origin and their family's history.

4. If you're close by, consider visiting a museum, memorial, or educational center that focuses on the history of slavery or black history in America. Some examples are the Whitney Plantation (Wallace, LA), the Ozarks Afro-American Heritage Museum (Ash Grove, MO), the Charles H. Wright Museum of African American History (Detroit, MI), the Lest We Forget Museum of Slavery (Philadelphia, PA), the National Underground Railroad Freedom Center (Cincinnati, OH), the National Memorial for Peace and Justice (Montgomery, AL), or the National Museum of African American History and Culture (Washington, DC).

Q: Congratulations on publishing your debut novel, *These Ghosts Are Family*! What has the experience of publishing this book been like? How much different is it from the experience of writing the book?

A: It's exciting to see how a book actually makes its way into the world and how different people interpret it. I love the cover and have loved witnessing that process and how it evolved to the final version. What really surprised me is how much work other people are putting into the book. When you're writing the book, it's not really a collaborative process. But now I see all the people who play a role in getting that final version out there—editors, the editorial assistant, copywriters, marketing and publicity, etc. People besides me are working so hard on this and it really makes me want to be more thoughtful of that labor when I read and consider other people's work.

Q: Much like the Paisley/Solomon family, you grew up with a big family. What are the best things about being part of a big family? What are some of the difficulties?

A: The best part of being a part of a big family is that you feel like you will always have someone to turn to in difficult times. It can feel like a security blanket. The drawback is that when people are not getting along, you have to choose sides and that choice can alienate yourself from dozens of other members of your family.

Q: You're a public librarian, as is one of the characters in your book, and books must be a large part of your life. What books inspired you as you were writing *These Ghosts Are Family*? What types of books did you love as a child? Do you see touches of any of them in your book?

A: Many books inspired me in different ways. Some of the books I re-read as I was writing this book were *The Dew Breaker* by Edwidge Danticat, *Homegoing* by Yaa Gyasi, *White Teeth* by Zadie Smith, *No Telephone to Heaven* by Michelle Cliff, *A Mercy* and *Beloved* by Toni Morrison, *The Dragon Can't Dance* by Earl Lovelace, *Brother Man* by Roger Mais, and *The Twelve Tribes of Hattie* by Ayana Mathis. Structurally, it was really inspired by Danticat,

Gyasi, and Mathis. I am always inspired by Toni Morrison, especially the way she writes about memory, the supernatural, and women's trauma.

As a child, I was kind of a misanthrope, but I hid it very well. I liked books that were about people or animals living in isolation. I loved *Julie of the Wolves* and *Island of the Blue Dolphins*. My favorite picture book was *The Story of Ferdinand* about a bull who didn't want to fight in the arena like the other bulls; instead he just wanted to sit under his favorite tree alone and smell flowers. When I was in middle school, my favorite book for some time was *The Catcher in the Rye*. I was always drawn to characters who seemed complicated, who were liked and accepted by some and rejected and disliked by others. I think those kinds of characters are still present in my work.

Q: *Kirkus Reviews* gave a glowing review of your book, noting that one of the themes is that "we all hunger for something . . . love, acceptance, freedom, an understanding of the past to know who we are, because our lives are never just our own." How did you approach writing characters that feel so realized that we can understand what they hunger for? How did you consider what would motivate each character?

A: I tried to draw from my own experience when writing certain characters. I tried to recall a time when I had felt a similar emotion. Many times I asked myself, if I could say something to my parents, what would I say? I feel like both my parents had experienced difficult times with their own parents when they were young, so I tried to imagine what they would say to their own parents if they had the chance. They never really liked to talk about their feelings, so sometimes I tried to imagine I was them, how I'd feel. I guess it's like being an actor, getting into character. I had to keep writing and revising until I knew those emotions and motivations intimately.

Q: You moved to the United States from Jamaica when you were only five years old. What was it like to move from the Caribbean to New York City? What was your experience like growing up in the city? What parts of your experience would feel familiar to readers of your book?

A: When I first moved to the US, we lived in Richmond Hill, Queens. That neighborhood is very West Indian—its nickname is Little Guyana—but also filled with people from over the world. Most of my friends were from the Caribbean. All of them were immigrants or the children of immigrants.

It was a perfect first entry point into life in the United States. No one belonged, so everyone belonged. Up until sixth grade, all my friends really understood me, my life, and my family in a way I would probably never find again until college. In seventh grade, I was accepted to a magnet school on the Upper East Side of Manhattan, which I attended through high school. Black and brown kids were a minority there, unlike in the rest of the city. That was a real culture shock to me. It showed me that there are different worlds in one city. That we are not all living in the same reality.

Q: *These Ghosts Are Family* is told from alternating perspectives of eight generations of a family. Were there any challenges in writing the book with so many voices? Or was it helpful to have those voices provide different perspectives in order to tell a more cohesive and complete story?

A: I wanted to show how the same trauma was still visible across generations but warped itself as it moved through time and jumped from character to character. It really isn't any one character's story, it's the story of a family, so it felt necessary to include as many voices as possible.

Q: *These Ghosts Are Family* covers more than two hundred years of history, spanning colonialism in Jamaica to life in Harlem in the present day. What did your research process look like? Did anything in your research surprise you?

A: In the beginning, I read nonfiction books on the history of Jamaica. I hadn't exactly pinpointed the historical time periods I wanted to include. Then, as I narrowed it down, I read historical newspapers, specifically old editions of the *Jamaica Gleaner* to understand how people spoke, what the mood was, the culture of that period in time. I don't think the research itself surprised me, as much as how so little of the research actually ended up in the book. I was very focused on getting details right, so I read and read, but sometimes I'd look at the version I wrote before I started researching and realize that I didn't need to change much. The voices were similar to what I had imagined.

Q: You've mentioned that this book took you a number of years to write, and that it went through a number of drafts. What kept you working on this project? Were there any key moments that helped you move forward to the next phase of writing?

A: I had some outside motivation from other writers I was working with. Sometimes when I had put it aside for a long time and had to come back to it, I'd make a very drastic change. That way it felt like I was writing something new and I felt reinvested in it again.

Q: You write the speech of the characters who live or were raised in Jamaica in a beautiful and evocative patois. Was that an intentional choice? Can you tell us more about the history of Jamaican patois? How did you feel about using language as part of a character's self-expression?

A: It felt natural to write in patois. I was raised hearing it, and even though I no longer speak it fluidly myself, it's still how my family speaks to me when we talk. I can't imagine writing a book about Jamaican people without having them speak in patois, but I did realize as I wrote that I was looking at it from my own class position. I was taught not to speak it outside our home, but inside was fine. I did know other Jamaican people who were upper class who had not been raised speaking patois at all. To them it was seen as a language of the middle class and the poor. I tried to change the dialect a bit depending on the character's age and class; that was the most challenging part. I'm not sure if I fully accomplished that goal.

Concerning the history, I recently read a really fantastic essay called "How I Learned to Embrace Jamaican Patois, the Language of my Youth," by Donna Hemans for *Electric Literature*, so I'll just quote her. She writes:

> To get here as a writer, I had to learn that our patois is the language of survivors, a pidgin language that originated as the common language among the enslaved Africans who spoke a multitude of languages and who, in order to survive and work together, fashioned our pidgin language to communicate. I had to unlearn the idea that these were broken, misspoken English words, as I had been taught, and learn instead the truth: that they were Akan, Igbo, and Yoruba words that, centuries later, are still part of our everyday dialect.

Q: What do you hope readers take away from *These Ghosts Are Family*? How would you hope they consider their own family history in light of what they've read in your pages?

A: Even though the subject is dark at times, I did hope to convey a message of hope and survival. Our ancestors have gotten through worse, and even with the baggage we're born with and the baggage we acquire, we can thrive and make life a little bit easier for someone else.